APRIL 1986

Bob Hawke is Prime Minister of Australia. Paul Keating is his Treasurer. John Howard is the Opposition Leader.

Police Academy 3: Back in Training is
riding high at the box office.

British journalist John McCarthy is kidnapped in Beirut.

An accident at the Chernobyl nuclear reactor in the Soviet Union claims several lives and pollutes the surrounding areas.

LESSONS IN LOVE
at the
SEASIDE SALON

LESSONS IN LOVE
at the
SEASIDE SALON

SOPHIE GREEN

hachette
AUSTRALIA

This book is for my readers, with love and thanks.
Without you embracing all the books that came before,
this book would not exist.

Published in Australia and New Zealand in 2025
by Hachette Australia
(an imprint of Hachette Australia Pty Limited)
Gadigal Country, Level 17, 207 Kent Street, Sydney, NSW 2000
www.hachette.com.au

Hachette Australia acknowledges and pays our respects to the past, present and
future Traditional Owners and Custodians of Country throughout Australia
and recognises the continuation of cultural, spiritual and educational practices
of Aboriginal and Torres Strait Islander peoples. Our head office is located on
the lands of the Gadigal people of the Eora Nation.

Copyright © Sophie Green 2025

 A catalogue record for this
book is available from the
National Library of Australia

ISBN: 978 0 7336 5309 4 (paperback)

Cover design by Christabella Designs
Cover images courtesy of Shutterstock
Typeset in 11.7/16.3 pt Sabon LT Pro by Bookhouse, Sydney
Printed and bound in Australia by McPherson's Printing Group

 The paper this book is printed on is certified against the
Forest Stewardship Council® Standards. McPherson's Printing
Group holds FSC® chain of custody certification SA-COC-005379.
FSC® promotes environmentally responsible, socially beneficial
and economically viable management of the world's forests.

CHAPTER ONE

'Pet, hand me those scissors, will you?' Trudy takes the cigarette out of her mouth and, with her other hand, takes the scissors from Evie, who has already whirled back to her client, who's sitting there with wet hair over her face, awaiting a fringe.

Stephanie, her name is. Came in saying she wanted a haircut like The Princess of Wales has and Evie tried to tell her that Diana has really thick hair that layers nicely whereas Stephanie has fine hair that won't sit the same way, but Stephanie insisted.

At that point Trudy stopped paying attention. She's seen it all before. In thirty-odd years of running the Seaside Salon she's had clients requesting all sorts, and usually whatever it is can't be done. Being a hairdresser means being an expert in managing unreasonable expectations while still trying to make the woman look beautiful. Because that's all they want, isn't it? To look beautiful. So that someone can notice them and give them a little lift in their day.

Trudy always hopes the salon itself will give her clients a lift in their days. When she opened it – a few decades ago now – she decked it out in peach: peach walls, peach benches, cream accents. She considered calling the salon Peaches and Cream, but her father advised against it. 'What if one day you wake up and want to change the décor?' he said. It was a reasonable question. And, sure enough, one day she decided it needed a change. In fact, she changes the décor of the salon about once a decade. In 1984 the walls became orange and the benches pink. Some might say it's a lurid colour scheme – and, true, the decorator thought Cyndi Lauper was the acme of style – but the clients love it.

'Ooh, Trudy,' one of them said the other day. 'I smile just thinking about this place. The bright colours make me happy.'

So, yes, Trudy gives her ladies a lift in their days, and that lifts her in turn. Even if sometimes she has to not so much lift them up as put them in their place.

Last week one of her regulars came in saying she wanted to look like that Krystle Carrington in *Dynasty*. Silly show. And, yes, Trudy watches it. Entertainment is a priority these days.

'You can't do that look, pet,' Trudy told her. 'You need more length on the sides and you just don't have it.'

Did the client listen? No. So Trudy did her best. That's all a person can ever do, isn't it? She put some streaks in the client's hair and layered on top and flicked the fringe out to the side, and the client was happy even though Trudy told her she'd need to spend an hour with a blow dryer at home to get the same effect. For all she knows the lady is wandering around the local shopping centre looking like a half-done Krystle Carrington and thinking she's the best thing since sliced bread. And why shouldn't she? Why shouldn't they all?

Trudy sighs as she starts trimming her client's hair. The woman is loud – she's new, and not local, which they know because she keeps saying she's up from *Sydney*, and don't they know that *Sydney* is just *so busy* and it's *so nice* being in quiet little Terrigal on the Central Coast for a few days instead. She probably thinks she's paying them a compliment but somehow those statements end up sounding like the person is looking down their nose at poor old Terrigal. If another person wants to take it that way, of course.

Trudy isn't offended. As her Laurie liked to say, everyone is entitled to their opinion.

It's been two years since he said anything like that. Or anything at all.

Two years since she lost the man who had been by her side, supporting her as she ran this little hairdressing salon by the sea. Originally it was called Trudy's – after she abandoned Peaches and Cream – and it was Laurie who suggested she change it to Seaside Salon. He thought it was reassuring – like a good memory, he told her.

She wished she could say she had only good memories of him but he was so sick in those last months that she has to work hard not to think of him thin and sallow as his body tried and failed to combat the cancer that snuck up on him. On them both. It's a cruelty, she reckons, to have your mind full of images of the man you love at his worst. With time, she hopes, the shock of his illness and what she saw, what she felt, will wear off and she'll be left with thoughts only of his big smile and his bushy eyebrows and that uneven shave he always had.

They used to go walking on the beach after she closed the salon for the day. That's a good memory. Every time she smells the salt air she thinks of him; she's been smelling it since she was a child, yet it reminds her of Laurie more than anything.

Some might say, then, that she's torturing herself by working so close to the ocean. She wouldn't change it, though; wouldn't leave it, even if it causes her pain. Who would? Terrigal is a glorious spot and she knows she's lucky that her father helped her buy this building in Church Street – one road back from the beach – in the 1950s, at a time when the place comprised not much more than a few fibro shacks and a dozen fishermen.

It's come a long way, this village she has known and loved all her life. For so long it was a well-kept secret, then the Sydney people found out about it and started coming here for their week-ends and their school holidays. Now the population of Terrigal is like the tide, always coming in and going out, and she's used to it. Likes it, in fact, because the incoming tide brings more clients and some of them return each holiday, and she likes that too, the consistent inconsistency of it. The way they're happy to see her. It makes her feel useful. There's still a place for her in this world even without Laurie in it. Even if there are days when she wonders what she's going to do with herself.

'We're out of Nescafé,' Evie mutters in Trudy's direction.

Trudy snaps back to attention. Someone wants a coffee, obviously. Probably Stephanie.

'There's a tin of International Roast in there,' Trudy mutters back, but obviously too loudly, because Stephanie makes a face that is visible even above the smoke coming from the cigarette she holds. Trudy lets the clients smoke in the salon because she's not about to give it up herself – losing Laurie was one thing, losing cigarettes would be one insult too many in a lifetime – and she can see from Stephanie's choice of slender cigarette and request for Diana hair that she fancies herself a classy lady and International Roast just won't do. Trudy understands, but sometimes circumstances warrant a compromise.

Evie makes a face as well. 'Really?'

'It's that or Bushells. Take your pick.'

Since her other hairdresser, Jane, left, it's been only Trudy and Evie in the salon, and when they both have clients there's no one available to run out for more Blend 43.

Jane was with her for ten years. Her best cutter, she was. Jane could take a lady with dead-straight hair and turn her into a Charlie's Angel with some artful layering – and a regular blow-dry, of course. Trudy thought of Jane as the daughter she never had. They confided in each other. Right up until the day Jane resigned, saying she needed to take a break.

It turned out she was taking a break so she could set up her own salon. On the beachfront. Where all the tourists walk past. Yes, yes, Trudy knows she's had a good run with Seaside Salon being the only salon in town and it was only a matter of time before another one opened. But *Jane* opening it . . . Trudy felt that like a physical wound. Jane knew how upset she was – is – about Laurie, and to go and do that was a cruelty Trudy truly didn't think she deserved. How much grief can a person bear? She's finding out. And it's far more than she wants to, that's for sure.

Trudy wishes – even more than usual – that Laurie were still here so she could talk to him about the other salon and what she can do to win back the regulars who followed Jane there. Although he'd probably tell her to let them go. Say they weren't regulars if they could so easily take off elsewhere. That she should forget about them and concentrate on the people who stayed, not the ones who left.

If only she and Evie could manage the ones who stayed on their own. All it takes is for Evie's son, Billy, to have a sick day and he's home from school and Evie has to be home with him. Those are the days when Trudy has to cancel clients – and once you start doing that, word gets around. That she's unreliable. Maybe she's lost her touch. Maybe her business is going down the sink.

So Trudy needs to find another hairdresser, preferably a good cutter, and she's looking for an apprentice too. Someone to do the washing and the sweeping, who can run around to the newsagent's to buy the *New Idea* and the *Woman's Day* and the other magazines the clients expect. And Trudy would quite like to reduce her hours if she can. Make time to see her son and his family in the city.

She becomes vaguely aware of Stephanie squawking at Evie and brings her attention back to the present.

'How can you only have International Roast?' Stephanie says.

'My fault!' Trudy sings out. 'I've been run off my feet, pet. Haven't made it to the shops in a few days. But don't worry – coffee's on the list.'

Stephanie huffs out a sigh then drags on her cigarette. 'I *suppose* it will *do*,' she says.

Trudy sees Evie smile tightly into the mirror.

'Won't be long,' she says in that fake-chirp Trudy knows well. It's the tone Evie uses when she's fed up and can't show it. They can never show it. Otherwise the client won't come back and probably also goes away and says mean things to their friends.

Her own client – the tourist – has actually been a dream. So far. She's been quiet, mostly; reading a magazine and letting Trudy get on with it.

Except now she's staring at her reflection in the mirror.

'I've never had a blow-dry,' she says, sounding almost afraid.

'Oh,' Trudy says, looking down at the dryer in her hand. The woman had a shampoo in preparation for her cut and Trudy usually dries them when their hair is wet. Doesn't everyone?

'Would you like one today?' she enquires.

'Will it be . . . poufy?' The woman's brow knits.

'Only if you want it to be.'

Her face relaxes into a smile. 'Yes, please,' she says.

'Righto.' Trudy turns on the dryer to its highest setting. She's vaguely aware of Evie putting down a coffee in front of Stephanie and another in front of her. 'Thanks, pet,' she mouths over the noise.

Evie wrinkles her nose in response. It's her cute little shorthand for 'you're welcome'. She always does it. Mainly because one or both of them are usually drying someone's hair and it's too noisy to speak.

After a few minutes the tourist client is patting her hair from underneath and grinning. Then she gives Trudy a tip on top of the fee and Trudy feels chuffed. The day is turning out better than she thought. Better than she's had in a while. Maybe it would be all right to have some hope.

Once Stephanie has left with the best Diana do Evie could manage, Trudy sits down for a few minutes of respite before her two o'clock turns up.

'You did well,' she says as Evie sweeps up hair. 'She was tricky.'

Evie shrugs. 'She's okay. Just has some unrealistic dreams.'

'Don't we all.'

Evie gives her a funny look – probably because they've never discussed their hopes and desires before.

'What's your dream?' she says.

Trudy smiles sadly. 'That my husband isn't dead any more.'

'Ah,' Evie says, looking up to smile quickly. 'I see what you mean.'

She keeps sweeping, away from Trudy, who is about to ask what Evie's dreams are when the two o'clock arrives early.

'Hello, pet,' she says to one of her longtime clients. Then she sits her down, goes to the back room to get a cape, and the routine starts again.

CHAPTER TWO

Anna glances around her bedroom. Her marital bedroom, so it's *their* bedroom. Their house. The house that she works so hard to keep lovely for Gary and their children. For herself too, obviously, because she wants to have a nice home. That's how she was raised. Her mother did it. Her mother's mother did it. Probably they all did it, back down the line, and while Anna occasionally likes to question things – religious beliefs, political-party platforms, the storylines of *Sons and Daughters* – she has never questioned that.

Which is, no doubt, a factor in her despair as she looks at Gary's worn shirt, socks and underpants on the floor – he never puts his clothes in the laundry basket, although somehow their children manage it – and at the shoes that need shining and the bed she needs to strip. She thinks about the casserole she has to make for dinner. There are just so many things that go in to keeping a nice home and while she doesn't expect someone else to do them, she wishes Gary wouldn't make them *harder*. Does it take that much time to put a shirt in a basket?

There are also all the things she has to think about. Thank goodness she keeps lists, otherwise she'd never remember. Gary's little law practice is busy – which is good for their income, but bad for their family life – and she resents the fact that he is so rarely home that he leaves her notes. Yesterday's asked her to buy a present for his partner's wife's birthday. How is she supposed to guess what the woman would like for her birthday? She barely knows her.

She barely knows Gary these days either. He's out the door when she's in the shower and he comes home after she goes to bed. All she is for him is a machine to do jobs. All he is for her, for their children, is the payer of bills.

This is, she thinks – and not for the first time – no way to have a marriage. Or a family. When did they stop treating each other as lovers, as confidants, as *people*, and start being cohabitants, parents, washers of clothes and payers of bills?

Anna doesn't know, and it makes her sad she didn't notice the change, because these days when she thinks about Gary – the man she joyfully chose to marry when she was old enough to be sure of what she wanted – she pictures only an outline of the man she loved. He's not filled in any more; not the way she knew him to be.

Maybe she isn't either. Maybe they're both husks, hollowed out by the demands of adult life and unable to locate the stuffing that once made them greet each day with anticipation rather than dismay.

It's not the kids' fault. She and Gary chose to have them. They discussed having them well before Anna became pregnant with Troy. True, they'd planned on leaving at least two years between children, and Anna shouldn't have believed the women who told her that you can't get pregnant while breastfeeding, because that's how Renee happened. But they were both delighted to have a little girl.

No, the kids have been the lights of their lives. And perhaps that's the issue: they shifted their attention to the children and took it off each other. Seriously, though, how was she meant to keep giving Gary the same amount of attention when she had helpless babies to look after? She was the one whose body was needed to feed them, whose time and care were needed to tend to them. Gary didn't have to breastfeed. Changing a few nappies was not at all the same thing. Yet he switched off from her too.

Was it because her body didn't look the same? She's often wondered but never asked. Because she didn't want to know the answer if it was 'yes'.

His body looks the same: trim, lightly muscled, a good shape. He hasn't even put on weight, whereas her body changes like the tide: ballooning with babies and periods, shrinking with breast-feeding and ovulation. It hasn't felt as if it's belonged to her for many years. It hasn't felt as if it belonged to him either.

They used to love being lovers. He would take his time with her, making it clear he found her desirable, delightful. After spending her teens and twenties feeling as if she was the target of slightly – sometimes strongly – aggressive interest from men, Gary made her feel safe while also being clear that he wanted her. He may not have directly understood that this was the way to elicit a worshipful response from her, so that she would want him as much as he wanted her, but it was. Why don't more men understand that? All the ones at the pub and the club who complain that 'no chicks want me' have to do is be kind, to see a woman as something to be cherished – not as a goal to be attained – and they'd have more luck. But maybe they can't see them that way. That might be it, yes: women are only ever targets for them, not people.

Anna was someone Gary cherished. Once. Not any more. They stopped taking pleasure in seeing each other right around the time he opened his practice and felt the pressure of making it work. Over time, long days at the office turned into late nights when he wouldn't come home until she was wiping off her make-up and getting into bed.

She'd waited for him, on so many of those nights. Waited for him to come home and *see* her. He didn't. So she started taking off the make-up after she got the kids to bed, piling up her hair and making a cup of tea to sip while she read her book. The tea would be long gone before her husband came home.

Except it's not home the way she wants it. A nice home requires more than having residents. It needs more than cooking and tidying and cleaning. A nice home needs a heart, and theirs has long since stopped beating. The question she now has to answer is: *What am I going to do about it?* Because she is not prepared to keep going like this. Not for one day longer. Not when she spends half the time wanting to scream at her walls with frustration that the life she thought they would be living has turned out to be an endless sequence of going through the motions, with no sense of what the goal may be other than to survive.

That's not what she wants. It's not what she wants for her children, either.

Sure, he's around today. It's Sunday. That's the one day he doesn't go into the office because his partner is religious and takes the Sabbath seriously. It's the first time in Anna's life that she's found religion to make sense. Brought up Catholic, schooled by nuns, she always thought the whole thing was ridiculous. Yet she's convinced that she and the kids wouldn't see Gary at all if it weren't for the Sabbath. He's a local solicitor, not the attorney-general, yet somehow he needs to work six days a week. Keeps telling her that with all the property developments going on and people moving to the Central Coast, he has his hands full with conveyancing.

This morning Gary has taken the kids jogging along Forresters Beach because that's another thing he does: fads. One year it was cold-water swimming. Another it was saunas. This year he has been insisting that the kids become runners, just because he wants to enter the City to Surf in August. For the past few weekends he's bundled them out the door early each Sunday, waking them up on a day when they should be allowed to be a little lazy. And she's let him, because it's the only time they have with him, and she supposes she should be grateful he wants to do something with them given that she has friends whose husbands work a lot less than Gary and don't even take their kids to cricket practice.

Anna thinks about this as she yanks the sheets from the bed and bundles them into her arms before stomping out the back to the laundry. She does a lot of stomping these days.

'Wait,' she says out loud, because another thing she does a lot of is talk to herself. That's what happens when your kids go to bed at kid time and your husband doesn't come home until vampire time. She inhales noisily as she shoves the sheets into the washing machine.

'There's something else going on,' she mutters, then she walks back to the bedroom to pick up his dirty clothes and pulls clean sheets out of the linen cupboard and starts to make the bed.

'I can't believe it,' she says to the air. What she means is that she can't believe she didn't figure it out before. *She* is who he doesn't want to see. *She* is who he doesn't want to be around. He is happy to spend time with the kids, obviously, because he's been doing things with them. Getting them up early. Out of the house. Away from *her*.

That makes her feel a little sick.

She should have realised it earlier.

He's having an affair.

That's it. That has to be why he's never here. Why he doesn't want to touch her. Hasn't touched her in months. Why he waits for her to be in the shower to leave for work. Why he comes home when she's asleep. So he doesn't have to see her awake.

Now she feels even sicker, to think he's been running around with someone and she's been too stupid to realise it. Is it his paralegal? She's been there for a year or so. Her name is Donna. She's at least a decade younger than him.

Oh yes, that sounds about right. It's Donna. He's staying at the office every night for Donna.

Do other people know?

No, she doesn't care about that. What she cares about – what she needs to bring into effect, right now – is getting him out of the house. For good. He can leave his dirty undies on Donna's floor. Anna is not going to keep making a home for him when he'd rather be somewhere else.

A noise at the back of the house tells her that Gary and the kids have returned from the beach. Which means she doesn't have long to figure out how she's going to handle this, but she is, indeed, going to handle it because suddenly she has reached her limit with this situation and she simply cannot *bear* the idea of Gary being in the house a minute longer.

'Mu-um,' Troy singsongs.

'Can you take your sister to the garden?' Anna calls. She didn't know she was going to ask him to do this, but since it's emerged from her mouth she must mean it. Funny how our minds can sometimes know things that we aren't consciously aware of – like how she's now sure her mind has been aware that Gary is having an affair and it took the rest of her this long to catch up. Or maybe it goes even further than that: her mind has known *for years* that he hasn't really been interested in this marriage, which is why he's spent increasing amounts of time away from her and their children, and she's been too stupid to figure it out. Until now.

She can't hit him with that straight up, though – he'll deny it. Why wouldn't he? If he's got away with it for this long, what reason does he have to own up to it now? No, she needs to find another lever to get him out. Because that's what she's decided to do. If he wants to be with someone else so badly he can spend all his time out of the house, he may as well be permanently out of the house.

Gary appears in their bedroom door, where she's pacing, hands on hips, her face so tense she feels as if she's going to grind her teeth to dust.

'G'day, love,' he says cheerfully, as if everything is wonderful. Probably because it is, for him.

'What do you think you're doing?' she says, keeping her voice down even though their bedroom is the furthest room from the garden, where she has sent the kids.

His brow furrows. They're the only lines on his face, and even then they're temporary. Sometimes she hates him for that. He has smooth, olive skin and a great head of thick hair, long eyelashes, full lips. Lovely cheekbones. He was stunning when they met and he's aged so well. Unlike her.

Yes, all right, she's superficial and she initially went out with him because he was the handsomest man she knew and she couldn't believe he was interested in her. She was a secretary in the legal office where he was a junior solicitor and he asked her out to dinner one night, and it went from there. Marriage. A house. Children.

It's the children who deserve better than a worse-than-part-time father – by which she means they deserve a mother who doesn't spend so much time worrying about why their father doesn't come home, and if Gary isn't living here any more she can stop worrying and just focus on being the best mum she can be. If she's going to be doing all this housework at least she can do it for people who don't leave their clothes on the floor.

'What do you mean?' Gary says, those lines still on his forehead.

Anna wonders if his mistress likes them.

'Sunday is the kids' only day off,' she says, setting up her argument. 'They don't want to go running.'

'Sure they do,' he says lightly.

'How do you know?'

'They didn't complain.'

'*Gary!*' she shrieks.

He jumps.

Fair enough, she's being a little dramatic. Because she feels a little dramatic.

'They see you so rarely,' she goes on, 'they're glad for any scrap of time you give them.'

The brow furrows deeper. She remembers the days when she used to kiss those furrows, laughingly saying they'd set in stone if she didn't. That was so long ago.

'What do you mean?' he says again.

'You are working seven days a week,' she says.

'No, I'm not – I'm home today.'

'And last Sunday?'

'Um . . .' He shrugs, looking sheepish.

'What about Saturdays, when I'm running them around to sport?'

'I told you, it's busy at the moment.'

'Well, I'm busy too. With *our children*.'

He laughs lightly. Too lightly. Because he has no idea what's coming.

'I'm bringing home the bacon,' he says, like it's funny. Like it's the best reason for never being here. Except it's never been a reason for her. It certainly wasn't the reason she married him. Laughter, lust, companionship, shared values – or so she thought: these were why she married him. Oh, and love. She loved him. Loved how he made her feel protected and safe. Instinctual things she'd never known she wanted but when she felt them around him – when she felt he would take away her worries, make her feel she could just *be her* – it was so strong she wanted to preserve it forever.

That's what has disappeared: the feeling of being protected. Of being safe. Without him here – when he's at the office most hours of the week – she has felt exposed. Vulnerable. And stressed. If she is going to feel vulnerable she can do without the extra stress. She's making a decision to put her wellbeing first, for once, knowing that what's good for her is good for the children, because if she's not functioning properly she can't look after them properly either.

'I think it's best if you move out,' she says.

'What?' He says it so softly it's as if he has no air left.

'Move out. You clearly don't want to be here. And I don't want to just be your maid.' She's tacked this on because it sounds like a rational argument, whereas *you're having an affair* does not.

'You're not –'

'Gary, I am.' She feels calm as she says it. Strong. Maybe she doesn't need him after all. Maybe all this time she hasn't needed his protection.

She can be her own protector. Although she wavers a little at that, because she doesn't *want* to be. Except he hasn't been looking after her for years anyway, she realises, and this makes her feel so sad it's as if a deep cavern has opened inside her and sucked into it all the good things about him – the things she fell in love with.

'We're done,' she says simply.

His mouth opens and she thinks she sees tears in his eyes, but he says nothing further.

She leaves the room and goes to the garden, where Renee and Troy are running in circles, laughing. Simple things can mean so much to children. To adults too. Love is simple. Or it can be. It should never be more complicated than *I love you* and *I love you too* because everything else should flow from that. But it becomes complicated as life goes on. As layers are added to it. Conditions too.

She added conditions for Gary without even realising it, and those conditions included actually being present in their marriage and in their home. That should be one of the marriage vows: *Do you promise to love, honour and actually show up for your wife instead of spending as much time as possible away from the marital home thereby rendering the marriage effectively dead even though you're too cowardly to say it?*

'Dad's going away,' she tells her children as they continue running and laughing.

'Where to?' Renee says hoarsely, giggling.

'I don't know.'

'Okay!'

Troy doesn't even seem to react to what she's said. Although why would he? He's eight. His world consists of what's happening right now. The past and the future haven't started to take root in him as they will later on, pushing and tugging at his psyche, offering up stories and interpretations of events and blurry memories that may be fantasies but he won't be able to tell the difference. These are the layers that complicate love. The layers that can be kept from turning into sediment, then stone, with careful attention and commitment. Mothers do that for their children: they offer them love which manifests as that attention, reminding their children that they see them, cherish them, that the past does not have to define them and the future is whatever they wish to make of it.

Someone has to do that for mothers too, though, and sometimes their own mothers aren't enough. Or even capable. If that attention doesn't come from anywhere, those foundations may turn to dust. Unless a mother determines to keep building them for herself.

'What shall we have for lunch?' she asks the children.

'Carrots!' Renee yells. Since she turned seven she has been obsessed with carrots for some reason.

'You'll turn orange if you eat any more of those,' Anna says with a laugh. 'Let's have a salad sandwich instead.'

The children murmur their agreement and set a course for the back door.

As they all walk inside the house is quiet. Anna doesn't know if Gary has packed a bag or simply walked out. It causes her immense sadness, for a moment or two, to realise that it won't make a difference to their lives either way. Then she turns her mind to sandwiches, knowing that once they're done she'll have a long list of other things to worry about and it will no longer include Gary.

CHAPTER THREE

Evie walks as fast as her short legs can take her, just shy of breaking into a trot, as she hurries from the Seaside Salon to the primary school, which is also in Terrigal, as is Evie's house.

She's late picking up her son, Billy. Why did she book in that last client? *Who books in a cut and colour at two o'clock and expects to get away at three?* Sure, some days she might be able to risk it but they're down a hairdresser so that means she's doing her own washes, which means everything's slower and they're getting backed up, which means it's three thirty-five now and Billy will be at the school gate with no one to meet him.

Trudy didn't say anything to her, either. Usually if Evie's cutting things fine with school times Trudy will send a 'Pet?' across the salon with a slightly warning tone and Evie doesn't need anything more than that to hurry up and get out the door.

Not today, though. Trudy's slipping.

Oh yes, that's right, blame Trudy. As if the woman doesn't have enough going on, what with being a widow and that bloody Jane taking off and setting up the new salon. The cheek of her! Evie never really got on with Jane but she'd been there for so long Evie had thought she must have had Jane all wrong.

As it turned out, she did not: Jane was a snake in the grass who slithered away with a good portion of Trudy's clients. It's not fair. Trudy may smoke too much and wallow in misery a little bit, but she's the kindest lady in the world.

While Evie couldn't manage without some of the school mums, who let Billy hang out at their homes on the afternoons she can't get away in time to pick him up, she also couldn't manage without Trudy. If Billy is off school sick he sometimes has to come to the salon if it's really too busy for her to stay home with him, and he's often there in the holidays, and Trudy never minds.

Sure, he's a quiet kid, always reading a book or playing with his yo-yo, so he doesn't cause any fuss. But Evie doesn't like to take advantage of Trudy's understanding, so she makes arrangements for him after school when she can. It can be exhausting, though, ensuring he has somewhere to be. She wishes, often, that she had a sister or mother nearby who could help her, but her mum died when Billy was a baby – he's seven now – and she doesn't have a sister. Two brothers, and they're not on the Central Coast.

'Hello, sweetheart!' It's Mrs Champion. She lives a few doors up from the school and sees all the parents and kids coming and going. At first Evie thought she was a bit nosy but now Evie thinks of her as a one-woman Neighbourhood Watch.

'I'm late, Mrs C!' Evie calls, more out of breath than she wants to be. She keeps promising herself she'll start doing aerobics because putt-putt golf – her preferred form of recreation – isn't really a fitness activity, but she hasn't managed it yet. The leg warmers are stopping her. She'll look stumpy in them, she's sure. Not like Jane Fonda at all.

'Are you off to the school?' Mrs Champion calls back.

Evie thinks it's a funny question. Where else would she be going?

'Yep!' She flashes a smile and keeps walking.

'But your lad's gone.'

Evie stops, her heart in her throat, then turns around to face Mrs Champion.

'*What?*'

'With his dad.' Mrs Champion smiles kindly. 'Isn't it his day?'

Evie scans her memory. She and Stevo have an arrangement for Billy. Four days out of five it's her picking him up – unless he's going home with a friend – and on Wednesdays it's Stevo. And today is . . .

Wednesday.

Her shoulders sag. No wonder Trudy didn't say anything. She probably thinks Evie's odd for rushing out the way she did, hardly saying goodbye. It's a strange day when your boss knows your school pick-up schedule better than you do. Not to mention the one-woman Neighbourhood Watch.

'I'm an idiot,' she groans.

'No, sweetheart,' Mrs Champion says, leaning on her gate, secateurs in hand. She's always cutting something, or acting as if she is. 'You're a busy mum. Don't be too hard on yourself.'

Evie smiles gratefully. 'Could you just forget you ever saw me?'

'Now, why would I want to do that? I'm always happy to see you.'

Evie sighs. 'Thanks, Mrs C.'

Mrs Champion peers at her. 'He's a nice man, that Steven.'

'Stevo.'

'Not Steven?'

'Not since he was Billy's age.' Evie waves a hand. 'He prefers Stevo.'

Mrs Champion nods slowly, as if she's considering something, but she doesn't say anything.

'We're not together,' Evie adds, although she doesn't owe Mrs Champion the explanation.

Again, Mrs Champion nods. 'Oh well. Just because you make good parents doesn't mean you're meant to be together, eh?'

'No. Anyway, now that I've got some time I'd best get home and start dinner. Bye!'

She doesn't really have to rush off since she's no longer late for Billy, but nor does she want to engage in a conversation about

Stevo. Although Mrs Champion probably knows their business anyway, because Steve works at the fish shop at the Skillion where all the locals go, right where the boats come in – his father opened it and now Stevo runs it. The hours are long but when Billy started school Stevo was adamant he wanted to pick him up on Wednesdays, and he closes early in order to do it.

There has never been any doubt that Stevo loves his son, and he's a great father. That is not the reason why they're no longer together. That reason is that they never really fit. Evie wanted a man who looked like Paul McCartney and ideally wrote songs like him too. Stevo has dirty blond hair, no doe eyes, and has never met a musical instrument he likes.

They met at a party at the surf club. Stevo asked her out, and they hung out, then Evie got pregnant and Stevo didn't take off but he didn't exactly want to stick around either. Not because of the baby – he was rapt about that – but because they both knew they didn't love each other.

They tried to make a go of it. Even lived together for a few months around the time Billy was born. And it wasn't that they argued or anything. They just . . . didn't care enough about each other, and even Billy couldn't make them.

So since Billy was a baby Evie has had him most of the time and Stevo takes as much time as he can get. Evie wants Billy to have stability so that's why she keeps him living with her, but she likes knowing she has some freedom if she wants it. Not that she's not free. She adores Billy. She loves being with him. She just wants more.

At thirty-three years of age, with some wear and tear on body and soul in the form of childbirth and disappointment and frustration and longing and the arm she broke as a ten-year-old, there is one big rite of human passage Evie has not yet experienced: love. The romantic sort. The sort she has read about, dreamt about, listened to songs about, obsessed over movies about.

She wants Love. Yes, with a capital L. The kind Trudy and her husband, Laurie, had. Right up until he died they acted like they couldn't get enough of each other. Yes, Trudy is bereft without him – but isn't that the price you pay when you love someone that much? When the love is so powerful that your life is forever altered? That's what she wants: to love someone so much that it would hurt if he weren't around any more. And she wants someone to love her that much too.

Yes, she had a child with a man she knew she didn't love and who didn't love her. But it brought her love in the form of Billy. Which is wonderful, huge, overwhelming and reassuring at the same time. Except she wants more, even as she thinks she may be greedy for wanting it.

She wants a romantic hero but he doesn't have to be a white knight. He doesn't even need to be handsome. He just needs to be strong and stable, and kind, preferably. And he needs to have interests. Maybe even hobbies. Women always have so many things going on in their lives they tend to have things to talk about, whereas the men she knows have work and sport and that's it. It does not make for interesting conversation. Which is important to her: if you're going to grow old with a man he needs to be able to hold a conversation. Because past a certain point joints start creaking and bits stop working and all that's left is who you are in company with each other.

That's what she wants. That's what she looks forward to: knowing someone when he's old. She hasn't felt that before, that she wants to know someone when he's old. Past sixty-four, that standard Beatles age.

The man who's right for her will be the one she wants to know when he's old. Also the one she wants to see naked. That's the part she doesn't tell other people about: the part that wants to be kissed and held and other things. All the other things. The man who's right for her will give her the best hugs, and when he holds her he'll make her feel safe. He'll take care of everything. Which isn't to say she can't take care of things – she's been taking care of them for years – but she doesn't want to take care of *everything*. So he can take care of a few things and in exchange she'll take care of him. It seems like a reasonable exchange. It's just so hard to find.

She is daydreaming about that love – the way she tends to do – the whole way home, and in the kitchen as she starts peeling potatoes for dinner, and she's still doing it when the back door opens and she hears her son's high-pitched tones and his father's lower ones.

Once she realised it was Wednesday she remembered that Stevo will have taken Billy to athletics. Billy's not much of a runner but he likes long jump. Given that he's seven, though, she's not going to hold him to anything. Unlike some of the other dads – so keen for their sons to play rugby league or don a baggy green – Stevo is relaxed about what Billy may or may not do on the sporting front. 'Whatever he likes to do is fine with me,' he told her.

They enter the kitchen from the laundry, Billy grinning, his cheeks flushed, Stevo patting his head.

'Mum!'

Billy hugs her round the legs and she clasps his shoulders, kissing the top of his head.

'Hi, darling.' She straightens and smiles at Stevo. 'Hi,' she says. They don't hug or kiss. That seems too formal for a relationship that is constant yet not close.

'How are ya?' He grins in the same way his son does – one side of his mouth lifting higher than the other, and the eye on the same side squinting. Evie doesn't know if it's a genetic thing or if Billy has learnt it by watching.

'Bit tired. You.'

'Stinking of fish. Aren't I, Billy-o?'

He ruffles his son's hair and Billy giggles. Then Stevo holds out a plastic bag.

'Brought you some fillets. Thought you may want to put them in the freezer.'

'Thank you,' she says. 'That's really kind.'

He shrugs. 'Least I can do, keep you two fed.'

Sometimes when he drops off Billy he has this air about him, as if he wants to be asked to stay for dinner. Sometimes she does, in fact, ask him because that seems like the right thing to do. But he never accepts. So she's not going to ask him to stay tonight.

'Anyway, I'm off,' he says, and he kisses his son's cheek. 'See ya, mate. Saturday, right? We'll go fishing.'

'Don't you get tired of fish?' Evie asks, because she's genuinely curious.

'Fishing's not about the fish, Evie.' He winks. 'It's about the peace and quiet. All right if I pick him up at eight?'

'Yep. I'll make sure he's awake.'

'Thanks. See ya then.' He waves to them both as he heads for the back door.

'Bye, Dad!' Billy calls after him, then he picks up his school bag and heads toward his bedroom.

She's lucky with her son: he never cries when Stevo leaves; never asks why Stevo doesn't live with them. Some of that is to do with Stevo and the fact that he's very much a part of Billy's life. Some of it has to be to do with her, even if most days she feels she doesn't give him enough attention. Nothing gets enough attention, though, including her. That's just life. She realises that now she's in the thick of it, being a proper adult.

That's why daydreams about capital-L Love are so nice. They take her away from her reality, if only for a few moments. That's all she needs. Some moments of escape from being her, the woman who can't find anyone to love her just the way she is. And that's the real dream, isn't it? That someone will love us as we are. Won't want to change us. Won't wish we were someone else. Acceptance.

Yes. That's it. Acceptance and also . . . appreciation. Adoration. Oh, how she wants to be adored. And to adore.

Billy reappears. 'What's for dinner, Mum?'

'Sausages. Sound all right?'

He nods, then looks at her hopefully, and she knows what it means.

'Okay, you can watch cartoons while I cook.'

He grins and skips into the living room, then she starts dicing the potatoes.

CHAPTER FOUR

Josie puts her Mini into gear and rolls it down the hill, out of the cul-de-sac and toward the intersection. Since learning to drive three years ago – as soon as she was able to get her learner's permit – this intersection has taken her everywhere she needs to go. She could turn right to go to the centre of Gosford and its shops, or left for the beaches.

She grew up in this cul-de-sac; she walked to school from it. None of the places she wants to be now, though, are in walking distance.

So she turns left at the intersection, because she's going to Terrigal. Although it's not that much of a drive from there to here, it gives her a chance to listen to the radio, which her parents don't like her doing because they prefer classical music whereas she prefers singers like Madonna, Cyndi Lauper and Whitney Houston. And Duran Duran. She *loves* them. She's had a crush on Simon Le Bon for the longest time. Even if boys were interested in her she'd only be interested back if one of them looked like Simon. Or John Taylor, in a pinch.

Her mum almost *died* when she discovered Josie liked Madonna, even though Josie tried to reassure her that she has no intention of being as racy as Madonna – she just likes the songs. And she likes to dance. Alone, in her bedroom. Sometimes she dances to 'Flashdance' and pretends she's the character Alex in the movie, dancing her way to a new life and a handsome boyfriend. She would never go to a nightclub or anything. For a start, she doesn't have any friends who would go with her. The girls she hangs out with are from church fellowship.

Josie is not religious, although her parents are a little. Uniting Church, so they're not too strict, but they're not much fun either. Her mum was brought up Methodist and told her how they weren't allowed to dance with boys 'in case it led to something'. *Leading to something* is the entirety of what Josie hopes for at nineteen years of age and never having been kissed.

She turns up the volume because that Donna Summer song 'She Works Hard for the Money' is on and, given that she's on her way to her first proper job, it seems appropriate.

Her window is down and the light breeze lifts her hair as she passes Brisbane Water on the right, with its scattering of small boats on its still surface. She pats the dashboard of her Mini, as she likes to do. This car means everything to her, even though it's poo-brown in colour and old and probably a bit daggy. She doesn't care because she knows it's worth the four years of working weekends and some nights at Gosford Maccas to pay for it. And getting past her parents' resistance.

'What do you need a car for?' her mother said when Josie told her she'd seen the ad in the classifieds for it.

Josie had rolled her eyes. 'What do you think?'

'We'll drive you wherever you want to go.' Her mother had sounded as if she wanted to cry and Josie got the concern, she really did – her mum's younger brother was seriously injured in a car accident in his teens, so her mum didn't want Josie to get her Ls, didn't want her to drive anywhere, thought that she and Josie's dad could drive her around for the rest of her life. As if that was going to work.

'You can't do that, Mum,' Josie had said with as much patience as she could muster. Because sometimes her mum's worrying really does get to be a little too much. Surely once your child leaves school you have to let the reins go a little?

That's what Josie thinks, anyway. She's been a model daughter. There was no running around with boys – because none of them wanted her, true, but she also didn't chase them, just stayed in her bedroom looking at magazines and listening to music and watching movies because her parents let her have a VHS player and TV in there. She tried hard at school, even though she wasn't that good at tests and things – reading's never been her favourite activity because the words all get jumbled on the page sometimes and no one believes her when she tells them. Still, she did her best. And she's still doing her best at tech, and she got herself this apprenticeship at the Seaside Salon.

Josie couldn't believe it when she saw the ad in the local paper placed by a woman named Trudy. She'd been looking for an apprenticeship position but there hadn't been a single one on the Central Coast. So she'd cut out the ad and she took it to one of her teachers at tech, who then called Trudy, who owns the salon, which was really nice of her because Josie is too shy to do anything like that. The teacher told her she'd have to get over the shyness, though, because being a hairdresser means talking to people.

'Just treat it like an acting job,' the teacher said.

Once, when she was in Year 8, she was in a play at school. It was the only time she was ever cast in a play and it wasn't a speaking role. Both she and the drama teacher knew her limitations. Still, she was scared about her non-speaking part because she was going to be on stage and people would see her, which meant they might not like her the way so many of the girls at school didn't like her. What if they told her they didn't like her? What if they were mean? She wasn't ready to have more members of the Josie Non-fan Club.

Her dad figured out she was nervous and said to her, 'Jos, it's like this: no one really knows what they're doing when they're doing it for the first time. They're just pretending they do. And through the pretending they get to figure out how to really do it. You see?'

She wasn't sure she did, at the time, but it made her feel better, and by the third and final night of the play she was more comfortable.

That's what she's going to have to do today, because she feels the beating wings of butterflies in her belly as she parks the car in the street she scoped out when she did a test run two days ago. She didn't want to have to worry about finding the salon on her first day.

She uses the short walk from the car to put her shoulders back and her chin up and a big smile on her face, acting as if she knows exactly what to do and where to go and how to be.

The Seaside Salon is not really the sort of place Josie imagined herself working in. Not working – *apprenticing*. She's still an apprentice. Can't get ahead of herself.

The salon looks a little old-fashioned from the outside. A few of the shops in Terrigal do. What is she saying? A few of the shops in Gosford do too, and Gosford is the busiest place on the coast. Even so, she didn't think she'd be working in a place that has mainly old ladies as clients, which is what it looks like through the windows as she swallows her nerves and prepares to open the door, putting on a big smile. She thought she might be in a salon that does modern haircuts – you know, the ones you see in the fashion magazines. Fashionable things interest her now.

Studying to be a hairdresser has been good for her, looks wise and confidence wise. Learning how to make other people look nice has helped her apply the same ideas to herself and she has a better hairdo and better clothes now than she did at school, plus she knows how to put on eyeliner – not as much as Madonna, but she learnt by copying Madonna, and now that her hair has blonde streaks she can carry off heavier eyeliner.

The other day she bumped into Sharnie, one of the school bitches, at the Gosford shops and she saw something different in

Sharnie's eyes: respect. Not something Josie saw in anyone's eyes while she was at school.

So while Josie is still shy she feels more confident than she did even a year ago, which means she's only slightly intimidated by the idea of starting work at a salon where she knows no one.

As she pushes open the door little bells tinkle and an older lady looks over from where she's standing behind a chair. She has thick hair and she's wearing a loose-fitting black dress. Practical in a salon, Josie thinks. There's another hairdresser on the other side of the shop who doesn't look over. She's pretty, with her hair piled on top of her head in a loose bun, and she has on a floral top with a lace collar and a tight skirt. Less practical than the black dress but the outfit suits her. She's combing out wet hair and chatting to her client.

'Hello, pet,' says the older hairdresser with a lovely smile. 'You're Josie, I'll wager.'

'Yes,' Josie says, feeling a little calmer. 'And I bet you're Trudy.'

'Correct.' Trudy's smile stays. 'And that's Evie.'

The other hairdresser looks up and waves a comb. 'Hi,' she says, then goes back to her client.

'Pull up a pew.' Trudy nods at an empty chair. 'Once I've finished here I'll give you the tour.' She glances around and snorts. 'Such as it is.'

'Thank you.' Josie smiles, grateful for the warm welcome.

'Love your outfit,' the client sitting in front of Trudy says, and Josie looks down as if she's forgotten what she put on: a tube skirt – like Madonna would wear but revealing nothing – over lacy tights with a lacy top and a singlet underneath to stop her mother saying anything about it being 'indecent'.

'Thanks!' She grins.

'There are mags behind you,' Trudy says.

Josie swivels in her chair. Magazines are always good for getting ideas for clothes and hair, so she likes to look at them even if she finds it hard to read the articles.

'Thanks,' she says again, then flips open *Mode*. She doesn't get this one at home.

It doesn't hold her interest for long, though, because her eyes roam over the salon décor. The pink and orange is an interesting combination, she has to admit – not one her mother would ever allow, but then her mother gets all her style cues from Jacqueline Onassis, who would be really unlikely to put pink and orange together.

The mirrors look a little old – their frames are worn – but they're clean. The place is tidy, and the windows that take up almost the whole front of the place make it look more spacious than it is. Even though the buildings on the other side of the road separate them from the beach, she can see the tops of the pine trees that line up next to the surf club along the promenade. They make her feel as if she's almost working at the beach, which is pretty cool.

So this place is pink and orange, and pretty cool.

She catches the eye of Trudy, who winks, and Josie smiles back.

Sure, this salon isn't what she expected, but it might be all right here. She starts reading the magazine properly and waits for Trudy to be ready for her.

CHAPTER FIVE

Another day, another opportunity for Trudy to drag herself around. Except today she's worked up the energy to go somewhere other than the salon.

She never used to be a dragger. She was a bounce-into-the-dayer. A go-getter, even. Her movement was always forward, never backward. Now she's either living in the past or revving in neutral.

It's not good. It's not right for a person to be stuck in the mire for so long.

Even her cat, Diogenes, thinks she's bad company. He used to curl up on her lap while she watched TV; now he leaves the room when she walks in. Not that she's surprised: he was always Laurie's cat more than hers. Laurie named him after he read a book about Greek philosophers. Diogenes was just called Kitten at that stage as they waited to find a name that fit him. For some reason Laurie preferred Diogenes to Plato or Sophocles for his pet's name. It makes Trudy smile to remember it. He had his quirks, her Laurie. Some might say that loving her was among them.

'Isn't that right, Dodge?' she says as the cat passes by en route to his bowl. That's the only way he gets close to her now: passing by. After Laurie died he was all over her, as if he was worried she would go away too. Then after a few months the ignoring phase began and has lasted ever since.

Does it count that she wants to ignore herself, too? There are nights when she's sitting on the couch, blanket over her knees if it's cold, telly on and nothing registering, and she starts listing all the things she thinks are wrong with her. All the reasons why she's a fool for not making the most of what's left of the rest of her life.

Except she doesn't *want to*, see. Rationally, yes, she knows what she should be doing. But her heart . . . oh, her heart tells her different things. It tells her that it's broken. That it will never be mended. And even though she thinks that's so dramatic, that she would never have picked herself as being a woman who let herself get carried away over a broken heart, she can't help it. It's just about the most powerful emotion of her life, and it's taken her completely by surprise.

She tried to talk to her son about it, figuring he might be feeling the same. When they spoke three weekends ago – he called her, which almost blew her socks off with the surprise of it – he asked how she was feeling, and she was honest with him when usually she jollies herself along for him.

'Low, Dylan. I'm feeling low,' she said.

Laurie named him too, after Dylan Thomas. Loved his poetry, did her Laurie. Except their Dylan, while economical with words the way a poet might be, has never been as eloquent.

'Oh,' was what he said. Then there was silence. Then he moved on to talk about his work.

At least today she has an outing, so it's not just another Sunday spent thinking about Laurie. She's at the club Laurie used to frequent in Wamberal, even though technically it's called the Terrigal Wamberal RSL. Sub branch, actually. Not a full club. She doesn't know what the difference is. This club is where her friends like to meet for dinner once a month. Them and their husbands. And she doesn't have a husband any more.

There are things no one tells you about being a widow, Trudy thinks with a sigh as she glances around the dining room. Such as the fact that you become aware of numbers. Specifically, odd numbers. Everyone else she knows is in a pair and she is a one, not half of a two. Which sounds like an odd concept but that's how it appears to her: she used to be half of a two. Or maybe half of a one, because she and Laurie always felt like a unit. They knew each other so well that they didn't have to talk all the time; they could exchange glances and understand each other.

Yet there were still mysteries between them, and she liked that. She didn't want him to know everything about her; for one thing, she is of the firm belief that women should have some mystery, and for another, some things are her business. No one is entitled to know all of your business. Some things are private, just as your thoughts are. Not once in her marriage did she ask Laurie what he was thinking, because she respected his privacy. He didn't ask her either, and she was happy about that because if he had she probably would have thought twice about him.

They met in 1948, at the beach. He was a lifesaver, and she admired him from afar. One of her friends knew him, knew his story – how he'd served in New Guinea during the war and been shot in the leg and evac'd home. Two of his friends died next to him and he wouldn't speak of it. None of the men she knew who served would. And she respected their silence because that was their business. Besides, how do you ever start talking about such a thing? *Where* do you start? What is the first sentence that leaves your mouth?

She thought about that sometimes as she lay next to him in bed, knowing he couldn't sleep. Or when he woke from a nightmare. Those nightmares would send him outside with his smokes, as if he needed a gear change: get out of bed, go outside, do something different. What a pity it was the smokes that likely killed him. Or maybe, looked at in another way, the war did kill him in the end.

'Ginger ale, Trude?'

She looks up and sees the kind face of Peter, who is married to her friend Lois.

'Sure, Pete, thanks.'

'Lois is chatting to someone.' He squints in the direction of the entrance to the club. 'Priscilla. Do you know her?'

Trudy shakes her head. 'Can't say I do.'

'Mystery woman, then. Righto – one ginger ale.' He holds up a finger, his usual signal for 'back in a tick'.

A minute later Lois bustles over. 'Hello, love.' A peck on the cheek for Trudy then she sits heavily in the seat opposite, across a Formica-covered table that has seen better days.

'Saw Priscilla. Do you know Priscilla? No. Wasn't sure. Anyway . . .' She exhales. 'Pete said there's a seafood special. Did you see that? Or maybe it's a fisherman's basket. Anyway. Chips. Prawns. Bit of fish. Sounds all right!' She laughs and coughs at the same time. Another smoker. And one who doesn't draw breath while talking if she can avoid it. It's partly why Trudy likes being around Lois: the woman is built-in entertainment because she talks nonstop but somehow gleans stories from others that she then tells Trudy, who decided long ago she doesn't need to read the local newspaper because she has Lois to tell her all the neighbourhood goings-on.

Since Laurie died she's been seeing Lois more – not for the distraction, but because Lois has been scooping her up and bringing her to the club. Which Trudy appreciates, even if it means she's the constant one to Lois and Peter's two. They never remark on it – never make her feel she's the odd woman out – and it's fine when it's just the three of them, but when they meet other friends, like they will tonight, Trudy notices how uneven the gatherings are. Or how she feels they are.

Lois looks around them. 'Do we need a bigger table? No? Yes? Hard to know how many will come. Anyway – oh, look, there's Joyce.' Lois waves enthusiastically in the direction of Joyce and her husband, Fred, who are walking toward them.

Trudy tries to smile but she's not Joyce's biggest fan. After Laurie died Joyce didn't call her, didn't come to the funeral, has never said anything about it. Once Trudy mentioned this to Lois, who went uncharacteristically quiet then said, 'We just don't know what goes on in people's lives.' Maybe not, Trudy thought, but that had never stopped Lois trying to find out. Except she didn't, not with Joyce, so Trudy has stayed quietly mystified, and upset, and instead of coming out and asking Joyce about it she tries to smile each time she sees her, and acts as if everything is fine, because she doesn't want to upset Lois.

'G'day, Loz,' Fred says as he kisses Lois on the cheek. He always calls her Loz – as if 'Lois' needs any shortening. Some people, Trudy has noticed, will do anything to get out of saying extra syllables.

'Trude,' he says as he grabs her arms and kisses her cheek too. Unlike his wife, Fred has talked to her about Laurie, who was his friend. They played golf together at Shelly Beach once a week until Laurie could no longer walk around without catching his breath every minute. He didn't want to use a cart. Said that as long as he had two legs he'd walk.

Stubborn, he was, her Laurie. Stubbornly clinging on to life even as its tide went out. 'I'm not interested in leaving you,' he kept saying. But in the end he had no choice.

'Yoohoo, Truu-dyy.'

She snaps back to the present and Lois in front of her, waving fingers in her face.

'Where did you go, love?' Lois says it lightly but she looks concerned.

Trudy shrugs. 'Somewhere over the rainbow.'

It's what she usually says when she wanders off into the land of her memories. It is such a comforting place to visit – so much nicer than the present day, with its familiar rhythms without Laurie in them, with nothing much to look forward to and nowhere else to be. She could make an effort to change things, she supposes, but change requires energy and determination, and she has neither. The one thing that would give her momentum is her son, Dylan, and his family, but he's too busy to drive up from Sydney to see her despite his promises of school-holiday visits, and she only has Sundays off, which means she'd have to go down and back in a day and that feels impossible as Laurie used to do all the driving.

Trudy *can* drive but she'd rather not. Her life is lived mostly on foot, walking from the house in Terrigal where they lived most of their married days to the salon where she has worked for her entire adult life. It's a small patch, her world, but it never felt small until he died.

Peter puts a ginger ale in front of her and she smiles her thanks.

'What do you think about the fisherman's basket, Joyce?' Lois asks and there's some murmuring between them.

Trudy doesn't pay attention because she's gone over the rainbow again, this time with a feeling in her chest that is stronger than the usual feeling she's been carrying since Laurie died, but just about as strong as the one that comes upon her at home some-times, when she's alone and thinking about him. It always precedes tears, and she doesn't want to cry, not here, not with uncaring Joyce and chattering Lois present, with gentle Peter and jocular Fred. If the tears are going to come she wants to be home on her couch with the cat, a book and a nip of Baileys.

To stop them she picks up the ginger ale and takes a slow sip and only stops sipping to put in her order for fish and chips, and attempt to hand money to Peter, who waves it away. She keeps sipping without really taking in any liquid until the feeling in her chest subsides. That's when she puts down the glass and smiles vaguely in Lois's direction, and tries to participate in the conver-sation about how the Terrigal bowling team were robbed at the last competition, all the while wondering how many years of her life will be lived like this, always the one, never the two again, and how many years of it she'll be able to stand.

CHAPTER SIX

'Thank you for picking me up,' Anna's mother, Ingrid, says as she pulls her seatbelt across and clicks it in.

'You're welcome.' Anna glances across. 'I like what you're wearing.'

Ingrid smiles in an insincere way and Anna grits her teeth. Her mother loves clothes as much as she loves going to the hairdresser, and Anna is interested in neither. Presumably the insincere smile is Ingrid's way of saying that she doesn't trust in anything Anna has to say about her attire. She's quite happy to get a lift to the Seaside Salon, though.

For as long as Anna can remember, Ingrid has had her hair done properly once a week. Even when they didn't have the money for it, while Anna was growing up, and she's always tried to figure out why her mother would spend money on something that seems frivolous. Ingrid has lived through austere times – which is what most of the first half of the twentieth century was – and she's always been cautious about money. The only clue Anna had was when she was thirteen and Ingrid told her that self-respect is priceless and any steps we can take toward making ourselves feel better are worth taking, no matter the cost.

Now Ingrid puts aside money from her pension to go to Trudy in Terrigal; she started seeing her after her last hairdresser retired. The ladies from Ingrid's VIEW club like Trudy, who lets them smoke and makes them as many coffees as they want and doesn't argue when they ask for three sugars, and has the Scotch Fingers at the ready along with a reminder to not tell their doctors that they're eating them.

It's funny, Anna thinks, because Trudy is clearly a responsible businesswoman who's been successfully keeping the salon going for decades, but she acts like a wayward teenager. Or maybe that's just for the VIEW club ladies. Anna wouldn't know what Trudy is like the rest of the time because she doesn't go to the salon otherwise. She cuts her own hair, washes it with the cheapest shampoo she can find, and conditions it when she remembers. It's unremarkable hair – limply straight, dun in colour – so there's no point trying harder. Although she imagines Trudy would say that's exactly why she *should* try harder, try to make more of what nature has given her.

Trudy herself has a thick, layered bob and she's always dressed plainly but smartly. Usually in black – 'It hides everything,' she told Anna once, with a wink. Anna thought maybe it was a hint that Anna had things to hide but she also knew she could be paranoid sometimes, which is what happens when you have a mother who is far more glamorous than you will ever be and you grow up convinced you're never going to measure up and that everyone is looking at her then looking at you and wondering how on earth you can be related.

In other words: she learnt young to hide everything, especially her feelings, and also any ambitions she had to be glamorous because as much as she loves her mother – and Anna has always been as close as you can be to a woman whom you think is secretly judging you for not living up to her standards – she resents her too. Not all the time. Always on the hairdresser visits, though, because that's when Ingrid looks the most done.

So Anna doesn't need to wear black to hide anything. She's already great at hiding.

She likes bringing Ingrid to her hair appointments, however, because they have a regular time to see each other and they chat in the car. Ingrid has no idea Anna resents her and Anna is determined she will never know, so taking her to the Seaside Salon each week is a good opportunity to show, at least, some piety.

While Ingrid gets her hair done Anna talks to the other ladies and even though she has never seen these catch-ups as a way of getting sewing business, it's come her way. Baby clothes for grandchildren, a blouse here, a granddaughter's formal dress there. Over the four years Anna's been coming to the Seaside Salon with her mother her business has increased. Which is what enabled her to feel she could manage on her own, financially, after she told Gary to leave last week.

Today is the first time she's seen Ingrid since. When she called to tell her what had happened her mother sounded unsurprised. At least she didn't sound glad.

'How are the children?' Ingrid asks as Anna drives the quiet streets. It's past the hour when school starts, and the peak-traffic period around the Coast has gone with it.

'They're fine. The same.'

'Without their father there?'

'Yes.'

Ingrid sniffs. Anna knows that sniff.

'*What*, Mama?'

'I know the man has been neglectful in some ways but he has supported the household.'

Anna clenches her jaw. 'Financially, you mean.'

'Mm.'

Anna is about to say that if financial support was all she needed she'd have tried harder to win Lotto, but she stops herself. Because – and it's occurred to her before – her mother has lived for decades with the consequences of having a husband who was not able to support the family financially.

When Anna was eleven years old her father dove into a swimming pool and broke his back. He never walked again. Their family life changed forever, as it had to, and it changed most for Anna and her mother. Anna's two brothers, both older than her, were allowed to carry on. Ingrid made sure they went to their sport on the weekends and saw their friends. They were allowed to study in the garden shed so that they had uninterrupted time. Anna had to come home after school each day and help her parents. Because her father couldn't work any more, her mother went back to working all the time. She was a nurse before she married and back to nursing she went, taking the shifts she could fit in during afternoons and evenings so that Anna could be on duty with her father. Sometimes she'd work on weekends, but if she did it never affected her ability to take the boys to sport.

Some days, the resentment Anna possessed toward her father and her brothers would press against the backs of her eyes, making it feel as though they were going to pop out. It was an odd sensation. Then again, she always felt herself to be odd. The odd girl out. The girl who had no time for ballet or netball or swimming or any of the activities the other girls at school would pursue. She had friends during school hours but not outside, because she could never go anywhere, never have anyone over to her house.

There was always housework. She learnt to cook at twelve. Her brothers would put in their orders after her mother left for work. How Anna hated that. Being at their beck and call. And now one lives in Hong Kong and one in Melbourne and her mother tells everyone how wonderful they are. How successful. *Because of me*, Anna wants to say. *Because I looked after them so they could study and do well.*

It took her far too long to realise she had replicated the situation with Gary. She felt stupid once she did. Ashamed that she hadn't picked it up earlier. Embarrassed for her lack of self-awareness. No doubt that's part of why she kicked him out – to cover her embarrassment – which isn't noble but it's real. But, also, he didn't have to take advantage of her like that. Couldn't he see she needed him for more than money?

Yes, okay, it didn't make entirely logical sense to feel she couldn't cope with him being gone all the time and now he's *really* gone all the time, but at least she doesn't have to worry about it any more. Doesn't have to keep calling him, asking when he'll be home. Come up with excuses to the kids as to why their father couldn't make this or that school or sport thing. It's the worry she's free from, and it was a bigger burden than she'd realised.

'Am I not allowed to say that?' Ingrid says when Anna stays silent.

Anna doesn't want to upset Ingrid. She loves her mother, which is why she never says all the things she has bottled up from the past. She understands Ingrid had been formed by her experiences and that it's not for Anna to judge them. Even if sometimes she thinks of telling her mother to get lost the way she told Gary to. But she knows if her mother weren't in her life she'd still love her, so it makes sense not to tell her to go away.

Thus she keeps focusing on that love, looping around her filial duties, balancing the weight of what she needs and wants, and what she feels she owes her mother. What she wants to give her because that's the nature of love: wanting to give to those you care for. It's why she's pulling up outside the Seaside Salon right now, taking her mother for her regular appointment, waiting patiently for her, even though the salon is of little interest to her.

'Of course you're allowed to say it,' she responds with a lightness in her tone. She turns off the engine, puts the car in gear and yanks on the hand brake, which feels a little loose. The car needs a service. Something to add to the to-do list.

Anna turns to look at her mother. 'I know what I did may not make sense to others, but I feel better, not worrying about why he's not coming home. Why he's . . . lying to me.'

'Lying to you?'

She hasn't told Ingrid about her affair theory and isn't sure she should – but she also doesn't want her mother thinking Gary is a saint.

'I just don't believe he has that much work,' she says, not looking her mother in the eye.

'So what do you think he's doing?' Her mother's voice is shrill.

Anna shrugs. 'I don't know and I don't want to know any more. Shall we go in?' She doesn't give her mother a chance to respond, instead jumping out of the car and helping Ingrid into the salon.

'Hello, Ingrid Bergman!' Trudy calls across the salon. She always calls Ingrid that and while Anna is tempted to think the joke is more than over after all this time, her mother *does* look a little like the Swedish film star.

'Gertrude,' Ingrid says – her usual riposte. Trudy hates her full name.

'Tit for tat, I see,' Trudy says. She points the comb at a spare chair in the corner, next to where Evie is combing out a client. 'That one's spare, pet. Be there in a mo.'

Anna smiles at Evie as they approach. Evie seems distracted, as usual. From what she's gleaned, she knows Evie is a single mum with one son who's around Renee's age, and she works at the salon in school hours, sometimes longer.

The single mum part hasn't registered with Anna before now but she guesses that's what she is too. Except it doesn't feel that different to how things were before.

'Hi, Evie,' she says, picking up a *Woman's Day* from the pile of magazines on the small table against the wall. 'Mind if I do the crossword in this one?'

'Go for it.' Evie puts a clip between her teeth as she teases her client's hair.

Anna smiles her thanks and glances at her mother, who has settled into a chair to wait for Trudy. There is an unfamiliar young woman sweeping the floor today, her eyes rimmed in black, her hair teased out. She looks cool in a way Anna could never.

The young woman catches her looking and Anna smiles quickly and looks away.

'Here she is, my movie star,' Trudy says as Ingrid approaches, shaking out a cape and fastening it at the back of Ingrid's neck. 'A trim today, I think?'

Ingrid nods, then Trudy turns in Anna's direction.

'I don't s'pose you booked in today?' Trudy raises an eyebrow.

'No,' Anna says. 'Should I have?'

Trudy and Ingrid exchange glances and Anna feels her cheeks go red.

'What?' she says.

'One day,' Trudy says, wagging the comb at her. 'One day you're going to let me – or Evie – have a go at that hair and you're going to be amazed at the result.'

'My hair's fine,' Anna mumbles, her cheeks still hot, as she picks up her pen and prepares to start the crossword.

'It's never just about the hair,' Evie says quietly, and this time she's the one glancing at Ingrid. 'Is it?'

Evie's client makes a small noise.

'Sorry, Mrs L,' Evie says. 'I didn't mean to tug so hard. But once we're finished it's going to look great for your lunch.'

The door opens and another client comes in. There's already one waiting.

Trudy and Evie glance at each other.

'Did you double book?' Trudy asks.

'No. You must have.'

'Not likely.' Trudy nods at the newcomer. 'Won't be long, take a seat.' She smiles at Ingrid in the mirror. 'We're flat chat since Jane left. If you know of a hairdresser looking for a job, let me know!'

Meanwhile Anna bites her bottom lip to stop it trembling because what Evie said has left her feeling exposed. Years ago, before she married, she was always doing her hair and her make-up, and she had fun with it. Is it her fault that she doesn't have time for those fripperies any more? No. And who are they all to tell her how things should be now? She can run her life, and her looks, her way.

Writing the first answer in the crossword, she keeps going without looking up until Trudy says her mother's hair is done.

CHAPTER SEVEN

Sunday afternoon. The one time she can simply sit and . . . be. Or smoke. Maybe have a little brandy and dry.

The other day Trudy mentioned to a new client, Janice, that she loves her Sunday afternoons because by then she's done all the housework and the weekly accounts for the salon, and she can relax.

'You could meditate!' Janice said brightly. She's a pixie-looking gal with spiky, layered and tinted hair. The sort that takes a fair bit of maintenance and which can signify that the human beneath the hair can be . . . tricky.

'Meditate?' Trudy made a sound that was on its way to being a snort. 'That's for vegetarians, isn't it?' She'd heard that people who meditate like to eat lentils. Or something like that. The Beatles went to India to meditate and came back vegetarian. Didn't they? Or was that just Linda McCartney? She read in a magazine that Linda doesn't eat meat.

'It's for everyone!' Janice swivelled around to look at Trudy for real, not in the mirror. 'I went to an ashram and did it! It's *so* calming.' She gave Trudy a pointed look, which Trudy thought was presumptuous, first because they'd known each other all of five minutes, so Janice couldn't know whether or not Trudy needed calming, and second because Janice's hairstyle signified that she was not, herself, a person given to calm.

'How interesting,' Trudy replied.

Janice turned back to face the mirror. 'Your aura could use some calming!'

Trudy dug her fingernails into her palm to stop her snapping. Sometimes the clients really pushed her buttons. 'Could it?'

'Oh yes.' Janice waved a hand up and down as if she was wafting incense. 'I have ESP. I can tell.'

Trudy smiled with her mouth closed and flicked out the cape. 'So – crew cut, you said?'

Janice's eyes widened. 'What! No. Why would you –'

'Sorry,' Trudy said. 'Got you confused with the bloke who has the next appointment.'

There was no such bloke, but at least Trudy could move the conversation along from meditation, which seemed to her a preposterous activity.

Except, as she sits here on her couch, ciggie in one hand, book in the other, Diogenes prowling around the house, the afternoon sun coming through the window as she looks out on her modest back garden beyond, it seems a little like meditating. She's still. She's calm. Her *aura* is calm. She laughs at that idea. She's pretty sure she doesn't have an aura and nor does anyone she knows.

So maybe there's something to the idea of meditation but she'll take it in her own fashion, with her Agatha Christies and her Dick Francises and their way of taking her mind off things. Like how Sunday afternoons never used to be spent on her couch – usually she and Laurie would go for a drive, or he'd play golf and she'd sit in the clubhouse with his friends' wives while the men played nine holes then came in complaining about how their handicaps were slipping. Friends she doesn't see too often any more.

Then the phone rings and the reminiscing is over.

Resting her cigarette in the ashtray next to her elbow, she picks up the handset. 'Trudy speaking.'

'Hi, Mum.'

'Darling!' He probably cringes when she calls him that but her Dylan will always be her darling.

'How are you?'

'Fine, darl, I'm fine.' It's a lie, but it's the sort of lie everyone tells when the truth is either going to take so long it will derail the conversation or you think the person you're lying to isn't that interested in the reply to begin with.

'That's good.' There's silence for a few seconds. 'So how's business?'

Trudy hesitates before she answers, considering whether another lie should be deployed. She hasn't spoken to Dylan for a while – she's called and left messages with his wife, Annemarie, but he hasn't called back until now – so he doesn't know about Jane setting up her own salon. It's a big thing for her. But maybe it won't seem that big to him, and she doesn't know if she wants to find that out. Still, it's something to talk about. Her son is a good, decent man but conversation is not his forte, so she usually has to come up with subjects if she wants their phone calls to last longer than two minutes.

'It's tricky,' she admits.

'Oh yeah?'

'Jane left.'

'Yeah, you said.'

'And opened her own salon.'

Silence.

'In the next street,' Trudy adds.

More silence.

It's in moments like these – the silent moments, that is – when Trudy sometimes longs for a daughter who could keep up her conversational end. She sees the mothers and daughters in the salon and they're always chatting. Even that Anna who comes in with Ingrid – she sits and reads magazines most of the time but they'll chat on for a few minutes here or there. Anna seems slightly scared of Ingrid, when she's not annoyed by her. This amuses Trudy because she thinks Ingrid is a dignified lady who is hell bent on preserving as much of that dignity as she can as she ages, which, yes, can make a person seem difficult because they need certain things – like regular visits to hairdressers – but she generally thinks it's a measure of how much they regard others as well as themselves. If you take care of yourself – if you value yourself highly enough to preserve your dignity – it means you're not asking someone else to do that work for you.

It's why she lies to Dylan – and anyone else who asks – about how she is. She says she's fine because that helps her preserve her dignity. Some might prefer to blurt out each and every feeling as they experience it but Trudy doesn't think that's dignified.

Dignity mattered a lot to Laurie as he was dying. He didn't want her seeing him at his worst; wanted to be in hospital for that so she didn't have to help him to the toilet, or shower him when he couldn't shower himself. Even though she told him that she loved him and that wouldn't change, he insisted she not help him with such things.

Oh, she misses him. Started missing him even when he was still alive. Her strong, steadfast, brave husband and the awful end he didn't deserve. Yet who does?

'That doesn't sound too good,' Dylan says after a few seconds.

She snaps back to the phone call. 'It's not. She's taking clients away.' Trudy clears her throat. 'Or, I guess, they're going to her.'

'Annemarie's sister had that.'

The sister owns a fish and chip shop in south-west Sydney and a rival venue opened three doors down. It was a drama at the time, but then the sister started doing hot dogs as well, which brought in the teenage boys, and she's been fine since. Trudy, however, has no plans to serve hot dogs at the salon.

'I remember,' she says. Then she has an idea. 'It'd be good to see Annemarie and the kids. And you, of course.'

'Sure, but –'

'Would you like to come up for lunch one Sunday? Maybe next week? The week after?'

Annemarie likes to see her own family on Sundays but perhaps she could make an exception. When Laurie was alive they used to come up and visit, so Trudy knows it's possible.

'Yeah, maybe. I dunno.'

She can hear a muffled sound. Dylan has put his hand over the phone and is talking to someone.

'Annemarie says she's busy the next few weekends.'

'Oh.' Trudy thinks. She doesn't want to drive to Sydney but she could get herself to the train in Gosford. 'How about I come down one Sunday instead?' she ventures. 'That way I could at least see you. Maybe the kids too?'

Over the past two years she's felt she's completely lost touch with Dylan's daughters, Irene and Bree.

'I'll check with Annemarie. Sorry, Mum, I've gotta go. Our neighbour's just come over.'

'Oh.'

'Love ya.'

'You too.'

He hangs up and Trudy is left listening to the dial tone. Her cigarette has extinguished itself but she doesn't feel like lighting another. Nor does she want to read more Agatha Christie.

Sitting back on the couch, she sighs. It's too early to make dinner. Which means it's too early to go to bed. Days are long when there's no one here to share them with, she thinks.

She closes her eyes and contemplates meditating, just to see what it's like, but instead she falls asleep.

CHAPTER EIGHT

Evie pulls up at the Forresters Beach putt-putt golf and switches off the engine. The place is packed, by the looks. She turns toward the back seat, where Billy is playing with a length of wool Trudy gave him the other day, making the shape of the Sydney Harbour Bridge between his fingers. He can entertain himself for hours with simple things, which is good – and especially helpful when she has lots of housework or she's cooking dinner.

'We're going to have a wait to get in, Billy,' she says.

He glances up from underneath the long eyelashes he gets from Stevo – definitely not from her, she needs about five coats of mascara – and gives her a sweet smile. ''S'okay,' he says and goes back to his Harbour Bridge.

A rap on her window makes her jump and she turns to see her friend Fran grinning, holding up a thumb, her daughter Tilly at her side.

Evie grins. 'C'mon, Billybub,' she says, then opens her door, greeting Fran with a kiss on the cheek as Tilly runs around the car to say hello to Billy.

'Good we could do this,' Fran says, still grinning.

Fran's a generally positive person and Evie finds it rubs off on her, which she needs sometimes. She can get mopey about the fact that she doesn't have a boyfriend, as much as she tries not to.

'You can't help the yearn, doll,' Fran said to her once in that idiosyncratic way she has, 'but you don't have to let it rule your life.'

Fran's been with her own Steve – clearly a popular name when he and Stevo were born – since they were all at high school together, and if she's ever had her own yearn for someone other than him, she's never let on.

'It is,' Evie says and she spies their other friends, Priss – short for Priscilla – and Juzzy, née Justine, hopping out of Priss's hatchback. Priss lived in Sydney for a few years then fell in love with a Coast boy, so she's back now. Juzzy has never left. The four of them have been solid since Year 7 and Evie has been grateful they've never judged her for not trying to make it work with Stevo, despite the fact they're all married and doing life by the book. Some people judged – people Evie didn't expect, like the aunt she was always close to – but you find out who your friends are when things get difficult.

'Hope you don't mind, but Steve's here,' Fran says just before the other two reach them.

'Oh?' Evie kind-of minds, because she thought this was a girls catch-up, but she isn't going to say that. Fran can obviously take her husband anywhere she likes.

Fran makes a face. 'Turns out he'd already organised to meet some mates here. They all want to be golfers – or so they say. Putt-putt seems to be the way in.'

'Hi, hi, hi,' Priss says as she walks up, kissing their cheeks, patting the kids on the head. Juzzy follows suit.

'No babysitting?' Priss says to Fran.

'Ah, Priss, a little NB for you – Steve looking after Tilly is not babysitting. She's his *daughter*.'

Priss rolls her eyes. 'All right. But Damien calls it babysitting.'

Fran nods. 'So he does. And Steve's here, actually. With mates. And Stevo . . .' She looks at Evie.

'He's on the Gold Coast for the weekend,' Evie says. 'But it's worked out because now Billy and Tilly can play with each other.'

Juzzy laughs. 'How you two ended up giving your kids matching names, I'll never know.'

'We're geniuses,' Fran says. 'Shall we go and line up?'

The children skip ahead while the women pay the entry fees and get in the queue that has formed to the entrance of the mini course.

The Forresters putt-putt has been popular since it opened, and it's an easy place for them all to meet, given that they're scattered around the Coast, so at least once a month they're here, usually without children. Next to it is a giant water slide Billy is desperate to get onto but Evie won't let him, and she's asked Stevo not to take him either – she's not keen on all that stagnating water in the pool at the bottom of the slide, no matter how much chlorine is in it.

As they're waiting their turn, Steve appears with three men standing behind him, and Evie immediately recognises one of them.

'Oliver!' she says with surprise. Although she shouldn't be so surprised – he's a friend of Steve's, and she met him when Billy was two, at a barbecue. He asked her out to dinner, which *was* a surprise because she thought no one would want to date her with a kid in tow. The only problem was that she didn't feel a spark for him. And she wanted that spark. The spark is what she's been searching for all these years. So she thanked him and said she appreciated him asking but she wasn't looking for a relationship because she needed to focus on Billy. He was gracious about it, and asked if they could be friends. Which they have been, sort of, in that she'll bump into him every now and then – the Coast not being all that big a community – and they'll chat as if no time has passed. She's never seen him with a girlfriend, but Steve mentioned a couple of years ago that Oliver was seeing someone. Evie had felt a pang of something – regret, maybe – at the time, but she didn't analyse it and didn't hold on to it.

'Evie!' he says now, hugging her. 'It's so good to see you.'

Billy presses into her leg.

'Hi, Billy,' Oliver says, holding out his hand for her son to shake. The last time Oliver saw Billy was at the Florida Hotel in Terrigal when he was four or five.

Her son smiles shyly.

The line moves forward incrementally and Evie goes with it.

'How are you?' Oliver asks. 'How's the salon?'

'Great,' Evie says. 'Busy. Busier than usual. We lost a hairdresser.'

Something passes over Oliver's face. 'Oh. That's interesting.'

'Why, are you wanting a haircut?' she teases. The last time she saw him Oliver's thick, dark hair was long, like a hippy's. The seventies had stopped a few years before but he was clinging on, it seemed, given that his favourite band is Fleetwood Mac. But now it's short and he looks better. Younger.

He laughs. 'I could join the army with this, huh?'

'You could.'

'Not long now,' Priss calls in her direction, nodding at the entrance gates ahead, and Evie nods her acknowledgement in return.

Oliver rubs the back of his head. 'Do you like it?' His hand drops. 'My brother did it.'

'Oh?' Evie searches her memory for a mention of a brother and comes up short.

'Sam,' Oliver says. 'He's been overseas for a few years.'

'Whereabouts?'

'Italy. We're Italian. He wanted to follow his roots. Or that's what he said.'

'You're Italian?'

'On Mum's side. Dad's English.' He grins; it's a knowing, sweet sort of thing. That grin was endearing when they met and she finds it endearing still, almost like Oliver knows a joke and he's deciding whether or not to tell it.

'Do you speak Italian?' She's always meant to learn a foreign language and she bought some cassettes from a bookshop once – for Italian, actually – but that's as far as it went.

'A little.' Oliver shrugs. 'Not as much as Mum would like. But she didn't want to speak it to us when we were growing up so it was hard to practise.'

'Why not?'

'She didn't want us to be different.'

Evie nods slowly. 'My mum's dad is Chinese. So, um . . .' She smiles ruefully. 'I know what you mean.'

'Really?' Oliver frowns, and she knows why – her eyes are blue and her hair is light brown, so she doesn't look as if she'd have Asian ancestry. Her mother thought it was a blessing when Evie was at school, with kids being cruel the way they are, whereas Evie loved her grandfather and wished they looked more alike. Often she dreamt about living with her grandparents instead of her parents, but it's the lot of a child to rarely get what they want.

The line shuffles forward again and now they're at the front of it.

'Um, I . . .' Oliver starts then looks mildly pained. 'I hope you don't mind . . . I have a favour to ask.'

'Right,' Evie says, wondering what it could be, considering he didn't know she'd be here. Or did he?

'My brother's actually a hairdresser. He was doing that in Italy. Doing really well.' Oliver smiles quickly. 'But he wanted to come home. *Mum* wanted him to come home. And, ah . . . he needs a job. So I was wondering if, ah . . . if, um . . .'

His brow knits and Evie wants to save him the worry and fill in the rest for him, but at the same time she thinks he should say it. If you're asking a person for a favour it's a good idea to actually *ask*.

'If you're a hairdresser short, would there be a spot for Sam?' he finally gets out.

She's mildly irritated that he's using this chance encounter to ask her for something, but she knows she'd do the same thing if it were her brother. Or maybe not, because her brothers don't like asking for help. For Billy. She'd do it for Billy. And for Stevo, because he's family too.

'Maybe,' she says to Oliver. 'I'll have to ask Trudy. It's her place.'

'All right, great, thanks, yeah, that's good, fine.' He sounds so relieved.

'We're on, Evie,' Juzzy says, taking her elbow as if she's saving her from the conversation.

'Good to see you,' Evie says to Oliver as the gate opens. 'I'll ask Trudy then call you, yeah?' He'll be in the phone book; everyone is.

'Thank you.' He smiles. 'I really appreciate it.'

'What are friends for?'

His eyes cloud momentarily. 'I don't want you to think I'm using you,' he says softly.

'You're not.' She pats his arm. 'You're helping your brother.'

Before she has a chance to say goodbye she's swept up in the tide of her friends, putting irons in hands, and when she turns back to wave to Oliver she sees him walking away with Steve and a couple of other men.

It's a shame, in some ways, that she didn't feel the spark for him, but you can't force it. As Priss once said, it's there or it isn't. Evie just wishes she knew what *there* felt like, because she's never had it.

But that's a conundrum for another time.

CHAPTER NINE

Anna thought that when you kicked a husband out of the house, it was his job to stay out. That would be the polite thing to do when your wife has made it clear she doesn't want you around, along with spending some time to contemplate your life and your decisions and working out if you've perhaps made some wrong ones. Like having an affair. Not that Anna has any proof of that, and after she blurted out her suspicion to Ingrid the other day, her mother cautioned her about getting too attached to the idea of something so serious before finding out if it's true.

'Those stories we tell ourselves can be very dangerous,' Ingrid said darkly and Anna wondered how she'd come to that conclusion, considering her mother has always seemed to live very much in stark reality, what with her husband being incapacitated for so many years. However, Anna didn't ask for more detail and Ingrid didn't offer it. Some things hover between mothers and daughters, undefined and unaddressed, and they can stay that way forever. Anna has some of those with Ingrid, and Renee will probably have a few with her, and that's just fine. They don't need to know everything about each other.

Although Ingrid did ask Anna if she wanted to 'see someone'. After saying it was a bit early to find a new man, Anna was informed that 'seeing someone' meant 'going to a psychiatrist'. She declined. Throwing Gary out wasn't anything that needed medical attention. It was the only rational thing to do in the circumstances.

Not that Gary thinks so, which is why he's sitting across from Anna holding a hot cuppa, drumming his fingertips on the kitchen table, not looking at her, biting his bottom lip.

'How long is this going to go on?' he's asking her, still drumming.

'What?'

'You not letting me live at home.' He looks up and she's surprised to see dismay in his eyes.

'This wasn't your home, Gary,' she says, trying not to sound snarky. 'It was your dormitory.'

His nostrils flare and he grips the cup tightly. 'That's unfair,' he says.

The kids are playing outside and she can hear Renee giggling. They haven't really noticed that their father isn't living there any more, and Anna is quite aware that it's because of the very reason she asked him to move out.

'Okay,' she says. 'Tell me why.'

He stares at her and she stares back as his mouth opens then closes then opens again.

'I know I wasn't here much,' he concedes. 'But it was only for a little while.'

'Two years,' she says, because she was keeping track. Of course, now she realises she was likely keeping track of how long his affair has been going on. Not that she's going to say that to him because he'll just deny it. And she has no proof. It's hard – nay, impossible – to think of anything else that would keep him away from her, from the kids, night after night after night. No one likes their job that much.

'It wasn't!' he says quickly, then frowns. 'Was it?'

'From when you took on Brendan,' she says. 'You told me having a partner would mean less work, not more. But it didn't.' She sighs, more from irritation than anything. Why is he putting her through this conversation? They're done. Not officially. Not legally. In her heart, though – that's where he really doesn't live any more. Because he can't. She won't let him.

'I know,' he says. 'I know. But he has a young family and –'

'So do you!'

Gary looks so confused right then – as if he has no idea what she could mean. How is it possible he can't understand?

'But it's my practice,' he says. 'I was trying to . . .' He lets go of the mug and runs his hand over his head. That's one thing that has changed about him since they married: his hairstyle. In the olden days he wore it longer; now he has it short all over. Easier, she supposes, to maintain for the busy lawyer on the go.

'Trying to what?' she prompts.

'Trying to look after everyone.' Now it's his turn to sigh. 'That's all I wanted to do.'

'So why didn't you?' She knows it's mean to say that but she also genuinely wants to know the answer. That is, she'd like to hear the excuse he's coming up with.

'Didn't I?' The dismay is back. 'We paid off the mortgage. The kids have everything they want.'

'Except your time,' she retorts. 'Do you really think money is the only thing our children want or need from you? That I need from you?'

'But . . .' He sighs again; this time it's ragged. Long. 'But I was providing for you,' he goes on. 'For the kids. That's my job. That's what I promised you when we married.'

Anna can't remember asking for such a promise, nor it being given – maybe because it wasn't something she required. What she remembers is him saying that with her by his side he felt like he could do anything, and she felt proud of that. She felt that was the balance they had: he would go out and do things, achieve things, that he wouldn't be able to do without her support, and she would have a good life, with a husband who adored her and the kids they both wanted.

He fulfilled his part of it, she guesses, except for this: he doesn't adore her any more. And it turns out that's the part she really cares about. Perhaps she'd care more about the providing if he wasn't doing that, but why can't she have both? She used to. He had her support right up until the end, because she ran his household for him and that enabled him to go out and do what he felt he needed to without having to worry about clean undies and food in the fridge. Men underestimate the worth of that, they really do – the fact that they wouldn't be able to put half the time and energy into their work if they also had to do the million small tasks women took care of for them.

They're staring at each other again but her mind is wandering, to the list of things she needs to tick off today, to planning for the week ahead so she can make sure the kids have everything they need for school, and remembering to take her mother to the shops after they go to the salon tomorrow.

'What do you want?' Gary says quietly. So quietly she almost doesn't hear it.

'Hm?' She's buying time because the question has flummoxed her – not because she doesn't know what she wants but because he's never asked her before. Not that she can remember.

'What do you want?' he repeats, his voice catching.

She narrows her eyes, trying to work out if he's genuinely upset or just trying one on. 'I want you to care about what happens in this house,' she says. 'But you don't.'

'Anna, I genuinely . . .' Another catch in his voice. Another ragged sigh. 'I love you,' he says.

She can't help the laugh that escapes from her lips and she can see how much it hurts him. That wasn't her intention, but she feels hurt herself and that's where it came from. All these years of supporting him so he could do what he wanted to do, only for him to consider her – their children – less and less worthy of his time. Because of another woman. Probably. Maybe.

'It's easy to say it,' she says.

'Because it's true,' he says firmly.

'Not so easy to show it, then. Is it?'

He looks confused again. 'But I do,' he insists.

'By working?'

'By *providing*.'

This is, she thinks, the point he'll keep repeating, probably long after they're divorced.

Divorce.

That's a word that actually hasn't popped into her head before. Is that what they're doing – divorce? Yet another thing she'll have to manage for both of them because he's not going to initiate it. Well, it's a year off anyway. One year they have to be separated. She knows that because her friend Tina just went through it.

'We're not getting anywhere here, Gary,' she says. 'But what I'd really like is for you to take more of an interest in the children.'

'I do!'

'Turning up for an hour or so on the weekend is not taking an interest.'

'So . . .' He frowns.

He really doesn't get it, does he? Maybe that's her fault. She made it all too easy for him to not be involved with anything in this household. Loosened his grip on their lives for him, then pulled off the last finger he was using to hold on.

'Troy has Saturday sport, Renee likes to go along. Maybe you could take them to that each weekend?'

'Will you come too?' He looks a little pathetic as he says it.

'No. It's for you to spend time with them. I do that every day. And night. And don't just take them then stand around talking to the other dads, please. Pay *attention*. They need to know you care.'

His mouth opens and she holds up her hand.

'I know you think you do,' she says, 'but you don't. They can tell.'

He nods slowly. 'All right,' he concedes.

She stands, hoping he'll take it for the signal to leave that she intends it to be.

'Where are you going now?' he says, slowly standing up.

'To the park.'

'Can I come?'

She sighs, considering her options. There are at least two loads of washing here, and she wants to make spag bol for dinner, and a casserole they can eat later in the week. It would be handy if she didn't have to go to the park.

'How about you take them?' she says.

'Oh.'

'Seriously, Gary? You can't handle taking your own children to the park? You need me to do it with you?'

His eyes water. 'It's not that,' he says. 'I just want to spend time with you.'

'You had years to do that,' she says. 'And you didn't. Don't make the same mistake with the kids.'

He closes his eyes for a second or two then opens them and looks toward the garden. 'I won't,' he promises. Then he picks up his car keys from the table and walks out the back door, calling to the children.

Anna heads for the laundry and starts the day's chores. It isn't until she comes across a stray sock of Gary's – who knows where on earth the other sock is, because the eternal mystery of washing is how socks become separated – that she feels something bubbling up that she really doesn't want to deal with. Not irritation, because she'd allow herself that – indeed, has been for months. Not anger. She's not given to anything so forceful, usually.

No . . .

A sob erupts from her chest and she's shocked by it.

What? WHY?

She's not sad about him being gone. She can't be. This is what she wanted.

Isn't it?

Sniffling back the tears that threaten to pour out of her because she really does not want to waste time on an emotional outburst, she switches on the radio in time for the bridge of Bonnie Tyler's 'Total Eclipse of the Heart' to waft out of it. Great. Not the song she wants to hear right now. Turning the knob through the AM dial she alights on a Lionel Richie song that is not about a broken heart and hums along to it.

Distractions. That's what she needs in order to get through whatever this is.

Distractions and a new version of herself, so she's not the Anna whose marriage went to hell.

Humming along to Lionel, she starts to daydream about who that Anna may be.

CHAPTER TEN

'Um . . .' Josie bites her bottom lip and looks around for the comb Trudy has just asked her for. Twice.

Now Trudy is jerking her head in the direction of the wheelie-tray thing that is on the other side of the salon. Seriously, Josie is starting to think Trudy is laying traps for her, putting the tools she asks for all over the place so Josie has to find them. Like a treasure hunt with no treasure, just the reward of combing someone's hair.

Josie scurries over to the tray only to find three combs of different sizes but the same colour: tortoiseshell. That's confusing. Oh, and the teeth are different on one comb compared to the next. How is she meant to know which comb Trudy wants?

Wait. Something's coming back to her: Trudy said the other day that combs need to match hair. Which Josie knows because she learnt it at tech but everything's great in theory till you're looking at someone's wet hair and trying to work out if it's fine or thick. Or neither.

The other day there was a lady in who Trudy told her was forty-five. Then Josie said something about her being old and Trudy looked upset. Whoops. Anyway, the lady's hair was thinning. Josie had learnt about that too. Something to do with menopause. Which is not something Josie thinks she needs to worry about, except here was the lady with the menopause hair and Josie didn't know whether the fact it was thinning meant it was fine hair, or could menopause hair still be thick? It's that sort of thing that confuses her when she's trying to choose a comb.

'Josie,' Trudy says.

Josie goes back to biting her lip. 'Oh.' She picks up the comb she thinks is right and carries it to Trudy, who raises her eyebrows. Josie can almost feel Evie raising hers too. She doesn't think Evie likes her because she barely speaks to her.

The other day some bloke called Sam turned up to talk to Trudy about a job and Evie hardly drew breath speaking to him. Yeah, the guy was good-looking – handsome, maybe? It was funny, because he was tall and dark-haired like the leading men are in the movies Josie likes except she didn't fancy him. He seemed really nice and he was interested in talking to Evie – or maybe Evie was interested in talking to him – and if a man like that had spoken to her a year or so ago Josie wouldn't have known what to say to him, because handsome men never speak to her, but these days she doesn't worry about them so much. Maybe it's because of the men she's met while she's been practising her hairdressing. A lot of men. A lot of women too. She's kind of immune to a good-looking guy now because no matter what he looks like he can turn out to be boring when you've got your hands on his head for an hour.

'Josie!'

Oh no. She's drifted off again. That happens sometimes – she gets into her own head. Her mother says that: *You're in your own head*. Josie isn't quite sure what it means because when she drifts off she feels like she's everywhere *but* in her own head.

She picks another comb and takes it over to Trudy, who peers down then gives her a single nod, so she guesses it's the right comb.

'Now you can prep the colour,' Trudy says. 'My cards out the back have the details for everyone's colours. Look for the one marked "Felicity".'

'Oh – all right,' Josie says meekly, then she turns and heads for the back room, which is where the colours are kept as well as their handbags and the fridge and the towels. And all the spare stuff. Trudy likes to have things on hand so they never run out.

The gowns for the clients all hang in a little cupboard in the salon. The first day Josie went looking for them out the back – everything else was out there, so she thought they must be there too – and the others were busy chatting so she didn't want to ask where they were. She felt like an idiot searching through the back room and not finding them. Which is how she used to feel at school, trying to spell a word she didn't know, and she'd try to work it out – she'd try really hard – but the teachers never cared about that. All they cared about was that she got it wrong.

Trudy isn't like her teachers, though. Once Josie found the gown – and the search probably only took a couple of minutes, although it seemed much longer – and put it on the client, Trudy smiled and winked at her and didn't say anything, although Josie was sure Trudy knew she'd had trouble finding it.

Still, today she feels pretty stupid, trying to figure out which comb is which, and now she's looking at the card for Felicity and at the colours on the shelves and worrying about mixing the colour for this client. If you get a colour wrong it can be a disaster. Really. Once during a class another student put a colour on someone and it turned out so bad. It was meant to be brown and it went orange on this woman, and oh god the woman was very upset.

So Josie takes her time to study the card then check the colours on the shelves and match them to what Trudy has written up. Josie may have trouble reading but she knows how to match words, because she recognises shapes. She also doesn't have a problem with numbers. Maths was her favourite subject, but also the source of some stick from her teachers, because they'd say she didn't jumble up her numbers, therefore they didn't believe her when she said her words were jumbled up.

Yeah, school was hard. She's glad it's over.

Once she mixes the colour she delivers it to Trudy, feeling a little sick in case it goes wrong but also kind of fine because she just knows Trudy would fix it if there were something amiss. Trudy just has that air about her.

'Would you like to take your lunch break now?' Trudy says to her.

'Okay!' Josie says, and it's such a relief because now she doesn't have to watch the colour going on and by the time she's back from lunch the client will probably have had her hair shampooed and any problems will have been handled by Trudy.

From the back room Josie picks up her handbag and her sandwich. Devon and tomato sauce – she liked having it at school and there's no sense changing something you like. And she doesn't have it every day. Some days it's Vegemite and lettuce – trying to be healthy. Her mum tells her to eat more vegetables but the meals at home are full of vegies, so why should her lunch be?

Each day she's gone to a new spot for lunch. Once she walked all the way to the Skillion and she didn't realise how long it took her, so she was late getting back. All Trudy said was, 'Maybe wear a watch next time, pet.' Josie was given a Swatch last Christmas by her parents, and she managed to lose it so doesn't even have a watch to wear. There's a clock in the salon so she doesn't need one there, and one on the outside of Terrigal Surf Life Saving Club, so since that Skillion day she's stayed within sight of the club and used that clock to mark time.

That's why she plonks herself down on a seat not far from the club, underneath one of the pine trees. There's seagull poo – she guesses it's from seagulls, she has no actual proof – on one side so she takes the other side and opens up her sandwich wrapper.

It's nice there. Peaceful. Her brain races a lot – she has all these thoughts, and worries, and things she wants to say, but she thinks they'll sound stupid if they leave her mouth so she keeps them all inside, which makes her brain feel crowded. In the past only listening to music or watching a movie made it better but now she finds that looking at the water calms it down too. If she just sits and watches the waves while she eats her sandwich, time passes and she doesn't worry about anything. Funny how you can get all the way to being an adult and find out something like that. Funny how upset you can be that you didn't find it out when you were younger. Maybe it would have helped.

Water drips near her feet and she looks up to see a tall guy in one of those short-sleeved wetsuits, holding a surfboard. He has blond hair that's kind of going every which way, and zinc cream on his nose. He's cute. And her immediate thought is that she's in his way, which is ridiculous because she's on a seat that is literally cemented to the ground so she can hardly have got in anyone's way.

'Hi,' he says.

Now some drops of water land on her skin, but she doesn't mind.

'Hi.' She has to squint a little to look at him.

'You work at the salon,' he says.

She frowns, because she can't remember seeing him there. 'Um . . . yeah.'

He nods. 'I take my nan there on Monday mornings. I don't go in. But I saw you this week. Looked like you were working there.'

'I'm an apprentice,' she says.

'Oh yeah?' He tosses his head the way boys do when they've been underwater, as if they're dogs shaking off a bath. 'Me too.'

'Where?'

'Mechanic's.' He jerks his chin in the direction of the shops. 'A coupla streets back.'

Now it's her turn to nod.

'Name's Brett.'

'Josie.'

He grins; his teeth are white and his smile is electric and she can't help smiling back.

'That's such a pretty name,' he says. 'For a pretty girl.'

Her smile drops because she's so surprised – he's calling her pretty? Her cheeks feel hot and she looks down.

'Anyway, better get going.' He dips the front of his board as if he's bowing to her. 'See ya, Josie.'

'Bye,' she says meekly, looking after him as he walks away, only to see him turn around and wave.

The rest of her sandwich sits uneaten in its Glad Wrap because there is something in her stomach that makes her not want to eat any more. Nerves, maybe? Or excitement. Both. Neither. Who knows. Who cares! A cute boy called her pretty.

CHAPTER ELEVEN

It's been a while since Trudy's had a bloke working in the salon. There was Carlos, that nice Spanish lad – that was quite a few years ago. He made it clear from the start he wasn't likely to stay more than a year – 'I wish to see the world, *señora*,' he told her, and at the time Trudy was mildly offended because she thought she still qualified to be a *señorita*. She used to look young for her age; smoking took care of that but it's too late to change now and she has no regrets.

After Carlos there was Greg, who had a boyfriend and never mentioned the man's name in front of the clients because he believed that if the boyfriend's existence was known it could cause issues. Trudy didn't tell him her clientele had done and seen a lot – including a war or two – and were the least likely people to judge anyone, but she didn't know for sure, and Greg's experience of life was quite different to hers so it wasn't for her to tell him what to do. Greg lasted a couple of years then moved to Brisbane. She raised her eyebrows at that news – if he thought the Central Coast was conservative, the Joh Bjelke-Petersen regime north of the border would be an adjustment – but from the occasional letter he wrote he seemed to be content.

Since Greg she's had only women working for her – not by design, it's just how it turned out. So when Sam walked through the door this morning it was almost as if there was a shift in the ballast of the place. In a good way.

'Hello!' he said in a deep voice, smiling broadly.

Nice teeth, Trudy had noticed when he first came in the other day to say hello. Not that she usually assesses people as though they were horses, but when someone smiles it's hard to avoid noticing their teeth.

Evie hadn't said anything about Sam being so handsome when she asked Trudy if she'd consider giving him a trial. Then again, Trudy is a little vague on whether or not Evie had even met him. She knows his brother, and was sparing with the details so maybe they used to go out – although she thinks Evie would have told her that. They've chatted about almost everything over the six years Evie's been working for her. She started when Billy was one year old and she needed a job to support him; Trudy didn't ask questions about why Billy's father wasn't supporting him and Evie seemed grateful. Before she had Billy she'd been working at a salon at Long Jetty and Trudy never found out why she didn't go back there – because it didn't matter. Trudy could tell from the start that Evie had a knack for hair. So when she told Trudy about Sam, Trudy trusted her.

When Sam arrived he walked straight over to Trudy, taking her hand with both of his, as if they were long-lost friends. Usually that sort of greeting annoys her, because it always seems a little earnest – or fake-friendly – but he was still smiling and he looked deeply into her eyes and, well, the man was charming. *Is* charming.

He's now attending to his first client. Merle has been coming to the salon for decades and when Trudy asked if she'd mind being the try-out for the new bloke, she didn't hesitate.

'It's been a while since I've had a man run his fingers through my hair, Trudy,' she said. 'Count me in.'

Merle is one of her more game clients. Most of the ladies like their hair done the way they've always had it done. For those clients Trudy may suggest a change every few years, most often to a more practical hairdo for those who don't want to spend much time on themselves. Otherwise it's a wash and dry and a set, with the occasional trim. The bread and butter of her business, so she's not complaining. It's just nice to have a regular like Merle who came in one day having seen *101 Dalmatians* and asked for 'a Cruella De Vil' then, a few months later, 'a Liz Taylor'. Elizabeth Taylor has been the inspiration for a few of Merle's hairstyles over the years. They look nothing alike, but Trudy's always created a reasonable facsimile of La Liz's hair.

Today Sam's instructions are to give Merle a haircut – not just a trim. Merle's in her seventies now but her hair is strong so there's plenty to work with, and she's been growing it out for a while.

'I'm in my Martha Graham era,' she told Trudy a few months ago, although Trudy didn't know who that was so she said nothing in reply.

'Right, darl,' Sam says as he puts his fingertips to Merle's cheeks, a comb in one hand, tilting his head from side to side. 'Do you have ideas or would you like me to make a decision for you?'

Merle catches Trudy's eye in the mirror and winks. 'Surprise me,' she says to Sam, who looks gleeful.

'Such a great face,' he murmurs. 'Did you model?'

Merle snorts. 'Only for my husband when I bought a new brassiere.'

From the other side of the salon Evie makes a strangled noise, although her client is absorbed in a book and appears not to have heard anything. Evie looks a little shocked, although Trudy would have thought she'd be used to Merle by now. The woman can be outrageous.

Sam, however, is not at all shocked. In fact, he's laughing, his head thrown back.

'Has anyone ever told you that you look like Montgomery Clift?' Merle asks.

'Yes,' Sam says, running his fingers over her scalp as Merle closes her eyes.

'That's good, love,' she says. 'Keep doing that.'

Trudy's next client arrives and she looks around for Josie, who's been refolding the towels. The creases weren't sharp enough for her liking, apparently.

'Josie, pet, can you do a wash?' she calls out.

As her client sits by the basin, Trudy keeps one eye on Sam. Not that he needs monitoring – she can see from the way he's not only talking to Merle but cutting her hair that he has experience, and that he's good with clients – but she needs to check out what he's doing. This is her business, and it's already been dented by one former hairdresser. There may be no way to guard against a repeat of Jane's behaviour, but it makes Trudy feel better to think she's not rushing to give Sam a gold star. He'll have to earn it. Except she doesn't actually want him to feel watched, so she goes to the appointment book and pretends to be busy.

While she's there, positioned in the middle of the salon, between Sam and Evie, she notices Evie looking into the mirror, across at Sam. They've had minimal interaction today, apart from Sam waving his greeting just after he met Merle, which makes Trudy now believe firmly that they've never spent much time together. And also makes her believe that Evie must really like this Oliver fellow, since she's so willing to help his brother. Except she can't like him like *that* because she's looking at Sam as if he's a member of one of those pop bands the girls are into – Wham! or some such. She likes that George Michael's hair – very nicely layered, and the colour is good too. Apart from that, though, the man does nothing for her.

Then Evie's eyes meet hers in the mirror and she glances away. Trudy could swear her cheeks are pink. Interesting.

After Merle is done – her hair beautifully shaped, and a big smile on her face – Sam does another cut then a perm. Soon it's time for lunch, and Trudy invites him into the back room.

'Busy first day already,' she says, lighting her lunchtime ciga-rette and offering one to Sam, who smiles his thanks and takes it. She lights it for him.

Sam drags on the ciggie then narrows his eyes. 'I'm fairly sure you've been kind and given me some of your regulars. I hope they didn't mind?'

'Mind?' She chortles. 'Did you hear Merle saying you look like Monty Clift?'

He grins. 'She's very kind.'

'And correct.'

Sam laughs – that same full-throated laugh as before. It's always lovely being around people who seem to laugh with their whole beings. Their laughter uplifts everyone around them. Since Trudy could do with some uplift, it's another tick for Sam.

'Your clients seem lovely,' he says, flicking ash into her ashtray.

'I'm hiding the mean ones from you for now.'

Another laugh. 'I don't believe you for a second, darl. You're too lovely to have mean clients.'

'Oh, you'll get ahead,' Trudy says wryly, but she's secretly pleased.

'That's what my mother's always said.' He shrugs. 'She's still waiting.'

He frowns but it's gone quickly. Perhaps the smoke is bothering him. Perhaps his mother bothers him. Trudy isn't going to ask.

'Did you bring some tucker?' Trudy says, stubbing out her cigarette.

Sam nods. 'A sandwich.'

'I'll leave you to it.'

'You don't have to go.' Sam looks genuinely disappointed, bless him. 'Unless you do. Sorry – I know this is your salon and you may have things to do.'

'I'll have my lunch in a little while,' she says. 'You need a bit of time to yourself on your first day, I reckon. To figure out if you'll want to come back.'

'Oh, I will,' he says, holding her gaze.

Suddenly she feels as if she's known him forever. Perhaps he's just adept at making people feel comfortable, but it's irrelevant: the point is that she *does* feel comfortable, and glad that he's here. And not a moment too soon. She suspects he may be a secret weapon in keeping people from going to Jane's salon, or enticing them to return. She's definitely not above thinking that a handsome young man is motivation for ladies of all ages to come to a salon . . .

'Wonderful,' she says. 'Because I believe you'll be a hit.'

She heads back to the salon floor and once again catches the eye of Evie, who is frowning.

'All good, pet,' she says, thinking that perhaps Evie needs to be reassured about their new staff member, then she turns to greet the next client coming through the door.

CHAPTER TWELVE

S am has only been working at the salon for a few days but Evie feels as if they're old friends. He's very good at putting people at ease. He flatters the clients, telling them he's happy to see them, or that he likes their shoes, asking about their weeks, their families, their hobbies. It all seems sincere, that he is genuinely interested. Or at least that he looks for the best in everyone and finds it.

The other day he made even their grumpiest client, Mrs Klein, smile, and after she left, Trudy let out a whoop.

'Sammy-boy, you worked a miracle!' she cried, to his puzzlement.

'She's been coming here for years,' Evie explained. 'And not smiled once.'

'Until today.' Trudy kept combing out her client. 'Isn't that right, Babs?'

'Sure is,' Babs said. 'She's a terror, that Enid.'

'That might be a little harsh,' Trudy said, laughing.

Babs turned around so she was looking Trudy in the face. 'You try playing her at bowls then tell me what you'd call her.' Babs then nodded her head once and turned back around, picking up her cigarette.

Sam was working next to Evie, so it was she who saw his big smile.

'That's nice,' he said softly.

'It's more than nice!' Evie said. 'It's a miracle!'

He'd laughed, then given his full attention to his client.

Today he came in literally with a spring in his step. He starts at ten o'clock – part of the reason why Trudy wanted to take him on was so he could stay later in the day for the clients who need their hair done for a night out, so he starts later accordingly. It's Trudy's new thing: offering blow-dries only. Clients were asking for them. Evie thinks it's because of the TV shows – all those American actresses have blow-dries. So the Central Coast ladies all want the Krystle Carrington. Well, blow-dries takes work so they all come back wanting Trudy or Evie or Sam, now, to make it look like it did that first day they got it done. Which is good for business, not so good for their hair with all the heat.

'Morning!' Sam called as he arrived, handing Trudy a bunch of flowers.

'What are these for?' Trudy asked.

'For you. For the salon. I love having flowers around, don't you?'

Trudy agreed. And so did Evie, although she didn't say so, just silently marvelled at a man who could appreciate flowers. She's long thought that kind of man didn't exist. Her father never brought her mother flowers, even though her mother loved them. And Stevo . . . well, they didn't reach that flowers stage, which is funny, considering they managed to conceive a child together.

'How are you, Evie?' Sam said as he wandered her way. 'Did Billy go off to school okay?'

He knows all about Billy, and asks after him, and her, every day. No one has ever been this interested in her – including her own family members – and while she knows Sam is likely being polite, his conversation isn't just about the comings and goings in her life. He wants to know more, go deeper. It's flattering. It's . . .

She doesn't know what it is. When he looks at her with those big brown eyes and that thick, impressive hair, his square jaw and his high cheekbones and his perfect eyebrows . . . No, she can't think about him like this. They work together.

Besides, Trudy has noticed.

'Listen to you, chatterbox,' she said yesterday with this funny smile. They were in the back room and Evie was checking their supplies so she could do an order.

'Hm?' Evie kept looking in the cupboard.

'I think you've said more to that bloke in a week than you've said to me the whole year.'

That made Evie stop, because she hadn't realised she'd been talking that much, or that anyone was paying attention, and it made her feel a little embarrassed, like she was in Year 9 when her friends found out she had a crush on this guy Jason who arrived during second term. And they found out because she couldn't hide it. Everywhere he went, her eyes followed. She embarrassed *herself*, forget her friends doing it for her. But they did. Eventually Jason found out and he avoided her, which was worse. She hasn't had a crush since, and she's not sure if it's because she hasn't met anyone crush-worthy or if she just pushed down that part of herself. Stevo didn't count, because they kind of slipped and fell on each other.

'Oh,' she said in response to Trudy.

'Be careful there,' Trudy said, but it didn't sound like a warning. Just a friendly note. Or perhaps that was how Evie wanted to interpret it.

'So, Mary,' she says into the mirror, where Mary's eyes meet hers. 'What are we doing today?'

'Mmm.' Mary moves her head from side to side while not breaking her gaze into the mirror. It has a rather odd effect. 'Not sure. Time for a change, maybe?'

Mary tried a fringe last year, then decided she didn't like it. She's been growing it out. Her hair's been long forever so cutting some of it to make a fringe was a big step.

'What sort of change?' Evie asks, not wanting to guess.

'Off.' Mary nods once, definitively. 'Chop it off.'

'What?' Evie says, and detects Trudy's head turning in their direction. Yes, Trudy would understand the import of this.

'Yep.' Another nod. 'I want the Lady Di.'

That's the other haircut they've been asked for over the past few years. It also requires blow-drying, which the clients say they understand but don't really. It requires thick hair too, which the princess has and Mary does not. Moreover, Mary has always struck Evie as the no-nonsense type whose plain hairstyle suits her.

'Why?' Evie says.

'Less work,' Mary says.

'Um . . .' Evie turns in Trudy's direction and raises her eyebrows. Trudy responds in kind.

'It's not actually,' Evie goes on. 'What you have now just needs a shampoo and a condition and you're done. That Diana haircut needs blow-drying to look good. You don't blow-dry at the moment, do you?'

'No.'

'Do you really want to start?'

'Hubby tells me I'll look good with it.'

And there it is: wait long enough and the client tends to cough up the truth. So many times a lady will come in wanting something done that is ostensibly for her and it turns out that the husband wants it, usually because he's bored of her or he fancies a particular celebrity. Evie wants to point out that Mary's husband is no oil painting, yet here he is telling her what to do with her hair. She wishes she could ask Mary what her husband would look good with, but that likely wouldn't end anywhere positive, so like everyone who works in a service job she keeps her thoughts to herself and tries to figure out a way to make this right for the client.

'All right. Well. If you're sure . . .' Evie stares at Mary in the mirror, hoping she's making her point.

In response Mary pulls out a photo of Diana around the time she gave birth to Prince Harry, when her hair was long and thick from the pregnancy and she had these big, dramatic layers. It is not a look Mary will ever achieve. Especially since Diana matched it with eyeliner and lots of mascara. No wonder she's called 'Dynasty Di'.

'I want that,' Mary says and Evie thinks she can hear Trudy sighing from across the salon.

The next thing Evie knows Sam is beside her, his hip bumping hers as he bends over to look at the photo, and Evie wonders if he did it purposely, as if he wanted to touch her, and if that's the case she really wants to know, because she'll tuck it into a corner of her mind and pull out the memory when she's feeling down on herself. This beautiful man touched her on purpose. This man who looks like the man she's long had a crush on – Paul McCartney – with his doe eyes and thick hair, come to life right here in Terrigal.

Evie feels her heart rate quickening and she swallows and looks away. Oh dear. Maybe Trudy was right – she *should* be careful. Because this feels like desire, and she knows from reading romance novels that desire is inconvenient and essential and overwhelming and amazing, and she also knows that she has never felt it like this before.

'Darl,' Sam says, still bent over the photo.

When he calls the clients darl they titter, as Mary does now.

Then he straightens and puts a hand on Mary's head. 'I'm going to be blunt, darl,' he says. 'I'd love to see you keep this hair long.'

Mary opens her mouth and he holds up a hand.

'I don't care what hubby says. If he wants you to have short hair you can put it in a French roll from time to time, okay?' He winks. 'Long hair is something a lot of ladies want and can't grow, isn't that right, Evie?'

Now he's turned to her, gazing into her eyes, and Evie swallows again.

'Um, yes,' she says.

'So we don't lose the long if we don't have to, Mary.' He pats her head. 'But if you want to make some sort of change I'm sure Evie can work out something.' He smiles at Evie as if she's hung the moon, then goes back to his client.

'Isn't he lovely,' Mary whispers, looking like a giddy schoolgirl.

'He is,' Evie whispers back, taking Mary's lengths into her hands. 'Now, let's have a think about this.' She gazes down and sees, in a way she hasn't before, that Mary has lovely chestnut tones in her hair that could work well with some contrast. 'How about we do some streaks in your hair?' she suggests.

Mary blinks rapidly. 'Streaks? Oh no, that's for . . .'

Evie isn't sure what Mary was going to say but she can guess.

'For models?' Evie says.

Mary nods.

'They're for other people too,' Evie says. 'And I reckon they'll look great on you. Do you trust me?'

Now Mary smiles along with her nods. Evie grins back. This is part of what she really likes about this job: making clients happy. Her mother would tell her that she needs to make herself happy too – mums are always right about that stuff – and she does, but she'll settle for making these ladies happy in the meantime.

As she heads to the back room to mix the colour she catches Sam's eye and he smiles at her as if she's made the sun come out. *That* makes her happy. He makes her happy. Which is a lot to put on a man she barely knows but she can't help it. And she doesn't want to.

CHAPTER THIRTEEN

It's just before nine o'clock on Monday morning, so Trudy sips the last of her coffee while she thinks about not much at all. It's a tactic she's developed since Laurie died: not thinking. Not thinking means not remembering. Not remembering means that she can keep her grief at bay, even if it's just for a little while, because the not-thinking tends to last as long as one cup of coffee or one cigarette, whichever she can get her hands on.

To be clear: she thinks about *something* but it's nothing that can start her worrying or grieving, which are the two states she needs to avoid otherwise, as her GP said the other day, she'll succumb to stress.

Succumb to stress. What a phrase. It makes her sound like a goldfish in a bowl that gets moved around all the time – you know how fish can die if they're stressed? That's her. A goldfish in a bowl that's being moved, except she is also the bowl and the mover, which really does her head in sometimes.

It's when she gets to that point, of everything being stirred up – of feeling she may succumb to stress – that she knows it's time to make a coffee or light a ciggie. They're not so much vices as crutches, and what are crutches for if not to support a person through hard times? Instead of a broken leg she has a broken heart, and that's what she needs the crutches for.

There are other crutches: TV shows. Crosswords. Arnott's Lemon Crisp biscuits. They're moderate, as far as she's concerned. She's not putting away half a bottle of whiskey a night – her parents had a neighbour like that. 'Slow suicide' her father called it, and Trudy agrees with that. She doesn't want to kill herself slowly; she just needs some help in the here and now.

Her clients are a crutch of sorts, with their chatter and laughter and general lack of stress, and that's who she's awaiting. The first one is due in ten minutes and while she waits she thinks about her phone call with Dylan last night.

He rang her and after the hellos she was about to ask him how he was when he said, 'So about a visit.'

She was disoriented by the directness and it took her a second to realise he was referring to their previous phone call.

'Oh – yes?'

'How about Sunday week?'

She stood there, silent, not because she needed to think about whether she would be free that day – the answer was yes, she would be, because her social activity is paltry – but because she couldn't quite believe he was suggesting it. This is the son who needed five reminders to put away his clean laundry. And she always made him put it away – she wasn't going to do that for him. No doubt Annemarie is happy she trained him in chores, although they've never discussed it. She and Annemarie aren't close, even though Trudy had been determined not to be the clichéd mother-in-law who has a rocky relationship with her son's wife. So it isn't through lack of effort that she and Annemarie have never had a strong connection – it's through Annemarie's lack of interest in same.

'That'd be lovely, darling,' she said. 'I'll get the train.'

'I can pick you up at the station.'

'Good. Thanks, that'd be great.'

They worked out a time then the call ended and Trudy felt lighter – not that she realised she'd been carrying any sort of weight around about it. It's funny what goes on in a person's own body and mind without them being aware.

The door opens and Trudy smiles as Ingrid and her daughter, Anna, enter, followed by a flustered-looking Josie.

'Sorry, sorry, sorry,' Josie says breathily as she beetles for the back room.

'You're not late, pet!' Trudy calls after her. The girl seems to live in fear of getting in trouble for something, no matter how often Trudy assures her that she's doing a good job. She does things without needing to be asked; she has an eye for detail, not missing a hair on the salon floor or a strand of it out of place on a client's head; plus she's up on the latest hair trends, always looking in the magazines. She also asks for Trudy's advice regularly, which no previous apprentice ever had.

'No, we're early,' Ingrid says, smiling serenely. That's how she usually smiles, and it's in stark contrast to the demeanour of her daughter who is, Trudy thinks, tightly wound – 'strung like a Stradivarius', Laurie would have said.

Anna usually comes in with something to read, or she picks up a magazine from the pile, and sits in the spare chair in the corner, reading, doing the crossword, rarely smiling. Trudy would love to get her mitts on Anna's hair because she thinks there's potential, but she's never chased a client and she's not about to start. Perhaps, though, being in the salon will rub off on Anna one day.

'How are you, Anna?' Trudy says as the younger woman crosses the floor in front of her, not seeming to notice anyone else.

'Tired,' Anna says, plopping down in the chair and opening *New Idea*, which has another cover of The Princess of Wales and that hairstyle. The last blonde who caused that much fuss was Marilyn Monroe. Or Agnetha from ABBA.

'Oh?' Trudy is intrigued, because that's more intel than Anna usually shares. Typically she says 'Fine'.

'Two kids, work, no help.' Anna smiles tightly then holds up the magazine. 'Just need a little respite.'

'Sure,' Trudy says, understanding. But the *no help* thing is interesting: the last time Trudy heard, Anna had a husband. Which doesn't mean she had help, obviously – they're not all like Laurie was – but it's a curious thing to say. Still, Trudy won't push. Some customers are like dogs, panting all over you with their news, and others are like cats, taking their time to decide if you're worth inhabiting the same planet as them. Anna is definitely a cat.

'How's work, pet?' Trudy says. She knows Anna is a seamstress, and that some of her clients have given her work, but not much else.

'Fine. I'm mostly mending. Some alterations.'

'She makes things too,' Ingrid says, smiling at Trudy in the mirror. 'Really lovely dresses.'

Anna looks surprised.

'Dresses?' Trudy prompts. 'I can't even sew on a button properly. I can't imagine making a dress.'

Anna shrugs. 'It's easy once you know how.'

'She creates her own designs,' Ingrid says proudly and again Anna looks as if she's never heard those words before.

'They're not that good,' Anna mumbles.

'Darling, they are!'

'If you say so.'

'I know so.' Ingrid beams. 'Mothers know, don't they, Trudy?'

'We do,' Trudy agrees.

'Thanks, Mama,' Anna says distractedly, then she leafs through the magazine.

Ingrid frowns then her face relaxes.

'The usual?' Trudy asks and Ingrid nods.

By the time she's finished Ingrid, Evie has arrived, and at that point the salon starts to resemble a bus exchange. Clients in, clients out, hairdressers moving around like conductors taking tickets. The bustle is good. The bustle keeps Trudy going. Without it she'd have too much time to think.

An hour later Sam is there and tending to Bobbie, a client who had left to follow Jane but called to book in with 'the new gentleman'. Clearly word's got around about young Sam, and if he's bringing clients to the salon, she's all for it.

'Hello, pet,' she greets Bobbie, trying to keep a straight face because the woman's hair, previously dyed red, is now brown with huge stripes of blonde. It's not a look Trudy recognises, nor one that is flattering – are they meant to be streaks? Jane was always good at streaks.

Trudy didn't check to see what Bobbie's booked in for but she hopes it's a colour – although Sam will need a few hours to fix this mess.

Josie ushers Bobbie to Sam, who acts as if the woman is the best thing he's seen all day. Trudy has no idea where he finds the enthusiasm, but she loves him for it.

'Darl!' he says. 'That's quite the look. Are we keeping it or moving on?'

Bobbie sits with a thud. 'Moving on,' she says, then glances Trudy's way. Trudy smiles as warmly as she can, although she's enjoying this situation far more than she should. Not that she wants Jane to fail. Not much.

Going to check the book – because if Sam's fixing that mess his next client or two will need to be reassigned – Trudy spies Evie gazing wistfully at the back of Sam's head. Evie glances across and notices that Trudy has seen her, and she quickly looks away, her cheeks pink.

Trudy knows that look. She's seen it on countless girls and women talking about the men they love. Their eyes change and their lips part and no matter how many times Trudy sees it, she thinks it's sweet. Not on Evie, though. On Evie it's trouble.

She's well aware Evie needs a little bit of romance, shall we say, but she doesn't believe Evie will get that with Sam. He's not the romancing type – not with ladies. Trudy worked that out pretty quickly because she has been, as Laurie might say, around the traps. But Evie, it seems, hasn't a clue, given the way she's looking at Sam, and Trudy's not going to be the one to tell her, because even though they've known each other for a while, they're not close. Not in the way of discussing potential suitors. Evie would probably tell her to mind her own business if she said anything, and vice versa. Or 'vicky versa'. Laurie used to say that too.

Trudy is worried for Evie, though, because if she's already that far gone, any extrication will be painful. This phase of wanting someone – it's too early to call it love – is like being brainwashed, and nothing Trudy could say would persuade Evie differently. This will just have to play out, and Trudy will have to watch, and be ready to catch Evie when she falls.

Unless she's wrong about Sam. There's always a chance. She was wrong about the last male hairdresser she employed, who raced off with one of her best customers. Last Trudy heard they were in Brisbane running a salon together. Good luck to them.

'Now, darl,' Sam is saying as he tugs on Bobbie's ends, 'do you have time for a conditioning treatment?'

'Of course,' the woman says.

'Josie!' Trudy calls, and her apprentice emerges from the back room, tying up her hair. 'See if anyone would like a coffee, would you?'

Josie smiles and nods, and the door opens again, admitting the next client, and Trudy shakes off her worries for Evie and steps back into the bustle.

MAY 1986

Expo 86 takes place in Vancouver, British Columbia. During a visit, HRH Diana, The Princess of Wales, faints.

The album *So* by Peter Gabriel is released.

The Flying Doctors makes its debut on Australian television screens.

Hands Across America – a human chain comprised of over five million people – stretches from New York City to Long Beach, California.

CHAPTER FOURTEEN

'You look lovely, Mama,' Anna says as she comes to stand behind Ingrid and they glance at each other in the mirror. Anna knows how mirrors work, of course, yet she always finds it a little odd that you can meet someone else's eyes in a mirror. You're not looking right at each other outside of the mirror, yet you are *in the mirror*. Isn't that odd? Doesn't that seem like it goes against the laws of science or nature or something?

Maybe she's overthinking it. 'You are thinking too much,' her mother likes to say to her, and it takes all of Anna's self-control to not bite back when that happens, because she can't believe her mother doesn't realise that she has *relied* on Anna to do the thinking for so many years now.

Like this morning: Ingrid said she wanted to buy a new outfit. 'The bridge ladies have seen all my clothes,' she said. Anna has seen the bridge ladies and doesn't think they'll notice if Ingrid is repeating outfits, but her mother likes to look smart. Anna used to like to look smart and she'd quite like to look smart again, except it's a muscle that has to be used constantly to work effectively and she's let hers atrophy. Which is not her mother's fault, even though Anna sometimes resents her for looking so put-together all the time. Can't the woman slip, just once? Of course not. Appearances have to be maintained, just as they did when Anna's father had his accident. Back then Ingrid relied on Anna to help her with that maintenance – and she's still doing it.

The outfit-shopping needed some organisation. For Ingrid, buying clothes does not mean pitching up at the local shops and hoping for the best. It's a mission, so it needs planning and targets. Anna did a recce in Gosford and found a boutique she thought Ingrid would like, and that's where they're standing now, with Ingrid in a matching cerise jacket and skirt with blue trim – possibly too dressy for bridge, but then again Ingrid has her own standards.

'The colour isn't too . . . loud?' Ingrid asks, scanning herself up and down, her blonde helmet of hair barely moving as she does so.

Anna shakes her head. 'Nuh-uh. Hot pink would be too loud.'

'Unless it's shocking pink.'

They smile knowingly at each other. Anna has learnt some fashion lore at her mother's metaphorical feet, and Ingrid worships at the altar of Elsa Schiaparelli, who was synonymous with shocking pink.

Their little in-jokes remind Anna they have things in common outside of just trying to make it through each day, which is what has marked most of their lives together.

'We're decided, then,' Ingrid declares, then disappears into the change room to put on her slacks and turtleneck.

Back in the car, Anna looks at her watch, considering all the other things that need to be done today.

'You wanted to go to Noraville,' she states as she starts the engine.

'If you have time.' Ingrid puts on her Jackie Onassis sunglasses and Anna stops herself from laughing, as she usually does. Her mother is not at all like the soignée Jackie. Ingrid is elegant in her own way, but it's a very different way to Jackie, so the big, dark sunglasses don't fit her overall look. But she loves them and Anna supposes that's all that matters.

Noraville is the cemetery where her father lies in ashes. The advantage of only having ashes to bury is that one plot can fit a whole family, and given their straitened circumstances at the time of his death, it made sense to just buy the one plot and make plans for them all to go in it, also in ashes.

He died when Anna was twenty-three, far too late for her to go to university with her friends from school – she hadn't been able to even think about it before that, because she had to be at home to help. In that time after school, though, she took up sewing, and became good at it. She did piecework for a local dressmaker and sometimes dreamt of starting her own fashion business. Now she only makes the occasional dress she designs herself, and Ingrid's never asked her to make one, which is why Anna was surprised to hear her talking about them at the salon the other day.

The drive takes a while and they pass it mostly not talking, listening to classical music on the radio. There's no need for a mother and daughter to talk all the time, Anna supposes, although she'd like to think she and Renee would always have something to talk about.

When they arrive, Anna follows Ingrid to the grave.

'It seems like a long time,' Ingrid says as they stand, both with their hands folded in front of them. It's something Anna does when she's standing still; no doubt she learnt it from her mother.

'It *is* a long time, Mama,' Anna murmurs.

'And yet it's not.' Ingrid has a faraway smile. 'He was a marvellous dancer, your father.'

Anna restrains herself from sighing, because Ingrid loves to retell the story of how she met her husband, and Anna knows it inside out. That's not the point, though, is it? Anna recognised long ago that Ingrid's retelling is like a talisman, warding off the full impact of the past. If Ingrid keeps retelling the old stories it's as if she hasn't moved on from them. As if she's still there, at the dance, seeing Ingrid's father for the first time as he crossed the floor, bowed, held out his hand and asked her to join him.

'Such grace,' Ingrid says.

Anna could take the story from there because it doesn't change in the retelling. However, she knows better: the talisman only works if it's Ingrid who wields it.

'He hated being in that chair,' Ingrid goes on, and that's part of the story too – the back-and-forth between past and present.

Today, though, Anna isn't in the mood for indulging it. 'We all hated it,' she says.

Her mother blinks as if she's coming out of a trance. 'What?'

'Mama, we all hated him being in that chair. Especially you. And me.'

More blinking. 'I didn't . . .' Ingrid purses her lips and turns her head away.

Anna glances down at the headstone. *Barnaby Powell. Loved and missed.*

'Of course you did,' Anna says. 'Between work and home duties, you barely slept until he died.' She swallows, preparing to say something she never has before. 'Nor did I. We were both exhausted.'

She leaves it hanging there: the implication that her brothers didn't endure the same thing. It's what she and Ingrid have never talked about, this bald fact of their family, that Anna was sacrificed to her brothers' futures. It's not the sort of thing a daughter can raise with her mother unless she wants to risk never being spoken to again.

'We were,' her mother concedes with what sounds like sadness.

Anna clears her throat. 'And my brothers were not.'

There's a sharp sniff and while Anna doesn't look at her mother she knows there will be a glare so piercing it might put a hole in her.

'They needed to be their best,' Ingrid says. 'They had to get to university. To achieve.'

There's silence between them for a few seconds. Maybe thirty. Maybe more.

'And me?' Anna asks, trying not to sound like she's begging. Now she turns to meet her mother's eyes.

96

'You?' Ingrid says. 'What did you need university for? You have Gary.'

It hits Anna like a punch to her chest, this stark admission that her husband was seen as her be-all and end-all. As if she needed nothing and no one else. As if she didn't need herself.

'*Had* Gary, Mama. He's not around any more.'

'Yes. Well.' More lip-pursing. 'You could fix that.'

'So I could go back to what I was when I was young – taking care of other people and never of myself?' She tries not to sound angry but it's hard.

'That's what we do,' her mother says. 'That's our place.'

Anna has always known her mother thought this, because it's how the situation arose originally, but it still hurts to hear it said.

'I want to be alone with my husband,' Ingrid says tersely.

Anna stares at her for a second or two, seeing her mother's irises waver just a little.

Then she turns and walks back to the car, leaving Ingrid to converse with a man who is long dead, and who left them in spirit even longer before that.

CHAPTER FIFTEEN

'You're sure you don't mind?' Evie says as she creates a nest of pillows on the couch in the back room, Billy standing by the door, wan and listless.

'When have I ever minded?' Trudy replies and Evie smiles gratefully.

Trudy has, in fact, never minded when Billy has had to spend time at the salon when he can't be at school, whether it's because he's sick or there's an outbreak of nits. Telling parents to keep their children at home is fine when the dad goes off to work and the mum is around and flexible with her arrangements; it doesn't work too well when Mum is also Dad when it comes to the day-to-day.

Stevo can't take Billy on sick days, even if he wants to – there's nowhere for Billy to rest at his shop. Whereas Trudy has always made it clear that Billy is welcome. 'Never a bother,' she says.

Probably because he's a quiet kid. Thoughtful, or at least Evie likes to think so. Maybe he's sullen instead. Hard to tell the difference with boys sometimes. He could be sulking or he could be contemplating the meaning of life and the expression on his face wouldn't change. Whereas if he were a girl . . .

Girls are tricky, with their scheming, but their emotions tend to be written on their faces. Until they hit their teenage years and they learn to hide them, mainly out of self-protection. Look upset when your high-school nemesis calls you a fat slag and you're doomed until the end of Year 12. Far better to practise controlling your expressions so that no matter what someone says to you, it's pushed down. Back. Away. It means that when some sleazy bloke hits on you in a pub and you realise – in a flash, the way women are trained to – that rejecting him in a particular way could make your life a whole lot worse, you draw on those school years of never revealing what you really think and instead say to him, 'Aren't you sweet? Sorry, I have a boyfriend.' The sleaze will guess that you don't have a boyfriend but he's saved face, and you've possibly saved your life because he won't follow you to your car later. Of course, he may call you a stuck-up bitch but that's the better option.

It amazes Evie, the things girls and women have to navigate every day just to stay alive. Which is why she knows it's easier to have a son. She doesn't have to worry about him being cracked onto by a sleaze in a pub. Mostly she has to worry about nits. Or a stomach bug, which is what he has now. Poor kid can't have anything left to vomit up; he'll probably sleep for the rest of the day.

'Bit poorly, are you, Billy-o?' Trudy says as he snuggles into the nest.

She's answered by a weak nod.

'There's lemonade here, sweetie,' Evie says, gesturing to the full glass on the table. 'If you feel like it.'

Another weak nod and he closes his eyes.

'Our very own Tiny Tim,' Trudy mutters, then winks at Evie.

The morning is a flurry of returning clients and a couple of new cuts, then Sam turns up for his late start, as he'll be closing today. Evie tries not to smile at him too cutely before he heads for the back room, and a couple of minutes pass before she remembers that Billy is in there and she really should have told Sam so he wasn't surprised. As it is, she feels the need to get back there, because Sam meeting her son feels momentous somehow.

'Sam!' she calls softly as she pushes open the door and finds him standing next to the couch, hands on hips, laughing. Billy is sitting up, also laughing.

'You've met,' she says redundantly, but she's taken aback that they already seem to like each other and she had nothing to do with it.

'Evie, your son is a card.' Sam grins at her and her stomach flip-flops, as it always does when he does so much as look in her direction.

'Is he?' She can't remember Billy being that funny for her.

'He's telling me a story about tadpoles.'

Sam keeps grinning and so does Billy, right until he looks at her, then adopts his Tiny Tim face again. He didn't fake the vomiting earlier but now Evie wonders if he isn't feeling much better than he made out when they arrived. Or perhaps the sleep did him good.

'Oh, the tadpoles,' she says. 'If it's not those it's silkworms.'

'Silkworms? Do you have any at the moment?'

Sam addresses this question to Billy and Evie feels a little jealous, which is ridiculous and also, probably, makes her a bad mother.

Billy shakes his head.

'My brother Oliver and I used to keep silkworms.' Sam grins. 'Never made any silk out them, though! But I have a mulberry tree in my back garden. So if you get any more worms, let me know and I'll bring you some leaves.'

Billy looks so delighted that Evie feels like running out and getting silkworms right now. But then she remembers how upset he was when the last lot died. There's only so much heartbreak she can inflict on her kid at any given time.

'He told me he's feeling better,' Sam says.

There's her pang of jealousy again, but this time Evie can't figure out if it's because Billy told Sam something she didn't know or because Sam is more interested in chatting to Billy than to her. Again, bad mother.

'That's great, but it's too late to take him to school, so he gets to stay.' She glances at the glass on the table. 'You had the lemonade,' she states.

Billy nods while his eyes remain locked on Sam. Clearly Sam has that effect on a range of people, and she loves him for it a little bit more. It's quite a skill, to make other people relaxed, if not happy. Not one she has, nor does she know how to cultivate it – she doesn't even know where she'd start. Maybe one day she'll ask him. Except that would probably mean revealing how he makes her feel, and she's not brave enough for that. How he makes her feel is special. Even though he is charming to everyone, his eyes hold hers for longer, his smiles for her are a little brighter.

'Ooh, a bit sweet on you, is he?' one of the regulars said the other day after she'd watched Sam and Evie interact while Evie brushed out her hair.

Evie didn't know the answer so she just smiled and said nothing. But she wants to think the answer is *yes*.

'Such a pin-up, isn't he?' another regular said, and again Evie smiled and said nothing, although that time she knew the answer was *yes*.

Sam has created quite the sensation in the salon, simply by existing – although he is a great hairdresser too – and that is a gift more than a skill. It's no wonder, then, that she can't stop thinking about him, this man who creates light and happiness and weaves both of them around her. While she knows it's partly his nature, she's also allowing herself to think that some of it is just for her. It's her he chats to the most; her he hovers around when there are rare quiet times. She may be flattering herself by thinking he sees some kind of light and happiness in her too, but why shouldn't she?

'Even if you don't have silkworms, maybe you should come round and see my mulberry tree,' Sam says to Billy, who looks delighted, although Evie feels odd about it: she wants to visit Sam's home on her own first. As an adult. While she loves that Sam is interested in her son, she really wants him to be interested in *her*. Although he is. Isn't he?

'Can we, Mum?' Billy asks.

'Of course, sweetie.' What else would she say? Ultimately she wants her son to be happy more than anything else in the world. 'I'll talk about it with Sam. Now he and I need to get back to work. Would you like to read for a while?'

Billy nods and she fishes his book out of her handbag, giving it to him, then closing the door after she and Sam leave.

'What a great kid,' Sam says, his voice soft, his smile wide.

'I like to think so.'

'That means you're a great mother.' He squeezes her arm and then turns away from her and toward the next client who's walked through the door.

Evie almost feels like crying, because no one ever tells her she's a great mother. 'Thank you,' she whispers.

CHAPTER SIXTEEN

'Are you sure you don't want me to pick you up this evening?' Evie says as she pulls into a parking spot near Gosford train station.

Trudy almost fainted when Evie offered to drive her here today. They've never seen each other on a Sunday. Not usually on a Saturday either, apart from school-formal season when the salon is packed to the hilt with teenagers wanting perms and teases and it's all hands on deck. So when Trudy mentioned she was heading to Sydney by train, she wasn't expecting Evie to offer a lift to the station. Except she did.

'You don't have a car, do you?' Evie asked as she was about to walk out the door to pick up Billy on Thursday.

Trudy can see how Evie would think that. After all, Trudy lives and works within a very small area, and she walks to the salon and the shops and back home.

'I do,' Trudy said. 'I'm just not that keen on driving. Laurie was the driver. I've hardly driven since . . .' There was no need to say it – Evie knew.

'I can take you to the station,' Evie had said.

Trudy could have managed to drive herself to the station, of course. Or made her way there by taxi, presumably. Or maybe there's a bus . . . When she'd suggested taking the train to Sydney she actually hadn't considered the logistics of it. So when Evie took that problem away from her, she felt grateful and surprised at how emotional she was about it. As she's not given to crying – even after Laurie died, she didn't cry much – the emotion she felt at Evie's gesture seemed too strong, and she's still feeling it as she unbuckles her seatbelt in Evie's car and prepares to exit.

'Thank you, pet,' she says. 'But I'll be fine this evening. You'll have Billy coming back and you'll be busy.'

'Trudy,' Evie says firmly, 'how do you think you'll get home from the station?'

'There must be a bus. Something.'

Evie raises her eyebrows. 'A bus on a Sunday night? You'll be lucky.' She smiles. 'Why don't you call me when you know which train you'll be on. You can leave a message on the answering machine if I'm not home.'

'What about Billy?'

'Billy can come with me to pick you up. He loves an adventure. He'll probably want me to put him on the train instead of taking him back home.'

'All right,' Trudy says, feeling that gratitude emotion rise, but she's not going be pathetic in front of Evie so she sniffs it back. 'Thank you.'

Evie waves her goodbye and Trudy heads for the platform.

When the train arrives it's mostly empty; she takes a window seat because there's a lot to see on this journey. Sometimes she and Laurie would take the train to see Dylan rather than Laurie driving, so she knows the track. The journey won't be too long – Dylan suggested they meet at Hornsby, which is where she'd have to get off the train anyway, as everyone has to change at Hornsby if they want to travel elsewhere in Sydney. If they were driving it would be at the end of the freeway, so it almost marks the spot where Sydney begins. For her, at least.

Dylan suggested they go to the RSL for lunch, as it's near the station. Trudy is happy with that – she likes a club.

The rhythm of the train makes her drowsy but she wants to keep watching the view. As the train nears the Hawkesbury River, Trudy marvels at the size of it. The magnificence of the setting. It looks more like an inland harbour than a river, dotted with islands and defined by inlets. Oysters are farmed down there. People have whole lives lived in, on and around that river and she knows nothing about them even though as the crow flies they're not that far away from her.

It's been so long since she's seen the Hawkesbury – at least two years. Maybe three, because in the last months of Laurie's life they didn't go anywhere much. They weren't exactly world travellers before that – Trudy doesn't even have a passport because she's never been able to take enough time away from the salon to travel very far – but they got out and about. Sundays were their day together and they would drive to Newcastle sometimes and have lunch, or to the Hunter Valley where they'd visit the vineyards. Trudy would sample the wine while Laurie watched. He never took a drop of alcohol when he was driving somewhere.

She knew his death would circumscribe her life but she hadn't considered that it would mean she'd stay so very close to home because there was no one to drive her around. Everything became smaller, and she's conscious that she needs to get out more, other-wise the boundaries of her world might close in on her so much they'll crush her.

Her thoughts occupy her until the train pulls in to Hornsby, and she sees her son at the end of the platform. At six feet two, he's easy enough to spot.

'G'day, Mum.' He stoops to hug her and Trudy notices some grey hairs – she shouldn't be surprised, as he's thirty-five now. When she had him she was twenty-two; at the time she felt so grown up, but when she thinks that Josie is nineteen, there's no way she could imagine her with a baby in three years' time. But who knows? Motherhood makes you grow up like nothing else.

'Annemarie not coming?' Trudy says, simultaneously miffed because she thinks it's a slight and pleased because she'll be able to have a proper conversation with Dylan.

'Oh yeah, she is – she's at the club with the kids. Thought we'd get a table early.'

'Righto.'

Trudy takes his arm as they stroll and he fills her in on his work week. He's in construction and there's always something being built in Sydney. This city is not for her; no city would be. The beach, the village attached to it, the peace at night, the brightness of the stars – these mean far too much to Trudy and she doubts she'd find them in this city that seems larger and louder each time she's here.

Arriving at the club's dining area – it's a cafe on its way to being a bistro – Trudy sees her granddaughters waving vigorously, then hopping off their seats and running over.

'Nana, Nana, Nana,' squeals the youngest, Bree, who is five to her sister Irene's six.

Trudy pulls out the presents she brought them – books from the Terrigal newsagent, who keeps a selection.

'Great idea,' says Annemarie as she stands and gives Trudy a kiss on the cheek. 'Now they'll be quiet.'

Trudy can't tell if Annemarie is happy about that or not, but she chooses to believe she is.

Once food and beverages are ordered, Trudy feels her shoulders relax and she smiles around the table.

'So, what's the news?' she says. It's something she says to her clients, who usually give her a recap at a million miles an hour then ask Trudy what they should do about their wayward child/ bitch of a sister/horrible co-worker or the bloke who won't ask them on a date (the latter answer is easy: forget about him).

'I'm learning to do nails,' says Annemarie with a hint of pride.

'Hm?' Trudy glances from her son to her daughter-in-law.

'Nails.' Annemarie holds up her hands and waggles her fingers, which seem to end in bright-red talons. 'Acrylics.'

Annemarie has, until now, shown very little interest in anything to do with grooming. She goes to the hairdresser for a trim every six months, which is about four months past the point Trudy would do it. Lipstick is a concept she has not fully embraced. And as for clothes . . . Well, Trudy may prefer an all-black uniform at the salon but outside of it she's fond of a dress in a nice pattern and is a firm believer that a decent pair of slacks can carry a person quite a long way. So this nail development is unusual. Accordingly, Trudy looks to Dylan for an explanation.

'She wants to run her own business,' he says, smiling. 'And she can do nails from home. Or in a salon.'

'Right,' Trudy says. He makes it sound easy, as if Annemarie can just do a little course and suddenly be the belle of the nails ball. Perhaps she can be, but in Trudy's experience a beauty business – which is what she'd call it – requires people skills, creativity and a little nous, and Annemarie is not famous for any of those. She's a wonderful mother – Trudy can't fault her there, the girls are well looked after and polite – and she must be a good wife otherwise Dylan wouldn't be so cheerful, but for any role beyond that Trudy has her doubts. Which makes her a mean mother-in-law so she'll keep them to herself.

'I was inspired by you, Trudy,' Annemarie says, her talons back under the table.

'Oh?'

'You've run that salon for so long. Years and years! So you must like doing it. And you had Dylan and everything.'

'I did,' Trudy says. 'But I couldn't have done it without Laurie supporting me. Not financially, I mean. Lifting me up. He was . . .' Her voice catches and she bites her lip to stop becoming upset. What is it with her today and these tears that threaten to appear? Except she knows: it's the reminders she keeps being given that

Laurie isn't here. Of all the ways he helped her. She means it when she says he lifted her up. Everyone who is trying to make something of their lives needs a person who tells them they can do it, and he was that for her.

Dylan reaches over to pat her hand. 'It's all right, Mum,' he says. 'I know Dad was irreplaceable.'

Yes, he was.

Not that she has plans to replace him, and she doesn't know how Dylan would feel about that if she did.

'Sorry to upset you, Trudy,' Annemarie says. 'Girls, stop kicking your chairs.'

'Sorry, Mummy,' the girls chorus as their drinks are put on the table.

'But would you mind if I ask you for some tips?' Annemarie goes on. 'You know – about how to start a business?'

Trudy is taken aback – partly because Annemarie wants to ask her for advice, which has never happened before, and partly because she doesn't believe she has anything useful to say. She doesn't think what she's done with the Seaside Salon is that noteworthy. This is her son's wife, though, so she has to make an effort.

'Sure,' she says. 'Call me when you're ready.'

'Great. Thanks.' Annemarie smiles then turns to her daughters. 'Now, drink that pink lemonade slowly, okay? You're only getting one.'

The lunch is pleasant, and the chatter is superficial, and by the time she reaches the payphone at the station Trudy is pleased she made the effort.

'Hello?' Evie says on the other end of the line.

'It's me, pet.'

'Hi! How was lunch? Actually, no, tell me in the car. What time does your train leave?'

'Five minutes.'

'See you at Gosford in an hour. Billy will be with me.'

'Sounds perfect.' Trudy hangs up and feels relieved, although she isn't sure why. Maybe it's because Evie is giving her a little touch of the care Laurie used to. And, in his way, Dylan did too.

So the day wasn't so hard after all. Without Laurie, she thought it might be.

As she waits for the train those tears are back, and this time she understands why: this was her first big test of being without him, the first family get-together without him, and it shouldn't have taken this long, but two years have passed both in a blur and been an eternity.

The tears are coming not because he's not here but because she passed the test. She got herself to Sydney. She made it through lunch. So this means she is moving on. Life is flowing without him and, after being stuck in a dam for so long, she is flowing with it. Leaving him behind.

CHAPTER SEVENTEEN

On Monday Brett brought his nan to the salon, just like he told Josie he did, only this time he came inside. He caught her eye immediately and waved hello. His smile was so big she thought his face would crack. And she loved it.

'Hi,' she said, so softly she didn't think he heard but she didn't want to alert the others in the salon.

'Hi,' he mouthed back, still smiling.

'Hello, young man,' Trudy said. 'We haven't seen you before.'

'I'm Brett,' he said, extending his hand to shake Trudy's.

That made Josie swoon inside. Good manners. She likes good manners – in anyone, not just in a man. But for some reason she liked them most on him.

'My nan comes to you on Mondays,' he continued, glancing in Josie's direction.

'So she does,' Trudy said, taking the arm of the elderly woman next to Brett. 'Hi, Jilly.'

Josie hoped Trudy didn't see her looking at Brett but she suspected she did, because Trudy never misses anything.

Brett winked at Josie before he left, and that's how she knew she'd see him again.

Now it's Wednesday and she's not surprised when she walks out of the Seaside Salon and turns right, heading in the direction of her car, and sees Brett. He is not holding a surfboard, or his nana's hand. Instead he's leaning against the wall, wearing a sloppy joe, King Gee long pants and work boots, his hair a little messy and a lot dreamy. He's grinning at her, his eyes crinkling a little at the edges.

Josie sighs involuntarily – the same noise she makes when she's watching a movie that lets her believe in romance or listening to one of her favourite love songs.

'Hi,' she says back, extending it, breathing it. *Hiiiiiii.* He probably thinks she sounds loopy. She feels loopy.

The other day, while she was eating lunch under a different pine tree, he found her again and stood there, dripping wet, asking her questions about her job and her car and what she likes to do on the weekends. As if she was the most interesting girl in the world. He made her feel that way. She was sure, at the time, that she made no sense whatsoever because she was distracted by how tight his wetsuit was and how clean his skin looked and how bright his teeth were against his tan. Did he notice that she was babbling? If he did, he didn't seem to care.

Afterward she realised how rude she'd been, not asking him anything about himself. She was brought up to have better manners than that. Well, now she has a chance to make up for it.

'How's your day been?' she says, hoisting the strap of her handbag further up her shoulder.

'Great!' he says still grinning. 'Now.'

Her eyes widen as she takes in what he's said.

'Where's your car?' he says.

'Grosvenor Road,' she says, nodding in the direction away from the water.

'May I walk you?' He dips his head a little, as if he's shy, except she doesn't believe he's shy because *he* approached *her*, but she also loves thinking that he's shy and he's talking to her anyway because he likes her so much, and . . .

And what if it's true? What if that is exactly what he's doing? Just like she's doing? Because *she's* shy. Too shy to be talking to a boy this handsome. The real Josie – the one who no boy looks at, the one who listens to her love songs and dreams about loving someone that much and being loved in return – could never be this bold. So the version of Josie that's here, talking to Brett, is the Seaside Salon Josie. That's the version of her who can chat to the customers and be outgoing and friendly all day. The version Trudy, Evie and Sam see, and the one they seem to like. She will keep that version going even outside of the salon if it means that Brett continues talking to her. That he will walk her to her car. And who knows? Maybe that version will become the real version if she keeps it up long enough. Which wouldn't be the worst thing in the world.

Every morning she puts on her Salon Josie persona in the car: shoulders back, head up, big smile. She's only been there a few weeks and she doesn't even need to do it consciously. As soon as she's out of the car she feels her body already in the shape of Salon Josie.

Now, walking next to Brett, she's not Salon Josie exactly but she's not far off her. Her shoulders are still back and she's still smiling. Because she wants to around him. That's part of it too: if you *want* to do something, *want* to be good at something, you figure it out because it's important to you. Being around Brett in a way that doesn't make him run for the hills is important to her.

'Here,' he says, holding out his hand, and for a second she wonders if she's meant to take it. 'Let me carry your bag.'

She blushes then hands it over, thinking for a second that he might be about to run off with it – that's what her mother would say he'd do – then feeling bad for having the thought. Besides, the bag is heavy: it holds her make-up bag, her wallet, two magazines, a can of hairspray, a brush, two apples she didn't get to eat, deodorant and her keys.

'Thank you,' she says. 'So did you surf today?'

'Nuh,' Brett says, glancing in the direction of the beach to his right. 'There wasn't much swell. Wouldn't have been worth getting wet.'

They chat about his day, working on cars, until they reach her Mini.

'Cool car,' Brett says approvingly.

'Really?' She isn't sure if he's being serious – the car is poo-brown, after all.

'The colour's great. You don't see it on the Minis that often. And these cars . . .' He grins, his eyes sweeping over the car from front to back. 'They just keep going. As long as you don't thrash them too much.'

He looks at her questioningly and she giggles.

'It's only going from home to here and back again most of the time,' she says.

'Where's home?'

He's standing a respectful distance from her but she feels something between them – like a magnetic pull coming from the core of her, connecting to his. It's odd and comforting all at the same time, as if it's inevitable they'll wind up stuck together even if she doesn't know how or why or when that might happen.

'Gosford. You?'

'Wamberal.'

It's the next beach up, to the north.

'Not too far, then.' She smiles.

'Not from here, no.' He shrugs. 'Too far from Sydney for my liking, though.'

'Oh. You want to live in Sydney?'

Josie knows people who can't wait to leave the Coast, to move to Sydney, where they imagine everything will be more exciting. The Coast has always been enough for her. Sydney is fast-paced and big and she doesn't even have the guts to drive the freeway to get there – yet.

'I'm not sure about living there,' he says. 'But I like to visit. And who knows? Maybe I'll live there one day. If I can find a beach I like as much as this one.'

'I, um . . .' She hesitates to admit the limited scope of her experiences to him, because what if he thinks that makes her boring? 'I don't go that often.'

He stares into her eyes and she wants desperately to know what he's thinking, because it feels like this is some kind of moment that determines whether he ever speaks to her again. She's the boring coastal girl; he's the coastal boy looking for adventure and realising he's not going to find it with her. If this were a movie, at least, that's what would happen here. She's not the main character, she's the girl the lead actor meets on the way to his sweetheart.

Brett smiles, his eyes crinkling again. She really likes how they do that.

'It's not for everyone,' he says. 'So . . .' He pauses, then grins. 'I'd love to take you out to dinner one night. Could I have your number? I'll ask the boys at work if they know any restaurants and call you once I've found a place.'

Another pause and she hopes he can't hear how loudly her heart is beating, because to her it sounds as if it's thumping all the way out of her ears.

DINNER? What?

After she recovers from the shock the first thing she thinks is that she can't tell her parents about this, so she's going to have to come up with a story to explain why she's going out at night.

'If you'd like to have dinner with me, that is.' Brett's words suggest uncertainty but his tone does not, and she really likes that too: he's not nervous, and he's not cocky either – he's confident. Like she wants to be.

'I, um . . .' *Breathe, Josie, breathe.* 'I would. Y-yes. Thank you.'

Now he grins so widely she can see his back teeth. 'Great!' Still with her handbag tucked under his arm, he pulls a notepad and pen from his back pocket with his other hand and holds them out to her. 'For your number,' he says.

Just before she takes them from him she remembers she lives at home and one of her parents will probably answer the phone and will want to know who the strange man is calling their daughter. No, that won't do.

'Um, I, uh . . .' How to get around this? Maybe she shouldn't even try. 'I live with my parents and it's their phone.'

He shrugs; he likes doing that. 'That's cool. So do I. But how about I see you at the surf club at lunchtime on Friday and we can talk then?'

Relief!

'That would be great.'

They stay standing, staring at each other, smiling, and she has no idea what to do next.

'I'd better give you your bag,' he says, handing it over.

'Oh – thanks.' She pulls out her keys.

'See you, Josie.' Now Brett grins shyly as he waits for her to unlock the driver-side door.

'See you on Friday,' she says.

He will never know how much it means to her that he waits for her to start the engine and pull away from the kerb, giving her a wave as she does, but it's enough to make her start crying as she drives off and turns left to head for the coast road that will carry her past Avoca and toward home, and she alternates between crying and laughing with surprise all the way to Gosford.

CHAPTER EIGHTEEN

The other day Babs, one of Trudy's regulars, told Evie, 'You have a spring in your step.'

Evie couldn't deny it. Because she can feel it, these days. Almost as if she wants to pirouette through the day, like Cinderella with her little birds flying around or whatever happens in the Disney movie. Or is it Snow White? One of them, with the birds. That's her. Although it's probably more accurate to say she's living as if she's in that Carpenters song about birds suddenly appearing when someone is near – 'Close to You', that's it. And the *you* in this case is Sam.

When Babs had said what she said she'd looked meaningfully from Evie to Sam and back again. Luckily Sam had his back turned otherwise Evie would have been embarrassed. Inside, she felt like giggling at the idea of someone noticing the change in her.

Stevo had said something about it too.

'You got a fella?' he asked this morning when he picked up Billy for sport. Then he was going to take Billy home for the night because Evie is heading out on the town with Fran.

'No!' Evie said. 'Why?'

Stevo had narrowed his eyes. 'You haven't been this happy in . . . ever.' He cocked his head, like he was sizing her up, and she felt a little guilty because he was basically saying she had never been this happy with *him*. Which was true. They weren't happy when they were together. She tried to get happy, and so did he, probably, but they weren't a match. It's a mystery to her why two such people can come together and make a kid as great as Billy.

When Billy was a baby Evie went to see a psychic who had a little crystal shop in the arcade across from Terrigal Beach. She was trying to figure out what to do about Stevo, which was really a way of trying to figure out what to do with herself. They knew they didn't belong together but she didn't want to be a single mum. Or so she thought.

'You have a son,' the psychic told her, which freaked out Evie because she hadn't told the psychic anything. Then the psychic took two puffs of her cigarette and blew the smoke in Evie's face, which made Evie wonder what she'd gotten herself into.

'He is a strong boy,' the psychic went on. 'Very strong. Strong enough to make his way into this world.' One puff, another blow. 'He brought you and his father together.' The psychic's eyes met hers. 'But now that job is done.'

Evie had felt cold at that instant, not from fear but recognition that the psychic was right. It had been the first and last time she went to a psychic, though, because she didn't want any more hard truths.

Now she wishes the psychic were still there so she could ask her about Sam. The crystal shop closed a couple of years ago and Evie has no idea how to track down a psychic, so instead she just wonders about Sam all on her own. She's not going to ask Trudy about it. But if she did she'd ask if Trudy thinks Sam likes her as much as she likes him. It's all she wants to know.

This crush is ridiculous – no one her age, and especially no *mother* should carry on like this – but she can't seem to shake it off. That's why she agreed to go out with Fran tonight when her old friend called to suggest it a few days ago.

'That band's on,' she'd said.

'Which band?'

'You know.'

Evie didn't know.

'You *know*! The one we liked. When we were in Year 12.'

Evie tried to think.

'Gawd, Evie, motherhood has sucked my brain out through my toes. I can't remember *anything*.'

'Same, Fran. I can't think of any band.'

'The Leatherjackets!' Fran said triumphantly. 'Thank god. I still have some neurons left.'

The Leatherjackets were a band from Woy Woy who named themselves after a fish but enjoyed the double entendre, especially as they played rockabilly. Evie and Fran used to sneak into their gigs when they were still under age, but it was worth it: The Leatherjackets were great. Some people thought they'd be the next big thing, but they never went further than the Coast. Then they broke up. Not for good, obviously, since they're playing at a pub in Gosford.

'Nice top,' Fran says as Evie hops in her car.

'Thanks.' Evie looks down at the shoulder-padded T-shirt with a sequinned heart on it that she bought at a boutique in Gosford after Fran issued her invitation. She has no idea what anyone wears to gigs these days but the top could be handy for any other social occasion that comes her way. *Not* that she has expectations of being invited to anything by anyone. Not really.

They pass the drive trading stories about their children's teachers and soon enough they're inside the pub, where Evie realises that the sequinned heart immediately marks her out as a dag. Everyone else is wearing band T-shirts – except Fran, who's wearing a black top with blue jeans.

Evie feels old and out of the loop. And here she is meant to be on top of trends and fashion because her clients expect her to know the latest. Okay, not all of them, because some of them just want a rinse and set. But a lot of them would think she knows the latest in everything.

'Drink?' Fran says, nodding toward the bar.

'About ten,' Evie says, making a face. 'So I can forget that I stick out like a sore thumb.'

Fran looks at her quizzically.

'The top,' Evie explains.

'Doll, precisely no one is going to care about that top. They're all too busy wondering if they're cool themselves. Besides, I like it. It's pretty.' She grins and goes to the bar.

Evie glances around and sees mostly men about her age, some trim, some not; some who look as if they've been dragged through a hedge backward and some with hair combed and T-shirt ironed. Is this her generation? When did they all start looking so much older? Would Sam think she's 'older'? She hasn't previously considered his age, or hers. He's Oliver's younger brother, and Oliver is her age. Maybe she's too old for Sam. Maybe he likes younger women.

She swallows, not wanting to contemplate all the variations of maybes she could consider over the course of the night.

'Nice top,' says a man's voice beside her, and she turns to see Simon, a boy she knew in high school. Although he's a man now, just as she's a woman.

'Simon!' she cries, genuinely pleased to see him. He was always decent and easy to talk to. A league player in winter, cricket in summer, surfer all year round, like most of the boys. Nuggety with muscle due to all the sport, and it looks as though he still does it all.

'G'day, Evie.' He kisses her on the cheek. 'How ya been?'

'Oh, you know.' She shrugs.

'Nah, I don't,' he says cheekily. 'So tell me.'

Where does she start? Given how small the Coast is, he might have heard she has a son. That she works at the Seaside Salon. People talk about other people. It's how life runs. But maybe he hasn't heard anything. So she'll start with what's most important to her.

'I'm a mum now.'

'Yeah?' He cocks his head to the side like a curious puppy.

'To Billy. He's seven.'

'Right. Right! Wow. A kid.' He runs his hand through his sun-bleached hair, which is nicely cut, she notices, and she wonders where he has it done.

'Do you have any?'

He grins and shakes his head. 'Nah. Haven't had the time.'

'Busy surfing?'

He keeps grinning. 'Something like that.'

Evie glances over to the bar and sees Fran picking up their drinks.

'I'm here with Fran,' she says to Simon. 'Do you remember her? Star hockey player.'

'Sure – Fran,' he says, but he's not grinning any more. Instead he's frowning in Fran's direction. 'Look, before she gets here,' he says, 'would you like to –'

'Simon Hardy, as I live and breathe!' Fran calls as she nears. 'How are you?'

'Great, Fran, thanks, yeah. Look, Evie, I . . .' He stops and looks to be considering something.

'Are you trying to ask her out, Si?' Fran says.

Evie wants to melt into a puddle. How can Fran be so bold? Mind you, she's always been like it, so Evie should be well past being mortified.

Simon laughs. 'Maybe.'

He looks into Evie's eyes and she realises she's probably meant to say something, but all she can think is how much she wishes it were Sam doing the asking. Then her answer would be an imme-diate *yes*. For Si Hardy, though . . . He never acted interested in her at school. So maybe he's desperate now? Why else would he want to ask her out so quickly when they haven't seen each other for years? Desperation isn't appealing to her, and she should know because she's been feeling a little desperate herself.

'Oh,' she says at last.

'I'll call you,' Simon says, and lifts his tinnie. 'Cheers. Enjoy the show.'

Then he's gone, probably to rejoin his mates, although Evie doesn't look because she's too busy glaring at Fran.

'Why did you say that?' she demands. 'Thanks for the drink, by the way.'

'The bloke was drooling.' Fran sips her Coke. She always drinks Coke. 'He's still cute,' she adds. 'So why don't you?'

'Because . . .' Evie sighs.

'Because why – you have so many other dates lined up?' Fran doesn't say it unkindly – she has often lamented that she can't understand why Evie hasn't been snapped up – but it stings regardless.

'Because there's someone else,' Evie blurts.

'*What?* Why haven't you told me this before?'

'There isn't anything much to tell. Yet.'

'So you've been on some dates?'

'No.'

Fran frowns. 'So . . .'

'We work together.'

'Right. So there's been flirting?'

'Yes.'

'He likes you.'

'He's really sweet to me.'

Fran takes another sip of Coke. 'Is he generally sweet to people?'

Evie takes a breath. 'Yes, but –'

'Evie, don't confuse attention for affection.'

Fran says it seriously but Evie wants to tell her that she *knows* that – it's not as if she hasn't rolled it around in her brain over and over and over and over . . .

Instead, she needs to make her case.

'I don't. I can tell he likes me by the way he looks at me,' she says, thinking of how Sam's eyes light up when he sees her. How he walked in the other day and said, 'I *love* your dress,' his hand reaching out to brush the fabric, his fingertip finding her thigh in a way that Evie did not think was an accident. She couldn't look at him in case he guessed what she was thinking. Except she wanted him to guess what she was thinking – and isn't that the conundrum for anyone who has a crush? They want the object of their crush to return their feelings, but that would mean making the feelings known and that prospect is mortifying, because what if the feelings aren't, in fact, returned?

All of it made Evie feel like she was back in high school, except she never had a crush of this intensity on anyone in high school. There was no one worthy. Not even Si Hardy.

'I need to see this in action to make sure,' Fran says.

This irritates Evie. 'You don't believe me?'

'I want to check the guy out! You're my friend. I want to make sure he's not just sleazing around, checking out every woman who comes into the salon.'

'He doesn't.'

Fran stays quiet.

'Promise,' Evie adds.

'All right, I believe you. But he's a co-worker. Is it a good idea to get involved? The salon is so small.'

'There's no involvement. Yet. We're just . . .' Evie can't help smiling as she thinks about the conversation she and Sam had in the back room the other day, how he asked after Billy, asked questions about her life. How interested he was in her.

'Let him ask you out, then.' Fran raises her eyebrows. 'I'm serious, Evie. He has to make the first move.'

Although Evie hopes he will, she has thought about taking the initiative herself.

'Why? We've had women's lib. We can ask them out if we want.'

'Because men will say yes to *everyone*.' Fran says and points her finger around the room. 'You could crack on to every guy here and he'll say yes to you, married, single, halfway single, whatever.'

'That's not true!' How can it be? The women's magazines all say men are hard to get.

'It is. You should hear the stories Steve has about his married mates and the women they go home with when they're all out on the town. They don't approach any of them. The women come to them and they don't say no.'

'But –'

'If he asks you out it's because he really wants to spend time with you,' Fran says. 'He could be with any woman who asks him, right? But you want to know that he really wants to see *you*. So wait for that. And if it doesn't come . . .' She shrugs. 'Then he's not for you.'

'But he is for me!' Evie feels stricken at the idea that she and Sam may not progress if she's unable to do anything about it. Can't she take charge of her own life? Fran doesn't know everything.

'Then it will all be fine.'

There's a noise from the stage and a scraggly looking man is testing the microphone.

'Looks like we're almost on here,' Fran say, taking another sip of Coke. Then she kisses Evie's cheek. 'You know I love you, doll. I just want you to be with someone who makes the effort because you're *worth that*.'

As the support band takes the stage Evie contemplates what Fran has said and can't help feeling despondent. She wants Sam. She's impatient for him, in fact. If she has to wait for him . . . how long will that take? Hasn't she waited long enough?

There's no way she's going to broach the subject with Fran again, though, so she concentrates on the music, and catches Simon's eye a couple of times, smiling, but not in a way that would encourage him. He's not Sam. He never will be.

CHAPTER NINETEEN

The radio is on softly enough to not wake the kids as Anna sits in her workroom with the pile of sewing she has to do. It's more mending, really. Hems to take up, buttons to sew back on. Some of it is alterations and she likes those – modifying a garment for its wearer, making it unique for her. It's usually a her. Men don't seem to worry about alterations unless it's for length or girth – usually taking up one and letting out another. She always has to explain that most pairs of men's pants don't have enough fabric to be let out but they always want her to try – 'They're my favourite pair, can't you do something?' She wants to tell them that *they* could do something, like buying a new pair, although that would mean losing business, so maybe she should just stick to the way things are.

She usually listens to the local radio station while she works; at night they have talkback and people call in with their woes. Currently there's a woman on saying 'my de facto' has gone to prison for three to five years and she's wondering what to tell the kids. Anna often wonders about the term 'de facto'. It even *sounds* temporary, as if it's waiting to be turned into something else, which she supposes it is. Her mother drilled into her that she was not to move in with a man unless they were at least engaged, because the man has to offer something of value in exchange for everything she would bring to his life. Clearly the caller to the local station didn't have the same sort of mother, because she's now complaining about having to work full time because the de facto left her with nothing and the dole isn't going to cover all the expenses. The radio host has no sympathy, telling her she shouldn't have got herself involved with a crim. The caller is, somewhat understandably, upset at this.

'*Shit*,' Anna says as she accidentally sticks a needle into her thumb. She forgot to put on her rubber thumb guard. After hustling the kids in from after-school sport, getting them through baths and dinner and homework, then sitting down with a cup of tea and the radio and the sewing, she forgot to do something so habitual she really shouldn't forget it.

She's got her period, that's what it is. Every month she feels vague for a couple of days, as if she's not really here, in this place, in this time. When Gary was around more he'd notice she was off and ask if she was okay. Sometimes he'd rub her lower back, which aches at such times. She misses that Gary. That Gary was subsumed into long-hours-working Gary and hasn't been seen for a while.

She sticks her thumb in her mouth so she doesn't get blood on the shirt she's mending and searches for her thumb guard in the tin of miscellany she keeps on her workbench.

'Mummy?' She looks up to see a sleepy Renee standing in the doorway, holding her beloved one-eyed teddy bear.

'What are you doing up, sweetie?' She put the kids to bed an hour ago.

'I can't sleep.' Renee yawns and ambles over, then puts her head on Anna's shoulder. It's one of the most precious things, Anna believes, when your child shows how much they trust you by putting their head on your shoulder. It's surrender on their part, and love and cosiness and sweetness. She will miss it when they're older and they think she's the un-coolest person alive. The switch that is flicked between child-sweetness and teenage-disdain has no due date but she wished it did so she would know when to have her last cuddle and snuggle and nuzzle with her babies.

'That's no good,' Anna says, kissing the top of Renee's head, knowing if she lets her stay there for a few minutes she'll fall asleep. It's a routine that's developed since Gary moved out. She starts humming a lullaby, 'Hush Little Baby', which Renee loves even though at seven years old she's past lullaby age.

A minute or so goes by and she hears Renee's breath slowing. *Success!*

But then a knock at the door makes them both jump and she could curse whoever it is – probably Gary. He called her around this time a couple of nights ago and she told him off for waking up the children.

'But I don't know what time they go to sleep,' he protested.

'Exactly,' she said then hung up on him.

They haven't spoken since, so it has to be him, come round to have the conversation he didn't get the other night.

'Stay there, darling,' she whispers to Renee, then gently lies her down.

A glance through the stained-glass panels on the door – the original owner's idea of a fancy embellishment, she has long thought – tells her she was right: it's Gary. He's seen her so she can't pretend she's not home.

'What did I tell you about this time of night?' she says as she opens the door.

'But . . .' He frowns then looks at his watch. 'I've just finished work.'

'Gary, your children are asleep.' Not entirely true, but he doesn't need to know that. '*Were* asleep.' She presses her lips together and glares at him despite being mildly pleased that he looks chastised.

'Sorry,' he says. 'Sorry, sorry.' And he does sound it.

Pulling her long cardigan around her to guard against the night air, she puts the snib on, steps outside and pulls the door to. Renee needs to go back to bed and, besides, if she sees her father she may think he'll be staying the night. Both kids have started asking about Gary lately; his absence seems to have made their hearts grow fonder.

'What do you want?' Her arms are folded, just so he really gets the message that she doesn't want him here.

It's only after she says it that she notices the bunch of roses in his hand. Soft pink and blooming, they are. Unlike his face, which is pale and creased. She feels bad for having a go at him but, honestly, why would he surprise her at this time of night? Although it's technically still his house, so she should be grateful he didn't just walk in and really give her a shock.

'I, ah . . .' He holds out the flowers. 'These are for you.'

She takes them – she doesn't want to be churlish – and their scent wafts up, so she sniffs it in and can't help a smile. 'Thank you,' she says. 'But what are they for?'

'Ah . . .' His eyebrows lift and she realises they're still outside and she should really invite him into the house he still owns.

'Sorry, come in,' she says, standing aside.

'Thanks,' he says. 'Are the kids . . .?'

'Asleep,' she repeats, because she wants him to think it's true.

He nods, and she feels like adding, *As they usually are when you get home.* But she doesn't. There's no point.

Ushering him past the door of her workroom, she walks to the sitting room and takes a spot on the couch. In the middle, so he's not tempted to sit beside her.

'What can I do for you?' she says and he looks pained in response.

'You can't – I'm not . . .' He sighs. 'I can't get anything right, can I?'

'Is that what this is about – trying to get things right?'

'Isn't it?' His frown is so deep she wonders if he might disappear inside it and, if so, how she would feel about that.

Sad. She'd be sad. Because despite it all, she still cares about him. The Gary she fell in love with is in there somewhere. She doesn't think he was faking it all those years; he's never been a good actor, not able to keep up a fake smile when they bumped into someone he didn't like or pretend her sister-in-law's cooking was great. It's just that she doesn't know what he's done with that Gary and she knows if he reappeared she'd love him again.

'Anna . . . what's happening?' he asks with a plaintive tone.

'What do you mean? Nothing's *happening*. It's *happened*.'

'To us.' That frown is still in place. 'What . . .' He sighs and it's ragged and Anna realises he may be about to cry.

That makes her want to cry, partly because she doesn't understand why sticking up for what she needs and what she wants should lead to her husband crying. Surely he should understand and support her. If he really loved her. Maybe he doesn't. That's definitely something she's been contemplating for a while, after months – years – of him working late every night.

'I love you,' he says, and it's strangled and desperate and it sounds like the plea of a condemned man, which she guesses he is.

She realises something then that has never occurred to her before: she has power in this situation. That's what he's just shown her, that she has the power to break him. And she doesn't want to. Even in this flush of knowing she has the power, she has no inclination to use it maliciously. Rather, she wishes she'd known it before, back when he was in the process of alienating himself from the house, from her, from the kids. She could have wielded it. Maybe she could have stopped what happened between them. Stopped the withering of their marriage.

She remembers something her mother said once – and she really does get irritated that her mother is so regularly wise, because Anna would like to have some of that wisdom herself one day.

'Women can control the moon and the stars, the tides and the heavens,' Ingrid said. 'That's why men are so scared of our power. That's why they tell us that we have none. But here is the thing, darling: with that power comes responsibility. And freedom. If we are prepared to accept that power, we can do what we want, when we want, as long as we uphold our responsibilities.'

Or it was something like that. Anna might be making it more grandiose in her memory because it sounded like such a shocking thing, really, to hear at the time, that she – Anna of the Central Coast, Anna of the sewing machine and the old Corolla and the hair she hasn't been looking after for years – might have the power to move worlds.

Yet here's the proof, in front of her: her husband, desolate because he isn't with her any more.

This moment, right here, feels like an opportunity for a reckoning. With her power. With what she can use it for. With him.

He's waiting for her to say something and she knows that he wants her to say she loves him, but she doesn't feel she can. It doesn't feel true. Not yet. Not again.

Instead she pats his hand, then his cheek. Caring gestures; not declarations of love but loving all the same.

'I know,' she says. 'But it's one thing to say it, Gary. It's another to show it.'

His mouth opens and he looks a little shocked. Probably because she's never said anything like that to him before.

'Then I want to show you,' he says. He sniffs and glances away, then huffs like a steam engine gathering pace. 'I would like to take you out to dinner,' he says, his voice sounding stronger than it has in months.

'Oh?' she says, trying to recall when they last went out for a meal, just the two of them. It was before they had children, she's sure.

'There's a French restaurant in Gosford,' he says.

The spiteful part of her wonders how he knows about that. When has he gone there? Who with?

Does it matter?

No, it doesn't. Not right now. Because she doesn't care. Does she?

'My mother will look after the children if we go there for dinner this Saturday night,' he continues.

So clearly his mother knows what's going on. Anna hasn't spoken to Sylvia for a while. They've never really been chums and her mother-in-law has been a disengaged grandparent at best.

'That's good of her,' she gets out, not wanting to give Sylvia too many credits.

'So . . . would you like to go with me?'

He looks so hopeful, like he did when they were first seeing each other, as if he couldn't believe she'd spend time with him. That's the version of both of them she liked the best.

'Yes. All right,' she says, and watches as he visibly relaxes.

'I'll pick up the kids at six,' he says, 'and take them to Mum's. Then I'll come back to pick you up.'

She opens her mouth, about to suggest that they just take the children on their way to dinner – but that's the arrangement of a couple who are still close and familiar, and she also doesn't want to try to organise things when he's taken the initiative.

'Sounds good,' she says.

He smiles, and it's brighter than anything she's seen for months.

'Thank you,' he says. 'I'll, uh . . . I'll let you get back to it.'

He gives her a peck on the cheek before she has a chance to work out what he's doing, then he's gone, and she wanders slowly back to her workroom and decides not to try to figure out what it all might mean right now.

Renee is curled up on the floor, asleep. Best to leave her there until Anna goes to bed herself. Which won't be for a while, because she feels a little agitated.

Sewing is a good distraction – she can focus and just be in the moment with her task. So, with thumb guard on, she picks up the piece she's mending and gets to work.

CHAPTER TWENTY

Josie has faced unruly hair, patchy hair, badly cared-for hair, hair that had been set on fire – possibly on purpose, although she never found out for sure – as well as hair that had been bleached for too many years, and quite a few heads of child hair that had been cut by mothers who then decided they didn't really know what they were doing and brought their unfortunate offspring to the salon for a proper cut. However, this is the first time she's done a layer cut on her own and even with Trudy hovering over her shoulder she's nervous.

'It's all right, sweetheart,' croons the client, who is Trudy's regular, Babs.

Babs volunteered for this, apparently. 'She likes you,' Trudy told Josie. 'And she especially likes the idea of a free haircut.'

The cut has to be free because it may turn out badly. That's the other reason why Babs was happy to do it: she doesn't mind if she ends up with short hair.

'Just start,' Babs says with a wink. 'What's the worst that can happen?'

That I'm chucked out of tech, Josie thinks, but instead of saying it she tries to smile at Babs at the mirror.

Babs's eyes are bright as they look into hers – well, as they bounce back at hers from the mirror. That's one of the funny things about being a hairdresser: you don't often look your clients properly in the face. Which means you're always seeing them reversed. Just like they're seeing you. Almost Josie's whole working day is spent as a mirror image of herself, literally. If she'd done better at school maybe she'd know a name for that. Is it a metaphor? No. A simile? No. A . . . wait . . . no, she can't think of it. Or maybe it's nothing fancy, she just thinks it should be, so if she had indeed been better at school she'd be able to write a poem about it or something. 'My Life as a Mirror'. 'My Life in the Mirror' – no, she prefers the first one.

Stop. She needs to focus on Babs. Partly because this haircut is a distraction from the thing that has been distracting her all day: Brett is taking her out to dinner tonight. She has lied to her parents about where she'll be, saying she's catching a movie with a friend, and of course they'll ask about the movie so she's going to say she saw *Crocodile Dundee* again. It's still running at the cinema in Gosford – she checked – and when they ask why she wanted to see it again, she's going to say it's because her friend hadn't seen it. Which will sound weird – because the whole of Australia has seen that film – but she does have a friend who grew up in a very religious family and she hardly knows anything about anything. So that's the friend she's going to draw into the lie, and she just has to make sure that friend never visits her house since her parents will probably quiz them both about the movie.

All this fuss just to go out to dinner with a boy. But Josie knows it will be worth it, because she really likes him. Now she just has to keep her mind on the job until he comes to collect her at the end of the day. Which – she notices by glancing at the clock – is only forty-five minutes away.

'So, um . . .' She swallows. 'You don't want a fringe?'

'God, no!' Babs looks amused and points to her face. 'With this moon? I'd look like Bert Newton. No, love, just some layers on top and the side.'

Trudy squeezes Josie's arm. 'It'll be fine. Just start.'

Swallowing again, Josie picks up her scissors. Each hairdresser has their own scissors – she learnt that early on. She and her friend from tech, Sue, bought theirs together, even though neither one of them knew anything about good scissors.

'Mind if I read?' Babs asks.

Josie shakes her head. Should she take that as a further sign that Babs trusts her?

'What are you reading, pet?' Trudy says as she starts to move away, much to Josie's alarm. Isn't Trudy going to monitor her?

Babs holds up a paperback. 'A bit of Michener.'

Trudy nods. 'It's a goodie, that one. It'll make you want to go to Hawaii, though.'

'Not the worst thing in the world.'

'All right, well, I'll leave you to it. Josie'll sing out if she needs anything.'

Josie's eyes widen. How will she *know* if she needs something? Maybe she'll cut all wonky and won't realise? Except if she asks for Trudy to stay it'll really seem like she doesn't know what she's doing.

Given that Babs already has the book open, she obviously doesn't mind. So there's only one thing for it. Josie takes a big breath and combs through Babs's wet hair, looking for the lengths she wants to shape. The time passes so quickly and she's so absorbed in what she's doing that she doesn't have a chance to be nervous again about Brett until she's sweeping the cape off Babs's shoulders just as the door opens, and Brett is standing there with flowers in his hand.

'Hi, Josie,' he says, sounding confident, which she loves. She wants the man who takes her out to sound happy about it. Every girl, every woman, deserves that.

'Hi, Brett.' She flushes, aware that the salon has gone quiet.

'This your young fella?' Babs asks with a cheeky grin.

'Oh, um, I . . .' Josie doesn't know how to answer that. Technically, for tonight Brett *is* her young fella – but after that, who knows?

'Hi, my name's Brett.'

His smile is so genuine and open that Josie's heart melts a little.

'Babs. And your girl here cuts a mean layer. Don't you think, Trude?'

'I do, Babs.' Trudy nods at Josie. 'Nice work, pet.'

Brett holds out the flowers to Josie. 'For you.' He grins.

Josie grins back. 'Thanks!' she says. 'I, um, I . . .' *Whyyyyy* does she get this tongue-tied around him? He's going to think she's an idiot!

'You can go, pet. I'll finish up here,' Trudy says.

'I'll just get my bag,' she says to Brett.

As she walks out of the salon, Brett turns toward her and he looks so happy Josie almost turns to see if there's a reason why back there. Except the reason is her, and a little part of her is beginning to understand that she can make Brett happy just by being her. It's quite something, to know that. Even if she will stop believing it in about thirty minutes' time, when she's worried about how she chews her food and whether it looks ladylike, and if she's pretty enough for him, and if he's going to want to see her again.

For now, though, as he holds out his hand to take her bag, and offers her the crook of his other elbow, she feels so light, so cherished, that she can put those doubts aside, especially as she's holding his flowers in her free arm.

'So how was your day?' he says.

They're walking slowly, as if he wants to take his time.

'I was a bit stressed at the end!' she says, laughing, and she tells him about the layer cut and how it all turned out okay.

By the time she's finished the story they've arrived at a little restaurant she's noticed before. It doesn't have many tables, and most of them are full. Brett gives his name and they're led to a spot at the back of the room. There's a lit candle on it and a single flower in a small vase. The waiter offers to take Josie's flowers and she hands them over.

'Have you been here before?' she asks Brett as they read their menus.

'No, but one of the guys at work likes it.' He glances around. 'It's nice, isn't it?'

'It is,' she breathes.

They order, a steak for him and fish for her, and while they wait for food he asks her questions about herself. No one ever has before – not like this. When you're making a new friend you might ask some things, but usually you find out about the friend simply by hanging out and doing stuff – information just comes up. But he's really asking her as if he wants to know.

Except what do you say about a life that has involved being a good girl at home and school, then learning to do hair and being an apprentice?

'You don't want to hear all of this,' she says eventually, just as their meals are placed on the table. 'I'm so boring.'

He frowns. 'Boring?'

'Yeah. I don't do that much.'

'Yes, you do. You deal with people all day. That's *hard*.' He laughs. 'Why do you think I work with cars?'

She hadn't thought of it like that before. Is her work really that hard? Maybe it is. Clients can be tricky, getting upset about things she doesn't think are that big of a deal.

'Thanks,' she says.

'What for?'

She smiles. 'For saying that. I guess it is hard sometimes. I feel like I do something important now!'

'You do,' he says, slicing into his steak. 'You help people feel good about themselves.'

The look he gives her then makes her feel like she could float off the chair. It's so warm and clear – like he really sees her. Like she's special. It's so unfamiliar a look to her that she can't hold it, so she peers down at her fish instead.

They spend the rest of the meal talking about their childhood holidays and which TV shows they like, then he walks her back to her car.

'Thank you so much,' she says as he opens her passenger door and puts her bag on the seat. 'I had such a good night.'

'Not as good as mine,' Brett says.

She wonders if he's going to kiss her. Then she panics, because she's never kissed anyone, which means she'd be so bad at it, and she would bet he's kissed lots of girls because he's so handsome.

There isn't a kiss, though. Not on the lips. Instead he pecks her cheek then holds open her driver-side door and waits while she rolls down the window.

'I'll see you soon,' he says, then he touches her cheek and walks off.

Her cheek feels warm all the way back to Gosford, but whether it's from his hand or the fact that she's smiling the whole time, she doesn't know.

CHAPTER TWENTY-ONE

It shouldn't be, Evie thinks, Josie the nineteen-year-old apprentice who is prattling on about her first date with some bloke, as they're in the kitchen making a cup of tea while there's a lull in their clientele. White with two for Evie because she's developed a sugar habit to go along with her Sam semi-obsession, while Josie has a dash of milk and no sugar and that's probably why she's a skinny minnie, and that's another thing Evie plans to resent her for as soon as she's over her resentment about the date.

No, it shouldn't be Josie. It should be her, Evie, telling her co-worker about her date with their other co-worker Sam, except she hasn't had one because he hasn't asked her out and despite what Fran said, Evie is so on the verge of asking him that she just may –

'We went to that cafe near the hotel,' Josie says as she switches off the kettle just after the whistle has blown, then she turns, her eyes wide and bright and full of hope.

Evie remembers that sort of hope. You can only have it when you haven't lived long enough to be disappointed by romantic relationships. Or, in her case, unromantic relationships. Some bloke fumbling with her buttons in the back seat of his car at the drive-in; another putting his hand between her legs as he stuck his tongue down her throat; another telling her, 'My mother will love you', over and over on a date then never calling her again. That wasn't a love life, it was a loveless life, and she's sick of living it.

Sam looks at her as if she's the best thing he sees all day and that has to mean something, doesn't it? It has to be the start of something, not the totality of it. That's what she tells herself at night, after Billy has gone to bed and she's sitting on the couch reading her Jackie Collins novels and dreaming of a more intense life than the one she's living now. Sure, Jackie's books aren't about romance so much as sex and power, but Evie will take any distraction she can get from wondering why Sam hasn't made a move on her.

The other day it was just the two of them left at closing and Evie thought it would be the perfect opportunity, so she swept the hair in his direction.

He grinned at her then nodded toward the floor. 'Missed a bit, darl,' he said.

That made her feel slightly sick and she wasn't sure why. It's the sort of thing she'd like to run past a friend – maybe an older version of Josie – but there's no one she'd trust with it. She knows Fran will get cross with her, and a lot of her other friendships are fairly shallow these days, all revolving around school activities because everyone she knows outside of the Seaside Salon is associated with Billy's school. She includes Stevo in that. But maybe not Oliver.

He called the salon the other day to talk to Sam. Evie answered the phone to him and they had a nice chat and she reflected, not for the first and probably not the last time, that it was really such a shame she didn't like him *that way*, because he's so easy to talk to. But so is Sam. Maybe the brothers are just really good at chatting? That's a little confusing for her, because if you're chatting to someone who's really good at conversation, how do you know if you really get along with them or if you're just the latest in a line of people they've been chatting to? And does it really matter? Does she need to be the special one?

Actually, yes, she does. For once in her life she wants to be special to someone other than her son. Obviously she is special to Billy because all mothers are to their children, if for no other reason than the children need them to survive. She wants someone to *choose* her, that's it. Billy didn't choose her. She chose him, in a sort-of way. She chose to keep him, even when everyone she knew told her not to go through with the pregnancy because it was clear to everyone – including her – that she and Stevo weren't going to last. It was clear to Stevo too, as it turned out, although he tried his best.

Trying one's best. It implies a lot, doesn't it? But not that the person is enjoying the experience. They're *trying*. They're *trying their best*. They're making a special effort not because they want to but because they have to. Evie wants more than someone trying their best for her, no matter how well-intentioned that is. She wants someone who believes she *is* the best. And she's aware that she may want this because she doesn't believe it about herself, but what are loved ones for if not to boost you? It's what she wants to do for someone else. She wants to be the champion for the man who loves her, and she wants him to be that for her.

Sam is the person she wants to champion. If only she could get him to see it. If only Josie would stop talking about how gentlemanly Brett is.

'I had fish. With a lemon sauce,' Josie is saying as Evie tunes back in. 'Have you ever had it? I'd never heard of it before!'

Fish in lemon sauce? Maybe she means lemon butter sauce. The restaurant sounds classy. Not that Evie would know because she hasn't eaten there. It's not the sort of place she'd go on her own.

'No, I've never had it,' Evie says. She's heard of it because she reads the *Women's Weekly* and it's the sort of recipe they have from time to time. Dinner-party classics. Margaret Fulton's best recipes. That sort of thing.

'It was yummy!'

Josie is almost breathless and there's something about her joy – the lack of smugness in it, the purity of it – that makes Evie think she's been a bitch, even it's just been internal. Josie deserves to be happy. They all do.

'Did you . . .' Evie swallows her bitchiness. 'Did you have dessert?'

'Chocolate mousse!' More glee from Josie as she pulls the teabag out of her mug.

'So have you, um . . . Have you heard from him again?'

'Well, he can't call me at home.' Josie looks from left to right as if they'll be overheard even though there's no one else there. 'My parents don't know about him.'

'Oh.' Evie nods. She understands: once upon a time she was a teenage girl living at home.

'So he waited for me before work this morning.' She grins.

Evie arrived later than Josie so she missed this.

'That's nice,' she says. 'So you'll go out with him again?'

'I guess!'

'Hello, lovely ladies,' Sam says as he walks in.

It's one of his late-starting days and Evie has been looking forward to seeing him for hours. Now she tries to control the hammer in her heart as she smiles at him.

'Hi, Sam,' she says, keeping her voice light. Casual. In that weird way a person does when they have a crush and don't want the object of the crush to know unless the crush is returned, in which case one of them is going to have to admit it or it'll go nowhere. She doesn't want it to have to be her to admit it. There's too much at stake.

'How was your date, darl?' he says to Josie.

'So good!' Josie almost squeals.

Evie picks up her mug, ready to depart. She doesn't need to hear this again. Not with Sam there.

'Tell me all about it,' he says, pulling out a chair at their tiny lunch table. He catches Evie's eye as she turns to go and winks at her.

It's enough, that wink. Enough to power her through the day. He's seen her. He's *seen* her. She matters to him.

It's pathetic to cling on to these sorts of signs, but she can't help it. She'll spend the rest of the day looking for more signs, then go home and analyse them, and wish there was someone else she could tell. But instead she'll wait until Billy goes to bed, and read her Jackie Collins, and wonder when her life is going to change.

CHAPTER TWENTY-TWO

As much as she doesn't want to, Anna has to admit that Gary has made an effort. For once.

Now she's being mean. *Now* she's being mean . . . ha! If she's honest with herself – and it's hard to be that, isn't it, a lot of the time – she's been mean to him in the past. But only over things that have mattered to her. Like time. And effort.

In the early years of their marriage he made an effort. With her, with the kids, with himself. He had hobbies back then. Interests, rather. 'Hobbies' makes it sound like he built model-train sets or balsa-wood miniatures. His *interests* included swimming and tennis. Things that kept him fit, kept him lean – kept him attractive, to her, because he still looked like the Gary she first met. It showed her that he cared, especially that he cared about her opinion. In a marriage – in any long-term relationship, and she includes friendship and family in that – if you stop caring about the opinion of those you love the most, you can't then be bewildered when they stop caring about your opinion. If they then, indeed, disconnect from you, believing you're no longer interested in preserving the relationship. It may be that to be is to do – was it Aristotle who wrote that? – but for Anna, to be is to care. The whole human enterprise falls apart if we stop caring about other people.

So she cared about Gary, and that meant she made an effort too. While she doesn't have her mother's quasi-obsession with appearances – to the point where she's not sure she's ever seen Ingrid's face completely bare – Anna has never believed that marriage is an opportunity to let oneself go. One of her friends, Jeanette, likes to crow about the fact she can slob around the house in a tracksuit and no make-up and hair that hasn't been brushed since Ronald Reagan became President and how her husband 'loves me just the way I am'. But that same friend also says her husband hasn't touched her in years. Anna wants to – but doesn't – say that if you behave as if your husband is your brother, with the tracksuit and the unkempt hair and so on, you can't be surprised if he treats you like his sister.

Not that Anna would ever appear that way in front of a family member either, because she respects them and she respects herself too. It's true she doesn't believe in the power of the hairdresser the way her mother does but she always made sure she looked nice around Gary, just as she expected him to look nice around her, because she cared about his good opinion. Once upon a time.

Anna – and Ingrid too – doesn't know when the belief started that we should demonstrate how much we love someone by being as lax as possible around him or her, but she doesn't approve of it. She loves her children more than anything, which means she wants to look nice for them. She wants them to be proud of her, as she is proud of them. It is inconceivable to her that she might show them how much she loves them by looking like she simply doesn't care. Or that she's given up. If she gives up on herself she simply can't take care of anyone else, and she very much wants to take care of them.

Of course, she had given up on Gary, once he pushed her to a certain point – yet now, as he pulls out the chair for her in this tiny French, or trying-to-be-French, restaurant in Gosford, she can see he hasn't altogether given up on himself, so she feels a sprouting of respect. Which may or may not grow into anything more. It will require light and warmth, and those two things are in short supply in their relationship. Is it even a relationship any more? She supposes it is, because they have the children. It just feels more like an interaction now. Which doesn't explain why she accepted his invitation to dinner, so maybe it is still a relationship. One that she needs to maintain because of the children.

The things mothers do and the things mothers *tell themselves* they should do for their children. Like, 'I'm staying for the children.' She feels the children need a mother who stands up for what she wants and for the integrity of her person. If that makes her a selfish bitch – and oh, she knows people think that about her, because Jeanette, among others, has told her – so be it.

'You look lovely,' Gary says once he's sitting across from her, his hand halfway across the table, as if he wants her to take it.

She glances at it instead then looks away. 'Thank you,' she says with a tight smile. Her hair is in a ponytail – an easy and neat way to present it – and she is wearing a purple dress with bigger shoulder pads than she usually wears, along with a pair of earrings the size of doorknockers which she likes because they feel almost like armour, even as they whack her in the cheek if she moves her head too quickly. She did her eyes tonight – eye make-up is not something she used to attempt but since Gary left she's been experimenting and she finds it fun.

'Would you like wine?' he asks, picking up the wine list that was left on the table by the maître d'.

'A glass would be nice.' More than one and she may start to forget she doesn't like him any more. Wine can do that to a person.

'Red? White?'

He seems so nervous. The Gary she knew was never like this.

'You can choose,' she says, and he looks like he's won a prize.

The waiter takes their drinks order and leaves them with menus.

'I don't know that I'll have the escargot,' she says, scanning the list of dishes far richer than she's used to. Her mother once told her that all French cooking tastes wonderful because everything has a tonne of butter in it, but butter is something Anna eats rarely. So she'll have the fish. That tends to be the lightest fare on a French menu.

'Me either!' Gary almost giggles and she stares at him.

'Are you all right?' she says.

'What?'

'You seem a little off. Are you unwell?'

'No. What? Why?' Now his eyes are darting around. Then he sighs loudly. 'I'm a bit nervous,' he confesses.

'Why?'

'We haven't . . .' He gestures to the table. 'It's been a while since we've been out to dinner, just the two of us.'

She runs through the calculations in her head. Renee is seven, and she thinks the last time she and Gary had dinner alone was when she was pregnant. After Renee was born it was harder to find someone to babysit two kids instead of one Troy, so they didn't attempt it. Perhaps that's where things started to go wrong.

'Not since Renee,' she says softly.

He nods slowly. 'No.' He nods again. 'I'm sorry.'

'For what?'

'I should have tried harder.'

Their eyes meet and she's not sure if what he said refers to dinners out or their relationship in general. She'll take the first option to be safe.

'It was busy, having two little ones so close together,' she says, letting them both off the hook. 'I guess we . . .' She shrugs.

'Forgot?' he suggests.

He's right – they did forget to make time for each other. But that's also not an acceptable excuse because she had to remember a lot more than he did. He had to remember to go to work and mow the lawn. She had to remember every little detail of the household and the children's health and their teeth and their toilet habits and their haircuts and their school lunches and their uniforms and their friends and their friends' birthdays and their friends' mothers' names and their teachers' names . . .

Little wonder she forgot to organise a dinner out with her husband. Big wonder it should be something she'd even have to consider.

'You mean *you* forgot,' is the shorthand way she chooses to express all the resentment and loneliness that has been bubbling away inside her for years.

'No, I . . . it was . . .' He closes his eyes for a few seconds. 'Yes,' he says when he opens them again. 'I forgot.'

He puts both his hands on the table this time and yet again she thinks he wants to take hers, but she keeps them in her lap, where they're twisting her serviette.

'I didn't mean to,' he says, his brown eyes bright.

Anna weighs up her next move. She could keep drilling on this subject but there's no more oil in this well, really, because he's just admitted responsibility and to want more would be churlish. The option that would ensure they both have a pleasant evening would be for her to move on. But she doesn't want him to get the idea that he might be in with a chance with her, so she has to consider her words carefully.

'We often don't mean to do things, Gary,' she says, and she keeps her voice as soft as she can, so it doesn't sound like censure. 'But we do them and they have consequences.'

She feels herself becoming upset, and that surprises her, because she hasn't been upset about him. Anger probably counts as upset, true, but there hasn't been sadness. She hasn't felt sad about him not being at home, likely because that started happening so long ago, in increments.

Perhaps she was sad then, when she first realised he preferred his job to her. That may be what is now rising within her, pushing itself into her chest and her throat, pricking at the backs of her eyes.

Yes, she was sad then. She remembers it now. She would sit on the couch and cry because her husband didn't seem to want her any more.

Those memories – those experiences, for they now feel ongoing, in her body, in the turbulence of her mind – obviously still matter. Not that she wants him to know. This is her business, this sadness, and she has to work out what to do with it alone.

'That's in the past, though, isn't it,' she goes on, not believing a word of it yet seeing the relief on his face that she's given him a pass. 'So let's enjoy dinner, shall we?'

He reaches further across the table with one hand but she ignores it and holds up her menu again. By the time she lowers it he's focused on his and she doesn't know how long he left his hand there, waiting for hers, before he withdrew it.

CHAPTER TWENTY-THREE

Whenever one of her clients complains about how her daughter won't get out of her hair, how she's always calling and asking for advice, or calling to complain about her own children, Trudy wants to tell that client to count herself lucky to have a child who stays in touch. And it's always the daughters they complain about, never the sons. Trudy used to think it was because they all thought their sons were amazing, and she felt sorry for the daughters as a result. Now she knows it's because they only ever hear from their daughters. The sons are like hers: not given to communicating.

It was wonderful to see Dylan and Annemarie and the girls at lunch in Hornsby but she hasn't heard from her son since. Yes, it's only been a couple of weeks but she's living on her own now and she's still grieving – wouldn't it occur to him that she may need someone to actually *care*?

True, some of her clients care. Evie cares. Now she knows Trudy needs caring for.

'Just tell me the next time you need a lift somewhere,' Evie said when she dropped Trudy home from the station after the Sydney jaunt.

'I don't want to be a bother.'

Evie guffawed. 'Do you really think I'd offer if you were a bother? Besides, Billy loves a car trip, don't you, Billybub?'

Billy had looked up from the book he was reading in the back seat – how he did that without becoming sick, Trudy didn't know – and smiled and nodded.

There's been no need for the taxi service since then but it's nice to know it's available.

The outing to Sydney served another purpose: it made her realise she actually likes going out and doing things. When she came home that night she felt energised, in a way she hadn't since Laurie became sick. It made her think, it really did, about the nature of her grieving and how maybe it has become this loop she's got herself stuck in, familiar and comforting despite itself.

She just needed a jolt. So she's continued to give herself one. Or two. She's going to the club more, and she's taken up walking with Gina, one of her regulars. Some of her regulars have become friends, and it's never felt awkward that they keep being clients because they all tell her she makes them feel like a million bucks and they'd never want to go to another salon.

It's Gina who's in the chair this morning, flipping through the *The Australian Women's Weekly* while Trudy gives her a trim.

'I don't know about that Joan Collins,' Gina says as she holds up a spread featuring 'the ladies of *Dynasty*'. 'Whaddyareckon she'd be like in real life?'

Trudy shrugs. She hasn't given it much thought. 'She's an actress, pet,' she says as she makes the smallest of snips. Gina's standing instruction is for only the very ends of the ends to be snipped off. She's been 'trying to grow my hair long' for decades now and although Trudy has told her that some curly hair doesn't grow that long and even if it does it can still look short, thanks to the bounce-up, Gina persists.

'What's your point, Trude?'

'That Alexis person is a character. I'm sure she's not like that in real life.'

Tiny snip, tiny snip.

'You're not cutting too much, are you?' Gina's tone is terse. She asks this every single time.

'Of course not. You'd hang, draw and quarter me if I did.'

'Too right.' Gina nods and turns the page, her face softening. 'Paul Hogan. I like him.'

Trudy smiles and shakes her head. Of course Gina likes Hoges – he looks like her husband, right down to the big grin.

The door opens and Trudy glances up to see Josie scurrying to greet the older gent who's just walked in. It's Josie's job to greet all the clients and check their appointments in the book.

'Hi!' she says brightly.

'Hello, miss,' the man says. He has good, thick white hair – a little shaggy, which is why he must be here. Trudy presumes he has an appointment with Sam, who's putting a client under the dryer so he'll be free any tick of the clock. Evie, meanwhile, is fussing over a first-time client who wanted streaks and is currently getting them.

'Do you have an appointment?' Josie asks.

The man looks around and catches Trudy's eye. He smiles and Trudy has a feeling – that feeling you get when you recognise someone but can't remember where you met them or what their name is. It's a feeling of mild social panic and normally she doesn't have it, because over the years she's become very good with names and faces.

'Trudy,' the man says.

In lieu of saying a name she doesn't know, Trudy smiles. 'Hello,' she says.

'You won't remember me,' the man says.

She feels the release of relief. 'Oh, right.'

'Solomon,' he says. 'Or Sol. That's what everyone calls me.'

'Right.'

'Laurie and I played bowls together.'

Now she remembers, thankfully. Laurie – who never lost the competitive streak he'd had as a younger man playing tennis – had taken up bowls when one of his golfing mates suggested it. She used to accompany him to the club Christmas parties, which is – she is now sure – when she met Sol.

'Ah,' she says. 'I knew I recognised you.'

'Did you?' He looks delighted.

Perhaps she shouldn't be surprised – he clearly remembered her, after all.

'Just didn't remember your name.' No harm in admitting it now.

'It's not a name people have top of mind,' he says, and it's kind of him. 'Not that common round these parts.'

Gina makes a noise and Trudy realises she's stalled on the tiny-snipping.

'Well, I . . .' she says and points the scissors in the direction of Gina's head.

'Oh, certainly,' he says.

Now it's Josie's turn to make a noise and Sol turns back to her.

'I don't have an appointment,' he confesses, then looks in Trudy's direction again. 'I hoped Trudy may be able to fit me in. Laurie spoke so highly of your skills.'

'Did he?' Trudy says, feeling a little emotional, almost as if Laurie left her one last message, two years later. She doesn't know why it's taken Sol so long to come in for a cut but she's glad of it now. Except she's solidly booked all day.

'Trudy doesn't have anything free today,' Josie says brightly. 'Maybe Sam could help you?'

In the mirror Trudy can see Sam turning and smiling with his usual neon brightness. That lad could power the lights at the Sydney Cricket Ground with that smile. And where Sam turns, Evie follows. There she is now, looking in his direction. Honestly, that girl needs to find a different target. Sam likes her but Trudy is quite sure he doesn't like her like *that*.

'Be happy to,' Sam says. 'I have some time now while Mrs Kim is under the dryer.'

Sol looks uncertainly from Trudy to Sam and back again. 'Oh. I, uh . . .'

There's something in his eyes: not sadness but . . . is it yearning? No, it can't be. He's too old for that. Once you're past a certain point it's not becoming to yearn.

Sam catches Trudy's eye in the mirror and understanding passes between them.

'Of course,' he says, 'if you'd like to wait for Trudy I'm sure Jos can find you an appointment sometime.'

Sol's face relaxes. 'Thank you,' he says.

Josie leads him over to the book while Sam nods once in Trudy's direction. She understands what he means: Sol wants to connect with her, probably to talk about Laurie. Well, she's going to let him, even if it will just make her sad. When she thinks too much about Laurie it makes her sad and maybe her misery will like having company.

CHAPTER TWENTY-FOUR

So Evie did it. She asked Sam out.

He was giving her all the signals and she was sick of waiting, and there was an article in *Cleo* or one of those magazines with a title 'Girls, Take the Initiative', which was all about how a woman should ask a man out if she likes him, because why should the man get to make all the decisions? Evie used to think she quite liked the man making the decisions about dating because she had enough decisions to make in other realms of her life, but then she wondered . . . If she wanted Sam, why shouldn't she go after him?

Therefore, she did.

Not that she said anything like, 'Do you want to go on a date?' Imagine if he'd come out and said 'no'? Instead, as they were in the back room together yesterday, she straightened her spine and said, 'Would you like to do something sometime?'

He'd turned to look at her, and, as ever, his face was so glorious to gaze at that she felt both enraptured and shallow at the same time. His face is not all there is to like about him! Except she can't help liking it a lot. No man this handsome has ever before paid her even a second's attention.

'You mean, like a date?' he'd said, winking, and she'd almost died. Not literally. But emotionally.

'Um.'

'Sure, darl. I'd *love* that.' He put a finger to his chin. 'There's an old movie playing in Avoca tomorrow night. Are you a fan of Lauren Bacall?'

Evie didn't know if she was or not as she hasn't contemplated the issue before, but the question implied that Sam knew a fair bit about Bacall so Evie crossed her fingers and nodded and said, 'Yes', even though she wasn't sure why he was asking her.

'Marilyn?'

'Monroe?'

He gave her a funny look. 'Of course! Who else?'

That one was easier to answer because Evie loved Marilyn, although admittedly more as an icon and less as an actress because she hadn't seen that many Marilyn movies.

'Yes!' she replied.

'Perfect!' Sam said. 'Because the movie is *How to Marry a Millionaire*. I was going to see it alone – who knew that the perfect person to see it with was in front of me all along?'

It was said so easily, so breezily, like it carried no weight whatsoever. But for her it was a statement the size of the moon and just as bright, and she almost gasped with the surprise of it. It's so rare that the very thing you've been dreaming of exists in the real world, yet here it was: Sam, the subject of her dreams and daydreams, wanting to spend time with her away from the salon.

Even better, Stevo had already asked for Billy to stay the weekend with him. Evie had thought she'd be home alone with *Hey Hey It's Saturday* and a frozen pizza.

Now they're sitting together in the dark, with Sam's leg close to hers and his hand on the other side of the arm rest, a movie flickering on the screen and a packet of Fantales getting warmer in her lap, and Evie can't remember the last time she took a breath. That's how tense she is. And excited. And nervous. And wondering what on earth is going on – or might be going on – between them.

They're watching the luminous Hollywood beauties simper and smoulder their way across the screen, and all Evie can think about is whether or not Sam actually meant it when he said this was a date. Or like a date. If this goes well, will he ask her out next time?

What if he's having a bad time, though? Oh no. Work will be so awkward. Not that she didn't think about that but she forgot it in the rush of asking him out.

There, she's breathing again. She can feel it. In, out. Despite her nervousness, she needs to try to stay calm. Fainting in the cinema is not romantically alluring.

God, she is *so* not ready to be romantically alluring. The last time a man saw her naked it was in a dark room and they'd both had too much to drink and she's not sure the bloke even saw much of her because he was so busy worrying about whether he was 'good enough'. No, he wasn't, but she was hardly going to say that, and all they did was roll around for a bit anyway and have a pash before he started snoring, which led to her getting dressed and leaving and never seeing him again.

Actually, she did see him again, at a pub, but she couldn't remember his name and they both pretended not to know each other.

She doesn't ever want to be in a position to have to pretend to not know Sam. It's corny to think it – and she's certainly not going to say it out loud – but she feels as if she's known Sam before, in another lifetime. At least one. Yes, yes, she's heard people say things like that and thought they were ridiculous, but now she knows it's because she hadn't found it yet. Hadn't found him.

Once she talked to Trudy about Laurie and how she was sure he was the man for her, and Trudy had said she just knew. 'It's a feeling, pet,' she said, 'and there's no mistaking it.'

Evie can't mistake this feeling. It's not butterflies fluttering in her stomach, it's eagles flapping their huge wings inside her whole chest, impossible to ignore or write off or pretend that it's just a crush. She's had crushes. They are feeble things compared to what she feels now. Moths, not even butterflies, let alone birds. Crushes

155

are silly and transient and they give you the equivalent of a sugar fix with no substance whatsoever.

Sam's leg and hand are still there. Right next to her. Oh, how she wants to touch them. She's not going to, though. That is definitely too forward. But it shocks her, how strongly she feels like doing it. How much of an *urge* it is. Not even an impulse. There's this force inside her that could make her reach out and touch him if she doesn't keep control of it. That's definitely something she's never felt before.

Is it lust? Partly. Sure. But that sounds too . . . shallow, too tawdry, not noble enough, for this experience she's having. It's stronger than feelings. It's . . . Oh god, no, she can't think the word. Can she?

It's destiny. Yes, that's what she believes. She was meant to meet Oliver so he could bring Sam into her life. What if she hadn't gone to putt-putt that day? Would Oliver even have contacted her about Sam working at the salon? Perhaps not. So it was destiny that put her at the putt-putt at the same time as Oliver.

Beside her Sam cackles and she blinks, coming back to the present.

'God, I love her,' he says softly as Marilyn looms on the screen. 'She's so funny.'

Funny is not a word Evie has associated with Marilyn Monroe but if Sam thinks she's funny, Evie will start watching her movies and figuring out why. Because she wants to know Sam better. Just like he wants to know her better – he's always asking her questions about Billy, for example.

Once the movie has finished they wander out into the cool early-winter air, hearing the sound of waves breaking on Avoca Beach. She wants to take his hand, but she knows that's too much, too soon. They've only had this one maybe-date.

'I'm so glad you wanted to come to this movie,' Sam says as they stroll toward his car, other moviegoers also taking their time to leave the cinema. There's never much of a rush in these parts. Why would anyone hurry? The Coast lifestyle is laidback no matter where you go.

'Thank you for suggesting it,' Evie says, hoping she doesn't sound too keen. It never pays to sound as keen as you feel.

'I'd love to do it again,' he says, fishing his car keys out of his pocket and turning to give her a big smile.

'So would I,' she says after a beat, holding back her keenness. 'Great!'

He opens the passenger door and sees her in, and her heart leaps because he has manners, just as her mother said men always should, and she tries not to read too much into it, but manners are so rare and it's so hard not to get excited about them.

When he drops her home he's even better mannered: not so much as a kiss on the cheek. But he walks her to her door.

'See you Monday morning?' he says with a wink. 'For those ladies and their gossip. I love it!'

'Me too,' she squeaks out, before she waves him goodbye and lets herself inside.

She sits on the couch for an hour staring into space, and later, when she goes to bed, she stares at the ceiling and tries to quiet the racing of her heart, knowing she doesn't want to, will never want to, because finally, at thirty-three years of age, she is in love.

CHAPTER TWENTY-FIVE

After Gary left – actually, she needs to stop thinking of it like that, because technically she kicked him out, as her mother keeps reminding her – Anna realised that while she rarely saw him at home, he had still occupied a large part of her brain space. She had to run the household and do all the things he needed in order to go to his job, like wash and iron his clothes, take his suits to the dry cleaner, make food for him to take to work, keep the house clean and everything that went along with that so that he didn't have to even think about it; and she also had to do all the thinking about their home and family. All the worrying. All the remembering: bills to pay and birthday cards to send and dinner-party invitations to turn down because he could never guarantee he'd make them. But mostly the worrying, about the kids and their schooling and the future and her mother and his parents and his sister and her family . . . The housework is tiring but the worrying is exhausting.

It's not as if she could turn it off either, because if she didn't do it, who would? Their children needed her to worry about them. It's part of the mum job description. But it shouldn't be part of the wife job description. Her husband should make it easy to be with him, not hard. She had never expected to be one of those wives who complained about hubby-this and hubby-that, yet she'd find herself at school pick-up doing so. It wasn't likeable, to her or anyone else. She resented Gary for putting her in that position.

So with him gone she's cut out the worrying and the whingeing, and lo and behold she has more time and energy for other things. Which is why she finds herself at jazz ballet with Ingrid on a Thursday morning. The other class time was Monday morning, but as that's the start of the school week she didn't feel like she could organise herself to do it on a Monday, so Thursday it is.

Before taking the kids to school she got herself into tights and a leotard – something she hasn't donned since childhood ballet classes, and she's not sure if anyone even wears that sort of gear to dance classes any more – and put flats on her feet. The teacher told her she could go barefoot today and then, if she wants to come back, there are special shoes to buy. That sounds like quite a commitment, and she's a little anti-commitment at the moment, but she'll try to keep an open mind.

'Hi, Mama,' she says as Ingrid gets into the car. A while ago Anna tried going to Ingrid's door to pick her up for the salon and Ingrid snapped, 'I'm not decrepit!' so since then she's waited in the car at the appointed time. Presumably her mother will tell her when she feels she's decrepit enough for social niceties to take place. In the meantime Anna gives her a peck on the cheek to say hello, then they're off.

Ingrid looks as lithe in tights as she did when Anna was a child; Ingrid did ballet classes then. 'Never too late to look your best, darling,' she would say as she pinched the non-existent fat on her thigh. As a teenager Anna thought this was a ridiculous attitude – that was the 1960s, after all, when the social conventions of previous decades were being chucked out – but now she tends to think that looking one's best is more an act of rebellion than letting it all hang out.

'A ponytail today, I see?' Ingrid says.

'I don't want my neck getting sweaty.' Anna self-consciously touches her hair. Whenever her mother remarks on her appearance she feels like she's failed some kind of test.

'Don't worry, darling – the fitter you get, the less you'll sweat.'

That's something else Ingrid has been saying for years. It didn't help that Anna's childhood ballet teacher used to admiringly say that Ingrid had legs like Cyd Charisse, hinting that Anna could have them too if she just persevered with the ballet. Genetics didn't help her out in that instance, though, because Ingrid is several centimetres taller than her daughter.

'Sure,' Anna says, because agreeing is easiest. Then she stays quiet for a few seconds; there's something else she wants to discuss with her mother and she's working out how to start the conversation. Her mother is direct – when she wants to criticise Anna, that is. At other times she can circle around a subject. But they don't have time for circling today, because the jazz ballet studio is only a fifteen-minute drive.

'Did you ever want to leave Papa?' she asks.

She hears a sharp intake of breath.

'Why would you ask me that?' Ingrid says sternly.

But that's not a 'no', Anna thinks.

'Why do you think?'

'Don't be impertinent!'

'Don't be obtuse.'

'That's a big word for you.'

The barb lands as Ingrid no doubt intended it to, and Anna didn't deflect it in time. You'd think she'd have had enough practice, except she always wants to give her mother the benefit of the doubt. Ingrid's own mother verged on the tyrannical and Anna long ago acknowledged that Ingrid had to make a serious effort in order to not be the same. Just as Anna has to work at not slipping into default critique mode with her children. It's hard, because you have to keep working at it, but if you love your kids you do all you can.

Anyway, Anna was never that good at English at school and Ingrid knows it, so she would think *obtuse* to be too big a word. Except she hasn't noticed that Anna has recently taken up crosswords, partly to improve her vocabulary, and she has an Oxford Dictionary as a regular companion at home.

There's no point going through all that now, though. Time is ticking away along with the kilometres.

'Maybe,' Anna concedes. Then she waits. Ingrid's temper tends to flare and die in the space of seconds. Again, an improvement from her grandmother's, which would flare and rage for days.

'It wasn't easy after your father . . .' Ingrid starts. She doesn't need to say the rest, because they lived it.

'No.'

'The easiest thing would have been to leave,' Ingrid goes on. 'My mother told me to.'

No surprises there: Anna's grandmother didn't like inconvenience and Ingrid's disabled husband would definitely have fit that category.

'But he was still my husband,' Ingrid says quietly. 'He was still your father. It was harder, yes. There were times . . .' Her sigh is deep and long. 'Of course I thought of leaving,' she murmurs. 'I'm not a saint.'

Anna is so surprised at her mother's candour she decides to go for some of her own. 'First I've heard of it,' she says. Then she risks a sideways glance and sees Ingrid's raised eyebrows. Then the beginning of a smile.

'Don't be impertinent,' Ingrid says again but it's soft this time. Almost loving.

'Sometimes I can't help it.'

The studio's street is coming up and Anna puts on her right blinker.

'I know it was hard for you, in particular,' Ingrid says. 'I relied on you so much.'

This is the biggest admission she has ever made and Anna feels something lurch inside her.

Ingrid sniffs. 'But I needed you. I couldn't have managed without you. You . . .'

Anna pulls into a parking spot and turns toward her mother with the engine still running. They stare at each other and Anna knows what her mother wants to say.

You kept me in the marriage. I couldn't have done it without you.

She knows it because it's what she would say to Renee in the same situation, and she and Ingrid are not so different that she has to struggle to understand.

'I know, Mum,' she says.

It's the sort of moment where, in a movie, they might hug. They're not huggers, though. Not with each other.

'Let's do some jazz ballet,' Anna says instead.

Ingrid peers across Anna to the studio building. 'I don't like the look of it.'

It's so in character of Ingrid to criticise something before she experiences it that Anna laughs.

'Maybe it will live up to your expectations,' she says, then she switches off the engine and heaves open the car door, waiting for Ingrid to arrive beside her before they walk up the path.

CHAPTER TWENTY-SIX

'Josie, pet, what's going on?'

Trudy frowns in the direction of her apprentice, who is dancing around as if the floor is on fire and sighing and huffing and doing all sorts. It's been going on for about five minutes.

'Oh, nothing.'

'Clearly that's a lie.' Trudy stubs out her cigarette in the ashtray then picks up both and walks toward the back room, nodding at Josie to follow her.

'Cough it up,' she says after pushing the door half closed. Evie and Sam aren't likely to eavesdrop but she thinks Josie deserves some privacy.

'My mum made an appointment,' Josie blurts.

From the look on the younger woman's face Trudy guesses this appointment is not something she wants.

'At two o'clock,' Josie goes on.

Trudy glances up at the clock on the wall above the sink and sees that it's five to two. Which would explain the fire-dancing.

'With you,' Josie adds.

'Ah, so she's the Erin in the book.' The name has a big N next to it, which means new client.

'I didn't know until this morning,' Josie rushes on. 'I think Sam or Evie took the call.'

'You're saying all this like it's a bad thing.'

'It is!'

Josie's face crumples and Trudy wants to pull her into a hug, but as her boss that's probably not a great idea. She needs to retain some authority and hugging won't do that.

'You don't get along with your mum?'

'I do. Mostly.' Josie does some more sighing.

Trudy hasn't known the girl to be this emotional but maybe her mother brings it out in her. 'So what's the problem?'

'She doesn't like me having this job!'

'Then why would she come here for an appointment?'

'Probably to gather information she can use to tell me to stop working here!' Josie's voice has gone up a register.

Trudy wants to help calm her employee but not negate what she's said because she doesn't know the facts. 'Why don't you give her the benefit of the doubt, pet? Maybe she just wants to see what you're up to. A mother likes to know what her child's doing, especially when she's just starting out in the world.'

She thinks of her mother, who used to drop round to the salon in the early days, bringing Trudy lunch. Trudy liked it; she never thought it was an intrusion. But her relationship with her mother was usually calm and respectful, and she doesn't know anything about Josie's mum.

'Trudy!' Sam calls and Trudy reckons it's because the lady herself has arrived.

'Could be her now,' she says to Josie, who bites her lip and nods. 'You'd better come and say hello.'

More nodding.

'Believe the best, pet. Especially in your mum.'

Josie sniffs but at least she stops biting her lip.

Heading out of the back room, Trudy sees an older version of Josie standing just inside the doorway with a neatly done plait wound around the top of her head, Heidi style. Interesting choice for a middle-aged woman, but also a practical one for the lady who wants long hair yet doesn't want to deal with it too much. Those women tend to want to have the hair for show – a night out, or a school event, or a wedding – and think it's worth dealing with it the rest of the time just for that. On those occasions they'll come to the salon to have it done properly and Trudy can play then. She loves doing those hairdos. But given what Josie told her, she has a feeling Erin has not come here for one of them.

'Hello,' Trudy says, smiling. 'Erin?'

'Yes.' Erin's smile is tentative. 'Hello.' She glances over Trudy's shoulder; presumably Josie is there. 'Hello, darling.'

'Hi, Mum.'

Josie pulls level with Trudy, who can sense Sam and Evie's heads swivelling in their direction.

'Your mum?' Sam asks.

'Come and take this seat,' Trudy says. 'Josie, cape and towel, please.'

Josie flits away and Trudy meets Erin's eyes in the mirror.

'So, Erin, what can I do for you today? Cut? Colour? Wash? Blow-dry?'

There's probably a note about this in the book but due to the chat with Josie she didn't have time to check.

'I think . . .'

The eyes that look back at Trudy are Josie's, just with lines at the corners and a little a sag on the eyelids. Time is cruel, Trudy thinks, but also inevitable, and part of what they do in this salon is help people manage it. Cuts and colours should change as a woman ages, and Trudy will advise if a client has been hanging on to a cut for too long, so that it ages her rather than making her look the way she did when she first had it done in her youth. Or she'll suggest a softer colour for an ageing face, as that means less heavy make-up. She remembers Elizabeth Taylor going from dark-brown hair to a silvery blonde and how it took years off her, partly because she no longer needed to have heavy brows and lips in order not to look washed out beneath the dark hair. There are tricks to the show and she knows most of them.

'A cut,' Erin says at last and Trudy hears Josie gasp.

'All right,' Trudy says. 'A cut of length or a new look?'

'A new look.'

'Mum!'

Erin's eyes flash. 'What, darling?'

'You said you'd never cut your hair!'

'Well, you said Trudy is very good and I've never really had a hairdresser I could trust, so I thought I'd find out if I can trust her.'

Trudy has been around enough to appreciate that she's been given a compliment as a way of balancing an implicit threat. Erin wants her to prove her trustworthiness, it seems. Fine. She can handle it.

'Do you have an idea of what you want?' she says to her new client.

'No.' Erin's eyes move to Josie's and Trudy can almost feel something crackle between them.

'Josie – what do you think?' she asks her apprentice because this is as good a learning experience as any, and Josie is unlikely to encounter a more fraught situation than this one, at least not for a while.

'I, um . . .'

She sticks her chin out a little and Trudy thinks, *Good girl*.

'I think Mum should have a long bob. With a Lady Di fringe.'

Currently Erin has a bare forehead so clearly a fringe has not appealed to her recently, if ever, but as Trudy studies her face she can see that Josie is right: it would suit a fringe, and the long bob would frame her face in an attractive way.

'Good girl.' This time she says it aloud, partly so Erin can hear. 'You're right.'

Now Erin looks a little nervous.

'What do you reckon, Erin? Long bob and a sweeping fringe? Like Di after she had Harry.'

The princess had grown her hair long for a little while then cut it short again after the media made a fuss. But Trudy probably wouldn't be the only hairdresser who kept photos of that brief period where they got to see how that famous cut looked when it grew out. It was hair history, so she had felt moved to document it.

'Can we take a little bit off first and see what it looks like?' Erin says, and as her eyes meet Trudy's once more, there is fear in them and Trudy feels for this woman who is trying to do something here – support her daughter, perhaps, and move beyond what's comfortable for her in order to do so – yet doesn't appear to be ready for it.

'Sure. Josie will brush out your hair, then we'll see what we're dealing with.'

She has time for a quick ciggie before she settles in for what she thinks may be an afternoon of negotiation, and when she returns Josie is looking tense but Erin is smiling, so Trudy picks up her scissors and makes a start.

While she's trimming the ends Erin makes a face as if she's in pain.

Trudy stops and looks at her in the mirror. 'Everything all right, pet?'

'Oh. Yes. I'm just worried you're going to take too much.'

'Gently, gently.' Trudy puts on the smile she uses when a client is overreacting and she would like them to stop. It's almost beatific, that smile. She learnt it from the nuns at her primary school. 'You do want a new style, though?' she goes on.

'Mm-hm.' Erin nods then smiles herself.

'So can I start to shape it?'

'All – all right.' Erin glances toward Josie, who has been floating around them for the past minute or so.

'Honestly, Mum, she's the best,' Josie says.

Erin presses her lips together. 'Go ahead,' she says to Trudy, who starts to snip with more purpose.

'Thank you,' Erin says quietly after a couple of minutes have passed.

'For what, pet?'

'For looking after my girl.'

Their eyes meet in the mirror.

Trudy smiles knowingly. 'I think she's pretty good at looking after herself.' She wonders just who Erin thinks her daughter is, because the Josie at the salon is capable and responsible. So she decides to say it.

'She is great with clients. And I wouldn't trust just anyone with my clients, because I've been here a long time.'

Erin seems quietly pleased, her smile small but persistent. 'That's good,' she murmurs. 'We did raise her to have manners.'

'It's more than manners.' Trudy winks at Josie, whose eyes are wide. 'She has a talent for putting people at ease. Believe me, I'm rapt she's here.'

Erin nods but only looks at her daughter in the mirror for a second. Almost as if she doesn't want Josie to see that she's proud. She is, though – Trudy can tell.

When Trudy has finished giving Erin the long bob, she calls Josie over. 'What do you think, pet?'

Josie breaks out in a grin. 'I love it! Mum?'

Erin pats the underside of her hair. 'Yes, it's good.' She nods. 'Very good.'

Trudy waves off payment but Erin insists, then she watches as Josie walks her mother outside. There's no hug or kiss; just a pat on the shoulder from mother to daughter. It's an odd formality given that Josie lives at home, but it's not for Trudy to judge someone else's family.

Josie is smiling as she comes back inside, and Trudy is somewhat startled when she's given a quick hug.

'Thanks so much,' Josie says. 'She's really happy.'

'Excellent news. Now.' Trudy peers into the book. 'I have time for a ten-minute break. If anyone's looking for me, I'll be out the back.' Out the back with a coffee, of course, but she doesn't need to say that.

For the next ten minutes – actually, fifteen, because her client is running late – Trudy thinks about mothers and daughters, about whether she would have been like Erin if she'd had a daughter, and indulges in a few more what-ifs before she emerges again.

CHAPTER TWENTY-SEVEN

The winter sun casts a rich yellow light across the water at Killcare as Josie stretches out her legs on the towel and squints as she looks out to the tinny with two fishermen in it, their rods propped up.

'Tell me if you're cold,' Brett says as he spreads out a towel for himself and sits beside her.

It was his idea to come here for their second date. He didn't use the word date, but that's what it is. Josie's friend Sue was really firm about it when she told her.

'Did he ask you or did you ask him?' Sue said.

'As if I'd ask him!'

'All right, all right.' Sue had kept chewing her gum, then nodded enthusiastically. 'Definitely a date. Where's he taking you?'

'He said it's a surprise.'

'Just as long as he doesn't take you somewhere weird.'

'Like where?'

'That rollerskating rink at Long Jetty.'

'Why would that be weird?'

'Do you know any blokes who rollerskate?'

Sue had looked so serious when she said it, but Josie couldn't take her seriously – why would Brett want to go rollerskating? Except afterward she found herself worrying about it, which just went to show she was gullible like her mother always said, so maybe that means she's gullible enough to think it's a date. Except Sue was really sure it was.

Brett had wanted to pick her up at home but as it's a Sunday she told him not to – that would involve her parents looking out the living-room window and seeing her getting in his car, which she'd have to explain later, and it just wasn't worth the hassle. Instead she said she'd meet him at the nearby jetty at Brisbane Water. Well, actually, first she said she could meet him wherever he had planned to take her, but he insisted on picking her up because it was a surprise.

The surprise, it turned out, was that he'd bought prawns and some bread rolls, and he brought a lemon from home and a knife to cut it with, then he picked her up and drove her to Killcare, taking towels out of the boot, and now they're sitting in the warm sun and he's peeling the prawns, which is really such a nice thing for him to do.

'Thanks,' she says, gesturing to the prawn-shell carnage on the paper. 'You had to get all messy.'

'No worries,' he says with a grin, then he walks to the water's edge and rinses his hands. 'Easiest place in the world to peel prawns,' he says as he returns, shaking off the water.

He cuts open the bread rolls then tucks prawns inside, squeezing lemon over them, before handing a roll to Josie. It's one of the sweetest things anyone has ever done for her: so simple yet caring. Thoughtful, that's what he is.

She knows what Sue would say: *He just wants to get in your pants.* She knows what she would say back: *What if I just want to get in his?* Except she wouldn't say that, because even the thought of it makes her blush. And feel curious. And, sometimes, giddy. It's not as though she hasn't had crushes on boys, and wondered what it would be like to . . . you know, *do things.* But she hasn't done things.

'Pretty good prawns,' Brett murmurs. 'Salty.'

'I wonder where they caught them.'

'Tuggerah Lake. That's where he usually goes.'

'Oh?'

The casual way he says it, the 'usually', suggests he's familiar with this prawn catcher and that intrigues her. She wants to know the story. She wants to know him. It feels comforting and strange and exciting and settled all at the same time. Is this what falling in love is? Sue couldn't tell her because it's never happened to her, she said. Once she thought she got close but the bloke got back together with his ex and moved to Newcastle.

'Yeah.' Brett grins. 'My neighbour. Terry. He catches them at Tuggerah and sells them out of his garage. Everyone knows about it, so he does well.' He keeps grinning as he takes another bite of his roll.

'I really, um . . .' She pauses. 'I really appreciate you doing this. It's . . . it's lovely.' She doesn't know how to tell a boy he's being nice to her without it sounding silly – there's definitely a more sophisticated way to do it but she doesn't know what that is, and meanwhile she wants to let him know that she's noticed his effort.

'You're welcome.' More grinning. 'We could have gone to a restaurant but I thought you may like this.' He gestures to the water. 'It's so pretty here.'

Most of the beaches on the Central Coast are pretty, but obviously he likes this one more than others.

'Do you come to Killcare much?'

He nods. 'Killcare, MacMasters, Copacabana . . . They're all good. Do you like the beach?'

'Yeah. I don't go that often, though. Not sure why.' But she does know why: none of the girls from tech liked the beach because they all hated being seen in swimming costumes, and she understood because she was also self-conscious about it, but she really wanted to go more anyway. Just not alone.

'We'll have to change that.' His voice is light but he's looking at her with intent.

And did he just say 'we'? *We!*

'Oh?'

He puts down his roll on the towel. 'I really like you, Josie.'

She feels warm and her heart is beating faster, and she's not making it, it's just doing it on its own, and all she wants to do is ask him why he likes her – what's so special about her? – even as she's always wanted to be special to someone. Someone other than her parents, because that's a different kind of special – sometimes a suffocating kind of special – and when she daydreams about a boy saying to her exactly what Brett has just said she thinks about how the boy who thinks she's special is choosing to do so, whereas her parents have to think it, don't they? She's their child. They just love her. There's nothing in particular about her that has made them love her. But someone else has to choose her, and that's always seemed impossible. In this whole, big world, how could someone find her and choose her?

'I really like you too,' she says.

The other night, after dinner, he didn't try to kiss her and she was both disappointed and glad. Glad because she doesn't know how to kiss and disappointed because she wanted to be wanted.

Now he's leaning a little closer to her and she wonders what is meant to happen here. Will he start? Should she?

'You're fun,' he says. 'And kind.'

Fun and kind are not words she'd use to describe herself. Isn't it odd, she thinks, that other people can see us so differently – and who's to say if they're right or we are?

'Thank you,' she says. Then she tries to think of all the things she wants to tell him he is, but her mouth won't form the words.

'And I hope you don't mind me saying,' he goes on, 'but you're really pretty.' His smile is shy this time.

'No, I don't mind,' she says quickly. *Mind?* Why would she mind? She knows it shouldn't matter that he finds her pretty but it does. It really, really does.

She's still holding her prawn roll when he shifts closer to her and stares into her eyes, and also when he puts his lips on hers, and they feel warm and dry, surfer's lips, lips that have been out in the sun and bear its mark.

At some point she drops the roll, she must do, because several minutes later – or maybe it's an hour or more, she loses track of time – she finds it on the towel with a few grains of sand on it, and he smiles as she picks it up and keeps eating, because she doesn't want to talk, can't talk, has no words to tell him what it meant to her that he kissed her like that, with tenderness and passion balanced, with one hand on her cheek and the other arm around her. She felt like a woman, that's it. Like a proper adult, like a woman a man wants. If that's what love feels like, she wants more of it, and even if it's not, she wants more of it.

When he drives her back to her car he holds her hand in between shifting gears, and they don't say much, and it's perfect.

JUNE 1986

Madonna's album *True Blue* is released.

Return to Eden is on Australia's TV screens.

Argentinian football player Diego Maradona scores
with the 'Hand of God' against England.

The feature film *Ferris Bueller's Day Off*,
starring Matthew Broderick, is released.

HRH Prince William turns four.

CHAPTER TWENTY-EIGHT

In come some of their retirement-home ladies, a little slower each week, Evie reckons, although that could be just her perception because she's impatient each week for Sam to show up. This is the one morning he starts around the same time she does and she loves knowing they'll have the whole day together. That's at least seven hours of her being able to surreptitiously glance at him and talk to him and maybe, if the timing works out, have lunch together.

Given that they haven't spent any more time together outside of the salon since they went to the movies, Evie suspects he has no idea she has a crush on him. Which is good on the one hand – the at-least-it's-not-awkward hand – but bad on the other, which is the hand that desperately wants him to sweep her into his arms.

So she needs to *do something* in order to make him realise it. She's just not sure what. Seduction has never been in her repertoire and she can hardly turn herself into Kathleen Turner overnight. The sort of confidence of a woman like that probably involves some kind of training class, or an older female relative who knows what's what.

No, she just needs to be even nicer to him at work, and try to spend as much time with him as possible. Which is why she beams when he strolls in, smiling, not at her directly but close enough.

'Good morning, lovely ladies!' he announces as he heads for the back room, where he will leave the battered brown satchel he brings every day.

'Good morning, Sam!' some of the clients coo back, and Evie feels that pang of jealousy she always gets when another woman says his name, even if she knows that woman is not a legitimate rival for his affections. Which is the case for all of the retirement-home ladies, who are several decades older than him, for one thing.

'Ev-e-lyyynnn,' he singsongs as he brushes past her on the way to his chair. He started using her full name after their night at the movies. She doesn't know why, and she doesn't know how he knows she's an Evelyn and not an Eve who added a syllable. Trudy had to have been the one who told him. Otherwise it's a lucky guess, and as she hasn't corrected him he'd presume, as he should, that he has the name right.

'Such a character,' says Mrs Behar, an irregular client. Some of the ladies come weekly, some fortnightly, some when they feel like it. The irregulars know the drill if they wander in without an appointment: regulars have first dibs on chairs so they may have to wait a while, but given most of them are well into their seventies or eighties they don't have jobs or children to attend to, so they never object to waiting. It just happens that Mrs Behar is in luck today as a couple of the regulars haven't turned up, or maybe they're running late.

'He is.' Evie smiles as she feels Mrs Behar's hair. She hasn't done her hair before, which means she wants to get to know its texture before they start. Unusually for a woman of her age, the hair is not entirely grey – she still has quite a few dark strands. It's long and straight, and Mrs Behar wears it in a bun, so Evie guesses she's just having a trim.

'So . . . a centimetre or two off?' she asks.

'No.' Mrs Behar shakes her head.

'No?'

'All off.'

Evie's mouth drops open. 'All?' She hadn't planned on a complete makeover this morning.

'I want it short.'

'But . . .' Evie picks up lengths that are healthy and in no need of chopping. 'Haven't you always had it long?'

Mrs Behar holds up a hand. 'I'm sick of it. It takes me all night to wash.'

'Oh . . . okay. So . . .' Evie narrows her eyes as she looks at Mrs Behar's face and tries to think of a cut that would suit her. She has a round face and a short hairstyle could make her look a little like mutton-dressed-as-lamb. Or, as Trudy would call it, having 'a case of the mutts'.

'You really want it all off?' Evie checks.

'I want it short and easy to care for.'

'How about a bob?'

Another shake of the head. 'No.'

Evie feels as if she's dealing with a toddler: every answer is *no*.

'All right. Well, I'm not sure having it really short will suit you. How about I chop it shoulder length to start and we take it from there?'

Mrs Behar purses her lips. 'All right.'

Evie relaxes a little. Now she needs to get a tougher pair of scissors – cutting off that much hair requires something closer to shears.

When she returns with Trudy's tough scissors, she notices that Mrs Behar is observing Sam, who is laughing as he chats to his client and Josie, who is no doubt about to wash the client's hair, as that's her usual job.

Mrs Behar sighs. 'Bit of a waste, isn't it?'

'Hm?' Evie starts brushing. She wants to see how much hair she's dealing with.

'That young man – Sam, isn't it?'

'Yes.'

'Bit of a waste that he doesn't like the ladies. Such a good-looking fellow.' Another sigh. 'Oh well. I'm too old for him anyway so it's just as well!' She titters.

Evie's hand stops brushing and she feels her throat tighten. It's funny how quickly someone's words can have an impact but perhaps that's because she registers them as true in a way they could never be true if she said them to herself.

'What do you mean?' she forces herself to say because she wants to hear it – *it, it, it,* the truth of the matter, the end of her dreams – out loud.

Mrs Behar's eyes meet hers in the mirror. 'You don't know?'

'Um . . .' Doesn't she, though? Doesn't she, in the core of herself, know this?

How she could not know is because she didn't want to. She's in love with him. He *can't* be gay. There is nothing about her that would indicate she'd fall for a gay guy and, yes, she knows, you can't help who you fall in love with, but how stupid could she be to not really know this from the start? To fall for his attentions thinking they were romantic when they were just friendly? Or maybe they have been romantic, but in a Victorian way – all looking, no touching. It's the no touching, though, that has thrown her. Except it makes sense now, if Mrs Behar is to be believed.

'Oh, I apologise,' Mrs Behar says. 'Perhaps he hasn't said anything. But it seems obvious to me.'

Evie resumes brushing. 'We, um . . . We haven't discussed it.' She can feel Mrs Behar watching her reflection closely.

'Ah, I see,' Mrs Behar says.

Evie bites her lip to stop herself crying. Are her feelings that obvious, in all their pathetic, desperate glory?

They're both silent for a while as Evie continues to brush.

'You wouldn't be the first,' Mrs Behar says softly, her eyes flitting over to Sam then back. 'You won't be the last. It is part of life, isn't it, to want what we can't have.'

Evie sucks in a breath and keeps biting that lip until it feels as if she'll draw blood, because if she lets it go she may howl.

'Perhaps,' she squeaks out, and she meets Mrs Behar's eyes because to do otherwise would be to give in to the shame entirely, and she sees understanding there, and sympathy, not pity, and for a second she feels better, then she doesn't.

'Let's get you sorted,' she almost whispers, still brushing, wishing she could be like the Wicked Witch of the West and melt into the floor, leaving only a hat behind, but instead she'll focus on doing her job and giving Mrs Behar the best haircut on the Central Coast.

'Indeed,' Mrs Behar says.

For the remainder of the appointment they talk about nothing much, and Evie remembers none of it as she spends the rest of the day trying to avoid Sam, who would no doubt be confused but she can't worry about him. She needs to get out of here and spend a goodly amount of time going over every interaction she's ever had to see if she's missed signs that are so obvious that even Mrs Behar could see them.

But once she is home, with Billy tucked in bed, she turns the television on, turns it up loud and sobs into her couch.

CHAPTER TWENTY-NINE

Right, this is it.

Anna blows air out of her open mouth as she stares at herself in the mirror at the Seaside Salon and thinks that she looks like a fish trapped in a bowl, with no other direction to take. She closes her mouth as she inhales and opens as she exhales. Not even consciously. As if she's *nervous* or something. Which is ridiculous, because this is a hairdressing salon and all she's doing is having a haircut. Maybe even a hairstyle.

It was a spur-of-the moment thing. When she walked into the Seaside Salon this morning with Ingrid she found herself asking Trudy if she had any free time.

'For . . .?' Trudy arched an eyebrow.

'Me.'

Anna wondered what on earth she was doing. She'd had thoughts about changing her hair. Now she's not with Gary any more it makes sense to change other things, to take some positive steps to take care of herself in other ways. Or maybe just to do something different. Changing hair seems easy – the hairdresser does it for you.

'You,' Trudy had said. 'Well, well.'

Trudy glanced at Ingrid in the mirror, then Anna saw her catch the eye of Evie, who was in the middle of painting on a colour.

'I want a change.' Anna kept staring at her reflection. She was sick of that reflection. Going through the motions of brushing her hair and putting on some lippy and mascara doesn't amount to anything other than habit. She wants something different.

Trudy's eyes twinkled. 'How much of a change?'

Anna took a deep breath. 'Whatever you think.'

Trudy turned to Evie and grinned. 'Don't hear that often, do we, Evie?'

Evie shook her head.

Anna's eyes met Ingrid's in the mirror and she saw something unfamiliar in them: curiosity.

'What do you think, Mama?' she asked.

'You have lovely hair, Anna,' Ingrid said. 'I've always thought so.'

That was probably a lie, because Ingrid had never said anything like that to her, but she let it go.

'But a change is, as they say, as good as a holiday,' Ingrid went on.

'Righto,' Trudy said. 'I can fit you in after your mum.'

The problem with that, though, is that Anna has had a chance to think about it since. Does she really want to have to fuss with her hair? Maybe she could just . . . put it in plaits or something? That would be different. Not necessarily great. But different. Easier than hairspray and teasing and who knows what else she'll have to do. No, she doesn't need the bother of a hairstyle. She has enough on her plate.

She puts her hands on the arms of the chair, about to push herself up to standing, when she feels hands on her shoulders and looks up into the mirror to see Trudy giving her a knowing look.

'Fleeing, are we?' Trudy says.

'Oh, um . . .' Using the mirror, Anna glances to the other side of the salon, where Ingrid is laughing along with Sam, who's brought her a cup of tea.

Sam is very good with the older ladies who come to the salon – charming without it seeming disingenuous, probably because it's not. The sorts of questions he asks the ladies indicate that he's a genuinely curious person, interested in their lives. Anna likes him, even if she's never actually had a conversation with him. Yet she's observed how he treats her mother like a person, not an old lady like so many others do, and she appreciates it.

'She's trying to make a run for it, Ingrid,' Trudy calls over the noise of clients and hairdressers chatting, and Anna is mortified.

'She'll be fine,' Ingrid calls back then catches Anna's eye and winks, and smiles in that comforting way mothers have.

'What are you worried about?' Trudy asks, her hands still on Anna's shoulders. 'That I'll make you look bad? Because I won't. At the very least, that's not good for business so it's a terrible idea. But I also don't want to make you look bad, pet, because you deserve to look *great*.' She picks up the cape and towel that are draped over her arm and arranges first towel then cape over Anna's shoulders before pinning the cape closed with a hair clip. 'So, we're going to give you something that is easy to maintain and which also makes you feel good, okay?'

Anna nods slowly, then swallows. Tending to her hair is another job she'll have to add to the morning routine. Does she really want to do that?

'No blow-drying required,' Trudy says, as if reading her thoughts. 'Maybe a bit of spray. That's all.' Trudy tilts her head from side to side, her eyes narrowed. 'I've been thinking about this for a while,' she says.

'You have?'

'Mm. It's good to be able to picture what you'll look like, then I cut to that.' She picks up some of Anna's hair. 'A fringe and some layers, I think,' she says. 'The layers will give you a little volume and because you have a wave to your hair they'll sit nicely. If it were dead straight they wouldn't work. And the fringe is an easy embellishment, shall we say. It'll draw a person to look at your eyes, and you have such lovely eyes.'

'Do I?' Anna stares into her own eyes and tries to understand what Trudy means.

'They're green, which is unusual, and you have those naturally long lashes. Yes, they're lovely. Some of us would kill for those lashes.' Trudy smiles. 'Josie,' she calls, and the young woman speeds over. Anna has noticed her scurrying around when she's here but they haven't spoken to each other yet.

'Hi,' Anna says.

'Hi.' Josie smiles shyly.

'Do you mind if Josie does your fringe? I'll be here. I promise she won't butcher it.'

Josie's eyes widen and Trudy cackles.

'Relax, pet,' she says. 'I'm joking. You've done fringes before. You'll be fine.'

Anna isn't sure, though – while an apprentice hairdresser needs to get practice, why should the practice be on *her*? However, as she doesn't want to go against Trudy, she tries to arrange her face so she looks agreeable.

'You have such good hair,' Josie says.

Anna is wondering if she says that to everyone when Josie picks up some of her strands and inspects them closely.

'Nice body,' the young woman goes on, then their eyes meet in the mirror. 'Have you had a fringe before?'

Anna recalls an unfortunate time in her teens when she had a too-short cut that had made her look as if she hadn't been able to decide if she wanted a fringe or not. It's possible the hairdresser did it because he hated her; at that age Anna hated herself, in the way that serious-minded teenage girls who long to be understood tend to do.

'Once,' is her reply to Josie. 'It wasn't very good.'

Josie grins. 'I'll make this one good. I promise.'

Again, Anna tries to look agreeable. It's important, she has found, for getting along in the world. A person's intention can be misinterpreted by others at the slightest provocation and she so wants to have a peaceful life. That can be somewhat ensured if she always looks agreeable while hiding her true feelings.

A friend of hers who has been seeing a psychologist said – upon Anna telling her about her agreeable tendencies – 'But don't you just want to *be yourself*?' Being oneself was the psychologist's favourite thing to talk about, Anna knew, because the friend mentioned it regularly.

'I *am* being myself,' she protested. 'Being myself means living in a way that doesn't upset other people.'

The friend huffed at that as if she'd said something ridiculous, muttered about how Gloria Steinem didn't wear skivvies just so Anna could spend her life appeasing others, and changed the subject to the Royal Family.

So Anna stays true to herself as Josie first washes her hair then starts cutting, and again when Trudy takes over to do the layers while Josie watches. She smiles vaguely even as she feels like a caged specimen, and when Trudy blow-dries her hair despite saying blow-drying wouldn't be needed. Or maybe it's not needed outside of the salon. Anna will have to check.

She loses herself, though, when Trudy turns her around and shows her the hairdo, in that she veers dramatically away from appeasement toward expressing happiness. Because in front of her is a woman she doesn't recognise but who looks ten times more interesting and glamorous than the one who walked into the Seaside Salon.

'Trudy!' she squeals. 'Josie!'

Trudy nods and smiles like a proud parent. 'Good, hey?' she says.

'I can't – I don't – I . . .' Anna gulps down a breath. 'How?'

'It's the magic of a good cut, pet. It's all about the lines and the angles. Josie has the talent' – she taps the side of her nose – 'and she is learning fast how to work with it. I knew she'd do the right thing. All I had to do was make sure my cut worked with hers.' She pats Anna's shoulders. 'So,' she says, 'wash it, condition it, let it air dry, okay? It'll fall into shape. And if you want something extra, come in for a blowy, all right?'

'Something extra?'

Trudy fluffs her ends. 'Like for a date.'

Anna's brain goes to Gary standing at her door with flowers and hopefulness. No, he doesn't deserve the blowy.

'I, ah . . . probably not!' She attempts a laugh.

'Righto. Whatever you say.'

Anna pays Trudy for her cut and Ingrid's blow-dry then grins as she walks toward her mother, who is gazing at her as if she's the most beautiful girl alive.

'Stunning,' Ingrid says. 'You look wonderful. You look . . . like yourself.'

Anna's breath catches and she feels like crying, which is so weird – except what Ingrid said is what Anna also thought when she looked in the mirror. All this time she believed she was just being herself when it turns out it was a facsimile of her. Maybe. She'll find out for sure once she gets used to this hairstyle.

As they leave the salon Ingrid turns to her and says, 'Let's have a coffee to celebrate my daughter coming back to me.'

Again Anna is surprised, but this time it's because she didn't realise a hairstyle could have that much power. Except if it couldn't, why would Ingrid come here every week?

This is something she plans to ponder as she waits for her hair to dry tomorrow morning.

CHAPTER THIRTY

Trudy doesn't often leave the salon for lunch. It's her morning, noon and sometimes her night, that place, because that's what happens when you run a small business – so why would she leave the premises to go . . . where? To the hamburger place on the corner? The ice-cream shop in the other direction? The sandwich shop near the beach? She brings her lunch from home and that means the back room at the salon is usually just fine.

Today, however, she feels the need for the sun on her face. It's winter sun, so it's not going to hit her like a blast furnace, and she'll be able to sit by the water while she eats her curried egg sandwich and tries not to think.

It occurred to her recently that thinking a lot is a problem. If she starts thinking, her thoughts are bound to turn to Laurie, then she's off down not so much memory lane as maudlin motorway, remembering all the reasons why she misses him so much. And that motorway can be about ten lanes wide and seem to lead inexorably to a destination she can't name and suspects she doesn't want to reach, because every time she's on it she experiences dread. It's the dread she wants to avoid, because she's feeling it settle in her bones, in her blood, in her tissues. Whether it's the dread of being without Laurie forever or of someday forgetting what it was like to be married to him, she doesn't know. But regardless, she doesn't like it.

Sunshine is life's great disinfectant, as her mother used to say, so it seems like her solution today. Along with sea air. Who doesn't like a good sniff of the salt?

So, sandwich in handbag, she sets off from the salon toward the beach, although she doesn't get far before she is stopped in her tracks by the sight of Sol heading in her direction, slowly; he's told her he has a bad hip, 'although I can't remember which one', which she didn't find as funny as he no doubt intended it to be.

'Trudy!' he says, his face alight.

'Oh, hello, Sol,' she says in that tone she gets – in fact, most women she knows get – when they can't avoid a social entanglement yet don't want to open any kind of door for further interaction. It's something learnt at mothers' knees and has probably been going on for millennia, which is why it's so instinctual. Or it is for her. And she doesn't want to stop and chat – she wants sun, sea air and sandwich.

'How are you?' he says eagerly, as if she's going to have a fascinating answer for him.

'I'm heading out for lunch.'

'Oh?'

She holds up her handbag. 'A sandwich by the seaside.'

He nods. 'What a good idea.'

Then he looks at her. *Really* looks at her, in a way that makes her feel exposed. As if he sees her grief, her loneliness, her sleepless nights, her occasional sense of hopelessness, her dismay that her son hardly contacts her . . .

She feels empty so much of the time, and that's what she thinks Sol is seeing now. It's unsettling, because she was so sure she'd done a great job of hiding that emptiness from everyone. Even as she has wished someone would notice it. However, here he is, possibly noticing it, and she is afraid it means she hasn't been so good at hiding it, really, which makes her wonder if she's been wandering around with some kind of hole in her heart that everyone can see. The sort of hole that can't be filled, that might make her feel ashamed that she isn't stronger, more capable, more resilient. All the things an adult is meant to be. All the things she has not felt, not one day, since Laurie died.

He was those things for her, and she didn't really want to have to be them for herself. There's only so much a woman can handle in her life, and when she has to do it all it wears her out. She is wearing out. Worn out, even. It's not what she wants, although she doesn't know how to end it without it being the end. And she's not ready for that. For all the grief she feels, for how hard the past two years have been, she still wants to be here, on this planet, trying to find a way forward. That's something.

'I don't mean this to sound untoward,' Sol says.

Trudy thinks that she hasn't heard *untoward* for quite a while.

'I would very much like to take you out for lunch,' he continues. 'Or dinner, perhaps. Yes, dinner might be preferable, since you have your business.'

He keeps looking at her. *Looking*-looking, and she feels she can't glance away or it would be rude somehow. Yet she has to ask him something, because she needs to know.

'Why?' she says.

He looks amused. 'Why?'

'Mm.'

'I suppose I could be flippant and reply, "Why not?"' His eyes are twinkling and she likes the way they do that. It makes him seem lively.

'You could,' she says, and something lets go in her. She's having an adult conversation – a proper exchange between two people who know they're at the same stage of life and don't have time to waste – for the first time since . . . well, since Laurie died.

'But the truth is, Trudy . . . I presume you want the truth?'

What a question. A big, all-encompassing question. Or not. There are little truths and big truths. A little truth is giving direct information in response to a question. A big truth is saying 'I love

190

you' – except that's also a little truth, because it should be a daily affirmation.

So maybe they're all big truths. Maybe every time we're honest with ourselves and others it goes to the bigger whole of how to be in this world, how to make life meaningful, how to roll out the carpet for the rest of our lives. Or for that day alone.

Yes, she's been doing too much thinking since Laurie died but it can sometimes lead her to good places, and one of those places is the recognition that truth is good. So that's what she'll ask for.

'I do,' she says.

'I was a little jealous of Laurie,' he says, and his eyes look even more alight. 'You're an impressive woman.'

She's taken aback by that. Her, a little hairdresser from Terrigal, impressive? That's a word she'd reserve for prime ministers and monarchs. Maybe Maggie Tabberer. Not herself. Impressive people are people who have achieved great things. Her life has been small – by choice and circumstance – and she has never minded it, and she certainly wouldn't make a claim to being impressive.

So she doesn't know what to say back to him except, 'Oh?'

'Indeed. He was a lucky man, I always thought. And, of course, I would never have said anything, but . . .'

He looks at her again, in that same piercing way, and she understands: he's waited for two years to approach her. That's respectful and she likes it, even if she's not sure whether or not to accept his invitation.

It's merely an invitation, though, and she shouldn't overthink it. Definitely shouldn't do that. Dinner does not oblige her to anything other than a conversation, and it will also be a change, and she knows she needs to make some sorts of changes. Who knows? Maybe her life will be less small as a result.

After Laurie died one of her clients brought her a book called *You Can Heal Your Life* by a woman called Louise L Hay. Trudy thought it was a tad presumptuous of the client – what did the woman think she should heal, exactly? – but it turned out to be a comfort at times. Trudy has struggled to completely understand how her thoughts affect her physical wellbeing, the way Louise says they do, except she can see the evidence of it in her life: she thinks herself into holes, and over the past few months she has noticed that she feels heavy and sluggish, which she has put down to being older, except it coincided with the wake of Laurie's death. So she's prepared to concede that there's something in it and that it would be good to change things. Change will only come, though, if she commits to it and the discomfort that can come with it. Like having dinner with a man who isn't her husband.

'That's kind of you,' she says to Sol. 'And I would like to accept your invitation.'

'Wonderful!' he says. 'May I call you at the salon to arrange a day and time?'

How polite he is, she thinks. And how nice it is.

'I'll give you my home number,' she says, and is unsurprised when he whips out a notebook and pencil from his back pants pocket.

After he's written it down he puts the items back in his pocket and nods again. 'I shall call you this evening,' he says. 'And now I'll let you go on your way.'

'Thank you.' She smiles, and it feels as if it's the first time she has today.

'You're welcome.' Then he makes a gesture as if he's doffing an invisible cap, and she finds it charming.

As Sol stands back to let her continue walking down the path, she keeps smiling, and as she crosses the street to head for the beach she feels lighter than she has for a long time. So perhaps that Louise Hay is onto something about thoughts and wellbeing. That's what Trudy will contemplate as she eats her curried eggs.

CHAPTER THIRTY-ONE

It's Evie's second time going to the movies with Sam and regardless of what Mrs Behar said, she is sure this is a date. Because this time *Sam* asked *her*, not the other way around.

On Thursday he said to her, 'You look nice,' and glanced up and down at her.

She flushed at the compliment, and also because he noticed, as she has been making an effort, even if it's just in her accessories. A fortnight ago she bought some scrunchies in neon colours, and she's been tying up her hair like Madonna used to – a little messy – hoping that it looks carefree. That's in addition to the hot-pink lipstick she's been wearing, and she's also doing her eyes.

'I love old movies,' he said the other day as he boiled the kettle in the back room.

'Oh?' She couldn't think of anything else to say. Was he expecting her to say she loved them too? Because she presumed he already did, given the movie they saw together. Was she *meant* to love them too? Is she meant to love everything he loves or be her own woman? The magazines she reads are divided on the issue.

'Have you ever seen *Blossoms in the Dust*? Greer Garson. *Love* her.'

Evie shook her head. She hadn't grown up in a movie-centric household – her parents thought reading to be a better way of spending time.

'*To Catch a Thief*!' he said. 'Grace Kelly!' He looked rapturous. 'God, she was beautiful. And *Cary Grant* – so debonair.'

She murmured her agreement but said nothing more in case she jinxed whatever was about to happen, because she had a feeling about what he was leading up to.

'*High Society*?' he went on. 'Sinatra, Crosby, Kelly. *The best!* And of course . . .' He closed his eyes briefly. '*Giant*. Rock Hudson. James Dean. Elizabeth Taylor.' He looked at her expectantly. She had, in fact, heard of *Giant* – probably everyone had – and told him so.

'Great,' Sam said. 'Because there's a showing of it at this old picture place in Gosford. One session only. Saturday night.'

She smiled encouragingly.

'Should we go?' he said, nudging her.

She counted to five in her mind so she didn't shout 'yes'.

'Do you think your ex would mind looking after Billy?'

The way he said 'your ex' rather than Stevo's name made him sound slightly jealous, she thought. *Your ex*. It's not a label even she gives Stevo, because he's always just Stevo and he feels like family more than he feels like her ex. So she was a little thrilled when Sam said it. Thrilled that maybe he was jealous. Also thrilled that he was asking her out on a Saturday, because that's definitely date night.

Now she's fussing over what to wear. Not that she has many options: despite her new interest in accessories, clothes have never been that important to her. At nineteen Josie has a better wardrobe than Evie ever had. Maybe Josie could give her some tips, because if Evie keeps seeing Sam outside of work she'll want to look her best.

The best she can come up with tonight, however, is a flowery blouse with her favourite jeans and some daggy court shoes of the style favoured by The Princess of Wales – a low heel, so Diana doesn't tower over Charles – although Evie wishes she had Diana's long legs to go with the shoes.

'You look so nice!' Sam says as she opens the door to him, then he kisses her on the cheek and she can feel herself blushing.

He drives her into Gosford, chatting the whole way, which puts her at ease – not that she should feel ill at ease, given they work together and chat all the time, but going out socially is different. Or she wants it to be different, not just chatting about clients and their hair.

Sam finds a parking spot near the cinema and offers her his arm as they walk. It's almost enough to make her swoon, and she's about to be brave and tell him so – because she really needs to say something, to make sure she acknowledges that this is more than them being work buddies – when she realises she can't. And the reason she can't is Sam's brother, Oliver, who is standing outside the cinema.

What are the chances, she wonders, of him happening to come to the same movie they're going to? Not good, she knows. Which means Sam and Oliver have arranged this. Which means . . . this is not a date. No, that can't be right. It's definitely a date! It has to be! Except the fact of Oliver standing in front of her, looking really pleased to see her, suggests that, yet again, she and Sam aren't seeing eye to eye on the direction of their connection.

Evie knows what she has to do: not let either man see she is disappointed – in fact, profoundly upset. Because they didn't know what she was expecting. They didn't know she had hopes and dreams and desires that she'd loaded onto a moment or a minute or an hour, or a movie. And they shouldn't know, because those hopes and dreams and desires are hers. They're tender. They're delicate. So delicate they can be destroyed in the milliseconds it will take to wrangle with that truth and work out how to rearrange her face and feelings so she doesn't reveal them.

Because those hopes and dreams are too precious. It's impossible to reveal to the object of her crush – okay, it's a little more intense than that but she doesn't know what else to call it – that by inviting his brother along to the same movie he's indicating, as powerfully as anything could, that he doesn't feel the same way about her. What if Sam thinks her crush on him is funny? That is the most mortifying thing she can contemplate at this moment in time. It's worse than being in Year 11 and thinking that Damo on the cricket team is a spunk then having one of the girls tell him, and him sniggering with his mates and calling out, 'As if!' as she walked past.

So much worse because it isn't a crush she has on Sam. It is much more developed than that. It's layered. It's considered. And it's nothing she can control. She would if she could because no one wants to feel as wretched as she does right then. As silly, as inadequate, as *ashamed*. Yes, she's ashamed. And he can't know. Nor can Oliver, because god knows what Oliver would think. He'd probably laugh at her too because *as if* beautiful Sam would be interested in her. As if. Yes, that's what her life feels like it's amounting to: aggregations of as-ifs.

All this contemplation takes milliseconds and in that flash of time Evie has to come up with a smile that suggests she is pleased to see Oliver but not overly pleased; a smile that indicates that she is not confused about him being there, not upset – even though these are both true – because to offer otherwise would be to make things uncomfortable for him and for Sam and, of course, she can't do that. She has to make sure that everyone feels fine, except her. That's her job as a woman, isn't it? As a mother, especially. Don't let on you're upset, ever. Don't make life uncomfortable for other people. Don't ask for what you want and don't ever, ever, *ever* get what you want. That's for women who a man like Sam would fall in love with, and she is not one of them.

'Hi – hi, Oliver,' she says, her voice catching despite her resolve.

Oliver's face lights up. At least he's happy to see her. And she knows she likes his company. It won't be enough, though, to get her through however many hours of *Giant* there are. What she would really like to do is go home and cry, but she'll have to keep the tears packed in her throat until Sam drops her off. Then she'll have to think about how to behave around him in the salon on Monday.

Maybe she should quit her job. That's an option. It would save her some discomfort. Of course, Trudy would want to know why she's going and she won't be able to tell her, plus she won't find another salon as conveniently located because while there's another salon in Terrigal, she couldn't work there – Trudy would find out and that would make life uncomfortable.

So, all round, she's not in a good spot and that makes her feel even more like crying. Oh *god*, why doesn't life get easier when you get older? When she was a kid she thought all mums and dads had things sorted out, yet here she is, a mother, and she is so far from being sorted out it's ridiculous.

'Evie!' Oliver moves as if to hug her but she stays still so he stops. 'Sam didn't tell me you were coming.'

Sam looks pleased about this, and that's when it occurs to Evie that he may be trying to get her and Oliver together. Doesn't he know their history? What has Oliver told – or not told – him? Worse than that, has he been thinking about bringing them together the whole time? That means he's never going to feel anything for her. She's never going to be able to convince him to love her, no matter how hard she tries. And there was a skerrick of hope in her, until about a minute ago, that she could indeed try.

'Right, let's get tickets,' Sam says, grinning at her, then at Oliver. 'My treat.'

Evie moves to stand on the other side of Sam so she doesn't walk in next to Oliver. This may be a set-up but that doesn't mean she has to go along with it.

'I'll get choc tops,' Oliver says once the tickets are bought, then Evie and Sam are alone again.

'Hope you don't mind,' Sam says, screwing up his face and half-giggling. 'I know you haven't seen each other for a while and he's *really* fond of you.'

As his eyebrows go up, Evie's spirits go down.

'Not at all,' she lies, but when she follows him into the cinema it feels like a trip to the gallows, and it's no comfort, as she sits in the dark with Oliver somehow on one side of her and Sam on the other, to know that she put the noose around her own neck.

CHAPTER THIRTY-TWO

'So Troy has to go to Kariong,' Anna says as she hands over her son's sports bag to his father, 'and Renee has a party at The Entrance.'

'Kariong to The Entrance?' Gary is frowning and Anna knows why: he's calculating how much driving he has to do. *Too bad,* she thinks: it's the sort of driving she's been doing for years, making sure their children go where they need to, so they can participate in activities and have friends. He thinks he has it so hard working in an office? Well, he can find out just what it's like driving around the Central Coast on a Saturday when all the day-trippers come up from Sydney and down from Newcastle and the traffic turns into more of a snarl than it does on weekdays.

'Yep,' she says, beaming at him as if going from Kariong to The Entrance is the best thing that will ever happen to him. He offered to take the kids more on weekends, and this is what it entails, so he'll just have to get used to it.

'Um, well . . .' His frown deepens. 'Do you have the addresses?'

She hands him a piece of paper and his mouth hangs open.

'I, uh . . .'

Poor Gary – the day is turning out to be more complex than he likely envisioned, but that's what happens when you have to remember a lot of things and make sure they happen almost simultaneously.

She sighs. 'The kids know where to go.' He probably only ever drives from home – whether it's here or the place he's staying now – to the office and maybe, once in a blue moon, to the shops, although she wouldn't mind betting he's hired someone to do his shopping and cleaning.

'What are . . . what are you going to do?' He puts the bag in his boot.

'Whatever I like!' It's such a strange concept she's still figuring out whether she should do practical things with the time or just relax. Does she even know how to relax? Possibly not.

'All right, kids!' she calls.

Renee skips down the front steps, followed by Troy and his messy hair. If he were going to school Anna would say something about it, but he's about to play footy so there's no point. Hair and boy and uniform will come back messed-up and dirty.

She hugs them goodbye, and Gary gets a peck on the cheek, then she almost skips herself after she's waved them off.

What to do, what to do . . . She smiles vaguely as she looks around the living room. Nothing that needs doing here. The washing is in hand. The shopping too. She's up to date with her mending. Probably she should have made plans with friends but all her friends are taking their kids to sport.

It's weird, having weekend time to herself. It's also weird being separated, even if she did bring it on herself. None of her friends are divorced or even thinking about it, so she's the lone ranger there. Which means she'll have to make this up as she goes.

The beach. She could go to the beach! With a book! And just sit and read! Maybe even have fish and chips for lunch. It's too cold for a swim so she won't take a costume, but that makes things simple. What she's wearing is fine. Which means . . .

Her eyes light on the novel she's reading, on the side table next to the couch. Putting it in her handbag, she picks up the keys and heads to the car.

Terrigal is her beach of choice, always, because even though it gets busy, it's so appealing with the Skillion sweeping up to one side. Plus she likes the buzz of people enjoying themselves.

Once she arrives she tucks her beach mat under her arm and has the pick of spots. On a winter's day only the surfers have laid any claim to the sand, their towels and thongs and house keys strewn here and there. No one would take anything – that's just not how things are done.

Closer to the shoreline she sees a woman hunched over, staring at the water, and thinks the shape of her head is familiar. Oh yes, it's the younger hairdresser from the Seaside Salon – Evie.

Now Anna has a conundrum: should she leave her alone and risk being seen as Evie leaves, and therefore Evie will know that Anna likely saw her and didn't approach? Or does she give up on her plan to read and say hello, taking the risk that it may turn into socialising?

Then Evie's shoulders shake and, looking more closely, Anna can see she's upset. That does it: she's not leaving a woman she knows distressed on the sand. She wouldn't want to be left distressed on the sand.

'Hi,' she says as she stands over Evie.

The woman looks up, and it's clear she's been crying. Then she squints and Anna realises the sun is above her. She moves slightly.

'I'm Anna. I bring my mum to the salon. Her name is Ingrid.'

'Oh . . .' Evie sniffles and drops her gaze. 'Hi.'

'Can I sit down?' Anna doesn't actually give Evie the choice: she's committed to it this far, so she might as well go all the way. Beach mat rolled out, bag dropped, Anna sits and extends her legs next to this woman she barely knows. 'I came here to read,' she says cheerfully. 'But, ah . . .'

There's another sniffling sound and Evie turns to look at her with what Anna can only think is despair.

'Sorry,' Evie mumbles. 'I'm not very good company.'

'I didn't think you would be!'

Now Evie looks upset.

'That came out badly,' Anna goes on. 'I meant that I can see you're upset. But I didn't want to walk away.' She thinks of the nights she spent at home, getting upset about Gary not appearing, wishing someone might knock on her door, saying they wanted to keep her company. Sure, it's probably wrong to project her wishes onto Evie, but do any of us really want to be alone when we're in distress? *Seriously?* Are we even meant to be? There are billions of people on the planet and somehow we're meant to take care of the heavy stuff alone? No, Anna doesn't believe that. She also doesn't believe that the onus should be on the upset person to seek out support. The people around the upset person should be paying attention. And she's paying attention.

'Thanks,' Evie says, her voice muffled. She sniffles. 'Really.'

'So – what's going on?' No point easing into it, since they're already being honest.

Evie's laugh is hollow. 'Nothing. Absolutely nothing.' She briefly closes her eyes. 'That's the problem.'

'Is it . . . work?' Should Anna even be asking that, given she's now a client along with Ingrid?

'No.' Evie half-smiles in that way people have when they're really upset but trying to be reassuring at the same time.

'Family?'

A shake of the head.

'Love, then?'

Another half-smile, then Evie looks at the water again. 'Yes,' she concedes.

'Did you get dumped?' It seems the logical cause.

'Not really.'

'Did you dump someone and you regret it?'

Another shake of the head. 'Nothing like that.'

Anna stops to think about all the pathways love can take and how many of them can end in distress. Maybe someone died.

Although she thinks Evie would have said that already. Sure, it's a bit like pulling teeth getting an answer out of her but Anna is the intruder here, and Evie possibly doesn't want to tell her. But a problem shared is indeed a problem halved.

'Tell me,' she says, because the guessing game could go on for a while otherwise.

Evie's face travels through about five expressions in one second – a smile, a crumple, a silent howl, a concertina'd forehead, lips pressed together. 'I love someone who doesn't love me,' she says.

'Oh.' Now Anna looks at the water, working out what to say next. She's actually never been in this situation, because the boys she liked in high school tended to like her back, so she doesn't have lived experience to offer. 'Has he said that he doesn't?' she asks.

'No, but I know he doesn't.'

'How could you know for sure if you haven't talked about it?'

Evie drops her head onto her bent knees and her hands knead the sand. 'I just know.'

Anna leans over and puts a hand between Evie's shoulder blades. It's the spot she uses when her children need to be reassured. That's because it's the spot Ingrid used with her. Still does sometimes. A steady hand, well placed, can make all the difference.

'Do you think he cares about you at all?' she asks.

Evie shrugs. 'As a friend.'

'Would he want his friend to be this upset?'

'I guess not.'

Seagulls are squawking around them, no doubt hoping for food, which neither of them has. The tourists have trained them into eating hot chips – not ideal seagull food – so they're a constant nuisance now.

'Will you regret not telling him? One day, I mean. One day when you're older, thinking about life. Will you regret it?'

Evie turns her head, her right ear resting on her knees, her forehead puckered. 'I think so.'

'He may not feel the same,' Anna says, because she has no idea, 'but if he really cares about you, I can't imagine he'd be upset to find out how you feel. If it were me, I wouldn't be.'

They hold each other's gaze and Anna thinks it's nice to be here, with the waves rolling into shore, the breeze cool but not cold, the sun just bright enough.

She pulls her hand back and sits up straight. 'You need to do what's best for you, of course,' she says. 'But that's my two cents.'

Evie smiles gratefully. 'Thanks,' she says. 'I feel like an idiot getting this upset.'

'Loving someone will never make you an idiot,' Anna says. 'It can feel like it sometimes because we get so swept up in it. But how can it ever be bad to care about someone so much? It's a compliment. It's a kindness. It's really beautiful, actually.' She smiles with what she hopes is reassurance. 'That's what I think, anyway.'

Evie inhales deeply and sighs loudly. 'Thanks,' she says.

Anna nods, then decides she can't stay here. Evie may not need to be alone in her distress but perhaps she does in her contemplation of it. So Anna stands and pulls up the mat.

'I'm going to leave you to it. Go and read my book.' She nods toward the surf club. 'Up there. I'll see you next week at the salon.'

'Thanks,' Evie says again.

Anna smiles as she turns to go, feeling slightly wistful about the fact that she can counsel Evie about her love life but be so disconnected from her own. It's not her time, this month, this season, this year, to be in love with Gary or anyone. Maybe it will be again. For now she'll just enjoy this beach and her book then rejoin her normal life later today.

CHAPTER THIRTY-THREE

For their third date, Brett asked Josie to a cafe in Blue Bay, near The Entrance. The Entrance is the more popular spot, attracting tourists who like the pelicans that tend to congregate in the area. Josie never recovered from her mother reading *Storm Boy* to her as a child, let alone seeing the movie, so she feels ambivalent about pelicans: drawn to them yet also sad when she sees them. She had told Brett this as they sat on the beach at Killcare, talking about books they'd loved as children – not the conversation she thought she'd be having, but she's learning that she shouldn't make up her mind about him in advance. Still, she couldn't believe he'd remember it. Let alone take her so seriously that, when he suggested Blue Bay as their destination, he said, 'I know we could go to The Entrance but I also know how you feel about pelicans.'

The thoughtfulness in that one sentence was enough to take her breath away. They were standing by her car at the end of another workday – because by now he turns up almost every day to walk her from the salon and see her safely into the driver's seat – and he was so matter-of-fact about it. Not saying it as if she's a weirdo for having a pelican problem.

'It's so pretty round there, though – how about Blue Bay?' was the way he phrased it.

She hasn't been to Blue Bay in . . . well, ever. There are so many beaches on the Central Coast and, as tends to happen when you live in a place that other people love to visit, you don't see it the way they do. Her cousin in Sydney says the same thing: people love going to Bondi Beach but unless you live near there you rarely think of it. Josie isn't sure if that means we tend to take things for granted or that we appreciate what we have. Maybe neither. Maybe it's laziness.

Brett is there to bust her out of that laziness by taking her to Blue Bay for lunch on this wintry Saturday that is slightly over-cast. He pulls back her chair for her and she sits down, beaming. Just happy to be with him. She's never felt this happy simply to be with someone. Other people can be complicated; hard to read, hard to predict, so she tries to be the good girl and behave in a way they expect, and usually fails. Brett seems to like her just to be her. It's harder to accept than she thought, because she's spent most of her life trying to be what others want her to be. Who is she and what does she really want? These are questions she's been asking herself as she drives to and from Terrigal each workday. The answers haven't yet appeared, apart from this one: she wants Brett.

'My mum says the sandwiches are great here,' Brett says, his white teeth flashing against his tan as he smiles.

'Did you tell your mum we were coming here today?'

He looks up from the menu. 'Yeah.' Another smile. 'I asked her where's a good place I could take you.'

'She knows about me?' Josie says in a rush.

He looks bemused. 'Sure. I told her about you when I met you.'

'Oh.' While she's thrilled about this, she wonders if he'll presume she's told her mother about him. Will he think her strange that she hasn't? Or maybe he won't judge at all. He's not the judgemental type. Or he doesn't seem to be.

'Is that okay?' He sounds worried and she finds it endearing.

'Of course! It's fine!'

He gives her a funny look then smiles. 'Don't worry,' he says, 'you don't have to meet her unless you want to.'

That's not what I was thinking, she wants to tell him. But before she can get it out the words get stuck in her throat because she sees something she never wanted to see: one of her mother's friends, walking into this little cafe in Blue Bay where she's sitting with a boy her parents don't know exists, let alone that she's on a date with him.

'Josephine, darling!' calls the friend, whose name is Miriam, which Josie knows all too well because Miriam likes to drop by unannounced and after she leaves her mother will sigh, shake her head and mutter, 'Oh, Miriam.'

It's impossible for Josie to pretend she's not her, because the most recent drop-in by Miriam was two nights ago and Josie has not changed at all in that time. Her hair is the same length and colour; her weight is the same. So there's no point pretending to be someone else, as tempting as that is because she really does not want to introduce Brett to Miriam of all people.

Brett twists toward the door in time to see Miriam rustling in their direction. Miriam always rustles. Josie is not sure why, but it's probably something to do with the fact that she likes to wear clothes with lots of details.

'Mwah mwah.' Miriam kisses Josie once on each cheek, almost as if she was expecting to see her and, indeed, that it's they who are meeting for lunch. 'Lovely to see you again so soon, darling,' she goes on, then turns her heavily mascara'd gaze to Brett. 'Who's this handsome young man?' she demands.

Josie wants to sink into her chair, but Brett just grins, then stands up, towering over the diminutive Miriam.

'Hi,' he says.

'This is Brett,' Josie says, not much above a whisper.

'Brian?' Miriam looks confused, although Josie is sure she heard it properly.

'Brett.' He's still grinning.

Whyyyyy? It will only encourage her!

'Brrrrrett.' Miriam rolls her *r*s as she says it and seems to enjoy doing so, given the spark in her eyes. 'And who are you, darling?'

'I'm Josie's boyfriend.'

He glances at Josie, so calm, so confident, and instead of feeling elated that he's called himself her boyfriend – *her boyfriend!* – she wants to tell him to take it back, immediately. Instead of this being the best moment of her life thus far, it feels as if she's being pulled into a black hole of imminent parental disapproval, because she knows for sure that the first thing Miriam will do when she leaves this place – something that might possibly even cause her to leave this place instead of staying for lunch or whatever she's doing here – is call Josie's mother and gossip about seeing Josie and meeting Brett. So when Josie arrives home this afternoon, after pretending she was 'just going for a drive', she'll have to tell her parents she has been lying to them.

It's going to be bad. Bad enough that she needs time to think about what to do and say and what she might need to do after she says what she'll absolutely have to say, which is that she's had three dates with Brett and she lied about all of them.

The lying. They'll focus on that first. After telling her since childhood that she never needs to lie to them, they'll sit her down and ask her to explain why she felt the need to do it. Why she couldn't tell them about him. Did she not love them? Did she not think they loved her? It will be a laying-on of guilt the likes of which she's never seen, and it's almost enough to make her want to stand up, tell Miriam that Brett is joking and this is the first date they've been on, and walk out.

Except she doesn't want that. Not at all. Because he called himself her boyfriend and somewhere under these layers of fear about what's going to happen when she arrives home, there's elation – total, amazing happiness – that he would feel that way. That he'd want to attach himself to her and tell someone about it.

He likes her. He really likes her. The incredible fact of that may be enough to get her through what's to come.

'Boyfriend?' Miriam says, turning to Josie. There's no rolling of the *r*s this time.

Josie looks at Brett, whose smile is wide and reassuring. His eyes are kind, and she imagines he's encouraging her to take on the mantle he's set down.

'Yes,' she says, holding his gaze, feeling herself smiling, not having made a decision to do so but it just happens, doesn't it, when the boy you think is really great tells someone else he's your boyfriend when you weren't even sure yet if that were true.

'Your mother hasn't said anything.' Miriam looks from one to the other.

'You're a friend of Josie's mother?' Brett asks.

Josie loves him a little for deflecting the enquiry away from her.

'*Old* friend. My name is Miriam.' She sends Josie a pointed stare, although Josie doesn't actually know what the point being made is.

'I haven't met Josie's mum yet. Or her dad.' He looks at Josie again. *It's going to be all right.* That's what the look says. Or what Josie wants it to say. 'We haven't been going out long,' Brett continues.

Miriam looks quite satisfied about something. 'How delightful,' she says. 'Well, I'd best be going.'

'You're not having lunch here?' Brett says.

For a second Josie wonders, with dread, if he's about to invite Miriam to join them.

'Here?' Miriam glances around. 'No. I saw Josephine through the window. That's the only reason I came in.'

Brett looks unfazed by Miriam's mild insult and Josie wants to hug him for it. She smiles as nicely as she can while hoping Miriam will leave immediately.

'No doubt I shall see you again, Brett.' Miriam's smile is faker than her blonde hair colour. 'Josephine, darling, I *know* I shall see you again. Toodle-oo.' And with a wave of her long-nailed fingers, she's gone.

Brett swiftly sits down. 'Quite a character,' he says.

Josie murmurs her agreement but feels the tension rising in her as she contemplates what's going to happen once she's home. She blinks back the tears that have unexpectedly formed.

'Hey.' Brett frowns, then reaches across the table and takes her hand. 'What's going on?'

'My parents don't know I've been seeing you,' she confesses, because she needs him as her co-conspirator now. 'She'll tell them. And then . . .' The tears packed into her throat make her voice raspy. 'They won't like it.'

'How do you know?' He squeezes her hand. 'I'm very likeable.'

She laughs involuntarily, then squeezes back. 'I know you are,' she says. 'But they want me to stay locked up at home for the rest of my life.'

'*That's* not going to happen.' He takes her other hand. 'We have too much to do. Places to see.'

We? We. We. What a magic word. Maybe he will be able to stand up to them with her. Maybe everything *will* be all right. It has to be sometime.

'Do we?' She smiles at him, even though she still feels unsettled.

'We do.'

He leans across the table and kisses her quickly, which makes her feel a whole lot better. Then they set about the business of ordering their lunch.

While they eat he keeps telling her funny stories, and she knows he's probably trying to distract her, and she thinks it's one of the kindest things anyone has done for her, because she's worrying – oh, how she's worrying – that Miriam will have scurried off to the nearest phone box to call Erin and tell her all about seeing Josie and a boy together.

'Hey,' he says as they're leaving, and he takes her hand in his and kisses her temple. 'It's not that bad.'

'Sorry,' she says, her voice strangled.

'For what?'

'I was bad company.'

He stops and stands in front of her. 'Did I say that?'

'No.'

He nods once. 'Right. Because you're not bad company.' He smiles and it's so warm her heart feels as if it wants to melt. 'You're my favourite company. And you don't ever have to apologise to me for having something on your mind.'

It's overwhelming, having him care for her this much. Really. It's . . .

She knows her parents love her. But this is different. Brett *chose* her.

'You're the best,' she whispers.

He laughs and takes her hand, kissing her on the lips this time. 'Nah, you are,' he says.

As he walks her back to the car, she forgets to worry, and she keeps forgetting all the way home.

CHAPTER THIRTY-FOUR

It's busier than usual today and Evie is glad, because it means she'll have to spend less time around Sam. Not that she wants to spend less time around him – if she had her way, she'd spend the rest of her life around him – but it's better if she does. Especially if he's never going to be interested in her.

There's a part of her that still wonders, though: even if he is gay, maybe he's not *all the way* gay. If there's a girlfriend in his past – while he was at school, for example – that would be evidence that he's interested in some females of the species. Wouldn't it?

Oliver. She needs to talk to Oliver. Who will probably think it's really strange that she wants to ask him if Sam might be interested in her but she's desperate.

She's never been desperate before. Not for a man. Not for anything. Ambivalence has been the bigger determinant of how her life has turned out. Which sounds lacklustre but it got her a son. She and Stevo were ambivalent about each other yet they managed to make a baby, so ambivalence can't be all bad. In fact, she prefers it – would prefer it a million times over – to the way she feels now, not sleeping well, being distracted during the day as she thinks about Sam and what she should do.

Meeting Sam was what it took to break her out of her pattern. Instead of the tepid temperature of ambivalence she felt fire. Thinking about him, being around him, would make her cheeks flame. It wasn't something she could control or understand; it just *was*. That's how she knows he's the man she's been meant to meet all these years. Not the one she was holding out for so much as the one she's been waiting for. So she can't accept that they can't be together. Which means she has to talk to Oliver about it. She'll call him tonight.

'Darl, excuse me, just getting this comb,' Sam says as he brushes past her. There go her cheeks again. 'You all right?' he says, grinning as he picks up the comb.

'Um – yes,' she says.

He looks at her quizzically. She knows why: normally she gives him long sentences, if not whole paragraphs, in response to any question. But she can hardly tell him that she spent the weekend crying over him, the way she's been crying over him for days now, trying to think of a solution which doesn't involve her not loving him, because it's been keeping her company, this love, for months now, and she doesn't want to live without it.

Still, he moves on and away from her to his client and she tries to focus on hers, although she kept the scissors moving while Sam was talking to her and now notices Mrs Grey putting a hand to the nape of her neck.

'Evie,' she barks, 'what are you doing?'

'Hm? Sorry?'

'Where has my *hair* gone?'

Evie looks down and sees she has snipped far more than Mrs Grey requested, so that her long bob has now become a shorter bob in one narrow section.

'Oh god,' she breathes.

'I can feel *air* on the back of my *neck*.'

Mrs Grey is quite agitated now and Evie understands why, but she really wishes Mrs Grey would try to stay calm. For all of their sakes.

'I'm sorry,' Evie squeaks. 'I'm, um . . . I'll even it off.'

'That will give me a short bob.' Mrs Grey glares at her in the mirror. 'And you know my feelings about short hair.'

Yes, Evie does, because Mrs Grey enjoys making them clear: women with short hair are asexual or, worse, they are 'women in sensible shoes', a group the church-going Mrs Grey absolutely does not approve of and could never countenance.

As Trudy appears by her side Evie feels she could weep with relief.

'What do we have here?' Trudy says, glancing from one woman to the other.

'I made a mistake,' Evie says. No point in avoiding it.

'A *huge* mistake,' Mrs Grey says, the glare intact.

'Now, Phyllis . . .' Trudy tilts her head from side to side, weighing up options. 'How would you feel about a change?' she goes on. 'Some layers? It'll be a little more work but I reckon it would suit you – give the hubby something new to admire, eh?'

Mrs Grey's eyes widen at that. 'Oh. Do you think?'

'It's good to keep them on their toes. Let them know you're not predictable, if you know what I mean.' Trudy turns toward Evie. 'Thoughts?'

'Um . . . yes, I can see it.' Evie scrutinises Mrs Grey's face in a way she hasn't before, because Mrs Grey has never wanted a change, she's always just wanted a trim. But a new cut means looking at the shape of her face, the shapes *in* her face, and thinking about what can work best for her. Indeed, as Evie looks closely, she can see that Trudy is right: a layered cut will do wonders for Mrs Grey.

'Yes,' Evie affirms. 'I think that would look fantastic.'

'Are you happy for Evie to do it, Phyllis?'

Mrs Grey's eyes meet Evie's and she nods slowly.

'*Wunderbar*,' Trudy says. She has a collection of affirmations in foreign languages that she trots out from time to time; Evie has become used to it.

Then Trudy leans closer to Evie and says softly, 'I know why you're distracted, pet, but you can't do this every time he's around.'

Evie gasps and looks away, feeling exposed. And stupid for having let the distraction have an impact on a client.

She nods, picks up her scissors and gets to work, and when Sam walks past later and stops to look at what she's done, she takes a step away from him.

'Love it, darl,' he says. 'That cut is *smashing*, Mrs Grey. Hubby's going to be *mad* for it when he sees it.'

Then he grins that dynamite grin and carries on, while Evie's heart keeps beating fast and her hand shakes a little as she writes Mrs Grey's next appointment in the book.

CHAPTER THIRTY-FIVE

'Ow!'

The client scowls in the mirror at Josie, who blinks then looks at her scissors as if they poked the woman in the neck all on their own. Then she sees her fingernails, bitten to the quick. Ever since she saw her mother's friend Miriam at the cafe in Blue Bay she has been chewing them. It's a habit that plagued her childhood and she grew out of it eventually, but now it's back. Not that there's anything left to chew. Apart from the inside of her cheek. She's been doing that a bit too.

'Sorry,' she says, feeling tears rising in her eyes and her throat getting tight. How could she have almost-stabbed this nice lady, a first-time client whose name is now escaping her?

It's because she hasn't been sleeping well. She's been convinced her parents are about to tell her that Miriam's called or visited or written them a letter – something, anything – to relay what she saw. It's on her mind all the time.

Yet Miriam hasn't done any of that. She's been silent. And that, Josie has realised, is worse. Now she actually wants the woman to say something to her parents so this tension can end. At least she'll find out what the consequences are and can move on. Or be locked in her room for the rest of her life. Because that's what her parents will probably do.

Why didn't she think about that? Why didn't she consider that being caught with Brett – with any boy – would mean that everything would change? They've always warned her against going on dates. Even her father says men are dangerous and that if Josie goes anywhere with one she could get in trouble.

They never said what kind of trouble. They never said that the trouble might actually be them and how they'd react.

She's been imagining different scenarios, different ways she could respond. Pretending that she and Brett are friends. That she knows him from tech or he's a friend's brother or a client.

Except she knows what Miriam saw. Knows she heard Brett call himself her boyfriend. That look in the older woman's eyes. *That look*. Of knowing. Of . . . smugness, almost. As if she'd caught Josie out. Because she did. Because Josie let her.

Stupid. STUPID. She's always been stupid.

'Josie, pet.'

She feels a hand on her shoulder. Trudy's.

'Pet, it's a good idea to breathe every now and again.' Trudy pats her then puffs on her cigarette. 'Of course, I'm not the person who can best advise on that,' she goes on, 'but I was worried you were going to faint.'

Josie catches her eye in the mirror and feels those tears again.

'Everything all right, Darlene?' Trudy asks the glowering client.

'Hm,' comes the response.

Darlene. That's right. That's her name.

'Do you want to keep going?' Trudy says softly in Josie's ear.

Josie nods. She's not going to ruin her job over this.

'Good. We all have bad days.' Another pat. 'Just come and see me when you're done.'

Trudy turns away before Josie can figure out if she's angry at her for being careless with the scissors.

'Sorry about that, Darlene,' Josie says meekly. 'It won't happen again. Just a trim, wasn't it?'

'Yes.' Darlene looks sceptical but she relaxes once Josie gets to work.

When she's finished the cut and Darlene has left, Josie goes to where Trudy is laughing along with Babs, one of her regulars.

'I'll just be a mo, Babs,' Trudy says, then she nods toward the back room.

Josie follows her there.

'What's going on, pet? You're jumpy,' Trudy says kindly.

'Sorry. Sorry. I'm really sorry.'

'I didn't ask for an apology.' Trudy sighs. 'I just want to know what's wrong.'

So Josie told her about Brett – because Trudy knows the bare minimum – and about Miriam and about her parents' likely reaction, the words almost hurling themselves out of her mouth, relieved to be freed from the prison of her whirring brain.

'I see,' Trudy says when she's finished. 'You didn't go on dates in high school?'

Josie shakes her head.

'Pretty girl like you – really?'

She shakes it again and Trudy shrugs.

'Then your parents should count themselves lucky you weren't raced off in Year 10 or something. The day was always going to come when you met someone. And you like him, this Brett?'

For the first time that day, Josie smiles. 'Yes. He's really kind.'

'The sort of bloke you'd like to introduce to your parents?'

'Well – yes.'

'The kind who will be polite when he's in their home?'

Josie nods vigorously.

'Right,' Trudy says. 'Maybe you're worrying about nothing, then.'

'But he's –'

'Your parents love you, I'm sure. They worry about you. We all worry about our kids. When you're a mum you'll worry too.'

Josie can't imagine being as strict with her children, making them feel as if they have to lie to her just to have a boyfriend or girlfriend.

'Maybe,' she says.

'Oh, you will.' Trudy looks at her watch. 'I'd best get back to Babs or she'll switch to Sam.'

Josie frowns, not understanding what she means.

'She thinks he's dishy,' Trudy explains. 'Wants to race him off.' She grabs Josie's shoulders and gives her a little shake. 'Everything will be okay,' she says firmly. 'When parents love their kids and their kid is as respectful and lovely as you, there's always a solution.'

For a second Josie wishes Trudy were her mum – except in a way she's her work mum. It's comforting to think that. To know there's an older lady who cares about her and has good advice. She doesn't have grandmothers, really – one died when she was young and the other lives in the country so she's rarely seen her.

'Thanks, Trudy.' She smiles.

'Pleasure, pet.' Trudy pinches her cheek. 'Now back to work and stop fretting. It won't get you anywhere. Believe me, I know.'

Josie follows her out and picks up the broom to sweep up some hair while she waits to do a wash or whatever is needed next.

For the rest of the day, whenever her eyes meet Trudy's there's a smile or a wink there for her, and that makes her feel Trudy is right and everything will be okay.

It's enough to put some lightness back into her step as she heads home, and she turns up the car radio loud and sings along.

CHAPTER THIRTY-SIX

This is a nice place, looking over Brisbane Water. Not a venue Trudy has been to before, but Sol offered to pick her up so she didn't have to know how to get there. He booked the table, told her a time he'd come for her and he was there on the dot, looking pleased with himself and even more pleased with her.

'Would you like wine with dinner?' Sol says as he holds the wine list their waiter gave him.

The waiter was older, and referred to her as Mrs Raymond – Sol is, of course, Mr Raymond – and she didn't object because the explanation would have been unwieldy and, besides, once she leaves here tonight the waiter won't remember her.

'Perhaps a glass,' she says.

'White? Red?'

She picks up the menu. 'I guess it depends on what I'm eating.'

'The tortellini is good.' Sol smiles in a way that suggests he doesn't mind if she doesn't take up his suggestion.

He's easy company. He was easy in the car, chatting away, leaving gaps for her to talk if she wanted, asking questions. She felt comfortable with him. It was pleasant. That's all. Pleasant. Not thrilling. Not the start of something. Not romantic. She didn't expect that, but she wondered if she'd feel it spontaneously due to the fact he's taking her out to dinner.

Laurie was romantic.

No, she has to stop comparing them. She has to stop letting her brain bring up Laurie so much, full stop. It's a habit.

When she was at lunch with Dylan and his family her son had said, with no small amount of irritation, 'You don't need to talk about Dad all the time.' She hadn't realised she did.

'It's only because you're here,' she'd protested.

He gave her a look. 'Mu-um,' he'd said, and he didn't have to say anything further. She'd been put on notice.

It's not as if she can talk to Sol about Laurie, though. While they were friends, it wouldn't be polite to go on about her dead husband to a man who has invited her to dinner after waiting a polite amount of time after that husband's death to approach her. If Sol had no manners or tact he would have bowled up to her the week after it happened, she supposes. She's heard of that happening. A woman from the club even had someone crack onto her at the funeral. Bold.

'I'm happy for you to order for me,' she hears herself saying, which is odd because she never said that to Laurie. There's something in her, though, that wants to have the decision-making taken out of her hands and put into someone else's, and Sol happens to be the current candidate.

Sol gives her a mysterious smile and sits back. 'No,' he says, 'I don't think the tortellini is right for you. Something else. Something else . . .' He scans the menu.

'You've been here a few times?'

He shrugs. 'Not many. I don't go out that often. Eating alone is not as much fun.'

The waiter reapproaches and Sol glances up.

'For the lady, please, the veal scaloppini and a glass of Chablis, and I'll have the ragu and a glass of the Bordeaux.'

The waiter bows his head, takes the menus and wine list and leaves them to it.

'Thank you,' Trudy says.

'You've very welcome.'

There's that mysterious smile again.

'How is your son?' Sol says.

Trudy is momentarily confused – she hasn't mentioned Dylan much to Sol – then remembers that Laurie would have talked about Dylan to his friends.

'He called me a few days ago.'

'Mm?' Sol is looking at her as if what she's said is unremarkable – which it should be.

'It doesn't happen that often,' she says lightly, as if she doesn't mind. There's no reason to not let Sol know that she minds, really – except it protects her. She doesn't want him thinking she's the sort of mother whose son contacts her rarely, even though she's on her own now and for all he knows she's fallen on her head somewhere.

'That doesn't sound right,' Sol says, his brows knitting.

'He's busy.'

'As are you.' He gives her a meaningful look.

'I'm sure Laurie told you that Dylan has a very busy job.' Dylan works for some agricultural business that he's always a little vague about. Or maybe it's the government and that's why he's vague. He has told her. She just can't remember the name of it. Remembering so many clients' names has meant that she doesn't retain other details. It's always been the case, so she doesn't think her inability to remember the company Dylan works for is of concern. Although perhaps she should. She's only fifty-seven years old so she can't be losing her mind. Or can she? There's probably no minimum age for that.

'Actually, he used to say that Dylan had a very busy *wife*.' Sol's eyes are twinkling.

Trudy gasps then laughs. 'Did he?' It sounds like something her Laurie would say. He could be quite feisty about certain things – and Annemarie was one of them. Spent too much time with her friends and going to boutiques, he always thought.

'He did. So, Dylan – how often do you see him?'

This time Trudy decides not to make light of it. 'Not enough.'

The waiter deposits their glasses of wine, to their murmured thanks.

'It's been months since the last time,' she goes on, staring at the cold glass of white wine in front of her, almost wishing it to be a crystal ball so she could tell when Dylan would have time for her again.

'I can't get to Sydney easily, which he knows,' she says. 'But he doesn't want to come up here. Or maybe his wife doesn't.' She waves a hand as if it's nothing, even though it is profoundly *something*. 'His children probably forget what I look like in between times.'

'You don't go to Sydney?'

'Not if I can avoid it.' Trudy smiles weakly. 'The freeway . . . I'm not mad on it.'

'It can be a speedway,' Sol says lightly. 'What if I were to drive you?'

'Oh.' It's a holding response because she's so surprised, first that he would offer something so generous, second that he would want to spend all that time in the car with her, third that this may mean he'd meet Dylan, and she's not sure if she's ready for that.

'Perhaps that's too audacious an offer.' Sol stares at his glass of wine.

'It's not,' she says, because she doesn't want to hurt his feelings. 'It's very kind. Just . . . unexpected.'

'And it does not require a response tonight.'

Their eyes meet and he lifts his glass.

'A toast – to pleasant evenings.'

She responds to his toast and they each sip their wine.

'Now,' he says, 'Laurie used to tell me which books you were reading.'

'Did he?'

'I love reading too, so he'd let me know if you enjoyed a particular book, then I'd go and buy it. So you see – you have been recommending books to me. We have been connected before this. You just didn't know it.' His smile is broad, and genuine.

For a second – maybe two – she feels as if he is deeply familiar. But he isn't, and she can't let herself indulge in such a flight of fancy. However, she notes that he's not only kind but adept at steering conversations. Quite the skill. Not one she believes she has needed, because her clients tend to talk at her rather than with her, but she appreciates it in others.

'Now I can ask you in person,' he says. 'Do you have anything to recommend?'

'That depends.'

'On?' There's mischief in his eyes and she quite likes it.

'On what you thought of the books Laurie told you about.'

He laughs. 'Some I liked. Some I didn't. But that's how it should be. And I can tell you for sure that I have missed having the recommendations these two years.'

At the mention of time passing, Trudy's face grows tight. Two years. Yes. No time at all. And such an aeon. It will always be both, because time is not as she used to understand it. Which means she can let the two years stop her – because it's not enough time to mourn her husband – or spur her on. To stagnate no longer. To actually connect with someone else. To get out of her head. To live. To feel.

'*The Prince of Tides*,' she says, naming a new book she bought because the bookseller told her it was good.

'A grand title.'

'It's good. Thought provoking. A novel.'

Sol nods slowly. 'Go on.'

'*Perfume.*'

His eyebrows shoot up.

'It's not what you'd think,' Trudy adds quickly. 'It's a novel too. About a killer who likes . . . scents, shall we say. Very unusual. But good. Absorbing.'

'I shall look them up,' he says.

'I'll lend them to you,' she blurts, surprising herself.

At that, he picks up his glass. 'Let's drink to that.'

They have a perfectly nice dinner, and chat about books and hairdressing and places he's been and she hasn't. When Sol drops her home she pops inside to retrieve the books, for which he is grateful. He does not mention driving to Sydney, and nor does she, but he shows her to her door, and kisses her hand, then waits for her to go safely back inside.

An hour later, as she drifts off to sleep, she doesn't think of him, but she doesn't think of Laurie either, and for once her mind is quite empty and she does not resist the pull of dreams.

CHAPTER THIRTY-SEVEN

Josie barely notices the drive home because she's half-daydreaming about Brett. Which she really shouldn't do when she's driving, but it's hard not to. He's been meeting her after work every day, even though she now knows he finishes work two hours earlier than she does.

'Don't you want to go home?' she asked him yesterday.

'Nah,' he said. 'Then I wouldn't see you.' He'd hugged her to his side as they walked toward her car, because that's what they usually do: walk to her car, then she goes home. Which means he spends all that time just waiting to see her for a few minutes.

'What do you do for two hours?'

'I surf!'

He didn't surf today, though: there were no waves. She would absolutely have understood if he hadn't waited for her when he had nothing else to do, but he did. As she emerged from the Seaside Salon he took her hand and kissed her on the lips – not for too long, because they were in front of the salon – and they walked around the corner where he kissed her some more.

It made her feel better, seeing him. He knows she's been worrying about her parents finding out about them – even though he wants that to happen, has told her that he wants to meet them because he's serious about her. It's the most wonderful thing she's ever heard and also the most stress-inducing because she can't imagine having that conversation with them.

The preferable thing to do is daydream about him and him alone, not what it would be like for her parents to meet him.

She's still daydreaming as she opens the front door of the house.

'Josie.'

Her mother appears in front of her and she jumps.

'Mum, you scared me,' she says, putting her keys on the table just inside the door.

Her mother's nostrils flare. 'Where have you been?'

'At work.' Josie frowns. 'Why?'

'You're later than usual.'

Her father joins them, his hands folded in front of him.

'I had a colour. She arrived late.' This was the truth, but she feels queasy as she says it, as if she's about to be exposed for lying even though she hasn't. Her time with Brett did not make her late – she was already late.

'If I call Trudy will she confirm this?' Her mother's voice sounds strangled.

'Yes.' Now Josie feels upset – why is her mother questioning her like this? Why would she care . . .

Oh. No. Her mother knows something.

'You're lying,' her mother says.

'I'm not.'

'Miriam *saw you!*' her mother screams.

Josie hadn't forgotten about Miriam but it's been almost a fortnight and she had started to believe that Miriam had forgotten about her. It feels like a betrayal even though she knew it was coming. Has always known, for years it seems, that this day would come when the life she wants for herself is on a path that her parents have barricaded and keep barricading because they don't want her going anywhere. Out of fear, not love. She is the only child they were able to have and her mother, in particular, never wants to let her go.

What they didn't count on was Brett. He knows how to clear that path for her. He's doing it already. Because of Brett she feels stronger than she ever has in her life. Not just Brett – the salon too. The work she does there. The person she *is* there. She is more capable than she realised. She's *good at things*. Clients tell her so. Trudy, Sam and Evie tell her so.

So she may have been stupid little Josie at school but she's not any more – and she never wants to go back to being her again, no matter how much her mother wants that.

There's no point pretending she doesn't know what Miriam saw. Which means she needs to draw on that new strength of hers and kick down those barricades.

'I saw her too,' she says as calmly as she can.

'*Who were you with?*'

'Brett.'

'*Brett?*' Erin's eyes are wild and she turns to Josie's father. 'Paolo – say something!'

Her father's mouth opens and closes, then he stops looking Josie in the eye.

Was he always this weak? Was her mother the one calling the shots all this time? Suddenly Josie pities him.

'How do you know him?' Erin's voice is lower but her anger is still clear.

There are different ways Josie could answer this but most of them would take her back to the start of her relationship with Brett: *I met him at the beach. He works in Terrigal. I see him around.* That's not what she wants to say. That's not what they are to each other any more.

'He's my boyfriend,' she says, and she feels power in that moment. Finally she knows there is someone who is just for her, who will stand with her. Because she knows he would. He has kept showing her he would. Kept showing up for her.

'Boyfriend,' her mother almost whispers. 'Boyfriend.'

Josie nods. 'Mm-hm.' Keep it light. Don't make things worse by giving any more information than her mother has asked for.

'You don't need a boyfriend.'

'I'm old enough to decide what I need.'

'You're a pretty girl – he's only after one thing!'

Is that what her mother thinks is valuable about her – the way she looks? Josie wants to protest – to tell Erin that she and Brett have conversations, that they've talked about how they both want to travel, that they both want kids someday, that they want to live on the Coast because they love it so much.

There is no point saying all of that, though. Her parents won't understand. So she says the first line that comes to her, feeling a tumult inside her, so many emotions moving and rolling: anger, fear, disdain, pity, despair – and love. But the love isn't strong enough to fight them in this moment, so she has to get out of here, at least for now.

'Well – he'll get it!' she shrieks and doesn't wait for a response. Just picks up her keys and her bag and rushes out of the house, to the car.

It's only then that her father does something. As she looks up from the driver's seat she sees him standing in front of the car, his eyes pleading with her – but for what she doesn't know. And her pity for him is threatening to turn into dislike, so she has to get away from it.

As she pulls away from the kerb he raises a hand. In farewell? Trying to call her back?

It's no use. She puts her foot down and heads away, away, away as fast as she can go.

She wants to go back to that beach Brett took her to. Killcare. She loved it there, with him. Unsure exactly how to get there, she heads for the road that will take her to the beaches and she'll find it from there. So she takes the Woy Woy Road that winds down, toward the water.

Her breathing is rapid. Panicky. She didn't notice it being like that at the house.

There was a woman in the salon the other day who was breathing like this.

'All right, pet?' Trudy said, even though the woman clearly wasn't. But it's how Trudy defuses situations. Josie has noticed this. If Trudy were here now she'd probably say, 'All right, pet?' then tell Josie to slow down.

She doesn't want to slow down, though. She wants to get to Killcare. She can't go to Brett because she doesn't know where he lives. Isn't that strange? They're so close but they don't know where each other lives. Maybe that's romantic.

Why is she breathing like this? Panic attack. That's what Trudy said in the salon to the woman. That she was having a panic attack. Then Trudy got her a paper bag and insisted the woman blow into it and that helped.

There's no paper bag in this car, though. Just her and her breathing.

Killcare. She has to make it. Can't stop until she makes it.

Except there are dark spots in front of her eyes now and she's really having trouble seeing, and this road has so many turns. There's nowhere to stop. She needs to stop.

Instead she sees a car coming around the bend and those spots are in front of her eyes, and she clips the car.

After that, she has no memory.

CHAPTER THIRTY-EIGHT

After avoiding Sam as best she could, he noticed. Of course he did, because normally Evie is all over him like a bad rash, as her mother might say.

He bailed her up in the back room one afternoon.

'Have I done something to upset you?' He looked upset himself.

'No!' she said quickly, and laughed falsely.

He still looked upset. 'Something's up,' he said. 'I know that.'

He stood there looking at her, which was both exactly what she wanted and unsettling.

'Can we go to dinner?' he asked. 'Have a chat?'

She could hardly say no – they're co-workers and refusing him might have made the Seaside Salon a less sunny place, not just for them but for Trudy and Josie too.

So now, sitting across from him in the Chinese restaurant on the main road at Bateau Bay, she feels nervous. Not able to speak properly. Which he may take as evidence that something's wrong, but really it's just how she's always been around him when she's not making a huge effort to control herself.

Spring rolls, san choy bow and prawn crisps have been put in front of them and Sam is dipping a roll in soy sauce and crunching into it. They've barely spoken since they sat down and it's strange. Normally he chats even when she doesn't.

'So,' he says, once he's swallowed his mouthful, putting down half of the spring roll and looking at her expectantly.

'Hm?'

She picks up a roll and goes to dip it in the soy sauce but he reaches across and puts his hand on hers.

'Stop avoiding the subject,' he says.

Obediently she puts the roll into the bowl in front of her. 'Which subject?' It's childish of her to say but she really doesn't want to be the one to define what they're talking about. That would make it real, both her feelings and her heartbreak.

'Evie.' He says it lightly but he looks so serious. And handsome.

Her whole heart is right here in front of her and she can't have it, and it feels as if someone has taken a sledgehammer and whacked her in the chest. She presses her lips together, trying to not cry.

Except didn't she try to tell herself that she might be able to have it? Have him? She can still cling on to that hope. Sam asked her to have dinner with him, after all.

'We need to talk,' he says, and now her hopes fire. 'Because you're *not* talking to me any more. Aren't we friends?'

Aren't we *more* than that? She wants to say this. She won't.

'Yes,' is what she says instead.

'I thought we were getting to be close,' he says. 'But something's changed. I think I've upset you and I don't know how. But I want to fix it. If you tell me what I've done to upset you, I won't do it again. I promise.' He smiles.

Oh, how she loves that smile.

Except how does she tell him it's not anything he's done but someone he *is*? How does she express the galaxy of emotions currently swirling inside her?

If you don't ask, you don't get. Her father used to say that. Want a discount at the fish shop? Ask for it. And likely get it. He would get a lot of things by asking, and people never seemed to mind the asking even if they couldn't give him what he wanted.

She may not be able to express the emotions but she can ask for what she wants. Can't she?

'You haven't done anything,' she says weakly, because even saying this feels like a bold start.

'Is there something else going on, then?' He looks so concerned.

Bless him. Yes, bless him. He is kind-hearted. Sincere. So good. She doesn't deserve him, with her ridiculous behaviour and her teenage crush.

'Mm,' she says, feeling nervous now. Shaky, even. She bites her bottom lip to try to steady herself because she knows this is the moment she needs to say something to him and *she can't, she can't, she can't*. But she must. Because if not now, when? There will never be another moment for her to try to claim the future she wants.

'I . . .' She breathes out. It sounds loud to her. Almost as if she can't quite get the air to leave her lungs.

The stakes are so high. The highest. She's no poker player. No card player at all. Nothing involving risk. Nothing involving change. What is she doing?

'Evie?' Sam prompts gently.

What she's doing is what she must.

'I love you,' she rushes out, looking at him, then looking away, then looking back, and he doesn't seem surprised, and that feels almost insulting. Shouldn't a declaration of love involve the other person gasping or crying out or something to mark the moment?

Instead he's leaning over to take her hand again, as if he's comforting her.

'I guessed,' he says, holding her hand firmly. 'It's all right.'

All right. *All right.*

Now she really wants to cry. Who says that being loved is just *all right*?

'It's not,' she says, and it almost hiccups out of her. 'Because you don't love me back.' Might as well get it out there.

233

He takes her other hand across the table and Evie worries that the soy sauce will go everywhere.

'I do love you,' he says.

And she is both intensely in this moment and outside of it. Aware of the dry warmth of his hands and wishing she weren't, because he's saying what she wants to hear but not in the way she dreamt of – not with passion, not with urgency. Not in an *I can't live without you* way, which is not the way she'd ever thought of being told anything until she met him and wished for nothing else.

'And I wish . . .' He sighs and lets go of her hands and sits back in his chair.

The soy sauce remains undisturbed. She stares at it. It helps, to have something to stare at when you feel you're at a major point in your life and it's completely out of your control, yet you are strangely sure of what's about to happen. Which is to say, she knows he's going to confirm that he's breaking her heart.

'I wish I could love you the way you deserve to be loved.'

He sounds so sad, and that makes her look up. Look at him.

A waitress comes over just then and Evie wants to scream at her to get away, but instead she smiles as the woman asks if they want more drinks. They both refuse.

Once she leaves, Sam sighs again. 'I can't love any woman like that,' he says, and his eyes are round and serious. 'I think you know what I mean.'

So there is her confirmation: there is absolutely no chance for her. For them. For her dreams to come true.

Her feet feel heavy. It's so odd. She really wants to get up and run out of here but instead she feels stuck, as though she couldn't even move one foot away from this table.

She hears a noise, as if someone is crying but not quite making it. As if the cry is half coming out of them.

The noise is coming from her.

Should she be embarrassed? Perhaps. But she doesn't even feel as if she's in her body. So maybe she's not the one crying. Her body is doing it all on its own.

'Oh, Evie.' Sam reaches across the table again and this time he cups her face in his hand.

You're making it worse! She wants to scream it at him, but also not. Because she would never want to scream at him. He's precious to her.

'I'm so sorry,' he's saying, gazing into her eyes, then he drops his hand. 'I didn't realise you felt quite like that about me.'

She sniffs back the tears that are not quite making it out of her.

'I knew you felt *something*,' he continues. 'I could tell by the way you looked at me.'

'I'm sorry,' she says quietly.

'For what?'

'I shouldn't have said anything.'

'Evie.' He says it softly but forcefully. 'Evie, please look at me.'

She does, and she sees the face she loves and will have to stop loving.

'It's the most amazing thing, to be loved by you,' Sam says. 'The greatest compliment. Honestly. And I'm not going to insult you by saying that if I were straight I'd want to be with you, because that's not how it works. Is it?'

She shakes her head, although she doesn't entirely agree with him: maybe it would work, the two of them. More likely, she then thinks, he would be a different man – a different Sam – and she wouldn't like him the way she does now. So he's right.

'But I do love you,' he says. 'You have such a big heart. So generous. You are caring and loyal and kind.'

'I'm boring,' she murmurs.

'Boring?' He snorts. 'Hardly, darl. You're so funny, the things you notice about people. Do you really think *I* would want to spend time around someone boring?'

He winks and she feels her face relax into a smile, although she's still not quite in her body. Mainly because she doesn't want to be. The fantasy she had of life with him was so much nicer than this reality in which they will never be together and she's going to have to find a way to live without the comfort of that love.

'No,' she says. 'You wouldn't.'

They sit in silence for a little while, then he smiles sadly.

'I hope you still want to be my friend,' he says.

Does she want that too? She thinks of how much she enjoys his company – has that been only because she thought there might be something more to it? No, she does genuinely like him. He amuses her, and it seems she amuses him. That's a start. Maybe it's everything.

'I do,' she says.

He looks so relieved. 'Great,' he says. 'Then you can help me hoover up this lot of food before our sweet and sour pork arrives.'

She laughs, even though she doesn't really feel like it, and picks up a lettuce leaf for the san choy bow.

The rest of the meal is spent in light conversation. It's pleasant, spending time with him, even as she wants to go home and lick her wounds.

Later, as she climbs into bed, she feels at last back in her own self, and once she turns out the light she lets herself cry, and she keeps crying until she falls asleep, waking up six hours later with tears on her cheeks.

CHAPTER THIRTY-NINE

With piles of sewing in her workroom, waiting for her children to go to bed, the rain causing a leak in the kitchen that Anna can't fix herself, a load of washing she forgot to put on today and a dinner the children didn't like, Anna finds herself irritated with the incessant small tasks that come with being an adult. What is even more irritating is that she can't switch off being an adult; it would be so nice, such a relief, to take a break from it every now and again.

Instead she has to deal with two children who are now sitting in front of her with serious faces, their baths done and dressing gowns on, ready for bed. They've been serious ever since they came home from school; quieter than usual when not whispering to each other.

She knew that having them close together in age might mean they'd be in cahoots as they grew older – possibly cahoots against their parents – and she has always loved the fact that they are close. Tonight, though, they seem to be winding each other up about something.

'Mama,' Renee says in a singsong tone. *Muh-maaa.*

'Yes, darling?'

Renee looks at Troy, who glances at Anna then back to his sister.

'I want to ask a . . .' She sighs and giggles and twists her hands around each other.

Anna waits. She doesn't like to prod the children into saying things because they'll come out with whatever it is eventually, and prodding them makes it seem she's too impatient to wait for them.

Renee and Troy look at each other again. He nods as if he's egging her on. They often communicate like this: wordlessly, gestures and eyes only. Like twins, someone once said, except Anna tends to think twins do it not because they're twins but because they grow up so closely together. For example, she'll often think something then her mother will say it. Who can explain that other than to say that they know each other very, very well?

'Do you still love Daddy?' Renee says quickly, then her eyes drop and the hands are twisting again, but not as much as Anna's guts are.

Oh crap, Anna thinks. This is not a question she wants to answer precisely because it's a question she's been asking herself as she tries to work out what she wants to do with her life. That's part of being an adult too: having to make decisions. So many decisions.

Last night she was making a skirt for this nice lady who lives down the street, and a question popped into her head.

Do I still want my husband?

It's been churning around in her mind ever since, because it's an important one, obviously, but also because it's a change from what she's heard other women wondering, which is whether their husbands still want *them*. That's the wrong way around, isn't it? She knows she's been trained so well to think about what everyone else wants – and a big part of turfing out Gary was because she was thinking about what *she* wants, as unpopular a stance as that is – that it feels revolutionary to ask herself what she wants. Not just once, but over and over.

Because here's what she's realised: if she's asking herself what she wants, and trying to give it to herself – like getting the new hairstyle, like taking care of herself better, like making a new friendship – she's happier. Less resentful. The things that people need her for don't seem so annoying, even onerous, now. There's a certain power that comes from doing something because she *wants* to not because she feels she *has* to. And what she's found is that, after making sure she does some things she wants to do, she is still very keen to take care of other people, to support them, to be generous with her time. The caring just comes from a better place. A place that doesn't involve her performing like a well-trained maid.

The fact that Renee has come up with a version of the question Anna has been asking herself is proof – if any were needed – of Anna's very theory about how family members can appear to read each other's minds.

'Of course,' she says to her daughter, because she can hardly say 'Maybe'. No child wants to hear their mother say that about their father. But she instantly realises the mistake she's made when Renee's face crumples.

'Then why doesn't he . . .' Renee makes that hiccup-crying sound that tears Anna's heart apart – as any crying sound from her daughter, or son, can.

'Why doesn't he . . .' More hiccup-crying. 'Come home?' Renee finishes.

'Oh, darling.' Anna goes to hug her daughter but Renee folds her arms and turns her head. Great. It seems the hiccup-crying was a manipulation.

Anna looks at Troy, whose face is impassive. That kid is an impressive actor a lot of the time and she would wonder where he got it from, except he's seen her and her mother putting on happy faces for people, pretending to like people they don't, all to keep the social wheels greased. Ingrid is more expert at it than Anna; then again, she's had more experience.

'We want Daddy to come home,' Troy says, his little chin jutting forward.

They're good, these two with their tandem act. Waterworks and stoic defiance – quite the duo.

'I know you miss him,' Anna says, even though they've actually shown hardly any signs of it. Or perhaps she just didn't want to see the signs because they didn't suit her.

'Everyone has a dad except us,' Renee wails, burrowing into Troy's shoulder.

Anna would think it cute if she didn't also think they're putting it on a little. There have been no tears about Gary thus far. Why now?

Wait . . . it's coming to her . . .

'They're having a Dads Day at school,' Troy says.

'Dads Day?' she says. 'I didn't see a letter about that.'

'There's a competition.' Troy blinks. 'A race.'

'Egg and spoon?' Anna guesses and Troy nods.

'I want Daddy to come,' he says.

'I see,' Anna says, biting her bottom lip. Her son has made a reasonable request, and although it still feels like her children have ambushed her, she needs to appease them.

'I'll organise it. And you do have a dad, darling,' she says to Renee. 'He's just not living here.'

'But I want him to!' Renee shrieks, before hopping up and stomping off. It's the perfect choreography for a seven-year-old's tantrum and Anna has to admire it, even as her heart breaks a little to see it.

I've done this, she thinks.

No, that's not true. *Gary* did this. Which makes her feel mad at him all over again – and she can't express that out loud because the children know only that their father isn't living here and clearly the snatches of time when they used to see him on weekends meant more to them than she realised.

'When's he coming back, Mu-um?' Troy asks in a whingey-whiny tone she hasn't heard since he wanted a Pac-Man game.

'I don't know,' she says. Which leaves the door open. She didn't say, 'He's not.' So she's given her son hope – and she doesn't yet know if it's false.

At least now she's clear on one thing: she will do what's best for her, because that is what's best for others. She should have learnt that from Ingrid a long time ago, because even when Anna's father was at his lowest Ingrid still tried to find a way to live well. To do something that was nice for herself. To maintain her dignity, she once said. Anna didn't understand it then but she does now.

The sound of Renee crying floats in from her bedroom.

'Let's go and see your sister,' she says, standing up and holding out her hand. These days Troy will take it sometimes, others not.

Tonight he does, and she squeezes it as they walk toward Renee, and Anna puts aside thoughts of her future and focuses on her now: two children who need her, two children she adores.

CHAPTER FORTY

'Josie! ... *Josie!*'

The voice is coming from somewhere far away. No – it's close. Is it?

'Josie, darling, please.'

Yes, it's close. It sounds like her mum's voice. But why would her mum be talking to her while she's asleep?

So it's a dream.

It's comfortable inside this dream. Whatever is happening in it. Not much. It isn't easy to observe your own dreams. It feels kind of weird, actually.

She feels someone taking hold of her hand. Now that's *really* weird.

A thumb is being rubbed over her thumb.

'Darling,' comes the whisper.

That's definitely her mum. But what does she want in this dream?

'She's not waking up,' she hears the voice – her mum – say. 'Why isn't she waking up?'

I'm not waking up because this is a dream!

She hears other noises now. A beeping. Rustling. Sounds that are further away from her than her mum's voice. This dream feels really real.

Her brain starts whirring. Maybe it's not a dream. But if it isn't, where is she?

An image flashes into her brain. She's driving round a bend on that windy road to Woy Woy.

Black spots in front of her eyes. She can't breathe.

A car, coming the other way.

Back. Back, back, back.

An argument with her parents. What was it about?

She can remember how it felt but not what they said.

Brett.

Was the argument about him?

'Josie, darling, please wake up,' her mother is whispering.

'Josephine.' It's her father's voice on her other side. 'We're sorry.'

Sorry for what? What's happened to her?

Now she has to find out.

But she's tired. Really, really tired.

It would be easier to go back to sleep.

She feels pressure on her shoulder.

'Josie,' says an unfamiliar voice, 'we need you to wake up.'

Who is that?

It's curiosity that makes Josie blink her eyes open to see an off-white ceiling and a neon light. Someone gasps.

There's a hand on her cheek.

'Darling, darling, darling.' It's her mother, so close to her. Too close. Josie wants to tell her to get off. Get away.

What's happened to me?

'There she is.' A more cheerful voice belonging to a smiling woman in a uniform.

Josie turns her head toward the beeping sound and sees her father, and machines, and a drip attached to her arm. The last – and first – time she had a drip was when she was a child and she had an ear infection that got out of control.

So the woman in the uniform is a nurse.

'Do you know where you are, Josie?' the nurse asks.

How would I know? she wants to say. *I've just woken up!*

'You're in hospital, love. You've had an accident.'

The bend. The car. The nothingness. Of course. An accident.

She has to get out of here. She has to check on the car. What happened to the car? She needs that car. It's her freedom.

Her job. She needs to get to work. So she needs to get out of this bed.

She moves.

But she can't. Her legs are too heavy. This thing is attached to her arm. It needs to come out!

'Darling, your legs are broken,' her mother says, stroking her forearm. 'And you've fractured your pelvis.'

'What?' That can't be right. She tries to move again but the heaviness is still there.

'You're in casts, Josie,' the nurse says and she makes it sound as if it's a great thing. 'You'll be stuck with them for a while.' The nurse is looking at the drip. 'I'll get the doctor,' she says. 'He'll want to know you're awake.'

After the nurse leaves Josie's parents crowd in and she wants to tell them to get away, but she has no power to make them go. No power to do anything. She's stuck. Trapped. Right where they want her.

'We love you so much,' her father says.

'Paolo, you're holding her hand too tightly,' her mother chides.

Josie hadn't noticed, though. There are so many sensations now: her legs that feel like lead, the twinges of pain she is aware of in her pelvis, her arm with a drip attached.

Oh god, how is she weeing? Is there . . . There's a bag at the end of the bed. Oh god. *Oh god.* It's so embarrassing.

She starts crying, and that's embarrassing too, but her parents are kissing her head and it feels comforting and she wants them there but she doesn't want them there. There's only one person she wants.

'Brett,' she whispers.

Her mother pulls back. 'Who?'

'Brett,' she says more firmly. 'I want to see him.'

'No one by that name has enquired after you,' her mother says.

Stop it! she wants to scream. *Stop acting like my school principal instead of my mother!*

A wave of nausea hits her. She wants to vomit and she looks around desperately.

The nurse, who has just returned, holds a plastic tray under her. 'You're all right, darling,' she says. 'It's the morphine.'

She rubs Josie's back and Josie closes her eyes and thinks that it's the loveliest, kindest thing anyone has ever done for her. Then the vomit really does rise and she is grateful for the tray and the hand still on her back.

'It's so unpleasant,' the nurse murmurs. 'You'll settle.'

Josie nods and takes the tissue the nurse hands her, wiping her mouth. She glances up and sees her parents. They look so worried. A flash of irritation – of anger, it might be – strikes her. They're only worried now because something's happened that they can't control. All they're interested in is controlling her.

After a minute or so has passed, she feels strong enough to do something about it.

'Would Brett know I'm here?'

Her parents exchange glances and she sees only how complicit they are in keeping him away from her. This feels worse than the pain in her body. This pain is in all of her. This pain *is* her.

She cries harder, and they likely think it's because of the accident, and she decides to let them, because lying in this bed, with everything that is wrong with her, there's nothing else she can do and no one to come to her rescue.

Brett was the one she hoped would save her from her life. He's not here. And any strength she feels to do it herself ebbs away as she decides to succumb to her misery.

So she closes her eyes and lets the tears silently flow down her face, not caring if her parents stay or go.

JULY 1986

The feature film *Aliens*, starring Sigourney Weaver, is released.

Convicted Australian drug smugglers Kevin Barlow
and Brian Chambers are executed in Malaysia.

The movie *Top Gun*, starring Tom Cruise, is released.

HRH Prince Andrew marries Sarah Ferguson
in Westminster Abbey.

Billy Joel releases his album *The Bridge*.

CHAPTER FORTY-ONE

The rain is coming down hard as Trudy flicks on the blinker to turn left out of Evie's street and head in the direction of Gosford Hospital, where they're going to visit Josie. It's taken Josie being in such a bad way to get her back behind the wheel; she was surprised by how upset she was about it, given that Josie hasn't been with her that long. There's something about the girl, though, that has burrowed its way into Trudy's heart.

Trudy has been on the phone to Josie's mum every day since Erin called to tell her that Josie had been in an accident. Well, Trudy couldn't believe it. Especially since the road Josie was on wasn't the road that takes her home from the salon, nor anywhere else she usually travels, it seems. Erin was baffled. Said her husband was a mess. Paolo, his name is.

Josie's last name is Martin so Trudy had presumed she had an English background, like a lot of people round here, but it turns out the name is Spanish – Paolo is from Madrid – not that Josie ever said anything about it. Which made Trudy wonder if Josie thought she couldn't tell her things about her life.

Except that boy comes around for her and she doesn't try to hide him. Brett. Nice lad. Trudy won't mention him to the parents, though, because the fact Josie meets him after work in Terrigal suggests he's not seeing her at home in Gosford.

Today's the first day Josie is having visitors who aren't family, Erin told her yesterday. So Trudy asked Evie if she'd like to come with her, since it's Sunday and they're both not working. She also asked Evie if Sam should come too and almost got her head bitten off.

Something's going on there. That is, something *else*. Trudy has been able to see that something is going on between Evie and Sam for a while – mainly on Evie's part, although she has thought that Sam leads Evie on, with all the chatting and flirting. Evie's had a sheltered life and she wouldn't realise that some flirty men aren't actually, you know, *interested*.

Not that Trudy's had a wildly unsheltered life but she's older, and with age comes a lot more experience with human behaviour.

'Everything all right, pet?' she asks. Evie is staring out the window, saying nothing. She didn't even put up a fight when Trudy offered to drive her to the hospital instead of the other way around.

'Sure,' Evie replies, but it has a tone to it which suggests she's definitely not sure.

'That was convincing.' Trudy peers through the windscreen. 'Geez, it's bucketing down. Hard to see anything. And I've got these wipers on full,' she goes on, not that Evie's likely to care. She's obviously wrapped up in something. Or someone.

'Yep.'

'Evelyn, I don't know what's got your goat but I wish you'd just spit it out.' Trudy grips the steering wheel tighter. She'd rather not have to be driving in such awful weather while she's doing the agony-aunt thing but you can't pick your timing.

'Why?'

Trudy senses Evie's head turning in her direction but she's not going to look at her because she has to look at the road.

They drive through a huge puddle and for a second Trudy considers praying that the engine doesn't stall, but she long ago stopped talking to God so she doesn't think He's going to listen this time.

'Why? Because I don't want you moping around Josie. The girl has enough problems.'

'I'm not moping.'

'What are you doing, then? Because the Evie I know hasn't shown up to work for a few days.'

'Sorry.' She sounds sulky.

'I didn't ask for an apology, silly girl. You know you can talk to me. I see you more than my own son. That has to count for something.'

'You wouldn't understand,' she mumbles.

'Don't presume things about people. It's rude.' Trudy is tetchy, but more at the weather than Evie.

Maybe that makes Evie sulk more, because she makes a huffing noise.

Trudy leaves it – she needs to focus on the road anyway. They can always sort it out later.

For a while the only noise in the car is the sound of rain on the roof and the wipers trying their hardest.

'It's Sam,' Evie says as they drive past Brisbane Water.

'What's he done?'

'Nothing.'

'Not helpful, Evie. If we're going to solve this thing, I need details.'

'I don't need anything solved,' Evie says tersely.

'Don't you?'

'I just need it to go away.'

'What is *it*?'

Another huffing sound. Trudy can't turn to look at her because of, well, the weather and having to be a responsible driver. Plus she's rusty so she needs to pay extra attention.

They're almost at the hospital, so time's running out to get Evie to talk to her, but she really doesn't want to walk into Josie's ward with the huffing and puffing going on. Like she said, Josie has enough to deal with.

'I'm in love with Sam,' Evie says with such force that it's almost as if a bomb has gone off in the car.

Trudy nearly rushes to answer but she understands this is a big confession from a shy girl, so she lets it marinate for a second.

'I see. Well, I can't say I'm shocked to hear this, pet.'

'*What?*'

She sounds quite upset but Trudy doesn't want to pussyfoot around this. In fact, she realises she should have nipped it in the bud when she saw it starting, not that you can stop a person having feelings.

'Pet, you don't have a poker face.'

'But . . .'

It sounds like Evie's crying so Trudy risks a glance and sees that she is. Oh dear.

The car park for the hospital is coming up, so Trudy puts on her blinker and finds them a spot. With the engine off, she undoes her seatbelt and turns toward the younger woman.

'I'll let you cry for another minute or so, but then you need to stop,' Trudy says firmly. 'There's nothing to cry about.'

'He doesn't love me back!'

'It happens in life. It's hard and it hurts but it happens. And you need to get a hold of yourself otherwise you're going to get into quite a state.'

Evie sniffles and her chest heaves. 'Maybe I want to be in a state,' she says.

Trudy thinks this is just about the crux of it: the girl hasn't let herself feel anything for years, just holding things together as a single mum with hardly any help from that moron she had a kid with, and then she sees a handsome bloke and ends up in a tizz and it makes her feel alive. It's easier to watch soap operas and let yourself ride the roller-coaster along with the characters – that way you get to feel things and it doesn't have an impact on real life. But what would Trudy know? She's just a slightly old duck who can't get over her dead husband, so clearly she feels too much.

'It's not good for you. You'll wear yourself out.'

Trudy has seen it with clients: ladies who invest far too much time and energy in a fella who then lets them down and they're in the salon crying and asking Trudy what hairstyle they should get in order to win the man back.

None, is what she wants to tell them. But it's not what they want to hear. They want her to wave a magic wand over them and give them a love potion they can take away with them. The worst part is that she knows, without ever having met these men, that they won't be worth the pain. Even Sam, god bless him, isn't worth the pain because she's fairly sure he knows what's been going on with Evie and he's enjoyed the adulation too much to stop it. Until now, of course, which is why she's so upset.

'You need to let this go,' Trudy says firmly, looking at Evie's blotchy cheeks and her hair that's all over the place from Evie running her hands through it, as she's doing now. 'And I'm being tough on you because it's good for you. Any man who doesn't love you back is not the man for you, I don't care how good-looking he is. And that's something else: good looks are just a fact. They don't make a man nice or not, they don't make him any better for you or not. They're just a *fact*.'

'But he's really sweet!'

Oh lord, she's still trying to justify it.

'In case you hadn't noticed, pet, he's sweet to everyone, including the eighty-year-olds and the teenagers. It's just him.'

Evie looks stricken, but Trudy decides to keep going and really drive the point home.

'I hate to say this to you, pet, but you're not special to him. Not like that. I'm sure he cares for you a great deal – I can see that by how he interacts with you – but it's nothing romantic. It never will be.'

There's more sniffling from Evie while Trudy starts to wonder if they'll get drenched going from the car to the hospital building.

'I know,' Evie says at last. 'He told me. That's why I'm so upset.'

'It's going to hurt for a while,' Trudy tells her kindly. 'Then it won't. So the only thing separating hurt from not-hurt is time. That's the best I can tell you. Also this: distract yourself. Get a new hobby. Make a new friend.'

Evie nods slowly then sits up straighter. 'I must look awful,' she says.

'Pretty bad, yes.' Trudy laughs. 'Come on, I'll fix you up then we'll try not to get wet and muss it all up again.'

CHAPTER FORTY-TWO

Nothing in Josie's life has prepared her for being captive in a bed in a hospital ward, completely reliant on other people, not even able to wee for herself. Or do other things.

That's really the worst part – worse than the pain that comes when her medication wears off and goes when she takes more of it. *Bodily functions.* Things no one has helped her with since she was a very small child – so small she can't remember her mum taking her to the toilet. It's really humiliating, having to ask a nurse to help you with . . . you know. YOU KNOW.

When she said something to her mum about it, Erin just said, 'Try having a baby, then you'll find out about humiliation. You're like a piece of meat on a slab and everyone's poking you.'

Was that meant to make her feel better? Especially since she had been the baby in question? She supposed her mother was trying to be sympathetic but it didn't work. And Josie really needs sympathy. Really, seriously. Her father, when he visits, looks miserable and says little, so she's not getting it from him. The nurses are brisk and their smiles don't seem genuine, and she can't really blame them when they have to spend all day tending to *you know*, among other things. What a horrible job. Josie couldn't do it. That's why she's doing hair. Was doing hair. Does she still have a job? Her apprenticeship is stuffed.

Except Trudy came to visit, with Evie. So that must mean Trudy still wants her around. She didn't say anything about the job other than 'you just take your time getting better'. Which could mean 'take your time because there's no job to come back to' or 'take your time and I'll hold it for you'.

At least those two were sympathetic. They gasped – loudly – when they walked in and saw her with her legs in casts.

'Oh god, Josie, you poor little thing!' Trudy cried when she entered the room.

Erin looked up from her magazine. 'Hello, Trudy,' she said. At least she put the magazine down and stood up to properly say hello. Most days she just sits in that chair and reads, and Josie wonders why she bothers coming here. Josie even said that to Erin the other day when she was feeling really low.

'Where else would I be?' her mother said. 'I know there's not much excitement for you having me around, but if I were at home I'd just be worrying about you.'

It wasn't about excitement, Josie wanted to tell her. It was about privacy. She has none. No point saying that, though, because Erin will get upset and make her feel guilty, and Josie can do without the guilt. It's bad enough her car was written off – she's been feeling bad about that for days.

Her mum and Trudy chatted along like old friends, which made Josie wonder how many times they'd spoken before. Evie gave Josie the chocolates she'd brought; Josie didn't tell her she couldn't eat chocolates because her stomach is sensitive at the moment and chocolates make her *you know*. These are things she actually wishes she could say to people because they might be sympathetic – we all have issues with digestion from time to time – but she knows her mother would flip, and as her mother is always around when Josie is conscious, that won't happen.

The only time her mother did give her some space was when Trudy and Evie visited.

'I'll just duck out for a while and leave you to chat,' Erin said, taking her book with her, so Josie knew she was going for a while.

They pulled up chairs on one side of the bed, which was considerate, because then Josie didn't need to turn her head from side to side to talk to them.

'How are you going, pet?' Trudy reached across and patted her hand.

There was such care in her voice and on her face that Josie started to cry.

'Um . . .' she said, sniffing and wiping her face with her hand until Trudy gave her a tissue.

Neither Trudy nor Evie looked uncomfortable, which Josie was so glad about. There's nothing worse than crying involuntarily and having people look as if they'd rather you sink into a hole in the ground.

'Better out than in,' Trudy said with a reassuring smile. 'I still cry over my Laurie and it helps me feel better.'

Josie has barely heard Laurie's name mentioned but she knows he's Trudy's late husband. So she guesses that Trudy has a lot of sadness about that. More sadness than her mother has about the babies she lost, although that's quite heavy too. And probably the reason why Erin won't leave the hospital unless Josie is asleep: she waited so long and went through so much to get Josie, then Josie almost did herself in over an argument about a boy who hasn't even been to see her.

Not that she wants him to see her in this state. No bloke would be attracted to a girl with her lower half in a cast and a WEE BAG at the end of the bed. She cringes each time a male doctor comes in to check on her – and there have been a few, which makes her feel like a freak show, everyone coming in to gawk – so she absolutely, no way, does not want Brett to see her.

Except . . .

Except she wants to know he cares. Is that weird? That she doesn't want to see him but she wants to know he wants to see her? Shouldn't there be a word for that kind of feeling? Maybe there is. She isn't good at words, after all.

While Trudy was here she wanted to ask if he'd been by the salon, but she didn't. It's been over a week since the accident, though, so wouldn't he be wondering where she is? The last time they saw each other he'd promised to arrange a drive to Newcastle so they could go to Merewether, which is one of his favourite beaches. He thought she'd love the baths there.

Turned out she didn't have to ask Trudy, because she volunteered some information.

'Your young man,' she said, and Josie held her breath. 'I saw him outside the shop on Tuesday, but he didn't come in. I was with a client so I couldn't go out to tell him. Haven't seen him since. Have you seen him, Evie?'

Evie shook her head. 'No, but I'm usually gone by the time Josie finishes. Gotta get Billy.'

So that was that. The visit was nice but Josie was tired after ten minutes and glad when her mother re-entered the room and suggested she needed a rest.

'We understand, pet,' Trudy said. 'Talking takes work, and you need your strength to get better.'

After they were gone, though, and it was just her and her mum again, Josie felt lonely. Which was strange, because her mum was right there, but it was the sort of loneliness that comes from thinking no one understands what you're going through and there's no way to tell them. She used to feel it at school when girls were mean to her. There was no one to talk to about it, no one who could say, 'Yes, I've been through that myself.' She just had to put her head down and get through it.

She does remember one thing from history class that keeps coming to mind, and her teachers wouldn't believe it if she told them that's what she retained. It's that thing Winston Churchill said during World War II: 'If you're going through hell, keep going.' She's not in a war, of course, but there are times when lying here in this bed, unable to get up, feeling like she's wasting away and wasting her life and wasting her time and wasting everyone else's, is a form of hell. Or maybe she's just bored. Anyway, that thing Churchill said helps, because it reminds her that she got through the hell that was school so she can get through this too.

If only Brett would call. Or something. Maybe then she wouldn't feel so alone.

CHAPTER FORTY-THREE

Whoever said time heals all wounds clearly had shallow wounds, Evie thinks, as she half-smiles at Sam when he passes while she's mixing colour. He keeps looking at her like some tragedy has occurred and all right, yes, she might have indulged in the idea that him not loving her is a tragedy but she hasn't said it to anyone else in those terms. It's also not a tragedy in the scheme of things. The Holocaust was a tragedy. And tragedy isn't even the right word for it, because it was millions of tragedies all bundled up in one word. A word that, among others, reminds her she has wounds to heal but they're wounds because she's still here. She has a chance to make them better, and she's trying to do that.

What does not help is the pressure she feels to keep being Sam's friend. He almost tries too hard to stay in her good graces when she really just wants to sulk behind her chair, at her own pace, in her own time, and once she's done she'll likely want to be his friend again, but for now . . . there are still those wounds to heal.

'Coffee, darl?' he says as he passes her again.

This time she wants to stomp her foot. He knows she has a client – that's why she's mixing the colour! Why would she want a coffee? She never has a beverage when she's with a client. Mainly because she doesn't have enough hands to work and sip at the same time.

At least stomping a foot – an action – is an improvement on sulking, which some would call inaction.

'No, thanks,' she says through a fake smile, holding up the colour pot. 'Busy.'

'Sure. Sure, sure.' He flashes his teeth at her. 'Just let me know when you want one and I'll make it.'

Why? She wants to yell at him. *A coffee won't compensate for breaking my heart.*

Except she broke her own heart, didn't she? Let herself have expectations he never indicated he could meet. Or wanted to meet. She dreamt herself up a whole life with him and he had no idea.

She shakes her head, hoping that will stop her obsessing over him, because she still is, only now it takes the form of constantly mulling over the same *Why not me?* thoughts that are completely redundant because it was never going to be her. Which is really the rub, isn't it?

As she exits the back room holding the colour, she glances up and stops, because Oliver is in the doorway, grinning at her.

'Hi!' he says.

Oh great – what does he want? First he crashed her non-date at the movies, now he's crashing her workplace. She could have kinder thoughts about him, obviously, but she blames him for putting Sam in her vicinity.

'How are you?' he says.

Does she imagine there's pity in his tone? Of course Sam would have told him the completely humiliating information that she was in love with him, and of course Oliver would know why Sam didn't love her the same way. She didn't consider this before but now she can add it to her list of regrets and ruminations. Perhaps she really should get a hobby, as Trudy suggested – that might distract her long enough for the list to shrivel up of its own accord.

'I'm great,' she says, although because her tone is flat it's completely unconvincing.

'Great,' he says, still grinning. 'I'm here for a haircut.'

'I'm booked up.'

His grin falters. 'Oh – no, I mean, Sam's doing it.'

Now she's the one who falters. *God*, how embarrassing. Why would she presume he's here to see her when his brother works in the salon?

'Of course,' she says. 'Sorry, default answer.' She smiles quickly then starts to move away.

'So you're good?' Oliver says. He's trailing after her and she wishes he wouldn't.

'Yep,' she says over her shoulder, then smiles at her client in the mirror. 'Mish, I think you're going to love this colour.'

She catches a glimpse in the mirror of Oliver looking crestfallen and feels bad. Although she shouldn't. He knows she's not good and he's asked after her twice, which to Evie smells of provocation – almost as if he wants to get a rise out of her. And it worked, because now she feels tetchy.

After half an hour she has Mish's colour on, where she'll leave it for about forty-five minutes, and it's almost time for her next client, who's having a trim and a wash and set, which she can mostly get done in the forty-five, although without Josie to wash it may take a little longer. Josie is fast and good. Washing is Evie's least favourite thing to do so she's slower than the others, which is counterintuitive – you'd think she'd speed through it – but her reluctance seems to slow her down.

In the chair next to hers Sam is pulling the cape off Oliver, then Oliver stands up. He's quite a bit taller than Sam, Evie notices. Why hasn't she before? Sam's not short, either.

They don't look like each other, apart from the dark hair. Sam's face is chiselled; Oliver's is slender, pointed. If she didn't know they were brothers, she wouldn't guess it.

'How's Billy?' Oliver says before she has a chance to get away. She doesn't want to loiter near Sam, even as he seems to want to loiter near her.

'He's good,' she replies, moving things around on her tray. Combs need to be kept in order, after all. 'Keeping busy with sport.'

'It'd be great to see him.'

Evie's head snaps up. What an odd thing to say. He barely knows Billy.

'Would it?' she replies.

Oliver blanches. 'I mean – I'd like to see him,' he says. 'It's been a while.'

'Right,' she says slowly.

There's no reason for you to see him.

'I mean . . .' He sighs. 'I'd like to see you both. Do something fun together.'

Evie becomes aware of Sam looking at her expectantly and wonders exactly what is going on. Does Oliver pity her? Poor, pathetic Evie with her crush on his gay brother?

Or is he trying to pursue her? If that's even what men do any more. And – she really doesn't like this idea – is Sam pushing him to? That would be really icky if true. Sam doesn't want her so he offloads her to his brother. It's the plot of a bad movie that would never get made because it's so pathetic.

No. No – she shouldn't be so negative. She was telling herself that this morning as a way of getting out of her slump. *Just because the sky feels like it's falling doesn't mean it is.* That was one thing she told herself. Another was: *Someone will love you.*

She didn't believe that one as much as she believed the other one. It's hard to convince yourself you're lovable when no one has, you know, loved you. *Like that.* Billy loves her, of course. Her mum loved her. But no one has *chosen* her. That's the part that stings.

'Maybe,' she says to Oliver, because what else can she say in the middle of the salon with everyone listening. Even Trudy's eyes are on stalks.

The salon door opens and with relief Evie sees it's her next client.

'I have to go,' she says.

'Can I call you?' Oliver says.

She says, 'Sure,' in as blasé a fashion as possible, and walks away from him.

As she's seating the client she's barely aware of him leaving, and only slightly more aware of Sam hovering, and when the hovering starts to annoy her she thinks that's a good sign: no longer can he do no wrong in her eyes.

So Oliver's visit served one purpose at least, because it moved her a little further on from Sam. Moving all the way along will take time, however. That's an expectation she *is* learning to manage.

'Coffee, darl?' Sam asks – again – as he passes her on the way to the back room.

This time she says, 'Yes,' just to shut him up, and feels a surge of something. She realises she may just be coming back to herself, one irritation at a time.

CHAPTER FORTY-FOUR

'So . . .' Anna rotates her glass on the coaster, which is harder than it looks like it should be.

'So . . .' Evie looks a little nervous, and Anna worries she might have made Evie feel obliged to come out for this drink. On a Friday night, when Evie probably has other things to do. Anna knows she has a young son – they have that in common – but Evie said it was fine, Billy's father usually takes him on Friday nights. Anna's left her kids with Ingrid, who doesn't look after them that often and complains when she does yet asks when she can have them again.

She asked Evie to come to the pub for dinner not because she saw her crying on the beach – well, yes, kind of because she saw her crying on the beach, as that's the reason they formed a connection beyond the salon – but mainly because she likes her, and she thinks it's returned, and it'd be nice to have a friend with a kid around the same age as hers. Come to think of it, they're probably at the same school – hers go to Terrigal Public, and Evie's must too. Why hasn't she seen Evie at anything there? Probably all the mum-things are during the day, and Evie can't attend them because she works. And her kids often take the bus to and from school, so she wouldn't see her then.

It's funny to think they've been closer in life than they realise, and they could have kept going without knowing each other better.

That's all connections in life, though, Anna guesses – they're made out of a combination of luck and timing and circumstance, which means we probably don't choose our friends so much as fate chooses them for us. It's nice, in a way – like we're destined to meet certain people. Then we have to keep up our end of it, of course, by putting in the work to keep the connections going. Hence the invitation to the pub.

The pub is one that she and Gary occasionally went to when they were together, the Avoca Beach Hotel. It's not actually on the beach, but that means it gets less of the tourist crowd so it's nice for an evening meal. And it's not too far from her place or from Evie's.

'Is your son at Terrigal Public?' Anna asks. May as well find out.

'Yes. You have a boy too?'

'Yes, and a girl. Troy and Renee.'

Evie frowns. 'Renee? There's a Renee in Billy's class.'

Anna smiles. 'Yes, I, ah . . . I think that's my daughter. I think our kids go to school together.'

Evie looks confused. 'How come we've never seen each other at school?'

'I was just wondering the same thing.'

They both laugh, and Anna feels herself relax a little, the way you do when you realise there are some things you don't have to explain to the other person. Some stories you may even have in common.

'Have you had a run-in with Mr Phelps yet?' Evie asks.

Mr Phelps is the unpopular principal, who, among other things, keeps firing male teachers, much to Anna's despair – she likes her kids having male role models due to the fact their father is barely around. Has been barely around. Yes, he's making more of an effort now, but that hardly compensates for the lack of effort before. *Anyway*, she's not here to talk to Evie about Gary. Although maybe they can compare notes about being single mums.

'Not yet. I'm waiting for it, though.'

Evie sips her drink. 'He really has it in for the boys. And the boy teachers.'

Anna nods her agreement and starts to sip her own wine when she sees something that makes her inhale that sip and start coughing.

'Are you okay?' Evie hops off her stool and comes round to put a hand on Anna's shoulder. 'I suppose water won't help – you inhaled, didn't you?'

Anna nods, still coughing, looking in the direction of the cause of her startling: Gary, in the company of some blonde woman, heading for a table in the corner.

So much for him wanting to spend more time with his kids. Not that he's been seeing them on Friday nights but is *this* what he's been doing with his time? Seeing someone? All while trying to get back together with her?

'That bastard,' she murmurs, the coughing abating as her lungs settle down.

'What?'

'My husband. Ex. Sort of. Husband.' She nods in the direction of the table, where Gary half has his back to her – thank goodness – and where she can also get a good look at the woman he's with. Anna hasn't seen her before, so she wouldn't be a school mum. That's something. Is she the paralegal? That's it, isn't it? He's getting it on with the new staff member. What a bloody cliché. She's married to a cliché! Was married to a cliché! Is still! Doesn't want to be!

Evie is looking at Gary's table and Anna is now worried they'll be spotted.

'That guy over there?' Evie asks.

'Yes. With the *blonde*.' Anna can hear something in her voice. Feel it, too. It couldn't be . . . could it? No. It can't be. Not . . . jealousy.

No way. She's not jealous of the blonde. *She doesn't want Gary back.* That's been her line for weeks now.

'Is he seeing someone?'

'Not that I knew of. In fact, he's been saying he wants to get back together.'

They both glance his way. He's definitely going to notice shortly.

'Would you like to leave? Go somewhere else?' Evie says.

'I would but . . . our fish and chips.' They put in an order when they got their drinks.

'Oh, stuff that. We can tell them to not make them. They probably haven't started.'

They both look to the kitchen, where there's not a lot of activity.

'No,' Anna says. 'No. Why should you have to change your night just because of my stupid marriage?'

'It's –'

'No, Evie, really. I need to get used to it.' She swallows. Does she, though? This jealousy – there's been nothing else to provoke it the whole time they've known each other, because he's never even looked at another woman sideways. 'But maybe we could move over there.' Anna jerks her chin toward a corner that's as far away from Gary as they can get, as well as being fairly dark.

'Good idea.'

Evie picks up their drinks and Anna their cutlery and tries not to be noticeable as she goes.

Once they're resettled, Evie has a quick glance in Gary's direction.

'So how long have you been split up?' she says.

'Not long. He was working so much. Never coming home while the kids were awake. So I thought he may as well leave. He didn't take it well. He's been . . .'

She was going to say, *He's been trying to come back*, but is that true any more?

Evie smiles at her – it's unguarded and warm, which is not how Evie smiles in the salon. 'Do you still love him?' she says.

'He's the father of my children, so . . .'

'Anna, you saw me blubbering on the beach.' Evie looks amused. 'I think we've kind of moved past the pretending stage.'

Anna is so taken aback she almost rocks off her stool. What is Evie seeing in her?

'I wasn't pretending,' she says. 'I just . . . I thought . . .'

'You thought you were over him until you saw him with the blonde chick.'

'Well . . . yes.'

Evie smiles again. 'You know how I knew I was over Billy's dad, if I was ever that into him?'

'You weren't into him?'

Evie waves a hand. 'Story for another time. But I saw him at the pub with this girl, right. I went there to see a friend for dinner, Billy was with me in a stroller. The girl was pretty, I guess. They were all over each other. And I felt nothing. Not a twinge. Not a pang. Nothing.' She sips her drink. 'Up till that point I thought maybe Stevo and I could work. You know – we got on well, we both loved Billy. We enjoyed each other's company. It was just . . .' She shrugs. 'Something was missing. And I found out what it was: I didn't want to see him naked.'

Anna bursts out laughing. 'But you managed to have a kid together!'

'It was dark. I was drunk.' Evie raises her glass. 'Here's to working out which men we want to see naked.'

After they've put their glasses down, she looks serious.

'I guess the question for you is whether you still want to see your husband naked.' She holds up a hand. 'And you don't have to answer that. I'm just offering it to you.'

From her new position Anna can't see Gary, but she can feel him there, across the room, and she desperately wants to know what he's doing. So she does care. She cares that someone else may get him. That someone *else* may see him naked. What does that tell her?

'Thank you,' she says to Evie. 'You've been a good friend and I hardly even know you.'

'You were a good friend when you didn't even know me at all.'

They sit and smile at each other for a few seconds, and Anna feels reassured that she's not barmy for suddenly realising she still fancies her husband after all. Evie doesn't seem to think it's strange.

'Number forty-three!' comes the call from the kitchen.

'I'll go,' Evie says.

Anna uses the opportunity to glance Gary's way. She doesn't quite know what to do with her new information about her feelings but she can't help thinking that fate brought her here so she could find out.

CHAPTER FORTY-FIVE

'Babs, pet, we've got you in already – for next Thursday.' Trudy points to a line in the appointment book.

'Really?' Babs bends down to look closely at Trudy's neatly inscribed entry then straightens. 'My memory's going.'

'Along with your knees.'

'You'll keep.'

'And your eyesight.'

'Thin ice, Trudy – thin ice.' Babs cackles and puts thirty dollars onto the book.

'Too much, pet,' Trudy says, picking up the ten and offering it back.

'You've been undercharging me for years,' Babs says. 'Keep it.'

Trudy shakes her head. 'You're in here every week. I can assure you I'm doing better out of you than the tourists who pop in twice a year.'

'You do me a favour, Trude,' Babs says, patting her freshly blow-dried head. 'I always look my best thanks to you.' She glances around the salon, which is empty apart from Sam chatting to his last client for the day. 'Tell me, how are Evie and Sam getting along?' she whispers theatrically. Luckily Sam has the blow dryer on otherwise he'd hear her.

'Fine,' Trudy says, arching an eyebrow. 'Why?'

'Ooh, I thought they were headed for the rocks, those two. She was a little too sweet on him. If you know what I mean.'

'I do. And it's all sorted now.'

In fact, Trudy wasn't sure of the exact state of Evie's heart because they haven't had a conversation about it since the trip to Gosford Hospital to see Josie, but Evie's looked brighter lately. She even mentioned she'd gone to the pub with Ingrid's daughter, Anna, which Trudy was happy about. The girl doesn't have a broad enough circle, in her opinion, which was probably why she fell hook and line for Sam's charms. Everyone loves him, including Trudy, and a woman who isn't used to a charming man can find herself thinking it's personal, when in actuality he's just like it with everyone. Trudy should have tried harder to warn her, but sometimes you do have to let adults be adults and come to their own realisations. They're the ones that tend to stick.

'And young Josie?' Babs says, dropping the whisper. 'How is she?'

'Upset. Miserable. Nothing for it but to wait.' Trudy sighs and shakes her head. She popped round to the hospital the other night and Josie was in a state, crying and telling her mother to get out.

Trudy had a chat to Erin outside and asked if there was anything she could do – perhaps she could come and sit with Josie sometimes instead of Erin doing it? What she really wanted to suggest was that Erin give Josie some time alone – no one wants witnesses when they feel wretched like that – but she barely knows the woman and it wouldn't be right. Which is funny, if you think about it, because prior to the accident she saw a lot more of Josie than her mum did, and she thinks she knows Josie pretty well now. Not as well as Erin – of course you know your child better than anyone – but enough to have a stab at some suggestions.

Erin was upset herself when they spoke.

'You could give me a cigarette,' she said, then laughed. 'I haven't smoked since Josie was a baby. But I want to. So badly.'

272

'I get it, pet,' Trudy said, and lit one for her. It's not for her to judge the woman and deny her a smoke. 'I've been smoking more since my Laurie died. Sometimes we just need something, maybe especially when we know it's bad for us.'

'Humans are funny,' she said, and Trudy agreed, but they didn't go any deeper than that.

Trudy snaps back to the present when Babs says, 'She has a long road ahead of her,' and she murmurs her agreement.

'Who's that young lad?' Babs gestures to the footpath, where Trudy sees Brett walking in half-circles.

'That's Josie's sweetheart. Brett.'

'What's he doing here?'

'Looking for her, I'd wager.'

'He doesn't know?'

'I guess not. The parents don't know him. Josie said they were all arguing about him when she got in the car and . . .' Trudy pulls a face. 'Some family friend had seen Josie and Brett together. Told the mum.'

'What a tattletale!'

'Come on, Babs, you love a gossip.'

'Not when it's going to hurt someone. I don't tell tales like *that*.'

'True.' She glances out and sees the boy's still turning himself inside out. 'I should go and talk to him.'

'Wait here, love,' Babs says. 'I'm off anyway. I'll send him in.'

'All right, pet, ta-ta.' Trudy pecks Babs on the cheek and watches as her longtime client steps outside and has a brief chat to Brett, who then opens the salon door and comes in.

'Hello, Brett,' Trudy says. 'You know you could have just come in. You're welcome here.'

'Hi, Trudy.' He looks unsettled. 'You were busy. I didn't want to disturb you.'

'No disturbance, pet. How have you been? We haven't see you for a few days.' She's fishing, of course, trying to find out if he's

273

looking for Josie because he wants to see her or if he wants to find out if he's been let off easily. There's no way to know how serious they were about each other before the accident, and Josie didn't say much at the hospital.

'I'm really worried,' he blurts. 'Josie hasn't been here. I don't have her number. Has she lost her job?'

'No, pet. Look, she's had an accident.'

His eyes widen. 'An accident! What? When? How is she?'

All the right questions, from instinct. Oh yes, he cares about her.

'It was a couple of weeks ago, probably not long after you last saw her. In her car. And she's not in a good way – she broke her legs, fractured her pelvis. She's going to be in hospital for a while.'

His eyes are going every which way, as if he's looking for something. 'I didn't know what was going on,' he says. 'I thought maybe she'd dropped me. Then I was worried something had happened to her, but you all seemed to be still working here so I thought she hadn't died or anything, otherwise maybe you'd have closed for a few days.'

He's talking a mile a minute and Trudy is worried he's going to pass out from lack of oxygen.

'Take a breath, Brett,' she advises. 'It's all right.'

'She'll think I don't care!' he says, and Trudy imagines that's right. 'But I do! I really do!'

Trudy reaches over and picks up his hand, patting it with her other. Her Dylan used to get wound up like this about his school work. So worried about his exams that he'd almost have a nervous breakdown. So she'd take his hand from time to time, like he was a little boy again, and it would always calm him. Deep down we're all still little kids wanting our mums to make things better, no matter how old we get.

'I know you do, pet,' Trudy says soothingly. 'Here's what we'll do, okay? I'll go and see her on the weekend and tell her you've been in to see me and that you want to visit.'

'I can't just go and see her? Where is she?'

There are two hospitals on the Coast – Wyong and Gosford – so it wouldn't make sense to keep him guessing, because he could figure it out fairly quickly. Still, it's not a clear-cut situation.

'She's at Gosford, but she's not seeing many visitors. And her mother is there a lot.' Trudy stares at him. '*A lot.*'

'That's okay,' he says.

Trudy realises then that he has no idea what Josie might or might not have told her parents about him.

'It's not, actually. Her parents only found out about you because some friend of theirs saw you and Josie together.'

His forehead creases. 'Oh yeah. We were in Blue Bay. Josie was really worried about that.'

'They had an argument. That was just before . . .'

No, she's said too much. She doesn't want to burden the boy. But from the look on his face she can see it's too late.

'An argument about me?' he says, and it comes out slightly strangled.

'None of this is your fault.'

'But . . .'

'Brett,' she says firmly, 'families are complicated. Every single one. This was not your fault. But you can't go and see her. Not yet. Let me handle it. Okay?'

He stares at her then nods slowly.

'Give me your number and I'll call you about it,' Trudy says. 'Let you know what's going on.'

He writes it in her appointment book. 'I really like her,' he says softly, and when his eyes meet Trudy's she sees just how much.

'I believe she really likes you too,' she says. 'So we'll just try to sort this out, all right?'

He nods. 'Thanks, Trudy.'

'You're a good lad.' Before she knows what she's doing she gives him a hug, but he so looked like he needed one, and when his arms tighten around her she knows she was right.

'I'll be in touch,' she says as she sees him out the door. When she turns back around she sees Sam waiting for her.

'Everything okay?' he asks.

'It will be. We have to believe that, don't we?'

He smiles, a little sadly. 'We do. I'm almost done here.'

'I'll be out the back,' she says, and she takes herself to the room that holds their bags and their colours and their tools and their towels, the place this salon couldn't function without and which is also a refuge from time to time. She turns on the radio and hears Pat Benatar's 'Love is a Battlefield' playing and thinks about what it means, that phrase, before starting to wash up the mugs in the sink, getting ready for the next day.

CHAPTER FORTY-SIX

Never in her life, even when she was at school, has Josie known so many days to be the same. Sure, she used to wear a uniform and take the same bus each day; her teachers were the same, the kids were the same. But there was variety in what she learnt – or didn't learn, as often turned out to be the case – and she felt she was moving toward something, which was leaving school and going out into the world.

Then she got to be out in the world, with a job and a car and a boy who liked her.

Spending all this time in a hospital bed, thinking – there's nothing else to do but think – she sees how the job, the car and the boy led her to be on that road to Woy Woy, driving too fast around that bend. Still, she wouldn't have traded them for anything. They were freedom for her. And now she has none. Now every day is frustration and pain and what feels like no progress even though the doctor said her body is healing, taking its time, as it needs to because they're big bones in the legs and the pelvis and they need time to be strong again.

She cherishes visitors when they come, breaking up the boredom. Trudy, once a week, keeping her up with salon gossip. Evie less frequently but no less welcome.

Her mother isn't spending as much time here, and Josie wonders if Trudy said something to her, because Josie mentioned she felt watched and it wasn't helping. Erin and Trudy have been talking – which she only knows because Trudy tells her.

'Had a chat to your mum,' she said on her last visit, although she didn't say much about the contents of the chat other than, 'Just checking in.'

Josie sighs as she looks out the window. Even the view is the same every day. At least the weather changes.

She hears a light knock on her open door and turns her head. And there's Brett. Or is it? Maybe it's a mirage. She's been imagining him coming to visit her so often she could be hallucinating him.

'Hi,' he says tentatively, taking a step inside the door.

'Hi,' she says back, but it sounds so quiet to her that maybe he didn't hear it. She tries to push herself up but it's hard with the casts and she feels so clunky and ugly and awkward, and if she'd known he was coming she'd have tied back her hair or something, made herself presentable, he has never seen her like this and he won't like her any more, she just knows it.

Except he's smiling at her in a way that makes her feel light inside, and now she can see he's holding flowers, and it's so nice, seeing him here, that she starts to cry and she wishes she wouldn't but she can't help it. The relief of seeing him. The joy of seeing him.

'Hi,' she says again, this time louder, and he steps toward her and now his arms are around her, and she can hug him back because her arms still work.

He's kissing her temple and now her lips and she holds on to him, not wanting to let go because maybe he'll disappear.

'I've been so worried about you,' he says into her hair.

She can smell the salt and sun on him and it's so familiar and so lovely that she cries even more.

'I thought you didn't want to see me,' she says into his shoulder.

When he pulls back he puts his hands around her face and stares into her eyes. 'I always want to see you,' he says.

She has always wanted someone to look at her the way he is looking at her now. There aren't words she can put to the feeling.

It's just a *feeling*. It's a knowing. The sense that he is right for her and she is right for him, even though if she had to fill out a questionnaire that asked each of them what their interests and hobbies were – the sort of thing you find in the magazines – they probably wouldn't be a match. Whoever is a good match on paper, though? Her parents' friends have sons who her mother thought would be perfect for Josie but when she met these young men she felt nothing other than irritation in most cases.

You know it when you see it. Trudy said that to her once when she was talking about her husband. Telling Josie how she and Laurie didn't really work on paper either – he liked dogs, she liked cats, among other things – but they wanted each other, and they kept wanting each other.

'How did you keep knowing?' Josie asked. 'All those years.'

'Some days you have to make a decision to keep knowing,' Trudy said. 'No one's perfect each day – no one's the same each day. It helps to remember the feeling you normally have around them, remember that it's the real feeling, not whatever's going on that's annoying you. Of course, if you start to have more bad days than good, that's when you should call it quits.' She'd smiled wistfully. 'Thankfully Laurie and I never reached that point.'

Josie wished she could have met Laurie, and seen what he and Trudy were like together. Maybe they'd be better role models than her parents, with her father always doing what her mother says and her mother changing her mind a lot.

One of the things she really likes about Brett is that he's consistent. He shows up when he says he'll show up, and if he tells her something he doesn't change his mind.

He has shown up for her here, too, when she's looking her worst and she can't even get out of bed to hug him properly.

'How did you know where I was?' she asks him as he strokes her hair, which is so comforting she wants to curl up and close her eyes and ask him to do it forever.

'Your mum told me.'

'My mum!'

This is so confusing it almost feels like a betrayal – why wouldn't Erin say she'd spoken to Brett? Why would she speak to him in the first place?

'Trudy called her,' he says. 'I was going to the salon to ask about you, and –'

'You were?' She smiles. All this time, he's been thinking about her. She was so wrong to believe otherwise.

He grins. 'Yeah. Trudy kept me up to date.'

'Not much to report,' Josie says, snorting.

Brett shrugs. 'I wanted to know. And one day she said she'd called your mum and told her how worried I was. Then she said to give your mum a call. So I did.'

It's hard to imagine how the conversation went, and Josie wishes she could have heard it – but all that matters is he's here, with her, and without her mother chaperoning.

If only it hadn't taken a car accident to get them here. If only her parents had trusted her in the first place. If, if, if . . .

Her whole world has seemed composed of *if* lately. *If only Brett were here.* That was one of them. Now he is. It's almost too much.

She presses her head into his chest, trying not to cry.

'Hey,' he says, rubbing her back. 'Hey, what's up?'

'I can't believe you're here.' Wrapping her arms as far around him as she can, she tries to stop the tears so they don't go on his shirt, but they flow anyway.

'I'm not leaving you,' he says, hugging her tighter than he ever has before. 'I'm going to help you. With your rehab.'

'You can't do that,' she says, straightening up. She doesn't want him to see her trying to walk properly again, all the incompetence and mess it will entail. How will he want her after that?

'I can,' he says, and he kisses her nose, laughing. 'And I will. Come here.'

As he hugs her again she lets herself go into it. Lets him hold her, feels the strength of his arms and his back and his spirit and his determination.

'This is just our start, Josie girl,' he says. 'And I'm not missing it.'

She stays cradled against him until she starts to fall asleep, and is barely aware as he lies her down on the bed and pulls the sheet up, then sits beside her and holds her hand.

CHAPTER FORTY-SEVEN

Right near this cafe at The Entrance is the field where Trudy and Laurie once took Dylan's children to the circus. The kids were staying for the weekend – Dylan must have talked Annemarie into letting that happen because she was never that fond of allowing the children to be away from her.

When Laurie was alive – yes, that's when Dylan used to visit more. When Trudy would see her grandchildren more.

She hadn't put it together until now, because the two years since Laurie's death have involved so much readjustment that she failed to realise that her son's physical absence from her life went along with her husband's.

So he doesn't want to see her without Laurie, is that it?

How can she not have known this?

Trudy gazes out from the cafe at people gathering around to watch pelicans on the water. Pelicans always look so patient, and slightly amused, like they're just entertaining the tourists for a while, then they'll spread those big wings and take off to a quieter beach.

The pelicans bring people to The Entrance. Not that they'd brought her here today. Sol has done that.

'Hopefully there's something you like on the menu,' he says, breaking into her thoughts. 'I haven't been here before but my daughter likes it.'

Sol doesn't talk about his daughter that often, possibly because Trudy doesn't ask. She's aware grief might have made her boring. It's difficult not to become completely introspective when you lose the centre of your world. You have to go inward to try to find another, even though you know it's not there. That it's gone forever. When one lives alone in the wake of that grief, it's even harder not to tunnel in and stay there, and it becomes harder still to make an effort to connect with other people. Then it becomes a habit to not try. Even though there are so many people who come and go from the salon, there aren't many she connects with, and fewer still who are genuinely interested enough to ask, 'How are you?'

Perhaps she doesn't ask *them*. That's another thing that goes when you're miserable: manners. But she's trying to be civil. Polite. That's why she's smiling and nodding and looking at the list of sandwiches and toasted sandwiches in order to see that, yes, there is something she likes.

Sol gives the waitress their order while Trudy gazes once more at the water and the pelicans and thinks about the last time the children stayed with her. It was that same trip, with the circus. Three years ago, it would be now. Laurie was ailing but they still had hope, not that the doctors gave them much.

'They're always popular,' Sol says, and she sees him gazing too at the water.

'They're magnificent birds. I never get tired of looking at them.'

Sol nods his agreement, then smiles at her. 'Have you thought any more about what I suggested?' he asks. 'About me driving you to Sydney to see your son?'

She has thought about it, and dismissed the idea, and thought about it again, and tried to predict how Dylan would react, and each time she thinks it would be a bad idea to introduce these two. Sol is her friend, nothing more. But Dylan will think it's more. Sol will think it's more.

Not that she can tell him any of that. So she settles for a lie.

'Honestly, I haven't had time,' she says. 'I've been run off my feet with Josie away.'

'How is the poor lass?'

'Not happy. Which is understandable.'

Trudy has taken to visiting Josie each Sunday afternoon, just after lunch, bringing a little cake or a bun because the hospital food is awful. The girl wants to go home, of course, but it would be impossible for her parents to manage her, since she can't walk anywhere yet.

'A difficult time for all,' Sol says seriously. 'She's lucky to have you looking out for her.'

'It's what anyone would do.' Trudy believes that. Not that she has proof.

'I doubt that. Most people, I find, can't be bothered thinking about others.'

He looks mildly amused as he says it, so she doesn't know if he's joking.

'That's a bit harsh, isn't it?'

'You think that because you can't imagine it.' He is gazing at her in a way that is adoring yet unsettling, because she's not sure she wants to be adored by him. 'That's how good your heart is.'

She glances away, not able to hold his stare. 'It's not too good,' she mutters. 'It's been doused in cigarette smoke for years.'

In fact, she'd like to douse it right now but she doesn't smoke that much around Sol – his clothes are immaculate and smoking may ruin them. Or, at least, make them smell.

'I see your heart.' He sits forward on his chair. 'Its endless capacity. You are welcoming to everyone in that salon.'

He's only been in two or three times, so she's not sure how he's worked that out.

'It's my job.'

He wobbles his head from side to side. 'Perhaps. But you mean it. I can tell. You care about everyone who walks through that door, even if they don't necessarily deserve it.'

'Everyone deserves it.'

'You see? That's what I mean. Good-hearted.'

He keeps smiling at her as the waitress puts down their little pots of tea and walks away.

'You are a wonderful woman, Trudy. I admire you greatly.'

She fidgets in her seat. 'So you keep saying.'

'Because I'm not sure you believe me.'

'That's because I don't think you're right!'

'Or you think I have ulterior motives, perhaps?'

That hangs in the air between them as he pours tea for her before taking hold of his own pot.

'I do,' he says, and their eyes meet. 'I want to see as much of you as I can. My life is greatly improved by having you in it.'

It's such a compliment. One of the best. Isn't it? As she digests it she thinks about who improves her life. Evie. Sam. Josie. Her clients. Her friends. Her son. Her grandchildren. Sol? Yes. He does. Not *greatly*, but he does improve it. They're sitting here in a nice place having a chat. That's an improvement to sitting at home feeling sorry for herself.

'Thank you,' she says.

There's something that needs to be said here. He's no doubt waiting for her to say how much she likes him – that's usual in these situations, she supposes. A sentiment is offered and the person who offers it tends to want it returned. But she's old enough now to want to be true to herself. She has to be: there's no one else to do it for her.

She clears her throat. 'I feel you may want more from me than I'm able to give,' she says.

They're still looking into each other's eyes and she doesn't see a shift in his. No disappointment appears. No dislike, either. Not a flash of anything different.

'Well, I'm glad you didn't say you *fear* I may want more.' His laugh is light, then he takes a sip of his tea and puts the cup back in the saucer. 'I have no interest in asking any more of you than you're prepared to give,' Sol says. 'I'm happy to simply have you in my life.'

That sentence right there – now, *that* is the biggest compliment he could have paid her. Not demanding anything. Not expecting anything.

Something unlocks inside her. Not love – no, not that. Her love is for Laurie. At least for now.

It's realisation: her life isn't empty and never has been. Laurie is gone but she has her salon, her friends, her clients, her staff; she has this beach and this area and these familiar streets and cherished places; she has books and music and bright mornings and beautiful dusks.

There is also a feeling of release. She's been holding on to something and she doesn't even know what it is, but it's gone now. Her chest feels loose where it was tight. Her shoulders relax. Why doesn't she know herself well enough to be able to identify what's going on? Why is she still such a mystery to herself even at this age?

These aren't questions she can answer now but she quite likes the idea that there's more to discover.

Ah, there it is: she feels differently about the future now. Before it was heavy and relentless. Now it appears to her as lighter. Maybe even carefree.

Has Sol given that to her? Perhaps. Or she may have created it for herself. By being here. Showing up each day – for life. Even on – especially on – the days when she hasn't felt like it. That's the best she can do for Laurie. For herself. For those she loves. Keep being here. Keep showing up each day.

There's a commotion by the water and they both turn to look to see the pelicans flapping their wings and taking off.

'I imagine that's it for today,' Sol says.

'Yes.' She smiles and their eyes meet. 'But there's always tomorrow.'

CHAPTER FORTY-EIGHT

Anna was surprised when Gary called and asked her out to dinner. She also had to restrain herself from asking why he wasn't asking the blonde instead. In the days since she saw them together she's been mulling over the sighting, then it turned to agitating, then it turned to boiling it up and letting it simmer unattended. Totally her fault, of course, because she chose to keep going back to the memory when she could have trained herself away from it. She's never been one to mull. Or hold a grudge. Witnessing her father's long decline meant she tended to keep things in context, which was partly why she asked Gary to leave in the first place: life is, she knows, too short to live badly if it can be avoided.

For some reason, though, the idea of Gary with a new woman really irked her. She's had trouble sleeping. There have been times when she's caught herself daydreaming about it at traffic lights. Luckily only one driver has had to honk a horn to wake her up.

What irritated her the most was how upset she felt when she saw him with that woman. It caused a schism within her, between the Anna she thought she was, completely over her husband and willing to move on, and the Anna who appeared to be lurking underneath that one, with different opinions and needs, and still, quite clearly, attached to Gary.

So after that night she stopped trusting herself and her responses to things. Did she really think that new school mum was a bitch or was it some insecure version of herself that was popping up and saying hello? Does she really want to be on her own, foot-loose and fancy-free, or is she merely telling herself a story to cope with the fact that her husband didn't want to spend time with her and their children to the tune of staying at work late every night?

It's really set her at odds with herself, all of this.

And then Gary called her. Wanting to take her somewhere nice.

A month ago she would have rolled her eyes and said, 'I suppose so.' This time she had to count to three so she didn't say 'yes' too quickly.

Curiosity. That's what it is. She just wants to know what he wants. Then she can go back to rolling her eyes.

Sure, sure, the other, subterranean version of her is saying. *Tell yourself the story that it's just curiosity. Ignore the jealousy you felt. Ignore the way you've been thinking about him since: as a man, not as an irritant.*

He is picking her up tonight. Her mother is staying with the children.

It's difficult to know whether or not Ingrid wants her back together with Gary. Indeed, it has always been difficult for Anna to know if her mother has ever liked Gary. Ingrid may be a woman of strong opinions but when it comes to her children's spouses, she keeps her own counsel.

'You look lovely,' Gary says after Anna opens the door wearing a new pink V-neck jumper with shoulder pads, made of a fluffy thread she started regretting once she put it on because it may shed all over her woollen camel-coloured skirt.

'Thank you,' she says, a little startled at the compliment.

He brightens. 'You've changed your hair.'

Involuntarily her hand goes to her head. 'Yes.' In their entire married life, this is the first time he's noticed a change in her appearance. Once she cut off a fair bit of hair and he said nothing.

Another time she wore thick black eyeliner just to see what he'd say – nothing. They went out to dinner with friends and she wore a low-cut top, which was not her sort of thing at all. No reaction.

'It looks great,' he says.

Suddenly she feels self-conscious and she brushes down the pink jumper.

'Thanks,' she says.

Their conversation in the car is perfunctory: he asks after the children, she gives him answers; she does not ask about his work and he doesn't volunteer any information.

He's brought her to a little bistro in Gosford she didn't even know existed. *Maybe he brought the blonde here*, she thought as they arrived, then tried to unthink it because it was ungenerous.

Yet she's not going to let the night end without asking him about that woman. If he's seeing someone, she wants to know. She *has* to know.

So she's not going to wait, she's going to ask now while they're in the lull between ordering their food and those meals arriving.

'This is a change from the Avoca Beach,' she says, smoothing her serviette over her legs.

'Hm?' He frowns and fiddles with his butter knife.

'The Avoca Beach. I had dinner there the other night.'

He looks up.

'And so did you,' she says.

Watching him closely, she sees no discomfort. He's always had a fairly open face so she'd notice it if it were there.

'Oh yeah,' he says, nodding slowly. 'I had dinner there with Fi.'

Anna swallows, knowing this is her moment of reckoning and she needs to stay calm.

'Who's Fi?' She tries to keep her voice light – so carefree! She doesn't care about this Fi! It doesn't work, because she almost chokes on the second word.

'Bracey's wife.'

'Bracey?'

'Dan Brace. From school.'

Anna tries to remember this person but can't.

'We were in the cricket team together,' Gary explains. 'Stayed in touch. Sort of.'

Still nothing. Does he have friends she has completely forgotten about? Or did he not tell her?

'He died.' Gary looks down, breathes out, looks back up at her. With meaning. Like this is information she's meant to know.

'Oh,' she says. Stalling for time.

'So, yeah, Fi's getting used to being on her own. To being lonely, I guess.' Another pause. 'They didn't have kids. Couldn't have them. So she's really alone.' He shrugs. 'She just needed a night out. So did I.'

Anna feels bad for making presumptions, but they *did* look cosy together. Which they would if Gary knew Dan that well. Why hasn't he mentioned them, though? Why hadn't she met them?

'We talked about you,' he continues.

'Me?'

'Yes.' He looks quizzical. 'Why wouldn't we? I told her you'd kicked me out.'

'You kicked yourself out,' she says sharply and her reward is his hurt face.

'Fi kind of said the same thing.'

'Really?'

'I told her how much I'd been working. She said Bracey always made her a priority no matter how much work he had. He just found a way to manage it all, she said. That's what you do once you have your priorities straight.'

He stares into her eyes. 'I have them straight now, Anna,' he says, and she finds herself holding her breath. 'You are my priority. You and Troy and Renee. I won't mess that up. Not again.'

With a flourish the waiter places sole in front of her and chicken in front of Gary, and she stares at her plate like it's an oracle.

Except her future does not lie there. Instead, it may take the form of the man sitting across from her.

'I know you don't have much of a reason to take me back,' he says, picking up his cutlery. 'But I'm asking you to try to think of one. And here's my reason for wanting to come back: I love you. I've never stopped. I just thought it was enough. You know? I thought all I had to do was love you and you'd know and that it would make everything fine. But I need to show you. The way you showed me, by taking care of our house and our kids and our friends.'

He puts down his cutlery and places his hands in his lap, almost as if he's about to pray. Is he? Has he turned religious in his absence? Anna won't know what to do with a religious husband.

'Please give me another chance,' he says quietly.

The eyes that meet hers are strong, determined. She likes it.

'You don't have to say anything now,' he adds, picking up knife and fork once more. 'Let's talk about something else.'

So she tells him about Troy's interest in learning to surf and how Renee wants to do ballet, and he listens. They talk about the holiday they once took to Manyana on the south coast and how they loved the fact there was hardly anyone there. Normal things. Family conversation. Yes, that's what it was. The sorts of things they always used to talk about.

It may make them a family again. She feels closer to that than she did.

When he drops her home they kiss goodnight. Not on the cheek. On the lips. It's brief, and she likes it, and when she goes inside she doesn't think about the blonde woman any more, she just thinks about the kiss and how it had felt like the first time.

CHAPTER FORTY-NINE

It was nice, having the fantasy of Sam's affection to keep her company while Billy was staying with his dad. On those long, empty weekend days Evie didn't feel so alone, because she would let her mind wander into maybes and one-days and isn't it funny how those can feel so real? How you can have memories of something that didn't exist? She is sure, for example, that she and Sam had a lovely house together, and that Billy was happy with Sam as his stepdad. That they'd taken holidays together and gone on long walks, just the two of them, and they'd never fallen out of love.

Those fake memories *feel* real – she has sensations in her body as she recalls them. Happiness, then the grief of knowing they won't become real. She's never before experienced grief for something that didn't exist. It makes her feel like an imposter, and that's increasing her misery.

She should never have let her fantasising get this far. With clear eyes, in hindsight, she can see that Sam never gave her any signs of being anything other than her friend. Yes, he was friendlier to her than anyone else in the salon – but you do that when you like someone. Also when you fancy someone, true. It's her fault for presuming things, though. She shouldn't have done that. He gave her an inch and she took two hundred miles.

There's so much she shouldn't have done. The shame of it sometimes feels worse than the grief.

Not that anyone's thinking about her that much – she can't imagine Trudy is spending time thinking she was a fool. In fact, Trudy has been really kind about the whole thing, along with having to manage a workplace in which she has one staff member recovering from a misplaced crush on another.

Sam could have left after her confession. No one would have blamed him. Instead he's carried on being his wonderful self, which doesn't help her get over him.

Argh, she needs to get out of this house. Go for a walk. Work off all this glumness. Maybe she should just keep walking and exhaust herself. That'd be a way to stop thinking.

Picking up her Walkman and shoving some cash and the house key in her jeans pocket, she heads out, trying not to slam the front door even though slamming doors has been in her repertoire lately. It's a way of working off the angst.

Out her gate and turning right, she sees a familiar figure closing a car door. Oliver. Oh great. She's trying to get over Sam and here's his brother, grinning at her as if she's got a bow wrapped around her. Why does he irritate her so much now? Maybe because he reminds her of how Sam came into her life.

'Oh. Hi,' she says, hoping he'll pick up on her tone, which is of the keep-away variety.

'I was just coming to see you!' His tone suggests that he has not, in fact, detected that she doesn't want to see him.

'Really?' She wants to ask why but no doubt he's about to tell her.

'Yeah. Ah – but you're going out.'

She stares at him.

He laughs nervously. 'Of course you are,' he says. 'That's why you're out the front of your house.' Glancing down, he says, 'Sneakers? Are you going for a walk?'

She nods.

'Can I come with you?'

He's wearing sneakers too. How convenient.

'Sure,' she says, because she can hardly say she doesn't want him to – he's Sam's brother, she's still working with Sam, so she has to be accommodating even as she resents doing it. 'I was just going to set off,' she says. 'No fixed destination.'

'Even better.' He smiles as if he means it. 'I love a ramble.'

She can't help laughing – who uses the word ramble any more?

'Sure,' she says again, then turns in the direction of the beach, which is down the hill and a nicer walking prospect than up the hill. The walk will take them by the salon, but it's past closing time for a Saturday so they won't risk running into Sam.

'So why did you come to see me?' She needs to know.

'I wanted to talk about Sam.'

Her blood runs cold. Funny how quickly thoughts manifest in the body. How they can change you so fast there must only be a millisecond between hearing something, reacting to it, then feeling it.

Cold, yes, she's cold. Because she can't imagine what Oliver is about to say to her, yet there's no way it can be good. There's no way it can be something like *he really loves you after all*.

'I'm really sorry,' he says.

They're walking slowly, so it wouldn't be dramatic to stop right then, except she doesn't know if she wants to look at his face. See the pity there. Because pity was in his voice.

'About what?' she asks.

'He told me . . .' Oliver sighs. 'Told me you had some feelings.'

'Oh god,' she breathes, wanting to turn around and run back to the house.

'He was upset. He thought he'd led you on.'

'He did!' Since the topic has been raised, she's going to run with it. 'He was so nice to me!'

Glancing at Oliver, she sees him frowning.

'You thought that meant he was keen on you?'

'Of course. Men just aren't . . .' She stops.

'Just aren't what?'

She doesn't respond.

'Just aren't that nice unless they're interested, is that it?' He sounds sad.

Of course, he's included in that. He's always been nice to her and he was interested in her for a while.

'Not usually.'

'You must know some badly behaved men,' he says softly.

'Most men I know aren't like that.'

'Then maybe you know better-than-average men.' Now she stops and turns toward him. 'What are you doing here? What do you want?'

The street sounds so quiet while she waits for him to respond. No cars going past. The occasional bird noise. No wind to move the trees.

'I wanted to apologise.'

'How is it your fault?'

'I should have told you he's gay. That way you wouldn't –'

'Why? That's ridiculous. Me falling for your brother isn't your responsibility.' Even if she'd like to make it so – that way she could absolve herself.

'I know. I just . . .' He sighs and puts his hands on his head. 'I would never want you to be upset, Evie. Never.' His hands drop. 'I only want the best for you.'

She has long known this about him, she thinks. After she told him they couldn't work romantically, he wasn't upset with her. He wanted to stay in her life. He wished her well. What she doesn't understand is why, considering she has never given him much time or done anything amazing – for him, for anyone. Sure, she takes care of Billy but being a mum isn't amazing, it's just a fact. Who is she, to be deserving of this man wanting the best for her? She decides to find out.

'Why?' she says.

Now a car drives past, its muffler clearly in need of replacing.

'I care about you,' he says once it's quiet again.

They're so exposed here on the street, yet the way he says it makes her feel as if she's in a cave with him, just the two of them.

'Yes, but . . . why?'

It's the biggest question she could ask him, yet also mundane. The moment feels freighted with something but she doesn't know what.

When he smiles it's full of warmth and understanding. 'Do we ever know why?' he says.

That's not an answer she understands, so she frowns.

'I love my brother because he's my brother,' he goes on. 'We're family. I love my friends but if you think about it, why do we love our friends? Because we know them. Because we grew up with them, maybe. Not usually because we stop and think about their personalities.'

'So . . . love is just familiarity?'

And why are they even talking about love?

'Maybe,' he says lightly. 'Maybe it's just something that happens. You know – you meet someone and you just like them, right? If they asked you why you liked them you couldn't really say. Once you get to know them you might be able to say, but it doesn't change the fact you liked them to begin with.' He smiles again.

He smiles a lot, she's noticed.

'I've always liked you,' Oliver says. 'I could try to explain it but it just . . . *is*. I don't need to do anything with it. Except I want to.'

Is he talking about apologising to her for Sam? Because she feels fine about Sam now, for some reason. Not embarrassed any more. Maybe Oliver has done that for her.

'I know you don't feel the same way,' he says. 'But I really hope you'll give me a chance to spend more time with you.' Another smile. 'Maybe you'll change your mind.'

She knew this was coming. On some level, this has always been coming. She and Oliver have always been moving toward each other. Over the past few years, in and out of each other's lives, him showing up, her not seeing it for what it was. Love. That's what he's talking about. That's what he's offering her.

That could be why, standing on this Terrigal street, with no wind and no cars and hardly any birds, it feels as if the world tilts on its axis and she has the choice to tilt with it or resist.

She closes her eyes, feels the air over her skin. Notices how seconds feel like minutes then hours, how time is changing shape and she is zooming backward and forward and it all feels more certain than it ever has.

When she opens her eyes he is standing right in front of her. As he has, in some ways, always been.

'Maybe I will,' she says.

CHAPTER FIFTY

It took her dead husband to get her live son to visit Trudy again. Dylan said something about how he hadn't been to Laurie's grave in a while – Trudy thinks he hasn't been since Laurie died, but she wasn't going to say it, not wanting to antagonise – and she suggested they visit together.

Trudy goes to the cemetery every now and again. She's torn on the matter. Some people like to visit dead relatives all the time, and possibly there's a tinge of martyrdom about it, or showing off, or maybe it's genuinely done out of love and she's a curmudgeon. However, she doesn't feel motivated to visit that often because Laurie's not in this cemetery. His remains are, but remains aren't a person. It's even in the word: *remains*. What remains of the man she held and loved and made love to is now disintegrating into the earth, as it should, because ashes to ashes and dust to dust and all that, but *he's* not there. He's gone. He's in the air and the trees and the sun. And he's also nowhere. There's nothing she can touch or feel of him, not at the cemetery, not anywhere. All she can do at the cemetery is look at his headstone.

She supposes she could talk to him. Or talk to the headstone. People do it – she's seen them pull up camp chairs and sit with thermoses. Who knows what they say. Maybe it's a form of therapy with a relative who can't talk back. For all she knows they're sitting there saying, 'You were a wretched so-and-so and I couldn't say it while you were alive so I'm saying it now.' She doubts it, though. Rage isn't as powerful as love. No one can make her believe it is. And it's love that brings a person to a gravesite with a camp chair and a thermos.

The only people she understands visiting regularly are parents of children who have died. That's a grief you could never comprehend, and she can see how visiting the grave might help you inch toward acceptance, at least. If you see the evidence that your child is dead, maybe you start to believe it. *Maybe.* She doesn't think she ever could. She hopes she never has to find out. Her son is strong and healthy, or so she believes. He's also walking with her to his father's grave.

'Thanks for coming,' she says, then she regrets it, because she shouldn't be thanking him for doing something that is the normal duty of a son: to show respect to his parents. It's a reflex to thank him because he does so little, but she shouldn't reward that. She should just say nothing.

'No worries,' he replies.

They're walking slowly, which befits being in a cemetery – what's the hurry when everyone around you is going nowhere?

'Here he is,' Dylan says, and he surprises Trudy by reaching down and tapping the headstone. 'Hi, Dad.'

She supposes she's now meant to greet her dead husband but she's not going to. She talks to Laurie all the time, wherever he is.

'It's weird that he's gone, isn't it?' Dylan crouches and scrutinises the headstone, as if he's never seen it before. It's possible he didn't read it at the time it was installed.

'It is.'

'Two years.'

'Yes.'

'There will never be anyone like him.'

Does she imagine there's a certain edge to his voice? As if he's warning her off thinking of another man? He couldn't have known that she wants to broach the subject of Sol with him.

Ideally it wouldn't have been in this location but she hasn't seen him otherwise.

'No, there won't,' she says.

He stands up and gives her a funny look. 'But?' he says.

'I didn't say that.'

'You didn't need to.'

How could he have guessed? It's been years since they've known each other well enough for him to read her like this. It makes her almost lose her nerve. Except she wants to have this conversation, no matter how uncomfortable it may turn out to be.

'I'm not looking to marry again,' she says, and it's true. 'But I need companionship.'

'You have friends.' There's definitely a certain tone in his voice now.

'Yes, but they have their own lives. I miss having someone who is in *my* life.'

'What – you want a boyfriend?'

He's laughing, and she knows he's laughing at her and she really doesn't like it.

'I didn't say that, Dylan,' she snaps. 'But I do have a friend.'

'You *what*?'

'I have a gentleman friend. Sol. He is very fond of me and I . . .' She folds her arms and half turns away from him, thinking about how to phrase this. 'I am becoming fond of him.'

'That's not right.' Dylan's face is thunderous. 'No, that's not right. You can't replace Dad.'

'I'm not trying to.'

'You are! Why can't you just stay faithful to him? Why isn't that enough?'

She has, of course, asked herself this question several times. Why isn't she satisfied being on her own, with Laurie's memory? Isn't it greedy of her to want to squeeze more from this life?

Her answer to herself has been: no. It's not greedy. She's alive. She may be alive for many more years. Wanting to fill that life with more than emptiness is not greed. It's human. Humans aren't designed to be alone. It's too hard. We need companionship. We need support. We need succour. Sol is offering that to her. Indeed, he is already giving it to her. Why shouldn't she take it? Why is she not as deserving of it as anyone else, just because her husband died younger than they expected?

She turns back to her son. 'If I were the one who'd died,' she says, 'would you think that your father should stay alone for the rest of his life?'

Dylan frowns. 'No. Why would he?'

Such simple words and yet so much meaning tangled in them. The double standard embedded in that 'no'. Dylan's evident confusion that she would even ask him such a thing.

'So why would I?' she says.

'It's different.'

'How?'

'Men need a woman in their lives.' He shrugs. 'We just do.'

'I agree. Your lives are greatly improved by having women in them. But I also think this woman needs a man in her life.'

'That's ridiculous.'

'So if you die before Annemarie, she needs to keep being alone?'

'Of course!'

'And if she dies, obviously you won't stay on your own. Does she know this?'

'She doesn't need to.'

Trudy thinks a woman should know that. Anyone in a relationship should know how the other thinks on these matters. She and Laurie didn't have a conversation about it because they were both pretending he wasn't going to die, but she knew her husband well enough to say that he would want her to make the most of her life, and if that meant bringing another man into it, he wouldn't disapprove. And he's not here to disapprove. He's gone. She's been faithful to a ghost for long enough.

'I don't want you seeing this man, Mum. It's not right.'

Dylan grew taller than her when he was fourteen but he was still her little boy for a long time. Perhaps even after he married, she still thought he needed her help. Then she had to learn to let him go so he could have his own family. So Annemarie wouldn't think she was interfering. No woman wants an interfering mother-in-law. He's not her little boy any more, though, and she doesn't need to look after him. She needs to look after herself. And that's the only demand she's prepared to meet.

'I don't care,' she says.

He looks startled. 'What?'

'I don't care. Dylan, I love you more than anything but I can't live my life on your terms. You don't get to dictate my life to me. And I don't know where you learnt to behave like that – your father never did.'

It's true Laurie never spoke to her like this but Dylan has some rather blustery friends who probably fancy themselves kings of various castles, so he might have learnt it from them.

Dylan opens his mouth then closes it, probably because he can't disagree with her.

'I'm not going to fight about this,' Trudy says. 'You either accept that I can make decisions for myself or you don't. I wasn't telling you about Sol to ask for permission. I was simply telling you so you knew.'

He looks down and away. She fancies he feels chastised but he'll never admit it.

'Now, why don't we spend a little longer here then you can drive me home,' she says.

He nods, then crouches over Laurie's grave once more. 'Do you mind if I have a bit of time alone with Dad?' It's said so quietly Trudy almost doesn't catch it.

'Of course.'

She wanders off down the row, looking at the headstones that contain scant details of lives. Whole existences reduced to dates and names, with the occasional accompanying phrase. But no more is needed. The occupants of these graves aren't here any more than Laurie is, so the headstones don't need to tell their stories. Those stories are carried in the hearts of those who love them, just as she carries Laurie's, and she always will, come what may, until she's laid here too.

Today, though – tomorrow too, and many days after, she hopes – she has a life to live. And no more time to waste.

CHAPTER FIFTY-ONE

After several weeks in hospital, and even though she's not entirely ready to go home in that she can't walk unassisted – and that includes going to the bathroom – Josie finds herself discharged with her pelvis and one leg healed enough that she can get around on crutches. And she finds that she wants to. Lying in bed all day is not her scene. Or it might have been – she might have once thought it was a nice idea on a rainy day or something – but she never wants to do it again. Ever, ever, ever. She also never wants to go to hospital again. Except she'll have to return for some outpatient stuff. Either her mum or dad will drive her, of course. She doesn't have a car any more, even if she were physically capable of driving it.

Her dad said that since the car was insured she'll get the money for it and she can buy something else. Living on the Coast does mean needing a car; she's now a little scared of driving, though. Maybe Brett could drive her where she needs to go.

He's been visiting. A lot. Once her mum gave him permission he took it as far as he could, coming after work, before visiting hours ended. They'd talk about everything and nothing: music, shows on TV, what his friends were doing, what the two of them planned to do together once she was able bodied.

Each time after he visited she would wonder if it was real. If he was real. Why does he want to spend so much time with her? He's so good-looking, and sporty, and he could have anyone.

Then she had to remind herself what Trudy said to her once: 'You never know how other people see you.' Just because she sees herself as a loser, the way she was in high school, doesn't mean Brett does. He didn't know her then. And he doesn't know what she thought of herself then. In some ways his regard for her is helping her overcome the way she felt at school, which she's been carrying around without entirely realising it – she didn't have time to think about it until she spent all those days in hospital with nothing else to do but think and watch television.

So he helps her, and one day she'll tell him. What she can't figure out is how – or even if – she helps him.

Once she gestured to her legs and said to him, 'I'm not much use to you like this.'

He gave her a funny look and took her hand and said, 'I don't think about how you can be of use to me. I just want to be around you. You make me happy.'

Never in her life has she thought she could make someone happy just by existing. Her mum would tell her that she did but Erin has always been so consumed by worry about her that she couldn't be called happy.

Josie has to trust it, though, doesn't she? What he said to her . . . He had no reason to make that up. There's something he sees in her that makes him happy. Which means she just has to keep being her. That should be easy. Except being back home with her parents, completely reliant on them in ways she hasn't been since she was a very small child, might make it hard.

That's why she needs something to focus on. The future. A plan. She has one. Her parents aren't going to like it. But she wants to tell them about it sooner rather than later, as the longer she's here, relying on them, the more betrayed they'll feel when she tells them.

305

Her mum made a nest for Josie on the couch in front of the TV. She has a view of the back garden, which is nice. It means that if she wants to sit and gaze out the window, there's something pleasant to look at. Birds come to the bird bath that her father installed a couple of years ago. She's been watching them dip into the water and not just drink it but let it run over their heads and wings.

It's this nest she's sitting in as Erin brings afternoon tea.

'I'm going to get fat if I keep having biscuits,' Josie says.

'You're not eating that much,' Erin says briskly, putting down the accoutrements.

'But I'm not doing much either.'

'You will. This is temporary.'

'I know.' Josie steels herself. 'That's what I want to talk to you about. Is Dad around?'

Erin straightens. 'Ah . . . yes. I think he is. Shall I get him?'

'Yes, please.'

Erin's brow furrows as she leaves the room and Josie feels her stomach churn. But she has to do this. Has to say it.

When Erin returns with Paolo, Josie tries to sit herself up straighter – a losing battle at the moment – and clears her throat.

'I really can't thank you enough for everything,' she says, trying to keep her voice light.

'Of course, darling,' her mother says. 'We just want to support you. You've had such an ordeal.'

Josie sighs. She can't accept that she's had an ordeal because she caused it. Her temper, her distraction, her recklessness. And she won't let Erin turn it into a reason for Josie not to do what she's about to say she wants to do.

'I really mean it,' she says, then she swallows. This is harder than she thought. 'And, um . . .' she goes on. 'When I'm better, I've been thinking . . .' Another swallow. 'Thinking that I, ah . . . I want to move out.'

Erin stares at her and Paolo stares at Erin.

'Move out?' Erin says shrilly. 'Why?'

'It's time I stopped relying on you for everything,' Josie says. She rehearsed that line, thinking it a checkmate of sorts, even as she knows Erin will try to find a way around it.

'But we love doing it!'

And there's the way.

'Don't we, Paolo?'

'Yes, of course,' he says, her father who knows his place in this household: supporter of his wife and his daughter, never to question his wife in particular and his daughter only when his wife wants him to join her in it. Sometimes Josie wishes he would say what he really thinks. Or maybe this is what he really thinks and her thoughts are unkind.

'We love you, my darling,' he says. 'We will take care of you forever.'

'But I don't want you to!' Josie worries she's yelling, although maybe it's just because the house is so quiet. 'I want to have my own place!'

Erin and Paolo look at each other.

'But . . . why?' her mother says. 'Don't you have everything you want here?'

'I'm an *adult*, Mum. I need to leave home eventually.'

'You didn't behave like an adult when you –' Erin stops, her cheeks bright red.

Josie hates her a little for saying that but also knows she's right, even as she wants to make a point.

'You didn't treat me like an adult,' she says firmly. 'You made out as if having a boyfriend was the worst thing in the world. You hadn't even met him. How could you know if it was bad or good?'

'So this is about Brett? You want to live with him?'

'No!' Josie doesn't feel ready for that. 'I don't even know where I'd live. I just . . .' She sighs again. 'I just want to see what it's like.'

Paolo puffs himself up a little. 'I don't think we can allow this, Josephine.'

'I'm an adult, Dad. You can't allow or not allow it.'

She really wishes she could walk away from them, but she knew when she started this that she couldn't and also that she'd want to. But it had to be done. She didn't want to spend the last of her recovery pretending she doesn't have plans for after it. She wants to spend that time making preparations for the life she plans to have once she can fully engage in it.

'We need to think about it,' her mother says, her version of not-allowing-it.

'Fine, think about it,' Josie says. 'But I'm doing it.'

'Josie –'

'Mum, I've made up my mind.'

She sounds resolute, although what she said isn't exactly the truth, because while she *has* made up her mind that she wants to move out, she's less sure about how to go about it. That will come next. Perhaps she can ask Trudy or Evie for advice.

There is silence, and no one seems inclined to break it.

Then Erin pours some tea and sits down heavily opposite Josie.

'We'll talk about it later,' she says, although she doesn't sound convinced.

It's a small victory, but also not a victory, because Josie doesn't want to be in a battle with her parents. She wants them to be happy for her. She wants to be happy for herself. And for them.

When she moves out it will be a huge change for them all. It's inevitable, though, and that's the part she has to ease them into.

They all sit and drink tea, and Josie eats one biscuit only. There's no more talk about anything other than Paolo's work. It's normal, and not. And they'll all have to get used to it.

CHAPTER FIFTY-TWO

'Billy, sweetheart, don't push your food around the plate.'
Evie smiles at her only child in what she hopes is a
loving-yet-firm way. Getting the balance right is one of the
hardest things to do as a parent, she's decided: you want your kid
to know you love him but also that he needs to listen to what you
say, because you're the adult and he's not and you need to show
him how to grow up.

There are some days she wishes her mum were still around to
be the adult, but then Evie remembers that she doesn't get to be
the kid any more. That stopped the day she had Billy.

Who is still pushing his food around his plate.

'Bill, kiddo, not a good idea, mate.' Stevo smiles at his son,
who listens this time – of course. Billy won't respect her but he
will respect his father.

Maybe this is how it's going to be from now on. Or maybe
she's just on edge. She wants to ask Stevo something because he's
the only man she *can* ask, but she feels weird about it. Ideally she's
not going to ask him in front of Billy, which is why she'd really
like her son to eat his dinner instead of play with it.

'How's your mum?' she asks Stevo as Billy restarts his chewing.

Stevo moves his head from side to side. 'Um . . . yeah, not great.'

'Oh?'

'Could be cancer.' He chews his steak as if he hasn't just announced something quite serious.

'Oh! Has she been unwell for a while?'

'A few months.'

'Months!' Evie wants to say all the typical things: *Why didn't she go to the doctor earlier? Why doesn't she care more about her health? This is Billy's only grandmother!* She doesn't, though, because that would not only be unhelpful but could be downright aggravating.

'Yeah.' More chewing. 'She thought it was nothing.' He shrugs. 'Turns out it might be something.'

'Finished!' Billy looks from his mother to his father as if he wants a prize for eating his dinner.

Maybe she should give him one, Evie thinks, then he wouldn't play with his food again. Or maybe he would, since she'd be rewarding him for playing with it *then* finishing. Again, being a parent is tricky. There's a lot to consider. Including dealing with your child's grandmother's serious illness that your child's father doesn't seem to be taking seriously.

'So when will she know?' Evie asks. 'If it's cancer?'

'Dunno. Wanna take your plate to the sink, Bill?'

Stevo has taken to calling their son Bill, and while initially Evie was irritated – they'd agreed he was always to be Billy – the boy himself doesn't object, so she can't.

That same boy obediently picks up his plate and deposits it in the sink. Evie knows she should start getting him to do chores but she hasn't yet, so she'll wash it later.

'You can go and read, sweetie,' she says.

Billy looks surprised. That's because when it's just the two of them, normally she doesn't send him away after dinner. She keeps him close, because he's company.

'I'll be in soon,' Stevo calls after him. Then he turns to her with an enquiring look in his eyes. 'So,' he says.

She raises her eyebrows, feigning ignorance and feeling silly for doing it.

He grins. 'C'mon. You want to say something.'

'I didn't know you knew me that well.'

He winks. 'Better than you think.'

It makes her feel more than a little transparent, hearing him say that, but they are family, she guesses. They didn't mean to be, but they are. With family comes familiarity, embedded right there in the root of the word.

'There's been . . .' She stops. How can she phrase this? She should have practised it.

'I was in love with someone,' she says. The word she was going to use was 'crush' but that didn't quite capture the impact of what she felt for Sam. May still feel. It's hard to switch it off.

'Oh yeah?' He takes a sip of his lemonade. Stevo likes soft drinks. Always has.

'Sam at work,' she says quickly.

'The gay guy?'

'What . . . how? How did you know he was gay?'

He shrugs. 'I've seen him a few times, round the place. I kinda worked it out.'

'By seeing him?'

'Sure.'

This makes her feel like even more of an idiot – how can Stevo, who barely knows Sam, have worked out that he was gay before she did? Oh, that's right: because Evie didn't want to see it. The truth didn't suit her fantasy.

'You didn't notice?' Stevo asks her, which makes her feel even worse.

'Obviously not!'

'Don't get huffy.'

'Don't tell me to not get huffy.'

He raises his hands in surrender. 'Is that what you wanted to talk about – being in love with Sam?'

'Not really. I'm getting to it.'

She *is* huffy, though, and not sure she wants to tell Stevo now. Maybe he'll dismantle her again with a perception she should have worked out on her own. Except she really does want his perspective on this.

'Sam's brother Oliver –'

'Oh yeah, I remember you talking about him. A while ago? You went out a couple of times.'

'He's the one who suggested Sam for the job in the first place.'

'Right.' Stevo takes another sip of his drink.

'He used to like me.' She pauses. 'He still does. He's being . . . really nice. Saying really nice things.'

Stevo stares at her. 'Yeah,' he draws out. 'Where's this going, Evie?'

'I thought I didn't like him like that. But maybe I do. But I don't know.'

'Jesus, woman.' Stevo rolls his eyes. 'You never could make up your mind, could ya?'

'That's not fair!'

'Sure, sure. So – what? You want me to tell you whether or not to go out with the guy?'

Is that what she wants? It would make things easier. That way, if it doesn't work out she can blame Stevo. Which is gutless and pathetic of her.

'Um . . . no,' she says, because she needs to be a grown-up. 'I want to know if you think people can develop feelings for someone when that someone is doing all the right things. You know, if they seem worth having feelings for.'

Stevo appears to consider this.

'Chicks are different to guys,' he says after a minute. 'Guys, we need to feel attraction, right?'

Evie almost feels time slip a little then, as if she is glimpsing what they could have been if only they hadn't got together while drunk, when they confused solving loneliness for the start of a grand passion.

'Right,' she says.

'Chicks . . . they don't need it right away. It's better if they like the bloke. Trust him. That's what I've worked out, anyway.'

She thinks about Oliver and realises she probably does trust him. He's always been steady. He's always treated her well. He's made it clear he holds her in high regard. Those are key ingredients.

'So . . . do you trust him?' Stevo asks it seriously. With care. She appreciates it.

'Yes, I think so.'

He grins. 'Do you think he's . . . y'know?'

She shifts her gaze so she can access a memory of Oliver, with his broad shoulders and wide smile, his lovely skin and his capable hands. These are things she has noticed and retained. That she shoved to the side when she was in the grip of Sam mania.

'Yes.'

Stevo keeps grinning. 'Then you have your answer.'

'But what do I do about it? I've rejected him before.'

'Ask him over for dinner. You know him well enough for that, yeah?'

She nods.

'So make him dinner. Listen to him talk. Just be there. Sometimes having a woman just *be there* is all we need.'

Their eyes meet and there's a sadness in his that surprises her.

'I'm sorry I couldn't be there for you,' she says softly.

'You didn't need to do that,' Stevo says, the sadness disappearing. 'You gave me my son.' He brightens further. 'Y'know, I could take Billy on weeknights if you ever want to . . . I dunno, go on a date.' He grins. 'Or to a dance class. Book club. Anything.'

'Thanks. I may take you up on that.'

'It's kinda stopped you, hasn't it?

'What do you mean?'

'Stopped you even thinking about being with someone. You can't go anywhere during the week.'

She hadn't thought about it in such stark terms but he's right: she never even let herself start thinking she could do anything other than be Billy's mum during the week. She's been grateful to Stevo for giving her weekend time, as if that would be enough, but if she really wants to be with someone and he wants to be with her, weekends alone won't be enough. They need to be able to perceive a life together. One that involves Billy, obviously, but that also means they could one day have a home together.

Stevo has been able to envisage that – he's just done nothing with it.

'Too busy with the fish, mate,' he said once when she asked him why he hadn't found anyone to settle down with.

Maybe it's the truth, or maybe he's felt as confined as she has, in his own way. Billy is both of their priority – she sees that now. Just because Stevo has only been around on the weekends doesn't mean he hasn't been a full-time father emotionally. They both love their son so much. It's just a pity they couldn't love each other enough to be together. You can't fake it, though – and they shouldn't try. Billy shouldn't have to live in a household where people pretend anything for his sake, because that's too much of a burden to put on a kid.

Instead, Stevo may just turn out to be her best mate and she his. That's a concept she never considered but it makes sense. They have the most important thing in their lives in common – what better basis for a friendship is there?

CHAPTER FIFTY-THREE

It seems to Anna that days can be slow but weeks pass quickly, and she is not sure how that happens. Her children were babies just a moment ago. Soon they will be teenagers. She won't notice any of it happening if she doesn't pay attention. Housework, mother work, sewing work, just existing, just trying to *be here*, can feel too much and never enough at the same time. It's not how she wants her life to be.

Yet she wonders – worries – that she's made some decisions out of that sense of it all being too much and never enough. She wonders – worries – if one of those decisions was telling Gary to leave. In the midst of everything that was too much and never enough, did she blame him for how she was feeling? Was he just a convenient target? Did she blame someone else – anything else – but herself?

Certainly she knows she has been changing her mind about all sorts of things of late. Where she used to slightly dread seeing her mother, now she looks forward to it because she has realised Ingrid is wise and possibly funny, although she keeps such a straight face it can be hard to tell.

That means she cheerfully takes her to the salon now. They chat more freely. The whole experience is more pleasant. And really all that's changed is Anna's outlook.

The same goes for the Seaside Salon, where they've just visited. Now they're at their usual cafe in Terrigal, taking their time with their hot beverages, enjoying the sea air.

'It feels nice getting that blow-dry done,' Anna says, touching her hair. 'Nice to have someone else doing it for me.'

'Indeed,' Ingrid says as she sips her cappuccino. 'You seem to like the salon now.'

'I do.' Anna smiles as she gazes across the road to the beach and remembers how good it was to sit and be tended to by Evie, chatting away about things, then having her head massaged during the shampoo . . . That's possibly the best part. Why did her mother never mention the head massage? It makes Anna wonder if everyone knew about this and just kept it secret because they don't want millions flocking to hairdressers. A head massage is surely one of the loveliest things one human can do for another, and addictive in its own way. Hence Anna happily booking an appointment each week at whatever time Evie can fit her in.

'You've worked it out.' Ingrid arches an eyebrow.

'What?'

'The value of the veneer.'

Anna laughs. 'What do you mean?'

'Our presentation to the world around us – it's armour. There's strength in it. And in turn it makes us feel better about ourselves. We are always putting our best foot forward.' Another sip of coffee. 'I learnt how important it was after your father became ill.'

Anna waits for her to go on.

'If I put effort into my appearance, it was an energy – you know? I was doing something for myself. I was making a statement to myself and everyone else that what had happened was not going to defeat me. And if I did it every day, well . . . it gained its own momentum.' She looks across to the ocean, smiling sadly. 'I wouldn't have survived without it,' she says.

That jolts Anna – to think her mother felt like that.

'I had no idea. Why didn't you say anything?' she asks.

'Because I had my dignity to maintain. And that's part of it too, you see – that act of presentation to the world, that's about dignity. I had to hold myself together for you and your brothers. Getting up each day and doing my hair, my make-up, choosing clothes, it was all *positive*. If I'd then talked to you about how I didn't feel I was coping – that would have been negative. No.' She shakes her head. 'I needed to keep it all moving. But I do realise it took its toll on you, in particular.'

'Your appearance?' Anna is confused.

'The whole situation. Your father effectively disappeared from your life even though he was physically present in the house. I see . . .' She stops then gives a little shake of her head as if she's clearing a thought.

'What?' Anna prompts.

'Gary,' Ingrid says. 'He disappeared too.'

They sit in silence, staring at each other.

'So?' Anna says at last.

'You couldn't do anything to change the situation with your father. But you could with Gary. And you did.'

Ingrid's face is impossible to read, so Anna doesn't know if she approves of what happened or not, but she does not like the feeling of being judged.

'Are you saying I shouldn't have told him to leave because you put up with it and therefore I should have?' Her voice rises along with her anger.

'*Did* I say that?'

'I don't know!' Anna glances around, convinced they can be overheard, but other patrons aren't looking their way.

'What I meant, my darling girl, is that you took action because you could after so many years of not being able to change what was, for all of us . . .' Her mother breathes out and it sounds as if she is letting go of years of pain. 'A very difficult time.'

A very difficult time. Such a simply worded phrase but it covers what was an aeon in the life of their family, and Anna couldn't have put it any better.

In that moment she understands that her mother is right: Gary had disappeared and on some level it reminded her of the abandonment she had felt when her father had been there in front of her but not there, and – if she went further into her psyche – her mother being the same. Because Ingrid necessarily gave her life over to her husband, and her sons had each other, which left Anna on her own. And this time Anna was determined to change it.

When she examines her behaviour toward Gary in this context she understands she never really gave him a chance to un-disappear. She warned him that he needed to be home more but she didn't ask why he felt so driven to work so much – because his absence was the beginning and end of it, as far as she was concerned.

For Gary, though, something else was going on. She thinks back to something he said to her at dinner, when she – yet again, and perhaps unfairly – raised the issue of his long hours.

'I was trying to save money,' he said, looking mystified. 'For you.'

'For me?' She was confused. She'd never asked him to save money.

'For a house.'

'We have a house.'

'A bigger house.'

'But I never said I wanted one.'

'I wanted to give you one. To show you . . .' He sighed. 'How much I love you.'

Then she was even more confused, because she didn't know what a bigger house had to do with love.

'You didn't think that being at home more would show me that? Show *us* that?'

'It wasn't meant to be forever. Just long enough to . . .'

His voice caught.

'You could have told me,' she said.

'I wanted it to be a surprise. A present.'

Sitting at that table, she had been cross more than anything: that he had decided this was what she wanted, without asking her. She didn't see that he'd been working to create something for his family, and that he thought she understood.

If either one of them had just said what they meant out loud to each other, they would never have reached the point they did.

It's not too late, though, to say those things. To mean more to each other. For Anna to stop feeling abandoned.

'What would you do,' Anna says to her mother, holding her gaze, 'if you were me?'

Ingrid's eyes widen. Probably because Anna doesn't usually ask her for advice.

'I would apologise,' her mother says.

'What?' That is not the advice Anna wanted to hear. Except that's not really the nature of advice – you can't dictate what someone else wants to tell you.

'There is power in an apology, my darling.'

Anna frowns. 'Says the woman who never says sorry.'

Ingrid makes a face. 'Point taken. But I could say that it's due to the fact that I have rarely felt powerful *enough* to apologise.' She pauses. 'To say sorry to someone who has caused you pain, for the express purpose of moving past that pain and forging the relationship anew, is to take on the responsibility of healing what has gone before and offering the opportunity of shared happiness in the future.'

She sighs, and Anna thinks she sees a faltering. But Ingrid's veneer is practised, and whatever faltering there is does not last.

'It is only for the brave,' Ingrid says. 'It is only for someone who is so sure of themselves they are prepared to risk that things may not turn out the way they hope, knowing that they will be all right, whatever comes.'

319

Anna thinks about what her mother has said. About where and how Ingrid learnt that. Because although she's not big on apologies as far as Anna knows, maybe she has been in other parts of her life. In the time before Anna. Or maybe it came from her grandmother or her great-grandmother. Maybe they were all strong enough to take those risks and that's why she is here now. That's why she exists at all.

'I'm sorry,' Anna says.

Ingrid's mouth opens slightly. 'For what?'

'For not trying harder to understand you,' Anna explains. 'I just focused on what I was going through. When Dad . . .'

She shakes off the memories. They're too hard, too dark, too much for this sunny cafe and this sparkling place. She sees people on talk shows on television saying they need to tell people everything that pains them, but Anna has never thought that what's in the dark needs to be dragged into the light. If it's dark, leave it there. Bringing it to the light doesn't make it light – it just brings a shadow to a place that used to be glorious.

There is much in her life that is light. Her children. Her home. Her mother – she can say that now. This little track she's on, with the salon, the school, the sewing, making friends, going places . . . It's not a big, flashy life but it is *light*. She has made it so. And she wants to share it.

'My darling,' Ingrid says, 'it was not your job to understand me. It was my job to raise you and I did that. Now, if we decide to be friends, that is another matter.' She smiles mischievously.

'I'd like that,' Anna says, then she reaches across and squeezes her mother's hand.

'Good.' Ingrid inspects her daughter's fingers. 'Now let's talk about those nails.'

CHAPTER FIFTY-FOUR

Talking to Dylan about Sol now seems like the easiest thing in the world, Trudy thinks, compared to bringing Sol to the club to meet her friends. Laurie's friends.

She didn't tell Peter and Lois, or Fred, that she'd be bringing Sol. Peter and Fred were Laurie's good friends but if she told Peter she'd have to tell Lois, who would then have told everyone she knew, just because she likes a gossip, not in a harmful way but she likes to be the first with the news. And if she'd told Fred he'd tell his wife, Joyce, who didn't care that Laurie died in the first place so she'd hardly care that Trudy has a new friend.

No, the element of surprise is better. She hopes.

She thought about how best to choreograph the whole thing – get there early, so she could watch for people arriving? Or wait until she thought they'd all be there, then walk in? That's the shock-value entrance, of course, but also the most efficient way to do it.

Efficiency has won the day, so she and Sol are arriving ten minutes after she arranged with the others to gather in the club's dining room.

'Now, you're sure about this?' Sol says as he offers Trudy his arm. She takes it; she always does. She likes that it's an easy way of being attached to someone, of showing a man you trust him, without holding hands, which she would find too ... much. At least at this point of their relationship.

Are they having a relationship? She supposes they must be. Even a friendship is a relationship. Any interaction with another is a relationship, whether at its beginning, middle or end.

'I am,' she says. 'I'm an adult and I'm allowed to make new friends.'

He gives her a look she can't read. 'Did you think you needed the permission of others?'

'Not that, but . . . It's normal to be worried, isn't it? They were Laurie's friends.'

'And yours.'

'It never feels that way after someone dies.'

She thinks about how those friendships have shifted in the years Laurie has been gone, how she has never felt on the same footing, because the others hadn't associated with her on her own before. They didn't know who she was without Laurie – just as she didn't. But she does now.

'I understand,' Sol says, and she knows he must because he's been through it himself – except she knows that men can have an easier time of it when their wives die. Other women scoop them up, not wanting them to fend for themselves. Whereas widows are considered to be able to cope. Or that they should be able to cope. That's her reading of it, anyway, from her own experience and what she's observed. Perhaps what she's unconsciously done to others too.

They reach the door of the club and Sol opens it for her.

Trudy feels queasy, and also like something is stuck in her throat.

Why is she doing this to herself? Oh, that's right: because she's allowed to have a friend. To move on. To not stay crystallised in amber because she's not a fossil.

Swallowing the stuck feeling, Trudy takes Sol's arm again and turns him left, in the direction of the dining room.

Peter is sitting in such a way that he sees them first, and Trudy watches his face change from confusion to mild shock, then he slips a mask of impassivity over it and stands up.

Lois follows his gaze and her mouth forms an O. Then there's the twinkle of impending gossip in her eye.

Fred also turns, and he smiles straightaway. A good sign.

Joyce glares. Who knows what's wrong with that woman, but for the first time Trudy doesn't care.

'Trude,' Peter says, kissing her on the cheek then holding out his hand to Sol, who takes it.

'Peter, I'd like you to meet my friend Sol. Sol, I'd like to introduce Peter. He was a friend of Laurie's.'

'And I'm a friend of yours,' Peter says, shaking Sol's hand vigorously.

'Trude, hi, hi, hi,' Lois says as she sweeps in, kissing Trudy, kissing Sol. 'Hi, darl, I'm Lois.'

Trudy introduces them properly then does the same with Fred and Joyce before they all go back to the table, which has only one spare seat. Of course – she didn't tell them there would be six for dinner.

'Oh,' Lois says, then she looks at Peter, who wordlessly retrieves a chair from another table and places it next to the other.

'Do we have enough room?' Trudy asks.

'Absolutely!' says Lois. 'Don't we, Joycey?'

Joyce makes a face then picks up her glass of wine.

'That's a magnificent brooch, Joyce,' says Sol, who is sitting next to her. Joyce's face softens. So Trudy hasn't been able to crack this woman for years yet Sol can do it with a few words? The man must have the magic touch, and she appreciates it.

'Thank you,' Joyce coos. 'I made it.'

'You made it! Tell me about it.'

With Joyce deftly handled, Trudy turns her attention to Lois and Peter.

'Ginger ale, Trude?' Peter says, standing again.

'Oh, I can –'

'No, you won't.' Peter smiles. 'What does Sol like to drink?'

Trudy gives the order and once Peter is gone, Lois pounces.

'So he's your new friend, is he? Handsome fellow. Where did you meet him? At the salon, I bet. You wouldn't think it's a place to meet men but clearly it's worked for you, Trude, good on you!'

Before Lois's imagination can run away from her, Trudy decides to intervene.

'Actually, he was a friend of Laurie's from bowls.'

Lois looks mildly scandalised, then leans in. 'You weren't . . .' She glances around. 'Having an *affair*?'

Trudy laughs so loudly that heads around them turn.

'When would I have had time for an affair?' she says, not caring who hears. If the worst that can be conjured about her and Sol together is that they might have been on before Laurie died, she can handle it. 'And I didn't even know the man until a few weeks ago.'

'Weeks?' Lois's eyes go even wider. 'You just seem like . . .'

'Yes?'

'Well, like you . . . fit together.' She giggles. 'Good on you, Trude. I thought you should be with someone. Truly, it's not good to be alone, is it? Pete and I talk about this. Whoever goes first – I mean, we could die together in a car crash, you never know – we've both said the other shouldn't be alone forever. It's not right, is it? We're social animals, Trude. That's what I always say.'

Trudy smiles as Lois continues to talk about how she's glad Trudy has found someone and Sol will need to join them each time they have dinner, and maybe he could play golf with Peter and Fred. Meanwhile Sol is fully engaged in conversation with Fred and Joyce, and something about it feels . . . right.

'Ginger ale, Trude,' Peter says as he puts her drink in front of her, then Sol's in front of him.

Trudy gently squeezes Sol's hand, and he squeezes back, and slowly she feels the hard shell of the past two years start to melt away.

AUGUST 1986

Lionel Richie's album *Dancing on the Ceiling* is released.

The Pablo Picasso painting *The Weeping Woman* is
stolen from the National Gallery of Victoria.

Paul Simon, formerly of Simon & Garfunkel,
releases the album *Graceland*.

Stand by Me, starring River Phoenix, is released.

Don Chipp retires from Parliament and his leadership of
the Australian Democrats. He is replaced by Janine Haines,
the first woman to lead an Australian political party.

Bon Jovi release their third album, *Slippery When Wet*.

Crowded House release their first album.

CHAPTER FIFTY-FIVE

While it's still winter, the chill is coming off the days a little – or maybe it's an unusually warm August. Or maybe Josie just feels warmer in Brett's presence, because they're sitting in her parents' garden at five o'clock and enjoying the golden light of the day's end.

She still can't quite believe that he is at her home, and that her parents have even gone out and left them alone. Then again, she suspects it's a ploy on Erin's part to keep Josie living at home: if she 'lets' Brett come to visit, Josie won't have any reason to move out.

Except her reasons for moving out include far more than Brett, and the reasons to stay are greatly outweighed.

The main reason to stay is the cost of living outside of home. Then there's the fact that a big change is always hard and moving out would be the biggest change of her life thus far.

Or would it? The accident – being so badly damaged and having to recover – has shown her she can manage difficult things, and sudden change, and be just fine. As terrible as it was, it did her a favour.

Her reasons to leave – apart from being able to spend time with Brett more easily – are that she can determine the shape of each day, and her life, without constantly having reference to what her mother in particular wants her to do. She can eat what she wants, spend the weekend doing what she wants, even go away if that suits her, and she doesn't have to worry about what Erin will say. Her mother will still have opinions, obviously, and she'll still worry about Josie, but Josie won't feel as overwhelmed by it all. The cloak of maternal love will not smother her the way it has thus far, even as she feels ungrateful for thinking it.

'I love this time of year,' Brett says, smiling to the sky. 'The waves are still good but spring's about to happen, so I can almost ditch the steamer.'

He's talking about his wetsuit. She knows this now because they've talked a lot about surfing, even to the point that he's offered to teach her how.

'Girls don't surf!' she said, because she didn't know any who did.

'Sure they do,' he replied. 'Pam Burridge – she's ace.'

Josie was barely aware of Pam Burridge but she agreed to learn, as soon as she was steady on her feet.

'We can get you in the water soon,' he says in the late-afternoon light, still smiling. 'I'll get you a spring suit.'

'What's that?'

'Short-sleeve wetsuit. I reckon you'll look great in it.' He raises his eyebrows and laughs, as if he's caught himself being suggestive. 'But you look great in everything.'

She blushes; he probably can't see it in this light even though their chairs are angled toward each other. They've been sitting and chatting for about half an hour. The temperature will drop as soon as the sun does, so they'll want to head inside soon.

'Did you get a surf in at lunchtime today?' she asks.

'Nah,' he says lightly. 'Too busy.'

'Oh.' She bites her lip. 'You could have gone after work. Instead of coming here.'

He gives her a funny look. 'Why would I want to do that?'

'Because you love it. Because it's fun.' When she invited him to come over she didn't mean to deprive him of his surf.

He reaches over and takes her hand. 'This is more fun.'

'Is it?' She keeps doubting him when he says things like that, even though he tells her not to.

'Absolutely. What's nicer than this?' Once more he lifts his head to the sky. 'Look at it. Perfect colour.' Then he looks at her again. 'And my perfect girl.'

She laughs, surprised, and points to her cast-bound limbs. 'Not so perfect.'

'Of course you are. And they'll be off soon.'

The day is indeed drawing closer when the plaster will come off and then she'll start the rehab process. Which will be tedious and she won't be able to move out until it's over, but moving out gives her a goal to work toward.

'Can't wait,' she says.

'Then we can have some adventures.' He waggles his eyebrows at her.

She giggles. 'What do you mean?'

'Some road trips, maybe. We could go north. And a bit of a day trip to Sydney. We could even stay overnight – my cousin has a place in Manly.'

She can feel it, sitting here in her parents' back garden: there's a fence around her now but her life is opening up in a way that it wouldn't without Brett. He makes plans. He *does* things. And he wants her to be part of it all. Road trips may not seem like much to some people but to her they mean going further than she ever has; seeing things, meeting people, becoming someone who has a full and interesting life.

'I'd love to do that,' she says.

'You want to travel overseas?'

She's dreamt of it, of course, but that's never seemed possible, financially or practically. Her mother would never let her go anywhere on her own and because she hasn't had many friends to date, she put it out of her mind. But with him . . .

'Yes, I do,' she says.

'Yeah?' He looks excited. 'Where to?'

'Everywhere!' It's out of her mouth before she realises how ludicrous it sounds. Who wants to go *everywhere*?

He laughs. 'Me too! Where will we go first?'

We. How sweet that sounds.

'I don't know! There are so many places to choose.'

He nods. 'We'll have to save up. So we have time to think about it.'

'You probably want to go somewhere you can surf, right?'

'Not really. The beaches are so good here. Why would I go anywhere else?' He screws up his face. His sweet, tanned, lovely, wonderful face. 'I reckon Italy is top of my list. Venice, yeah.'

'Venice?' She's surprised – she would have thought he'd like California or Florida or someplace where it's sunny.

'You don't think it's wild that the whole city is on the water?'

He looks so animated, and she thinks that this is yet another side of him to discover: the part that is curious about the world, that wants to see and experience things.

'And there's all the art and stuff. Yeah, I reckon Venice is the go.'

'I've love to go there. I'd love to go anywhere.'

'That makes it easy, then, doesn't it.'

He moves his chair closer to hers, a little to the side so he doesn't hit her cast-bound legs.

Thrillingly, she realises he wants to kiss her. It's still so new, this idea that this young man wants to kiss her, put his hands on her skin, be so close to her. Be as close to her as she wants to be to him. It all feels so natural, as well as amazing.

As they kiss it's as exciting as it was the first time. More so, actually, because now she knows to look forward to it. They keep kissing and she thinks about kissing him in Venice. In Rome and Florence. In Paris and London and New York City. So many places to go with him. So many places to be happy with him.

Once the kiss is over it's almost dark. Who knows how long they've been entwined.

The outside light goes on and Josie realises her parents must be home.

The back door opens and her mother steps out.

'Hello, Brett,' she says, smiling. It looks like a genuine smile, although maybe she's just good at pretending to be happy to see him.

'Hi, Mrs Martin,' he says, pronouncing it the Spanish way.

'Would you like to stay for dinner?' Erin asks.

Josie knows she can't hide her surprise at the invitation.

'I'd love to,' he says, getting to his feet. 'Can I help you with anything?'

Erin looks pleased. 'If you could help Josie inside, that would be wonderful.'

'Sure thing.'

As Erin closes the door Brett offers Josie his hands. She holds them and with what seems like hardly any effort he pulls her up and wraps his arm around her.

'I've got you,' he says, and she knows he means it for today, tomorrow and as far into the future as she can see.

'I've got you too,' she replies, nuzzling her nose against his neck.

'You sure do,' he says, laughing, and as he walks her inside she relaxes into him, feeling as light as air.

CHAPTER FIFTY-SIX

After she had Stevo over for dinner the other night, things shifted between them. They've always communicated well but now it feels as if they're in on something together. Not romantically – that's never going to happen. Instead they appear to be co-conspirators. It's almost as if he wants to help her get a boyfriend, whether it's Oliver or someone else, and she really wants Stevo to find someone as well.

At the end of that night Evie still wasn't sure if she should give Oliver a go but it was good to know she had time available should she choose to. A few days later she'd made up her mind, and she called him. He sounded surprised to hear from her.

'How have you been?' she said.

'Worried,' he said.

She waited for him to continue.

'I didn't know if I'd ever hear from you again.'

'Guess you can stop worrying, then.'

She swore she could hear him smiling into the phone.

'So, um . . .' She twisted the phone cord in her hand. 'Would you like to come over for dinner one night? Billy goes to his father's on a regular basis so, um, it would just be the two of us.'

She wanted to make it clear to him that this wasn't a clubby get-together with a kid around. It was dinner. It was . . . a date, maybe? Or something on the way to a date.

Oliver accepted her invitation and sounded very happy about it, so he's coming over tonight, which means she has to get away from the salon on time. Stevo is picking up Billy from school so Evie can go straight home and start preparing. She's going to keep it simple: pasta and a sauce, and she's made a cake for dessert. Despite never having been that keen on cooking – maybe because she has to do so much of it for Billy – she loves the idea of cooking for Oliver.

'It's flat out today, isn't it?' Sam says as he passes by her chair, rolling his eyes. 'Is every woman in town getting her hair done or something?'

Evie laughs. A few weeks ago she would have tried to decode what Sam was saying, in case it might have greater meaning for her. *He's flat out – that must mean he needs someone to help him and she could be that person.* Now she sees that none of it is personal to her. It never was. She just wanted it to be. She desperately wanted someone's words and feelings to be about her. But that wasn't Sam's business. It was hers. She should never have put it on him. If anything makes her feel abiding embarrassment bordering on shame, it's that.

'Maybe there's a big do on?' Evie tries to calculate what might be going on around the place. 'You know how some ladies get their hair done in advance and keep it away from water until the day.'

Anna walks in just as Evie goes to look up her next appointment.

'Hello, stranger!' Evie says ironically. Anna's been coming in once a week, and they've taken to chatting on the phone sometimes too. Like proper friends. In fact, they *are* proper friends.

'Hello.' Anna beams.

Earlier this week Anna told her that she and Gary are talking more and that she's happy about it. She looks relaxed. Her face has lost the tension it's been holding for months.

'How are you?' Anna says knowingly – Evie told her about Oliver coming to dinner, and it was Anna's cake recipe Evie used for her dessert.

'I'm . . . good.' Evie smiles bashfully. 'Really good. Looking forward to tonight.'

Anna glances over to where Sam is throwing his head back with laughter at something a client has said. 'Does he know?'

Evie shakes her head. 'Not unless Oliver has told him.'

'I bet he hasn't. When a man is serious about a woman he keeps his mouth shut until he's sure about what's going on.'

'Really?'

For some reason Evie doesn't know these sorts of things about men. Oh, that's right: the reason is that she hasn't had that much experience with them.

'Men are gossips, don't get me wrong – but my brothers didn't breathe a word about the women they ended up marrying before they were well into the relationships. Unlike other girlfriends. Couldn't shut them up about those.' She pauses. 'It's like they're superstitious or something. And they say women are weird!'

Evie nods and puts a cape on her friend. 'Wash and blow-dry?' she asks.

'Um . . . how much time do you have?'

'Why?'

'Do you have time to do a colour?' Anna's smile is bright and hopeful.

A colour usually requires notice, but Evie can hardly say no. Doesn't want to, in fact. She has a cut coming in about half an hour, which she can fit in while Anna's colour is taking. Then one more client in for a wash and blow-dry but Trudy might be able to help. Mainly because Trudy knows about the dinner tonight and will support Evie trying to get away on time.

'What do you have in mind?'

Anna holds her gaze in the mirror. 'I'd like to know what *you* have in mind.'

Evie thinks about this. Typically the clients have their own ideas for their hair, even if Evie doesn't agree with them. One lady wanted to go russet even though it really didn't suit her skin tone, which Evie gently told her; once it was done she blamed Evie for the fact she looked sallow, and Evie then had to spend another hour fixing the colour with more chocolatey tones. However, she'd prefer the clients make their own decisions as opposed to her having to do it. Choosing a colour for a client is a lot of responsibility. Especially when she knows the client well.

She swallows and looks at Anna's brown hair, which is an average sort of brown, nothing remarkable about it. Which can be good: it's kind of like a blank slate. But a woman who's had an average hair colour her entire life usually doesn't want to stand out. Which means your options, as her hairdresser, are limited to mildly enhancing the average colour.

Except she doesn't think that's what Anna wants. A woman who didn't want to stand out would not have kicked her husband out of the house.

'You could go blonde,' Evie says.

Anna's eyes widen. 'Ooh. Really?'

'Sure,' she says with a shrug. 'It would suit you. Your eyes are blue and the blonde would make them pop more.'

'You mean . . . blonde like Lady Di?'

'Diana is *quite* blonde,' Evie says, picking up some strands of Anna's hair. 'I'm thinking we start with some highlights and see how you like them. Then if you want to go blonder we can do it gradually. It's better for your hair if we don't go too hard too fast.'

'I trust you,' Anna says in such a way that it makes Evie smile. They didn't know each other even a few months ago. Now here's Anna saying she trusts her. Not that long ago, in the grip of her fantasies about Sam, Evie didn't even trust herself.

'Thank you,' Evie says. 'I'll do my best.'

'I know.' Anna smiles then sits further back in her chair. 'Let's do it.'

They chat while Evie does the streaks, and after Sam's seen his client out the door he comes over.

'Going blonde – I thoroughly approve,' he says with a wink to Anna in the mirror.

'Says the man with the darkest hair in town.'

He pats his layered head of hair. 'I may get streaks one day. Summer's coming.'

'Then I'll do them for you,' Evie says with a smile.

'Wouldn't want anyone else,' Sam says, then he quickly kisses her cheek before moving away.

'I heard that!' Trudy calls.

'I'll let you wash them out,' Sam says as he heads for the back room.

'Lucky me,' Trudy says then goes back to her client.

Anna catches Evie's eye in the mirror. 'Call me tomorrow and tell me how it goes,' she says in a stage whisper.

Evie smiles and nods. 'First thing.'

By the time she leaves, she practically walks on air back to her house. It takes her a while to work out why: she has something to look forward to. Something real. Not her fantasy of what might happen. Not her need for something amazing to change her life. She has a man and a dinner and anything could happen, and the uncertainty is delicious.

CHAPTER FIFTY-SEVEN

Anna can't say it's like the good old days to have Gary come to the kids' sport with her on a Saturday because he didn't used to attend sport. Or concerts. Or assemblies. Or anything apart from his office.

Not that she is going to hang on to that any more. Going over and over all the times she was upset about him working late has made her realise she wasted energy then and she's wasting energy now. Not that she's judging herself for it – that would be a waste too – but she will no longer indulge herself in it. Because it was an indulgence – it was oh-so-comforting to sit at home on the couch and think about how hard done by she was. How awful and mean Gary was for working late again.

Except she had no proof he was awful and mean. She had no proof of anything other than that he was working late. Everything else amounted to a heap of her *feelings* and they didn't prove anything at all.

So when he offered to pick them all up and take them to the pool for swimming training, she accepted.

He's sitting with her now on a bench at the pool while Troy does laps and Renee splashes around in the shallow end, amusing herself.

'I can do this each Saturday,' he says, and as she turns to look at him she catches a quick smile. 'If you'd like me to,' he adds.

The hair-trigger part of her wants to come back with, *If you don't have something better to do.* But she knows where that comes from now: fear and resentment. Her mother always had something better to do because her father needed constant tending. For most of Anna's life, those closest to her have always had better things to do than be with her. Gary was the same – or so she thought.

There's a way for them to move forward. It starts with her feeling strong enough to stand up for what she wants. Showing him, showing the world and most of all showing herself that she can ask for things. For time. That she is worthy of being given it. She may wish that someone else can do that work for her, but no one can.

'I would,' she tells Gary, fully turning toward him and smiling. 'I would love you to.'

He looks caught unawares. 'You would?'

'Mm-hm.'

Her eyes are on the pool again as she works out what she wants to say next. They have time – the kids will swim heats, and they each do three strokes, so they'll be in the water so long they'll look like Shar Peis when they finally emerge.

Yet they also don't have time. She knows, excruciatingly well, from what happened to her father, that the time she thinks she has – that anyone thinks they have – can be gone in a second. There is nothing to say that she could ponder her future with Gary for the next few weeks or months or years, then decide she's ready to do something about it only to discover that their time is up, for whatever reason. That it was up years or months or days before.

Her father, the way she remembers him, before he became his shadow-self, seems a moment in time away – she could reach across to pull back some veil and he'd be there. But he has been gone for so long she's not sure if the veil is still there or if it ever was.

Gary, the way he was when they married, is there too – she can reach across and pull back that veil and he'll be there, because he's still here, sitting beside her. She has another chance. They both do.

'I'm sorry,' she says, and she feels, in that moment, as if the earth clinks into place.

His face is a portrait of confusion. 'What do you mean?'

'I mean . . .' She closes her eyes briefly because she feels this thing in her chest – warmth, expansion, and also wholeness and rightness and *promise* and hope – and she wants to truly experience it. 'I mean that I'm sorry for what I did. For throwing you out.'

His head is tilted to one side, then he looks down and frowns. 'You don't need to apologise to me,' he says softly. 'I'm the one who needs to apologise. I didn't take care of you.'

'But you did,' she says. 'In the way you thought was right.'

That warmth from her chest is in her whole body now, almost as if she is radiating light and heat from her pores. To him. This is the power her mother was talking about. Damn that Ingrid, she's always right.

Anna smiles. 'I just want to let it all go,' she says. 'I don't want to hold on to that.'

'Do you mean . . . ?'

Troy shouts from the pool, waving up at them. They wave back.

'I mean I can sit at home for the rest of my life thinking you did something wrong,' Anna says. 'Or I can realise that we were both trying to do things right. In our own way.'

Gary takes her hand. She lets him.

'I've only ever wanted to do right by you,' he says.

'We can't just go back to how things were.'

'I know,' he says quickly.

'We need to talk more.'

'I know.'

Then she decides to say what's been on her mind these past few days. 'It would be easier to do that if you were at home.'

Their eyes meet and she realises she's nervous about how he's going to respond.

'I can move back tonight,' he says, hope in his voice.

She laughs. 'Let's just have dinner first. All of us.' She squeezes his hand. 'It's not that I don't want you back soon,' she says. 'But I think we need to explain it to the kids first.'

'Agreed.'

His smile is shy, and she can feel that hers is too.

They sit holding hands, like they used to do when they first started going out, and cheer their children through freestyle, breast-stroke, butterfly and splashing until Renee and Troy get out of the pool, skinny and dripping, and Anna and Gary wrap them in towels and take them home.

CHAPTER FIFTY-EIGHT

'So what is it today, Babs?' Trudy stubs out her cigarette and waves away the smoke in front of her face. That was her first cigarette of the day, which was late for her. She's been smoking less, though. Couldn't say why other than that she's not as interested in it. Or doesn't need it the way she used to.

'Didn't I tell you? Nephew's wedding this afternoon. So I need a nice wash and set.' Babs puts her handbag on the bench.

'That's all, pet? Nothing fancy?'

'No, I wouldn't want to take attention away from the bride.'

She says it so seriously Trudy can't help but chuckle. Then again, she admires Babs's self-belief. Every woman should have that much of it.

'All right. Wash and set it is. Phoebe, when you're free can you take Babs over for a wash?'

Phoebe is her new apprentice. They needed a set of hands and Josie's going to be off for a while. She can have a job when she's ready, and that's because Sam has told Trudy he's moving on at some point – he wants to go back to Europe. And while Josie may still technically be a student Trudy's happy to pay her properly and let her take Sam's spot. The girl has talent, and she's a hard worker. It won't be too long before she's on her feet again, literally.

Phoebe nods. She's washing someone else at the moment so Trudy and Babs have a few minutes.

'Where's the wedding?' Trudy asks.

'Kariong. Function centre or some such.' Babs is eyeing her in the mirror. 'I've heard a rumour about you, Gertrude.'

'Gertrude! No one calls me that.'

'Your mother did once.'

'Yes, she did.' Trudy says it with an edge, because she's not sure where Babs is going with this and doesn't know whether to worry about something she's going to say in front of the other clients.

'You' – Babs waves a finger at her – 'have a gentleman caller.'

Trudy relaxes. Is that all?

'Yes, I do,' she says.

'And you didn't tell me!' The note of outrage in Babs's voice could be real or feigned – it's hard to tell.

'None of your business, *Barbara*.'

'Don't call me that. It doesn't suit me.'

'Gertrude doesn't suit me either.' She puts her hands on her hips and raises her eyebrows.

'Fair. It's a harsh-sounding name.'

'I'll take that as a compliment.'

'Do.' Babs purses her lips and keeps eyeing Trudy. 'What's his name, this gentleman?'

'Sol.'

'Where do you know him from?'

'He played bowls with Laurie.'

'Bowls . . . bowls . . .' She presses her lips together harder than before. 'Not Sol Jacobs?'

Trudy feels like a child caught with her hand in the lolly jar. 'Yes,' she half whispers, taken aback. 'Obviously you know him?'

'I used to play bowls at that club.'

It's coming back to Trudy now: Babs started coming to the salon because she played bowls with Laurie. Which means, of course, that she'd have played it with Sol.

'Lovely fellow. So sad when his wife died. We all wanted him to find someone.' She brightens. 'And he has! Wonderful! Do you play bowls?'

'No.'

'Good. Don't start.' She makes a face. 'So *political*, those clubs. Waste of time.'

Phoebe appears, nervously tucking her hair behind her ears. 'I'm ready for you, Mrs . . . um . . .'

'Babs.' She pushes herself up from the chair. 'Call me Babs, love.'

Babs toddles off to the basins as Trudy thinks about the fact that she knows Sol. About the roads that lead us to people and how sometimes there are more of them than we think.

Evie is on the other side of the salon chatting away to Anna, who's in for her own wash and blow-dry. From what Trudy has gleaned, Oliver is turning out to be quite the nice companion for Evie.

There's another road that's led them all somewhere: Evie knew Oliver, Oliver suggested Sam for the job, and Sam has been a gem to have in the salon. And in his own way Sam led Evie back to Oliver. Perhaps he was always her destination.

She doesn't think Sol was always hers – but he didn't have to be. Because the road can change course and we won't even notice. And sometimes we'll decide to take a different road.

Trudy's been thinking about selling the business. Not now. Not even soon. But it's in her mind. She even talked to Sol about it, because he's been retired for a while, 'and I recommend it', he told her.

'We could travel,' he said, and she liked that idea, not having set foot much beyond Terrigal in her entire life.

Not that she needs more than Terrigal. Everything she wants and loves is here. Apart from Dylan, of course.

There's more of the world to see, though. More of life to live. Her clients have lives that spin in and out of this place, and for decades she has listened to their stories and thought those experiences will never be for her because she has to stay and work. Stay and keep up with her responsibilities.

She said something like that to Sol the other day. He said, 'But your primary responsibility is to yourself. If you are happy, the people around you are happy.'

'How does that work?' she asked, genuinely curious.

'That's the power of a woman,' he said. 'Whatever she feels, others feel. Those who love her feel it most. Happy, sad, whatever it is, that's amplified.' He smiled. 'I can't explain it, I just know it's true.'

'I'll take it into consideration,' she said, and he laughed and offered her his arm, which she took. Then they walked into the club and had dinner with Peter and Lois.

Since then she's been paying closer attention to the ladies around her, and she reckons he's right. When Evie's happy, she and Sam and Phoebe are happy, because Evie's mood radiates from her. It happens with the clients too. Whatever mood they bring with them into the salon affects everyone.

This could all be a way of Trudy trying to remind herself of the importance of her job, of course: if a woman looks good, she feels good, and that makes other people feel good. She thinks she's right about it, though – otherwise why would so many people come to her Seaside Salon over and over again? For years.

Babs is back, freshly washed.

'Time for the blow-dry,' she says, sitting down with a thump and smiling into the mirror. 'Make me beautiful, Trudy.'

'You already are, pet,' Trudy says as she picks up the implement. 'You already are.'

As she nears the end of the blow-dry she looks up to see the shape of someone she knows profoundly well outside the salon window, his back to her. Not that she'll hurry Babs through – no matter what goes on in her life, she won't compromise the clients. So it's not until Babs has paid and left that Trudy walks out the door to greet her son.

'Hello,' she says, looking up.

'Mum,' he says. He doesn't look either happy or sad to see her, but he gives her a hug and that's something.

'You're a long way from home.'

'Yeah.' He presses the ball of one foot on the pavement, as if he's trying to squash something. 'Annemarie told me I was being an idiot and it had gone on too long.'

'Oh?' Trudy isn't sure exactly what he – or Annemarie – is referring to.

Their eyes meet.

'She said you need to have your own life.'

'That's true.'

'That your . . . your boyfriend is none of my business.'

Trudy knows how big this admission is and decides to let him off easily. If you can't do that for your only child, who else can you?

'I prefer the term "man-friend",' she says.

Dylan makes a face. 'God – really?'

She laughs. 'Not really. But he's a fair bit older than a boy.'

Dylan nods. 'So am I.'

'This is true. But you'll always be my little boy. Which means I'll always miss you when I don't see you.'

'Annemarie said something like that too. Told me to imagine what it would be like if one of ours didn't see us for months on end.' He looks sad.

'And?' Trudy prompts.

'I'd hate it.'

Up high seagulls pass them, riding the late-afternoon wind toward the beach. There will be people there, Trudy knows, with fish and chips, and those gulls will be in search of bounty.

'How about you and Sol come to lunch sometime?' Dylan says.

Trudy turns her body toward him, which means she is looking back into the salon, where she can see Evie and Sam trying not to stare in her direction.

'That sounds good,' she says. 'Will you cook?'

'Of course not. You'd rather starve.'

It's an old joke between them: when he was a teenager Dylan decided he was going to try making dinner for his parents and tried to serve them half-cooked chicken. The next time he offered to make a meal, Laurie said he'd rather starve.

'I might,' Trudy says. 'But I wouldn't care. As long as you're there.'

'I always will be, Mum.'

She feels like pinching his cheek, just as she used to when he was half her size. There is, however, something she can offer instead.

'Come inside,' she says. 'You need a trim.'

Dylan laughs and runs a hand through his hair. 'I guess it's a little shaggy.'

'It's a lot shaggy. In you go.'

But he stands back for her to enter first, just as his father taught him to do.

After he's sitting in a chair, with a cape around him, Trudy picks up her scissors and as she snips they make plans for lunch, and for Christmas, and for Dylan to bring his family to Terrigal over the next summer holidays.

ACKNOWLEDGEMENTS

There were three sparks of inspiration for *Lessons in Love at the Seaside Salon*: the online comedy series *Hot Looks Salon* by Casey Dressler; the album *Girlhood* by Hayley Marsten; and the song 'Black Sand' by Matt Joe Gow and Kerryn Fields. Thank you to all of these artists for the specific and general inspiration their work gives.

At Hachette, thank you to Rebecca Saunders, Bec Allen, Louise Stark, Kate Taperell, Eliza Thompson, Lil Kovats and the Sales team, and . . . well, everyone, really!

Thank you to my agent, Melanie Ostell, for her intelligence, insight and support.

Thanks to editors Nicola O'Shea and Lauren Finger, and proof-reader Julia Cain, for snipping and combing as required.

Christa Moffitt continues to create stunning covers and I merely strive to write books worthy of them! Thank you, Christa.

Many thanks to Laura Benson for taking such good care of my books out in the world.

Love and thanks to Jen Bradley and Isabelle Benton for their friendship, and to the Australian country music community for holding space for me in it.

Thank you to Rachael Johns for being funny and generous and going on the *Dear Rach & Soph* adventure with me.

For their support, thank you to Vanessa Radnidge, Scott Henderson, Ashleigh Barton, Chris Kunz, Kate Sampson, Jill Wunderlich and Tammie Russell.

Thanks to my Bushcare buddies Ruth and Diana for being the best weeding company.

All my love to my parents, Robbie and David, and my brother, Nicholas, and to Frankie for being my other brother.